Midnight Raider

SHELLY THACKER

AVON BOOKS  NEW YORK

P9-DNE-246

MIDNIGHT RAIDER is an original publication of Avon Books. This work has never before appeared in book form. This work is a novel. Any similarity to actual persons or events is purely coincidental.

AVON BOOKS
A division of
The Hearst Corporation
1350 Avenue of the Americas
New York, New York 10019

Copyright © 1992 by Shelly Thacker Meinhardt
Published by arrangement with the author
Author photograph by Jim La Moore
Library of Congress Catalog Card Number: 91-92999
ISBN: 0-380-76293-5

First Avon Books Printing: February 1992

AVON TRADEMARK REG. U.S. PAT. OFF. AND IN OTHER COUNTRIES, MARCA REGISTRADA, HECHO EN U.S.A.

Printed in the U.S.A.

RA 10 9 8 7 6 5 4 3 2 1

Their eyes locked, his ablaze with emotions so strong and so savage Elizabeth couldn't begin to name them.

"G-get out or I'll—"

"You'll what?" he said softly. "Send your husband after me? I don't believe there *is* a husband, Elizabeth. I think that was a lie, too."

He yanked her against his chest. His face was cast in hard lines. His whole body shook with the force of some inner battle. Looking down at her, he groaned, then whispered, "You don't kiss like a wife." Suddenly his mouth came down on hers.

"Don't," she rasped.

"You kiss like a woman who hasn't been kissed often enough."

"Let me go!"

"Like a woman who has much to learn."

"MIDNIGHT RAIDER is irresistible to readers who want their love stories liberally laced with adventure, passion and intrigue. A great read!"

Kathe Robin,
Romantic Times

To Mum and Dad,
who continue to show me by example
that the dreams you dare to dream
really do come true.

Very special thanks to Angie Thayer, Carol Lucas, and Suzanne Brown for their endless supply of insight, enthusiasm, and support; to Kat and Gregg Thacker for time and assistance above and beyond the call of sibling generosity; to Amy Norton and Aaron Halabe, who glitter a mean bookmark; to Professor John Reed of Wayne State University for his resource list on eighteenth century criminal law; to Alfred Noyes; and most of all to Mark, who believed in me from that very first moonlit night in May.

Prologue

London, 1734

Elizabeth Thornhill had one thing left to live for. She clung to that thought with steely tenacity as the door to Mr. Charles Montaigne's study swung closed behind her. Sunlight streamed in the tall sash windows that offered a view of fashionable Cavendish Square. Elizabeth took no pleasure in the sun's warmth. Nor did she find reassurance in the well-remembered scent of wax and lemons that rose from the room's freshly polished oak floor. She pulled off her worn mittens but left her voluminous cloak on and her hood up, seeing no sense in revealing just how desperate her plight was.

She chewed the inside of her cheek while she waited for the white-wigged man hunched over an enormous Queen Anne desk to address her. He did not even look up from his ledger book. She started to speak, then stopped herself, unsure whether it would seem rude. Confound it, she had hoped this meeting would be over quickly, so she could be on her way. She needed to find herself some sort of employment. She had tried for a fortnight, only to be rebuffed at every turn. No one would hire her in her present state.

Today she would succeed. She must. Another night on the streets would be more than she could bear. Even the meanest lodgings would be better than sleeping in St. James Park, as she had the past few days. Remembering the damp grass and the bone-soaking cold and the men who prowled by moonlight made Elizabeth shiver.

1

"M . . . Mr. Montaigne?" she asked finally.

He waved her forward without replying, without even looking up.

Elizabeth took a deep breath to still her trembling and walked forward, her woolen skirt scratchy against her bare legs. She wore no undergarments; she had gotten fivepence for her pannier, twopence for her petticoat and three whole shillings for her stays. It still wasn't enough. Not nearly enough.

It seemed to take an inordinately long time to cross from the door to the desk. The study was nearly twice the size of the attic apartment she and her late husband had shared. It was beyond belief that one man lived alone in this entire townhouse.

"Sit." Montaigne indicated a seat in front of his desk. Marking his place in the ledger, he looked up at last.

Elizabeth sank into the spindle-legged chair, hoping it was sturdy enough to support her weight. She could not meet Montaigne's gaze, and instead found herself staring at the jeweled stickpin in his snowy lace cravat. The stone—she guessed it must be an emerald—matched the green satin of his coat and waistcoat.

She suddenly felt more shame and loneliness than she had ever known in the entire twenty-three years of her life. "Mr. Montaigne, I—"

"Have you brought my money, Mrs. Thornhill?"

"No, sir. I know I said in my note that I would have it by today—"

"I have been most patient with you, Mrs. Thornhill."

Elizabeth stared down at her chapped, reddened hands, twisted in the folds of her blue cloak. "I am sure my parents' solicitor is looking for me even now, Mr. Montaigne. My inheritance—"

"Yes, yes, your note was quite eloquent about that, and I certainly remember the high points: your entire family was killed in a fire a few weeks ago, and you have an inheritance which will arrive in London momentarily. Spare me the sad tales, madam. I have heard them all before."

Elizabeth felt her temper flare. She forced herself to

keep her tone level. "Please, Mr. Montaigne, I am telling you the truth. Grant me one more week." Begging was as unfamiliar and distasteful to her as several of the other things she had been forced to do in the past two weeks, from sleeping in doorways to fighting with the worst kind of riffraff over scraps of food. But she must not think of herself now; she was responsible for the life of another. "It is only seven shillings."

"*Only* seven shillings?" He snorted and picked up his ledger book, shaking it at her. "Have you any idea how many of your kind owe me seven shillings? If I let you get away with not repaying your late husband's debt, others will see no reason to repay their debts. Then those who owe me seven *pounds* shall begin to think twice, then the ones who owe seven *hundred*. No, Mrs. Thornhill. It is not good business."

Elizabeth looked at the silver inkwell on his desk, the leather-bound books, the lacquered chinoiserie bookends—probably all paid for by the misfortune of others. She could no longer keep her temper in check. "What can seven shillings possibly mean to a man of your wealth, sir? Surely you sell enough of your accursed gin in a single hour to make many times that amount."

"Do not deign to lecture me about what I choose to sell, madam," he snapped. "I am only providing the people with what they want. If I didn't do so, someone else would. To return to the subject of your debt, you insist you have no family?"

"None, Mr. Montaigne." She fought back a wave of emotion that threatened to choke off her voice. "As I explained in my note, my parents and sisters are dead."

He still didn't seem to believe her. "And there is no one here in London from whom you could obtain the money?"

"No. My husband and I only arrived from Northampton this spring, just after our wedding. He thought to find work—"

"Yes, yes, just like the cartloads of other bumpkins who flock to London every day. The men end up as thieves and the women make their money on their backs.''

He suddenly fell silent, and Elizabeth looked up. Her cheeks grew hot as the old man perused her face. His carefully powdered and rouged features were animated with an all-too-familiar expression.

''Yes, you would be worth a great deal more than seven shillings.'' He rubbed his chin with pale, liver-spotted fingers. ''Your eyes are the most—tell me, what color is that?''

Elizabeth answered through gritted teeth. ''I am told it is violet, Mr. Montaigne. Now as to my—''

''Violet.'' His gaze lingered over her face, then traveled downward, assessing. Suddenly his blue eyes narrowed and his lips twisted in disgust. ''It would seem, Mrs. Thornhill, that you are in no condition to repay me in that way.''

Elizabeth's hands moved in an unconscious protective gesture to cover her midsection. She had vainly hoped her cloak would conceal her condition, but there was no hiding that she was almost seven months pregnant.

Montaigne gave a disappointed shake of his head. ''I have friends who would pay a high price for exclusive use of your services. But until you drop the brat you are of no use to me.''

Elizabeth raised her chin and glared at Charles Montaigne, her hands clenched into fists. Enough was enough. True, she was only a country girl, but her father had been a prosperous innkeeper and a respected man of some means; he never could have known that arranging her marriage to ambitious young Geoffrey Thornhill, a friend of the family from nearby Coventry, would bring her to these straits.

Geoffrey hadn't found the better life he sought in London, but refused to return home a failure. He had drowned his disappointment in liquor until one night he was killed in a drunken brawl, leaving her with bills to pay in every gin shop in the East End, including one owned by the fine Mr. Charles Montaigne.

By then it was too late for Elizabeth to return to Northampton. The roads were in a deplorable state and she dared not travel in her condition. Her inheritance had not arrived yet, but she would find some way to make the seven shillings, an *honest* way. She had her child, her pride, and her wits, and she would find a way to survive.

"Mr. Montaigne, your money and your fine townhouse and your expensive clothes do not give you the right to abuse me. I have told you the truth. I have sold everything I own." Reaching up, she threw back her hood, smiling at his look of shock. Her once-luxuriant black hair had been shorn within an inch of her head.

A wigmaker had paid her three pounds, but even that had not been enough. "I have paid all of my husband's other debts. Yours was the smallest, and I did not expect it would be so troublesome to you. I give you my word you shall have your seven shillings by next week."

She rose from her chair with as much grace as she could manage and stared down at him. "*I*, sir, have no price." She turned to leave.

"No."

Already halfway across the chamber, Elizabeth stopped and slowly turned about. "Is there something else, Mr. Montaigne?"

"I said no, Mrs. Thornhill. You will not leave. I knew before you came here that you would not have the money. You shiftless country rabble never do. I have taken the liberty of swearing out a warrant against you with the magistrate at Fleet Prison."

Elizabeth suddenly found it hard to breathe. "You cannot mean it!" The polished oak floor and scroll-patterned ceiling seemed to be spinning about her and she closed her eyes against a wave of dizziness. "You cannot commit me to Fleet for *seven shillings*."

"Yes, I certainly can." His impassive voice did not change. "What I cannot do is run a business on sympathy. After a time, I may come fetch you. As I said, I have friends who would pay a great deal to have you."

Elizabeth's legs trembled but she fought the weakness that threatened to overwhelm her. She would not sink to her knees before him. "But my baby. I cannot give birth in Fleet Prison. You must at least allow me time—"

"No, Mrs. Thornhill. I have no doubt that if I allow you to leave this house, I will never see you again." He leaned to one side and tugged the tasseled bellpull beside his desk.

Before Elizabeth could think of what to do, what to say in her defense, two of Montaigne's footmen entered the room and took her by the arms. She struggled in their grasp. "You cannot do this! You cannot! Please!"

The silk-liveried footmen ignored her cries. They held her still and waited expectantly for their master's orders.

Charles Montaigne didn't spare Elizabeth another glance. "Escort this woman to Fleet Prison. I have already spoken with the magistrate. The gaoler has the appropriate papers."

For her baby's sake, Elizabeth stopped trying to fight as the servants dragged her out. Montaigne said not another word to her. Just before the study door closed, she could see him calmly reopening his ledger book, picking up his pen and resuming his work.

Outside, one of Montaigne's elegant coaches waited in the almost blinding sunlight of Cavendish Square. The footmen loaded Elizabeth inside with all the care they would show a sack of vegetables. By the time they arrived at Fleet a half hour later, she was numb with fear. Even in her brief time in London, she had heard horrible tales of the place.

Fleet. The notorious debtors' prison where the dregs of society and nobles alike, men, women, and children, were jailed until they paid their debts—or died. Sending someone here was tantamount to murder, and usually just as effective.

Elizabeth was handed over and processed with swift and terrifying efficiency. Within minutes, the gaoler escorted her to a cell, shoved her inside and locked the gate behind her.

Shaking so badly she could barely stand, Elizabeth squinted into the darkness, trying to make sense of the forms milling about. Her senses reeled from the stench of overflowing chamber pots and unwashed bodies.

"Look at the belly on 'er," a male voice chuckled from the shadows.

Then another voice rang out, this one feminine and lacking the slightest note of humor.

"Welcome to hell, missy."

Four weeks later she had grown used to the smells, the cold, the moans and sobs of her fellow prisoners. Hour upon hour of imprisonment had worn away her revulsion and fear until there was nothing left of either. Even the lack of light no longer bothered Elizabeth, though she could tell day from night only by the trickle of sunlight that occasionally shone down the empty chimney flue.

Every day, more debtors arrived. Elizabeth's cell was so full that the prisoners had to sleep packed together at night. Even that no longer bothered her. She had found she could stand almost anything. Except the awful pain in her belly.

It was so agonizing that she had been lost in a delirium for a time. In her mind, she was home in Northampton again with her sisters Eleanor and Emma, racing Father's coach horses pell-mell over every fence in the shire, warming her hands on a steaming mug of chocolate, reading a book borrowed from one of the inn guests in the kitchen, surrounded by the smell of smoked bacon and fresh coffee and the glow of candlelight . . .

Gradually, Elizabeth floated back to awareness. She did not know how long she had been unconscious. Like iron bands alternately squeezing and releasing her body, the pain still wracked her, though she knew she had delivered her son hours ago.

Her son, Elizabeth thought, a smile touching her chapped lips as she drifted awake. Her labor had come upon her unexpectedly, almost a whole month early. There had been no midwife to help her through it, no apothecary's potions to ease her suffering. The pain had been so horrible, lasting an entire day and into the night, that she thought she would surely die of it.

But when she saw her son, with his ten perfect fingers and ten perfect toes, his face round and chubby like a cherub's, his cries so loud and lusty, she forgot the pain. She forgot the prison, the hopelessness of her situation, forgot everything but this tiny person who was new and beautiful and completely hers. Her family was gone, but she was no longer alone.

Edward, she thought. She would call him Edward, after her father. She felt joy spring to life within her for the first time in months, along with a tiny bud of hope. Just after hearing his first cries, she had passed out.

Someone was squeezing her hand. Elizabeth opened her eyes and squinted up at the faces leaning over her.

"Georgiana?" she blinked. Yes, it was Lady Georgiana Petersham, Viscountess Alden, and beside her sat Nell Osgood. The two women had appointed themselves Elizabeth's protectors from the time she arrived in the cell. Like her, they were newcomers to Fleet—the viscountess jailed for her husband's gambling debts; Nell, a shopkeeper, entrapped by a false charge sworn out by a jealous competitor.

During the long days and nights when there was nothing but conversation to fill the darkness and chase away fear, the three of them had become close.

"Georgiana." Elizabeth weakly held out her arms. Her friends had done their best as midwives. "Give me my son."

"Elizabeth, lamb . . ." Georgiana's lower lip began to tremble. She squeezed Elizabeth's hand tighter. "I am so sorry. I am so sorry."

A bolt of panic shot through Elizabeth. "My son. Georgiana, where is my son? Give me my son!" She struggled to sit up, but her weakened body would not respond. Anguish and terror clashed in her before she even heard Georgiana's next words.

"I am sorry, lamb. He was so small. He lived only an hour." Tears rolled down Georgiana's full cheeks. "He was just so small—"

"No!" Elizabeth shook her head, fighting to pull her hand out of Georgiana's. "No, no, no. You are lying! Nell, where is he? I heard him cry. I held him in my arms. He can't be dead." Her frantic words came faster and louder as she tried to convince them they must be wrong. "He can't be dead. He can't be dead."

Georgiana and Nell exchanged a look, then Nell nodded, tears and a frown marring her pretty features. She lifted a small bundle from beside her and gently placed it in Elizabeth's outstretched, empty arms.

Elizabeth's mouth opened on a wordless cry of agony. She took the tiny form and cradled him to her breast. The ten perfect toes and ten perfect fingers were still, the cherub's face cold as a statue's beneath her fingers. His eyes would never open. He would never smile up at her. A sound began deep in Elizabeth's chest and came out as a strangled sob.

"Edward."

Too weak to hold onto him, too weak to even speak anything more than that single, choked word, she let Nell take her son from her arms. She stared up into the darkened cell, her joy shattered, her hope shredded like the tatters of the blue woolen gown she wore. Hot tears spilled down her cheeks. She felt them on her skin, but not in her heart. Her heart lay cold and numb as a stone in her chest. As cold and numb as her son's dead body.

As cold and numb as the silver in Charles Montaigne's damnable coffers.

Nell squeezed her shoulder. "Be brave, me girl, save yer strength, now, Bess. Ye've lost a bit o' blood, and ye need yer rest, ye do."

Elizabeth did not respond. As if from far away, she heard another prisoner's voice in the darkness.

"I get them shoes of hers when she dies."

Nell rounded on the woman. "Shut up or ye'll get me fist in yer nose, ye stinkin' whore."

Georgiana stroked Elizabeth's ragged hair. "Don't you listen to that, Elizabeth. You just be strong and get well."

Elizabeth did not respond. She gazed into the darkness, not even blinking. "Seven shillings," she whispered. "He's wealthy as a prince and he did this to me for seven shillings."

She saw the worried look Nell and Georgiana exchanged, but did not comprehend nor care that it had anything to do with her. She felt very odd, as if she were floating above her body, merely observing what was happening in the cell without being part of it.

"Rest now, lamb," Georgiana said.

Elizabeth closed her eyes obediently, but sleep did not come. She was aware of every sound and movement around her, every grunt and grumble, every nuance of life in this tiny cell deep in the bowels of Fleet. She felt cold and began to shiver, despite the fact that Nell and Georgiana had covered her with their own cloaks. She thought of telling them she was cold, but couldn't see the point.

She was dying, she thought calmly. She was dying and could find no will to fight it. What had she to live for now? Her son was gone. Her parents and sisters had died in a fire. Geoffrey had killed himself with gin. To live would mean to spend day after day in this fetid cell, with no hope of escape, until she died—or until Montaigne came to fetch her, to sell her to one of his wealthy friends.

No, she would say nothing to Nell and Georgiana. Better to die quietly.

She knew it was morning when the others in the cell began to stir. They shoved their way closer to the door, the stronger ones elbowing the weak and the children out of the way. Each was eager to be first to get the watery gruel passed out for breakfast. Georgiana, who had checked on her now and again through the night, placed a hand to Elizabeth's forehead.

"How do you feel, Elizabeth?"

Elizabeth looked up at her friend's haggard visage. "Don't worry about me." She closed her eyes again, wondering how many hours she had left.

At ten o'clock the crier came through the prison as he did every morning, with his daily report of London news.

"I bring you good tidings this Christmas Eve," the man began in a booming voice.

Christmas Eve, Elizabeth thought. How ironic to die on a day that celebrated birth.

The crier continued as he moved along the corridor, though he sounded oddly formal, as if he were reading from a scroll. "To mark this most joyous season, and to relieve the conditions in the Fleet, which has become most disagreeably overcrowded as a result of the large number of insolvent debtors in it, His Majesty King George the Second has in his most Christian generosity signed a proclamation—"

The man was almost drowned out as a murmur among the prisoners grew into anxious shouts of joy and disbelief.

"—forgiving the debts of all women prisoners, and those girls and boys aged less than seven years. They are to be set free on Christmas morning. God save the king."

The cheers in the cell rose to a deafening level, shaking Elizabeth from her detachment.

"W . . . what was that he said?" she whispered.

"We're free, Bess!" Nell cried. "Do ye 'ear me, we're to be set free tomorrow morning. You and me and Georgi, we'll be all right, we will."

"You hold on now, lamb, and we will get you to a physician." Georgiana leaned over Elizabeth and hugged her. "We shall take care of you. We'll all have a chance to start anew."

Elizabeth clung to that last sentence. To start anew? A new life?

Yes, she thought suddenly, and spoke with a voice much stronger than she would have thought possible. "There is but one thing I want from my new life."

She stared up at her friends, seeing not their faces, nor the horrid prison cell around them, but Charles Montaigne sitting in his elegant study.

"Vengeance."

Chapter 1

Pierce Wolverton, Earl of Darkridge, slowed his horse to a trot and scowled at the moonless expanse of Hounslow Heath. A touch of dampness in the May night had strengthened into a steady drizzle within the past hour. He flipped up the collar on his greatcoat and buttoned it against the chill. It was too dark for him to check his pocket watch—a silver beauty he had nicked from the Prince of Wales in younger, more reckless days—but he guessed the hour to be long past midnight. He swore in annoyance, his breath forming little puffs of steam that frosted his collar. The bloody coach was late.

Or had it been waylaid?

Pulling his tricorne lower over his forehead, Pierce adjusted his black mask. *Hellfire!* If Swift had struck again, he might just beat him to a pulp, and to hell with the three hundred pounds' reward. He wouldn't be out here at all tonight if not for his blasted rival.

Pierce only rarely attacked Charles Montaigne's coaches; Swift, on the other hand, had been raiding them regularly for three months. Montaigne was getting nervous, and that was the last thing Pierce wanted. If his own plan was to succeed, he had to stop the elusive Blackerby Swift.

He drew one of the twin flintlock pistols he carried in holsters on his saddle. It was his father's gun; he'd had the other made to match it. Pierce no longer felt rage when he touched the weapon, nor bitterness. The pistol that had taken his father's life aroused only a slow-burning determination now.

For fifteen years, he had used it to wreak havoc on

the men who betrayed his father in their South Seas investment scheme. In the beginning, mindless with grief and fury, he had recklessly preyed upon his wealthy peers as well, "friends" who had cast him out on the basis of rumor and believed him guilty of murder.

Catching a bullet in the leg and almost landing in the gaol one night had shown him the foolishness of letting his passions rule his actions. Ever since then, he had limited his attention to his fathers' former partners. Pierce learned the discipline of logic and practicality; his raids became selective and careful. He ruthlessly subjected his every motion to rigid control.

It was the only way to survive.

Soon, Pierce vowed, he would use the pistol for the last time. He would have enough money to buy back Wolverton Manor and all the estates stolen from his family. He had already ruined three of the partners; he intended the fourth's destruction to be particularly slow and humiliating. Pierce wanted Charles Montaigne to feel the desperation *he* had felt, that night Montaigne claimed Wolverton Manor and turned a fifteen-year-old boy and his mother out into the streets.

Slowing his horse to a walk, Pierce shifted restlessly in the saddle, staring up into the cloud-choked sky. It was a new moon, darkest night of the month. Thunder rumbled in the distance, and brief flashes of lightning lit the clouds. Pierce absently rubbed his thumb over the scar on his left cheek. Soon.

First he must capture Swift and turn him in. He wondered where his renowned fellow highwayman was. The newspaper reports of Swift's exploits placed him most frequently at Hounslow Heath; then again, the Heath was a favored haunt of many highwaymen, who relied on its woods for cover and its relatively good roads for fast escapes.

But coach drivers also knew how popular the Heath was, and armed themselves accordingly. They would be especially wary when it was this dark, likely to shoot at anything that moved. Only madmen and fools would be out tonight.

Pierce frowned ruefully at the thought. "And which are you?" he muttered. To hell with it. Three hours was long enough to search. Swift obviously wasn't going to show up, or the bloody rogue had already taken the coach closer to London. Pierce holstered his pistol.

"I don't know which y'are, guv'nor, but I got a claim on this 'ere bit o' road, I 'ave."

Pierce froze, one hand on his reins, the other still on his pistol. The husky voice came from behind him, speaking in the thickest Cockney accent he had ever heard. His memory quickly skimmed over the newspaper reports on Blackerby Swift. He could remember no mention of the man's voice.

"Out o' the saddle, guv. And I'd like to see some air 'round yer 'ands, if ye don't mind."

Making no move that might get him shot, Pierce swung one leg over his horse and leapt to the ground. "Courtesy of the road, friend. What say we take the coach together?"

He slowly turned around to size up the interloper, raising his hands slightly so that his left was only inches from his holstered pistol.

With a mixture of disappointment and annoyance he knew at once he was not facing his rival. This was clearly a lad, no more than sixteen or so. The upstart stood about a yard away, holding a pistol aimed dead center on Pierce's chest. He wore a greatcoat that swamped him, the collar wisely pulled up to conceal his identity. Pierce couldn't make out much else, other than a rakish tricorne and black mask. For one so young, the boy had courage to pull a gun on a much larger man—courage likely born of desperation.

Pierce returned the lad's steady gaze with an unyielding stare, a look that had unnerved more than one prison-toughened criminal and made many a sweet young innocent swoon. The boy did not waver.

Pierce ground his teeth and raised his hands higher.

He had learned long ago that courage and desperation made a volatile mix. "There is no need to be greedy, lad. Half the spoils for half the work. What say you?"

The boy cocked the weapon, ready to fire. "I'm not of a mind t' share."

Though he had been ready to leave, Pierce began to get angry. He had waited three hours in this miserable cold and drizzle. And though he had come here in search of Blackerby Swift, not Montaigne's silver, he did not relish the idea of going home entirely empty-handed. Most important, Pierce Wolverton did not take orders from anyone, least of all a wet-nosed brat with more grit than sense.

On the other hand, he didn't want to get killed by a wet-nosed brat with more grit than sense.

The boy impatiently waved his pistol toward the road. "Ye don't own the whole 'eath. Unless ye want me to cut ye a new buttonhole in yer nice coat, I'd be on me way. Who d'ye think y'are, anyway?"

Pierce didn't move. He decided to give the boy a serious answer to his sarcastic question. "The Night Raider."

The boy stood silent for a moment. "The Night Raider?" He backed up a step. "The one who killed Fast Jack Figgs single-handed last summer?"

"The same." Pierce noted the boy had lost his accent.

The lad recovered quickly. "I don't give a pig's arse who ye be. This coach is mine. Be on yer way." He came forward. As he took his second step, the unmistakable sound of horses and the rattle of a carriage reached them. The boy's attention wavered for just a second.

With a liquid movement, Pierce lunged for the weapon. It went off with a burst of fire. He grunted in pain and surprise as the bullet struck his arm.

In the sudden flash of light, he was staring straight at the lad's face. He caught a glimpse of a delicate, pale chin—and the most striking violet eyes he had ever seen, staring wide with surprise at the roaring pistol.

The force of his forward motion threw them to the ground, hard. Each simultaneously ground out a curse. Pierce landed on top, his left arm burning with pain just above the elbow. He knew then and there that grabbing for the gun wasn't the only error he had made tonight.

This was no lad.

Despite the thick greatcoats they both wore, there was no mistaking the lush curves of the body beneath his, the softness in all the right places.

"Bloody Christ!" Ignoring the pain in his arm, Pierce knocked the pistol from the girl's hand, grabbed her by the lapels and shook her. "What in the *hell* do you think you're playing at, woman?"

Trembling beneath him, she opened her mouth to answer, but before she could say a word, they heard the startled orders of the coachman. She seemed to utterly forget her current position.

"Damnation!" She pushed at him with her gloved hands. "Let me up. The shot scared them off!"

Pierce glared down at her with a mixture of astonishment, irritation and anger. Then he released her. Leaving her lying in the mud, he jumped up, grabbed his fallen tricorne and ran for his own horse. "They haven't got away yet."

"I told you, I'm not of a mind to share," the girl yelled after him.

Pierce ignored her, having wasted enough time on the dangerous little chit. He vaulted into the saddle and kicked his horse into a gallop, intent on getting something to show for his trouble this deuced night.

The girl took to her own horse and quickly caught up with him. "Very well, we'll take it together, then."

Pierce didn't respond, concentrating on the vehicle that was racing away ahead of them, its lanterns sending crazy slices of light dancing across the dark hills. It was a tall, broad wagon with a cloth covering, meant for transport rather than speed. Oddly, there were no men riding the rear axle, only a driver and a guard up front. He couldn't tell how they were armed.

Pierce dropped his reins and drew both his pistols. His stallion galloped faster once given its head, as he had trained it to do. He was only a few feet from the coach's rear wheels now. He darted a glance to his left. The girl was right beside him, her tricorne back on her head, empty pistol in her hand.

The guard fired. The shot whizzed through the air between their horses.

Pierce growled an order at her. "If you want to be helpful, go to the left side, damn it!"

She quickly obeyed, guiding her mount to the left and disappearing on the far side of the coach.

Pierce spurred his stallion into a final burst of speed and came alongside the driver. "Stand and deliver!"

Looking at the highwaymen on his left and right, the coachmen reined in his team. He raised his hands and elbowed the guard in the ribs. "It's not worth getting killed for."

The guard reluctantly threw down his flintlock and raised his hands as well. "We don't want any trouble."

"Good, then, you might just get out of this alive," Pierce snarled at them. He aimed a pistol at each. "Throw down that little chest there between you."

The driver quickly unstrapped it and made to toss it down to him.

"Wait." Pierce hesitated. His wounded left arm was throbbing so painfully even his gun felt heavy. The idea of catching the box of silver was less than appealing. He thought of the girl, but she was on the other side of the coach, where he couldn't see her. He decided to take the chance. Surely she had more sense than to try and cross him; if she didn't, she would pay for her mistake. "Throw it to my partner there, on your other side."

The man did as Pierce bade, then gasped. "God's mercy, it's the one what robbed me last month. It's Blackerby Swift!"

Pierce thought the cold night air was playing tricks with his hearing. That slip of a girl could not *possibly* be the notorious Blackerby Swift. The man had to be mistaken. One highwayman looked more or less like the next in a tricorne, mask and greatcoat.

As if reading his thoughts, the man yelled out again, this time addressing his companion. "He's got that same silver-plated pistol. I'm the one what told the *Daily Post* 'bout that."

A husky voice uttered an oath on the far side of the coach. "Never mind who we are, ye cove. Get yer team movin' 'fore we really give the papers something t' write about."

Pierce brandished his own pistols. "Yes, like two coachmen found dead on Hounslow Heath."

The driver needed no further urging. He picked up his reins and whipped the team into a gallop. Pierce gritted his teeth and kept his weapons drawn. He had a few questions for his mysterious partner.

But as soon as the coach sped away, he saw he had made his third mistake of the night.

She was gone.

Astonished, he peered into the darkness. She could not have slipped away across the fields so quickly. He looked up the road, seeing no sign of her. He only guessed her ruse when he looked in the direction the coach had taken.

The bold little chit must have galloped off alongside it! He urged his horse forward, but already knew it was too late to give chase. She would be long gone into the trees by now, taking all the money with her, along with any chance of getting his questions answered.

Pierce swore savagely under his breath. He didn't know how, or by God's truth, why, but Blackerby Swift, the infamous, notorious highwayman, *was a woman.*

For just an instant, he felt an unfamiliar stab of conscience. How could he turn a woman over to the "justice" of the London magistrates?

He ruthlessly forced the thought from his mind. *She* was the one who chose to play this dangerous game; he was merely going to end it. He had worked fifteen years to avenge his family's ruin, and he was too close to his goal to allow *anyone* to interfere.

He would capture Blackerby Swift and turn her in. And it didn't matter a damn who she was.

Chapter 2

"**L**ady Barnes-Finchley?"

Elizabeth didn't respond to the woman sitting beside her on the richly upholstered settee, nor was she paying attention to the feminine conversation that filled the Marquess and Marchioness of Rowland's dining room. She had come to this party to gather information about Montaigne, but instead couldn't stop worrying about her encounter on Hounslow Heath two weeks ago. A delicate china cup and saucer teetered precariously on the lap of her lavender silk gown, her steaming tea untouched, her apple tart not even nibbled.

Who *was* the highwayman she had wrestled with that night? Was it truly the Night Raider or only someone boasting? Whoever he was, that man now knew that Blackerby Swift was a woman. What if he went to the newspapers with the information? Elizabeth chewed the inside of her cheek. Damnation, she didn't need things to be any more difficult than they already were.

She tried to take a deep, calming breath but was foiled by the fashionable Watteau gown she wore. The low bodice, decorated with an echelle of navy blue velvet bows, was laced too tight. She tried to master the art of breathing in little gasps.

"I say, Lady Barnes-Finchley?"

A nudge in the shin from Georgiana, who sat on Elizabeth's right, brought her back to the present.

"You will have to excuse my niece, Lady Kimble," Georgiana apologized. "She always gets a bit sleepy after dinner." She gave Elizabeth a stern glance.

Elizabeth forced a smile. The inheritance she had

20

collected three months ago provided just enough for her, Georgiana and Nell to let a modest townhouse together and buy a few clothes and necessities. Georgiana, explaining that she had been out of the country on holiday, introduced Elizabeth to society as her niece, Lady Elizabeth Barnes-Finchley, recently returned from an extended stay on the Continent.

Elizabeth wore a wedding ring to spare herself unwanted attention from suitors, and gave out the story that her husband was in Italy attending to family investments. Georgiana had done all she could to teach her the ways of polite society, but Elizabeth was having the deuce of a time just remembering to respond to her title.

She would have to work harder; only as a lady could she blend in with the upper classes and learn what she needed to know about Montaigne, his business, and the comings and goings of his coaches. "I am sorry. You were saying, Lady Kimble?"

Lady Kimble darted a glance about the vast drawing room, her pinched face flushed with excitement. After supper the ladies had retired for tea and dessert, leaving the men to their port and political talk in the dining room. "I say, have you heard the latest about that outrageous Blackerby Swift?"

"No, I haven't." Elizabeth stifled a yawn and surreptitiously checked the charming little pocket watch attacked to the bottom of her fan. Her limbs felt heavy with fatigue. "*Do* tell me all about it."

It was almost nine, thank God. She and Georgiana would be leaving in an hour. She could hardly wait to change out of the stylish outfit she wore. The white lace at her elbows itched, her high-heeled shoes pinched, and the layers of petticoats were too warm for June. She also despised the thick cosmetics Nell had applied to cover the circles under her eyes and add some color to her cheeks.

Even her hair hurt. Georgiana had devised a clever little chignon to disguise the fact that Elizabeth's black tresses barely reached her shoulders, and it had involved a great deal of pulling and combing.

"Well," Lady Kimble began, speaking in a dramatic whisper. "Lady Hargreaves tells me—and she heard it straight from her lady's maid, who heard it from the scullery girl, who got it directly from a groom—that Swift robbed the Duchess of Wembly last Saturday. Right in New Bond Street, in broad daylight, no less!"

"Really?" Elizabeth tried to sound suitably shocked, and wondered how the devil such rumors got started. She hadn't been anywhere near New Bond Street on Saturday. "How terrifying."

"Yes! And the latest word is that the rogue named himself after the Blackerby Arms, that inn up in Northampton that burned down last year and killed all those people. Well, there was even a rumor that he might be the *son* of Edward Blackerby, the innkeeper. But then I heard yesterday that it couldn't be true because the man didn't have any sons."

"No," Elizabeth said softly, her amusement fading. "Only daughters."

"What's that?"

Elizabeth caught herself. "You say he had only daughters?"

"Yes, and a woman couldn't possibly be responsible for the daring attacks this Swift has carried off. The name must have some other meaning for the ruffian." Lady Kimble leaned in closer and lowered her voice even further. "They say he's quite handsome. It would be just *too* scandalous of course, but I for one would be willing to sacrifice a necklace or a few guineas for the chance to have, shall we say, a tête-à-tête with such a bold and handsome man. It would be quite a thrilling encounter. Can you imagine?"

"Quite," Georgiana said in the same whisper.

"Yes, thrilling," Elizabeth added.

The woman giggled. "Oh, I'm just *too* wicked for admitting all my secrets, aren't I?"

Elizabeth choked back a mad urge to scream. She was risking her life and this woman thought of the whole thing as an entertainment. When choosing her *nom de guerre,* she hadn't realized the amount of attention

Blackerby Swift would get from the newspapers—or that Londoners would make the connection with the inn in Northampton. It was too late now, and she didn't care. She needed only a few more weeks to finish her revenge and stop Montaigne from ever hurting another person as he had hurt her. Nothing else mattered.

"I say, Lady Alden." Lady Kimble turned to Georgiana. "You must tell me all about your holiday in France—that *is* where you have been since last summer?"

Elizabeth felt her friend stiffen at the doubtful tone in Lady Kimble's voice.

"France and Italy, in fact," Georgiana said smoothly. "Anthony took ill and we could not return home as soon as we planned. When he passed away, I decided to sell our estate here and remain on the Continent for a time. I simply couldn't face living in our old home without him."

"Yes, of course. Well, I suppose the rumors are only servants' gossip."

"Rumors?" Georgiana asked lightly.

"Rumors, my dear," Lady Kimble smiled smugly, "that when the viscount passed away, you *did* return and you were," she lowered her voice again, "imprisoned upon your arrival. Something about your husband's gambling debts. They say you sold your estate and still couldn't cover them."

"*Really,* Lady Kimble." Georgiana laughed, a long, rich chuckle that set the other woman back on her heels. "You know how stories start to fly when someone is absent from London for an extended time. I should think *you* would be able to sort such tales from the truth, my dear. I've always depended on you as such a reliable source."

Clearly embarrassed at being made light of, Lady Kimble fidgeted with her teacup. "Yes, well, certainly you may continue to do so. And you can also depend on me to quash that story if ever I hear it again."

The three of them fell silent; Elizabeth couldn't hold back a weary sigh. She used to love nothing better than to pass hour after hour talking with the guests at her father's inn, listening to tales of their travels or debating whatever issues were currently before Parliament. She had never attended school, but her education had been rich and varied.

By contrast, the gossip that passed for conversation among the upper classes seemed dull and vapid to her. The women never discussed anything of import. She was about to excuse herself when a servant entered through a side door, carrying a small bundle wrapped in fine lawn and white lace. A curious murmur trickled through the room.

"Come, everyone," their hostess beckoned, with a proud smile. "I know you are all just dying to see how much little Alfred has grown since his christening."

"Oh! It's the Marchioness's new baby." Lady Kimble set her cup aside and leapt up from the settee as quickly as her three-foot-wide pannier would allow. The women in the room quickly converged on the nurse.

Georgiana stood, but Elizabeth sat frozen in place, staring at the baby. Her mind had gone blank. She could not force herself to rise.

Georgiana's ruddy features softened as she looked down. She touched Elizabeth's arm. "It's all right, lamb, I'll make your excuses," she said gently. "You go outside and catch your breath."

Elizabeth nodded, her throat so tight she couldn't speak, and exited the drawing room as inconspicuously as possible. Thankfully, she could no longer see the baby through the bevy of cooing women, but the child began to fuss and cry. The sounds struck Elizabeth's heart like needles.

She slipped out the door and closed it, leaning against it for just a moment while she fought back a wave of sadness. Then she hiked up her lavender skirts with one hand and hurried down the wide hall toward the glass French doors at the back of the house, her steps echoing like pistol shots on the gleaming marble floor.

Once on the terrace outside, she ran to the stone railing and held on to it, gasping in aching sobs of the night air. *Don't think about it,* she urged herself. *Don't feel it.* She would be all right if she could just avoid thinking about the baby. Six months had passed, but the pain was still there just beneath the surface, as fresh as on that horrible December day. She dared not give in to her grief, certain she was not strong enough to survive it.

She squinted out at the neatly trimmed lawns that covered acres and acres of the Rowlands' estate. The pathways and gardens had been thoughtfully lit with lamps so guests might admire the flowers. The smell of the burning oil mingled on the breeze with the scents of roses and cherry blossoms. Elizabeth spied a small gazebo on the far side of the grounds. Breathing slowly to calm her pounding heart, she descended the long terrace steps and headed toward the little building, eager for the chance to be alone.

The gazebo turned out to be a small imitation temple, fashioned after the monuments of Greece. A large man-made pond flanked it on one side, a stand of Scotch pines on the other, carefully planted to look as if they grew there naturally. *All false,* Elizabeth thought as she walked to the edge of the water. She was quickly learning that nothing was as it seemed among the upper classes.

The full moon and flickering oil lamps traced ribbons of silver fire across the glassy black surface of the pond. Ruffled by a breeze, her reflection shifted and scattered into dozens of bright pieces. Elizabeth swallowed hard, staring at the splintering shards. It was exactly how she felt; every day it became more dangerous, harder to hold the pieces all together. Trembling, she put her hands over her face, blocking out the image.

She was just as false as the temple or the pond. By day she was Lady Elizabeth Barnes-Finchley, by night Blackerby Swift. She was digging herself into a pit of deceptions that she might never be able to escape.

How long could she keep going? Her strength and courage were at a perilously low ebb, and a slip in either disguise at any time could end her plans for Charles Montaigne—and her life.

Montaigne. The name alone tempered her rising panic.
She could feel the anger and hatred curling inside her,
burning like twin fires that fed upon one another. They
grew hotter with each passing day until they consumed
her, even invading her dreams. They drove her to attempt
the most reckless of raids, despite the fatigue that constantly plagued her, despite her fear.

Damn him, God damn him for what he had done to
her! The only course was the one she had chosen; she
could have no peace, no rest until Montaigne's downfall
quenched the flames.

"Please don't hide your face, Lady Barnes-Finchley,"
a squeaky voice requested from behind her. "It is far too
lovely."

Startled, Elizabeth spun around. She groaned when
she recognized the short man approaching along the path.
It was Lord Anthony something-or-other, an utter boor
who had bothered her ceaselessly during supper. His
squat body was encased in yellow silk, and he wore an
old-fashioned, full-bottomed periwig topped by a black
tricorne with a feather in it. He looked like a bumble bee
flown astray.

"Lord—er—Awkwright," Elizabeth greeted him, trying very hard to remember what Georgiana had said
about being cordial to the noblemen she met, no matter
how much she loathed their self-important attitudes.

"*Ark*wright, my lady," he corrected.

The smell of the perfumed pomatum in his wig smoth-
ered the pleasant scents in the air. Elizabeth retreated to
the far side of the temple. "Have the men finished their
port already?"

"No, but I happened to glance out the window, and
thought I saw a lady out here. It is dangerous to walk
about unescorted at night, Lady Barnes-Finchley. One
never knows what sort of ruffians one might encounter
out here in the country."

Elizabeth frowned. Ruffians she could handle; the only
"sort" she had to worry about was *his* sort—preening
lords with liquor on their breath, long on lust and short

on scruples. "I am quite well, I assure you, Lord Ark-wright. I wish to be left alone."

Damnation, was that too abrupt? She decided she didn't care. She was doing her best to carry out the social niceties as Georgiana had taught her, but sometimes it was asking too much.

He sidled up next to her, and Elizabeth found herself with no place left to retreat but the trees.

"I simply cannot leave you out here alone. However," he let his voice trail off suggestively, "if you do not wish to return to the party, my lady, I should be only too happy to offer my carriage."

Elizabeth almost slapped him, but couldn't remember if that was allowed in this situation or not. She had no interest in any sort of liaison with *any* man, and certainly not with an arrogant nobleman. "I remind you, sir, that I am a married woman."

"Yes, and I am sure your husband would thank me for seeing to your safety, were he here."

"Thank you for the generous offer, Lord Awkwright." She purposely mispronounced his name. "But I really do wish to be alone."

He moved closer. "Come, now, Lady Barnes-Finchley—may I call you Elizabeth?—allow me to escort you to my carriage."

"No." She said firmly. She wished she had her pistol. "You are too kind."

He suddenly grabbed her shoulders and stood on tip-toe. "I insist."

A voice startled them both before he could kiss her. It came from the evergreens behind her—a deep, resonant voice, like a rumble of thunder in the stillness of a sultry night, just before a storm. "The lady wishes to be left alone."

Elizabeth pushed free of the surprised Lord Arkwright and looked into the stand of Scotch pines. She found herself staring at a man she had never seen before. He drifted silently out of the trees, a shadow, then more than a shadow, as if God—or perhaps Satan—had breathed hot, vital life into a slice of the night sky.

His tall, angular frame was almost frightening in its powerful lines. Elizabeth backed up a step, feeling a warm prickle of danger up the back of her neck. A dark cloak fluttered about his back and shoulders, and her heart began thumping against her ribs; she felt an unreasoning fear that he might reach out and envelope her utterly. Her mind urged her to flee, but she could not bring her body to move as he came forward with sure, aggressive steps.

"Darkridge." Lord Arkwright snapped the name as if it were a curse. "I don't remember *your* being invited here. There are penalties for trespassing, you know."

The stranger walked to the little Greek temple and leaned against one of its pillars, his eyes never leaving Elizabeth's. He looked as solid and unmovable as the column of stone. "Calling me out, Arkwright?"

Tearing her gaze from the stranger, Elizabeth looked at her supper companion and saw fear in his face. He had, in fact, blanched to a shade lighter than his starched cravat. "No," he replied. "Certainly not."

"Then I suggest you return to your tea and cakes inside."

Lord Arkwright muttered something under his breath that Elizabeth couldn't quite make out, though it sounded like "bloody murderer." He held out his arm. "Come, Lady Barnes-Finchley."

"She stays," Darkridge stated.

"I am not leaving this lady alone in your company."

Darkridge's eyes narrowed to slits and his tone dropped to a growl. "I think you will."

Arkwright hesitated only a moment more. Then, with a quick, apologetic bow to Elizabeth, he made a hasty retreat.

"Lord Arkwright! Wait!" Elizabeth started after him. She could not believe the blasted coward would abandon her to this, this—God knew what sort of man.

"Don't go."

The stranger's words were not a request, but a command, his voice taut, controlled and thoroughly unnerving. Incensed, Elizabeth turned and started to speak, then forgot what she had been about to say.

He had silently moved closer until he was a few feet away, close enough so that if she reached out, she might touch the fine navy waistcoat that strained across his broad chest, or the white cravat that emphasized the angular, deeply tanned line of his jaw. He had a long scar on his left cheek, just below his ear.

Elizabeth found she had to look up even further before she could meet his gaze. Tiny beads of perspiration broke out on her upper lip. His eyes were brown, intense—and somehow familiar. She felt her stomach drop to her toes, then ricochet back. She had the feeling she should be able to place him, but couldn't think straight. "I . . . I have lost my desire to see the gardens," she managed at last. "And we have not been properly introduced."

Turning on her heel—in what she thought Georgiana would surely praise as the very picture of an affronted society lady—Elizabeth started to stalk away from the man.

She got exactly one step before the stranger's hand shot out and captured her wrist. With easy, confident strength he held her fast and slowly turned her around to face him.

He was smiling. No, not quite a smile, more a sarcastic grin that held some private humor. "Lord Pierce Wolverton, fourth Earl of Darkridge. So pleased to make your acquaintance."

He spoke with the smoothness of a man born and bred in Cavendish Square, but Elizabeth got the impression he would be more at ease trading curses with a Thames ferryman. If he were truly a lord, he was strangely attired, for he wore neither wig nor hat nor any face powder. His hair was tied in a simple queue at his neck, one dark brown lock straying over his right eye.

"I . . . I am . . ." Trapped by that unyielding, dusky gaze, Elizabeth could not remember by which name she should introduce herself. He was studying her face, her chin, and most of all her eyes. She found the intense interest both odd and disturbing. He still held her wrist, and the sensation of his long, strong fingers clasping her bare skin filled her with the strangest prickly warmth. "I am—"

"Lady Elizabeth Barnes-Finchley," he said with a cynical bite to his voice. He released her at last, seeming satisfied with his perusal. "I was told you would be here tonight."

Elizabeth felt unsteady on her feet, but a rising sense of alarm quickly cleared her head. "By whom? And how do you know who I am?" Had Arkwright said her name? She couldn't remember.

Lord Darkridge wandered around the side of the temple to the edge of the pond. "You, my lady, have swept London society off its feet. Every drawing room and concert hall is abuzz with talk of the beautiful young woman who arrived with her aunt from the Continent, three months ago. When I heard you had the most striking violet eyes, I simply had to meet you."

Elizabeth's heart began to pound. Was this merely a wealthy nobleman interested in seduction? Or did he somehow suspect that she was not what she seemed? "My eyes have brought you all this way out into the country? To attend a party where you are obviously *not* wanted?"

"Yes." He said the word harshly, and when he turned to look at her, Elizabeth thought she saw a flash of some emotion in his eyes—anger, or perhaps hurt. But when he spoke again, his voice returned to its rich, low tones. "I am something of a poet, you see. I asked where I might find you because I am currently working on a volume of odes to London's great beauties. I should like to include you."

She blinked at him in disbelief. As he stood at the edge of the water, framed by the light of the lamps and the moon, he looked like a dark god of war, just arrived in a new land, ready to conquer all he surveyed. The idea of this man as a poet was ludicrous; his flattery was obviously intended to lure her to his town house and into his bed. Elizabeth couldn't explain the twinge of disappointment she felt upon discovering he was no better than the other lords she had met.

"I would *not* be interested, Lord Darkridge." She started to walk back to the house. "I am sure my husband would take exception to such an idea."

He stepped in front of her before she could get more than a few paces. "Where *is* your husband, that he allows you to wander about unescorted like this?"

"In Italy," she said quickly. "Attending to business—"

"What sort of business?"

Elizabeth gritted her teeth to stop an oath, trying to remember she was supposed to be a highborn lady. "He doesn't discuss it with me," she said in dulcet tones. "Now you must excuse me—"

"But we have only just met. Or have you another engagement tonight?"

Elizabeth glared at his chest, annoyed at his persistence and distressed by his question. She could not shake the feeling that this man knew much more than he should, that she was not safe out here alone with him. "No, I haven't another engagement. But my aunt does not like to stay out late, and I am sure she is ready to return home."

Before she could move around him, he reached out and took her hand.

"Sir," she ground out, "if you are any kind of a gentleman, you will let me go. And if you do not, I shall scream."

Pierce did not heed her threat; he believed her, but found himself unwilling to let go. He had been wandering the grounds for an hour, trying to think of a way to get inside and find her, when she neatly presented herself, a pale wisp of lavender moonlight, floating over the lawn in her silk gown.

She hesitantly raised her head, and he felt the strangest clenching sensation in his gut. Her eyes, so bright—and somehow so haunted—drew him in like a song of bittersweet beauty. Her blunt, straight nose and slightly uneven lips didn't detract from her charm. On the contrary, they elevated her looks to the realm of the uncommon. This was no angel drifted down from heaven, made for poets to sing of; this was a woman as real and dark and intriguing as the night itself, a woman made for a man.

"You really must let me go," she said.

"No, I don't think I shall."

There was no mistaking her voice, either. The Cockney accent was gone, but the husky, throaty sensuality in its place held him enthralled. Hellfire, he should just let her leave. He couldn't for the life of him understand why he had stepped in front of her. His first look at her face had told him all he needed to know.

There was no doubt in his mind that Lady Elizabeth Barnes-Finchley and Blackerby Swift were one and the same. The London magistrates, however, would not believe him if he presented this girl, looking like she did now. They would laugh him out of the courtroom.

He would have to capture her at the scene of one of her crimes, in her disguise. He guessed that the *real* reason she was so eager to leave was that she intended to take Montaigne's midnight coach. He might catch her in the act this very night.

So why didn't he just let her go?

The moon bathed her skin in pearl-white light, from the delicate line of her chin to the shadowy edge of her shoulders. The upper curve of her full, high breasts was just visible above her décolletage, and Pierce's whole body tensed unexpectedly at the sudden image of this woman—Lady Elizabeth Barnes-Finchley, Blackerby Swift, or whoever the devil she claimed to be—lying naked beneath him, here on the grass.

His fingers itched to touch her, just there, at that vulnerable spot where lavender silk and white lace gave way to warm, soft woman.

The next instant, he lowered his lips to hers.

"Please." She jerked her head to one side, a note of panic in her voice. She tried to pull her hand out of his, and this time Pierce released her, amazed at his own impulsiveness. This wasn't like him at all; he hadn't paused a second to think about what he was doing.

She backed away a step and stood there, staring at him, those eyes of pure amethyst wide with confusion, her black lashes and brows stark against her skin, like ink strokes on a fresh white page. In an instant, her features changed from uncertainty to anger, and she hiked up her skirts and turned away. She walked off with a proud, graceful sway that sent Pierce's blood hammering through his veins.

He couldn't resist having the last word. "Good night, Lady Barnes-Finchley."

At the sound of his voice she broke into a run like a startled doe, fleeing from him toward the house in a flurry of shimmering silk.

Pierce smiled grimly and walked back toward the south end of the grounds, where he had tied his horse. Best to get this over with as soon as possible and pack her off to the authorities, before she confounded him any further. He flipped open his silver pocket watch. Nine-thirty. More than enough time to catch her on the North Road out of London. There was no reason to put this off, absolutely no reason.

He would take her tonight.

Chapter 3

The hackney coach carried Elizabeth and Georgiana along Park Lane and into Grosvenor Square. Elizabeth stared out the window at the rows of town houses they passed. Most had candles in the windows, the servants inside awaiting the return of their wealthy employers from supper or the latest concert at New Spring Garden. Elizabeth had kept silent since leaving the Rowlands' party, but it was impossible to hide her distress from Georgiana; the older woman had an almost uncanny way of sensing the emotions of others.

"Elizabeth, are you not going to tell me what's wrong?" Georgiana leaned forward, her snug gown of striped taffeta rustling. The deep carmine color emphasized the red in her hair and the ruddiness in her cheeks. "I know seeing the baby upset you—"

"No, I'm fine, really," Elizabeth said quickly, not wanting to even think about the child. She gave her friend a reassuring smile. She had known Georgiana less than a year, yet she felt closer to her, and to Nell, than to any friends she had ever known. She supposed it was similar to the friendships forged between men who had been through battle together. In a short time, they had become inseparable, despite great differences in their family backgrounds and social classes.

Georgiana gave her a doubtful look. "If you were fine, you would be talking yourself breathless, not staring pensively out the window."

Elizabeth shrugged her shoulders. "It was that awful Lord Arkwright. He followed me out into the gardens."

"You were quite adept at managing him during supper. I can't believe he could get you this flustered."

Elizabeth looked out the window again, absently twisting the wedding band she wore on her left hand. They were coming into the Strand, the fashionable market district where Nell had her shop. "In truth there *was* someone else." She took a deep breath. "A stranger. He said he had come to the party because he wanted to meet me."

"Good Heavens!" Georgiana exclaimed, a strong oath coming from her. "Who was he? What happened?"

"It was nothing I couldn't handle, Georgiana, really," Elizabeth insisted, knowing it was untrue. She had no idea what might have happened if she hadn't gotten away from the man when she did. Even now, miles away in the safety of the coach, she trembled at the memory of his powerful strength holding her still, his commanding voice calling after her in the darkness. "His name was Pierce Wolverton, Earl of Darkridge." He had definitely made a potent—and disturbing—impression on her; usually she had the deuce of a time keeping names and titles straight.

"Darkridge!" Georgiana sat up, her blue-gray eyes wide. "My God!"

Elizabeth looked at her in astonishment. "What *is* it about the man that makes everyone say his name as if it were a curse? Who the devil is he?"

"The devil, precisely. Listen to me, Elizabeth, if ever you see him again, stay away from him. The man has been an outcast for years."

Elizabeth frowned. It wasn't like Georgiana to judge someone unfairly. If she thought Pierce Wolverton terrible, he must indeed be terrible. "But why does everyone seem frightened of him? What did he do?"

Now it was Georgiana who shifted uncomfortably and averted her gaze. "They say he killed his father."

"His *father*?"

"It happened fifteen years ago. It was all very mysterious, but it seems he killed his father during a drunken argument. He and his mother disappeared from society then, and no one knows what happened to her. It's rumored he killed her as well. They say he's not entirely sane.''

Elizabeth was aghast. "But how is it he was never tried for murder?''

"There was not enough evidence, I suppose.'' Georgiana shrugged. "In any case, he returned to London a few years ago, and he seems to have done quite well for himself. He's very wealthy. He spends his time at the most disreputable sort of gentlemen's clubs, but every so often he'll turn up at a party or one of the music halls. His title still wins him a few invitations here and there from the more daring hostesses.''

Elizabeth absorbed all this with a shiver. To think she had been alone with the man! Still, she found it difficult to believe he was unbalanced. Although he had frightened her tonight, he had seemed quite rational.

Georgiana gave her a worried look. "Elizabeth, it is certainly understandable that an encounter with Lord Darkridge would upset you. Perhaps you shouldn't venture out tonight. I have . . .'' She rubbed her temples. "I have such a strange feeling about this.''

Elizabeth's heart skipped a beat. In the months she had known Georgiana, she had come to respect the older woman's "strange feelings.'' The premonitions came true with disturbing regularity. After a moment, she shook her head. "I must. You know the Trust needs the money. Even with the profits from Nell's shop, it's barely getting by.''

"But we've paid the debts of fifty-six women so far,'' Georgiana argued. "We're doing what we set out to do. I would say our London Women and Children's Trust is a grand success.''

Elizabeth smiled patiently. Georgiana and Nell were constantly trying to persuade her to curtail her raids. "A success, yes, but I would not call it grand. We've saved fifty-six from being sent to prison, but they're only a raindrop in the barrel. There are *so* many more.''

"But how long can you go on like this? I've seen the strain it's putting on you. So has Nell. If you're caught, you'll be *hanged*. Montaigne is not taking this lying down. I understand he increased the bounty to four hundred pounds.''

"Only if I'm taken alive," Elizabeth said with carefree confidence she didn't feel. "It's only two hundred if I'm—"

"Elizabeth!" Georgiana cried vehemently. "This is nothing to be made light of!"

"I'm sorry, Georgiana. I don't mean to upset you, but I must finish what I started," Elizabeth said firmly. "It won't be much longer now. I overheard some of the men talking at supper. It seems my raids are making Montaigne nervous. He plans to purchase one huge shipment of gin, sometime this summer, so he won't have to risk his twice-monthly coach runs anymore. All I need to do—"

"Don't say it." Georgiana winced. "I know what you're thinking, but you can't be serious. He'll have scores of men to guard it!"

"It's worth the risk. All I need to do is find out when and where it's to take place. I can finish him in one final blow.''

"But surely he'll keep the time and place secret."

Elizabeth chewed her lower lip. "Yes, I thought of that. His solicitor is holding a masquerade ball next week. I think I shall attend and find out if the man knows any of the details.''

Georgiana threw up her hands in exasperation. "You're not listening. *Think* of what you are doing. You may ruin Montaigne, but at what price?''

Elizabeth looked out at the cold moonlight and felt an equally cold determination grip her heart. She was willing to risk any price to have her revenge. "Charles Montaigne took from me the one thing I treasured most in the world. I mean to take the one thing *he* treasures most: his money. All of it." She knew her tone was harsh and unyielding, but she didn't care. "I'm going to give him a taste of the misery he's forced on so many others, Georgiana. And his money will make sure that other women and . . .'' her voice faltered, ''and their babies never have to suffer what I suffered.''

She turned back toward her friend and forced a brave smile. Reaching out, she squeezed Georgiana's hand. ''What we *all* suffered.''

Before they could discuss it any further, the coach came to a halt in front of a line of stylish shops. The driver helped them alight, and Georgiana slipped him an extra copper for his trouble before sending him on his way.

Several of the establishments still had candles burning. They could see masters and their apprentices within, cleaning up from the long day's business and preparing to open for their aristocratic patrons at seven the next morning.

They walked past windows displaying an opulent array of goods: clocks, pewter and china, millinery and ribbons, pyramids of fruit, the latest wigs. They stopped before a pair of tall windows crowded with silks, velvets, Scottish plaids and fine English linens. The heavy sign hanging over the entrance read, *N. Osgood, Draper.*

Elizabeth felt a little jump of excitement in her stomach, the now-familiar combination of anticipation and fear that always accompanied her transformation into Blackerby Swift.

'' 'Ello ladies,'' Nell called as she opened the door, a broad shopkeeper's grin lighting her pretty face. She wiped at a strand of blond hair that had slipped from her bun, then smoothed the skirt of her blue cotton gown. ''Welcome to Osgood's. What can I interest ye in this evenin'? A fine Norwich crepe, per'aps? Or . . .'' Her voice trailed off as she looked up and down the street. Assured that no one was about, she hustled them inside and closed the door behind them, locking it and pulling the shades.

''Where the blast ye been?'' She greeted them, hands on her trim hips. ''It's almost eleven. If ye keep comin' in so late, it'll look suspicious.''

Georgiana puffed up like a ruffled hen. ''We've taken every precaution. If we come too early, we might encounter customers. And we hire a different coach each time. No one has reason to suspect we are anything more than a pair of ladies doing a bit of late-night shopping on our way home from Covent Garden."

"Well, see that ye be a bit earlier next time," Nell grumbled.

Elizabeth smiled, knowing Nell's gruffness was her way of saying she had been concerned about them. "If the two of you have finished your argument for the evening, would someone *please* help me out of this dress?" She reached behind her and fiddled with the laces as she walked through a maze of satin-upholstered chairs, past counters piled high with bolts of fabric.

Nell followed her to the back of the shop and unlocked a door that concealed a narrow stairway. The small apartments above, which usually served as the shopkeeper's home, held what would seem to a visitor an unusual array of items.

Elizabeth had already pulled the pins from her hair and was running her fingers through it as she turned into the small bedroom at the top of the stairs. The room contained no bed, only a small wardrobe, a washstand, and a table in one corner, with a black tricorne and a silver-embossed pistol on it. She took off the wedding band she wore and lay it next to the gun, trying to ignore the pinprick of guilt she felt as she slipped out of one false role and into another.

With Nell's help, she quickly shed her gown, stays, pannier and petticoats. "Why is it, you suppose," she asked, trying to dispel the worried mood that creased her friend's brow, "that women are the only ones who have to wear such uncomfortable undergarments?"

"Hmph," Nell grumbled, taking a white cotton shirt, stockings, and black breeches from the wardrobe. "Because women always think they need t' be improvin' themselves, and men always think they're bloody perfect just as they are. A man would never admit to wearin' a special contraption to make 'is shoulders look bigger, nor 'is—"

"*Nell,*" Elizabeth admonished, knowing what other

body part her friend was about to mention. "If Georgiana caught you talking like that—"

"She'd give me a tongue lashin' that would last a fortnight, I know, Bess, I know."

Elizabeth couldn't suppress a grin. It was Nell's outspoken personality as well as her skill as a draper that made Osgood's a favorite stop for London ladies. Nell had run the shop alone since her husband's death four years ago, until a competitor began pursuing her with marriage on his mind; when she spurned his advances, he swore out an enormous false debt against her and landed her in Fleet. Fortunately, her well-trained clerks had kept the place running until she could return, and her time in prison only added to her flamboyant reputation, bringing in more customers than ever.

"There." Nell helped Elizabeth into a matching black waistcoat and coat, then handed her the pair of light, square-toed jackboots they'd had specially made in her size. "Cor, Bess, ye look convincin', but I 'ate that ye 'ave t' do this."

Taking her first truly deep breath of the day, Elizabeth stood still while Nell brushed her hair and tied it in a queue at her neck. "You know it's no use to try and talk me out of this, Nell."

"I still say ye should let me try me 'and at it."

"Except that you can't ride a horse at more than a trot without falling off." Elizabeth grinned.

"I know, I know. And there's no way Georgi could pass as a man. She'd be as out o' place as I'd be at one o' them fancy society parties. Can ye picture 'er in a frock coat an' breeches? 'Oldin' a gun on some poor dandiprat?" She slipped into an imitation of Georgiana's sweet, lilting voice, " 'If you please, my lord, might I ask you to hand over your money, if it's no trouble?' "

"Nell," Elizabeth admonished again, laughing despite herself. Nell and Georgiana baited one another constantly, and had almost nothing in common, but she knew they felt a deep affection for one another underneath it all.

Nell helped Elizabeth don her greatcoat, then handed

her the black tricorne and the silver-trimmed pistol. "Ye promise me ye'll be careful tonight, now."

Elizabeth accepted the heavy weapon reluctantly. She was not a very good shot, and the idea of hurting anyone in the course of her raids made her physically ill. When she had accidentally wounded that other highwayman two weeks ago, she hadn't been able to sleep for almost three days. She hadn't loaded the weapon since then, and had promised herself it would stay that way.

She supposed it was odd that a person with her sensibilities could be a successful highwayman, but so far the facade of ruthlessness, the threat of violence, and a fast horse had been enough to see her through.

"I give you my word I'll be careful," Elizabeth finally said. Flashing a confident smile, she added in the Cockney accent Nell had spent weeks teaching her, " 'Ere, now, ye cove. I'm a lass what's always careful, don't you know?"

"Don't ye know," Nell corrected crossly.

"Don't ye know," Elizabeth repeated, leading the way out of the room and back down the stairs. She slipped the pistol into her right pocket. Checking the left, she found her pocket watch, and the black mask that would complete her disguise once on the road. Her body was already growing tense, her pulse quickening. No matter how many times she had been out, or how right her cause, she couldn't shake a deep feeling of anxiety.

For no matter how she made light of it, the fact was that she had become a wanted criminal.

Georgiana waited for them at the foot of the stairs, pacing, one hand on her forehead as if she felt faint. "Are you sure you have to go out, Elizabeth? I really *do* have a strange feeling about this tonight." She stopped pacing, squeezing her eyes shut with a wince. "Oh, dear. This is quite strong."

Elizabeth gulped and silently busied herself adjusting her tricorne. She looked at Nell, who frowned back at her. "I'm with Georgi. Let this one go, Bess. Ye need yer rest."

Elizabeth hesitated, then at last shook her head. This

was too important, to her and to the scores of women facing debtors' prison—women and children preyed upon by Montaigne and others like him. Every guinea, every shilling meant salvation to someone who would otherwise suffer the horrors of Fleet or Ludgate or Whitechapel.

She couldn't let anything stop her, not even her friends' good intentions. "I'll be fine, really." She buttoned her greatcoat and pulled up the collar, then gave each of them a hug. "Now you two stop worrying about me and start thinking about all we'll be able to accomplish with Montaigne's money."

Giving them a wink, she slipped out the back door and into the darkened streets of London's West End.

Even after months of living here, Elizabeth still could not get over the differences between the West End and the East End. The alley she walked in was free of refuse, the homes well-kept and spacious; the East End street where she had lived in an attic with her husband had been crowded with beggars, gin vendors, rats, and filth.

Every day Geoffrey had gone out looking for work, and every day he came back empty-handed, ranting about how unfair the tailor's guild was, reeking of liquor, frustrated, and angry.

She shivered at the memory, and forced herself to concentrate on tonight's raid. Charles Montaigne's coaches left London twice a month with orders for gin distillers in the north. His suppliers refused to deal in the paper currency that was becoming so popular among London merchants, so the coaches were always loaded with silver or gold. Elizabeth—or rather, Blackerby Swift—was draining Montaigne's gin business dry, shilling by shilling.

She rubbed her neck, feeling too hot in the heavy greatcoat. The weather had grown much warmer since the last time she had been out, two weeks ago. She hadn't told Georgiana or Nell about her encounter with the Night Raider. They worried too much about her as it was. Elizabeth could well imagine how upset Georgiana would be about the Night Raider, after seeing how troubled she was over Lord Darkridge. . . .

She stopped a few paces further on. Lord Darkridge . . . and the Night Raider. She hadn't thought to put the two together until just now. Between the darkness and storm clouds, she had seen very little that night, but the deep voice and powerful form were certainly similar. Could the infamous Pierce Wolverton also be one of England's most infamous highwaymen?

She dismissed the idea and walked on. What reason would a wealthy earl possibly have for risking his neck on the roads? He would have to be mad.

She stopped again. Mad was precisely what everyone said the Earl of Darkridge was.

Forcing the thought from her mind, Elizabeth resolutely kept going. She had enough real problems to worry about; there was no sense scaring herself with phantoms. She arrived at the stable where she kept her horse, and twenty minutes later she was riding along the Great North Road, her heart beating fast, her every sense alert for some sign of Montaigne's midnight coach.

The full moon splashed silver-blue light over the hills. The cries of a night bird, the sharp scent of crushed leaves on the breeze, the swish of wings overhead—all were unnerving, yet alluring. All part of the night.

It was almost frightening how easily she became part of it, how gently she surrendered to the darkness and allowed it to envelope her. She tied on her mask. Blackerby Swift took over, and Elizabeth slipped away. Playing Lady Barnes-Finchley was a chore, but if the truth were told, she felt a combination of freedom and danger in this other role that was somehow irresistible.

She was fortunate this night, and only had to ride a few miles north of the city before she spotted the coach ahead. It was a short, squat carriage with two men up front and an armed footman on the rear axle. She bent low over her horse's neck, slipping her hand into her pocket and grasping her pistol. She withdrew it, her heart hammering, and urged her mount into a faster pace.

She raced up beside the coach and took aim at the driver. ''Yer money or yer lives, gents!''

It was then she noticed, too late, a pair of men riding in front of the coach. Guards!

''It'll be *your* life tonight, Swift!'' one of them shouted. He raised a gun, its barrel glinting in the moonlight.

Elizabeth jerked her mount to a stop. The guard fired as she wheeled about.

The shot went wild. She dug her heels into her horse's flanks and the animal leapt forward. The footman's blunderbuss roared, spewing a load of lead shot. Elizabeth gasped as several pieces struck her leg. The bulk of the explosion hit her horse in the shoulder and the stallion screamed, a wild neigh that shattered the night.

Elizabeth ignored the fiery pain in her thigh. Feeling nothing but stark terror, she forced the animal to keep going. She galloped back the way she had come, desperately trying to gain distance.

The guards gave chase. She left the road and turned into the fields, hoping to lose them in the trees beyond. She darted a look over her shoulder, and now saw a *third* man—this one masked and garbed all in black—behind the other two.

''Damnation!'' She spurred her failing horse onward. Two more shots rang out, one right after the other, then a third. Something hit Elizabeth's side with a force that half knocked her from the saddle. She yelled out in pain and surprise, clutching at her horse's neck, clinging to his mane and reins while he bucked and pitched in panic.

Her foot twisted in the stirrup. She tried to kick free, terrified of falling helpless beneath his hooves. At last she worked her foot free, but couldn't hold on any longer. She fell to the ground and her horse galloped away.

She rolled onto her back, moaning with pain. Where were her pursuers? They would be upon her any moment. She clamped a hand to her side, feeling the wetness that soaked her shirt. There was blood all over, on her waistcoat, her coat . . . Good Lord, it was every-where.

She heard another shot and looked up, certain she was about to be killed. To her amazement, she saw that one of the guards had disappeared. The other was locked in a hand-to-hand struggle with the black-cloaked rider. The guard was obviously getting the worst of it; flailing wildly at his opponent, he snatched the man's mask away.

Just before she passed out, Elizabeth realized, with stunning clarity, that the highwayman was Pierce Wol-verton.

Chapter 4

Pierce jerked his stallion to a halt, torn between riding off and running toward the crumpled form that lay so still on the moon-washed hillside. The acrid scent of gunpowder from his now-empty pistols clung to the air around him. One of the guards lay moaning on the grass a few yards back; the other, the man who had shot Elizabeth, wasn't making any sound at all. Pierce looked over his shoulder. The coach was long gone, its driver having left the dangerous job of bringing down the highwayman to his guards.

Pierce holstered his pistols. Why was he hesitating? This fit perfectly into his plans. He could just leave her here. If she didn't die, someone would find her on the morrow. Blackerby Swift's career would be very neatly ended.

He glared at the slim figure in the ridiculously large greatcoat. She might even be dead already.

"Hellfire and bloody damnation," he ground out, dropping the reins and throwing himself from the saddle.

He covered the distance in a few strides and knelt beside her. He couldn't explain why, but it chilled him to think of leaving Elizabeth—or whatever the devil her real name was—to die out here.

He quickly unbuttoned her greatcoat and started to unbutton the frock coat beneath when he felt the blood. *Blood on his hands.* His chest constricted. He stared at the slick redness of it on his palm and a torrent of memories crashed down on him with mind-numbing suddenness.

The moonlit June hillside disappeared from his vision,

replaced by the gold damask wallpaper in the study at Wolverton Manor, *flecked with blood*, the polished floorboards, *red with blood. His father's blood, everywhere. The gun in Pierce's hand was slick with it. No. Help me, someone help me. Montaigne just stood there in the doorway. Pierce began to tremble, screaming. God help me . . . I can't get my father's blood off my hands.*

Pierce reeled under the weight of the images. He put out a hand to steady himself, feeling the bristly dryness of grass, not the slippery floorboards of his father's study. Even so, he had to close his eyes and sit unmoving for a long moment while he got his breathing under control. He shook his head to clear it.

Opening his eyes, he focused on the girl. She was real, and she was still alive—and all too helpless.

He clenched his fists, suddenly angry. Blast the chit, anyway! He had come here to capture her, not to rescue her. She had already caused him more than enough trouble, and now she was causing more. What the hell was he supposed to do with her? Where the devil was he to take her?

He could think of only one practical answer. Cursing again, he tore a strip of cloth from her shirt and bound her wound as best he could. Then he slipped one arm under Elizabeth's shoulders and the other under her knees. He lifted her up, doing his best to ignore the blood that stained his shirtfront, and carried her to his horse. She was surprisingly light for a woman with such lush curves.

He savagely cut that line of thought short. He was not going to allow himself to become entangled with this woman in *any* way. The only reason he wasn't leaving her here to die was that she was worth more alive. He was still going to turn her in, he told himself firmly. Mounting with some difficulty, he kicked his horse into a gallop and rode south, toward London.

He held Elizabeth against his chest, and tried not to notice how very soft and warm she felt in his arms.

Elizabeth knew only darkness, everywhere, so utterly black she couldn't see at all, no matter how much she squinted and strained her eyes. She felt as if she were floating on a coal-black fog. Fear gripped her heart. Was this death? She could not die, not yet. She had too much left to do. Vengeance. She wasn't finished yet. Despair pulled at her. Then a man appeared, drifting out of the fog like a dark specter, his head bowed, his face hidden beneath the brim of a black tricorne. He reached out to her. His leather-gloved fingers touched her cheek, traced her lips, then cupped her chin, lingering there, trembling as if with longing, or was it anger?

"*No,*" she insisted. "*I must keep moving. They will find me. They are looking for me.*"

He began to raise his head. She could almost see his face . . .

But it was only a dream.

Elizabeth opened her eyes and for an instant thought she had catapulted from one dream into another. Darkness surrounded her, but this darkness was not so complete and terrifying as the other had been. She blinked, her eyes gradually adjusting to the light from candles that burned somewhere to her right. She swallowed and found her throat tight, her lips dry. She was in a bed. Her head felt strangely light, her limbs heavy.

Then the pain hit her, a sting in her left thigh and a sharp, burning sensation just below her ribs. She inhaled sharply and her hand moved to still the throbbing in her side. Her fingers met not blood but the softness of a clean cotton shirt, and beneath it a bandage. Moving her limbs experimentally, she found it was all she wore—a man's shirt, much too long to be one of those Nell had specially made for her.

She squinted to bring her surroundings into focus. She lay in a massive bed, its canopy and covers of navy satin. Gingerly turning her head, she peered at the room's other furnishings, trying to discern where she was. She could make out only a wardrobe, writing desk and chair, and a washstand, all of dark wood, carved along heavy, masculine lines with little decoration. Elizabeth's heart pounded. How the deuce had she come to be in a man's bedroom? She remembered the guards chasing her, the shot that knocked her from her horse, then nothing more.

The door opened. A tall, male figure filled the entry and light spilled in with him. He made no move to come closer. She tried to speak twice before she managed to form coherent words. "W . . . who are you?"

The man at the door bowed ever so slightly, and in the shifting light she could see he had blond hair. "Quinn, miss, the butler," came the soft reply. Crossing the room, he placed a pitcher on the washstand.

"*Whose* butler?"

Instead of answering, he left, closing the door behind him. Elizabeth felt dizzy, her head spinning with fright, worry and curiosity. She tried to raise herself to her elbows, but found she could not. The pain in her side was too great. Where was she? And who the devil was her savior—or her captor?

She had only a moment to wait for her answer, for the door opened again. This time the man who entered was different, and carrying a candle that lit his darkly handsome features.

"*You!*" Elizabeth breathed, fear taking over. Even the throbbing of her wound was forgotten as the Earl of Darkridge crossed the room and came to stand beside the bed. He wore only a pair of dark breeches and a loose white shirt that was half unbuttoned, revealing the corded muscles of his chest and neck in a stark, disturbing display.

He looked down at her with an unreadable gaze. "How do you feel?"

As his deep voice surrounded her, the horrible things Elizabeth had recently heard about Pierce Wolverton cascaded through her thoughts. *Murderer. Madman. Killed his own father.* And now he knew her identity. He knew she was Blackerby Swift.

But as he stood there, awaiting her answer with cool detachment, another image formed in her mind. After she had fallen from her horse, Pierce Wolverton was the highwayman she had seen unmasked!

She knew in that moment that her earlier guess, which

had seemed so farfetched, had been right. The dark eyes, the commanding voice, the tall, broad-shouldered form *were* the same. Lord Darkridge was the Night Raider. She had no doubt that if he removed that shirt, she would see a fairly recent bullet wound on his left arm, where she had accidentally shot him.

She licked her dry lips and decided it was best not to let on that she knew his double identity, at least until she found out what he wanted with her. Rather than answering his question, she asked one of her own. "Are you going to turn me in?"

He arched one mahogany-colored eyebrow. "Turn you in for what?"

Elizabeth tried to remain calm. The coldhearted devil was toying with her, like a cat teasing its captured prey. She wouldn't play the part of a frightened mouse. "I think we both know."

"Do we?"

He sat on the edge of the bed and Elizabeth was suddenly all too aware of her own indecent state of undress. She also concluded that this was his house, his room, and *his* bed. The idea that he might have put her in his own bedchamber rather than a guest room added a new skip of fear to her already racing heart. "Stop it. You know who I am."

The candle in his hand flickered, casting a slim shaft of golden light over his upper body. The glow brought the hard angles of his face into sharp relief and highlighted the scar on his left cheek. Still she could read no feeling at all in his guarded, distant expression. After a moment, he smiled, but there was no warmth in it; it was instead the satisfied look of a predator who had cornered his quarry.

"Yes, I do know who you are, Lady Barnes-Finchley," he stated. "Or Blackerby Swift, or whatever you choose to call yourself. I could hand you over to the authorities right now and collect a very tidy sum."

Elizabeth stiffened with panic, yet she could hear the tone of an offer in his voice. "Or?"

"The alternative depends entirely on you."

"W . . . what do you mean?"

"Agree to cease your attacks on Charles Montaigne's coaches, and I might be persuaded not to turn you in."

"Why?" The mention of Montaigne's name made Elizabeth forget her vulnerability for a moment. "Why do you want me to stop? Do you work for him?"

He uttered a short, humorless bark of laughter. "Hardly. I have plans of my own for Charles Montaigne. You are interfering with those plans."

"What is Montaigne to you? Or is it his money you want?"

He remained silent, and Elizabeth frowned. She was obviously not going to get an answer, but she could guess what the blackguard wanted. Perhaps he had some quarrel with Montaigne and meant to kill him. Or perhaps he had run through his own family fortune and needed funds to pay for his expensive town house, his fine clothes and the high life of a nobleman.

Whatever his reasons, she was not about to let him stop her, not when Montaigne's money could be put to good use for London's poor women and children.

She lowered her gaze. "And if I do not agree to your terms?"

"I will force you to stop. Turning you over to the authorities is not the only way to accomplish my ends."

Elizabeth felt a chill, her imagination filling in the unspoken part of his threat. She was entirely at his mercy. He could kill her right now, and Blackerby Swift would simply disappear.

But if he meant to kill her, he had already had ample time and opportunity. He had, in fact, *saved* her life . . . or had he?

The bullet wound in her side throbbed. She winced and rubbed at it, remembering again that Georgiana had called Pierce Wolverton a murderer and a madman. "Was it you who shot me?"

"No."

Though it was difficult to judge his emotions, especially from that terse answer, he appeared to take offense at her question. Elizabeth chewed the inside of her cheek, then decided to gamble and play the one card she held. "Lord Darkridge, I do not believe you would murder a defenseless woman. And if you turn me in, or in any way reveal my identity, I shall reveal yours."

His gaze turned decidedly menacing. "What do you mean?"

"I . . . I saw you." She took a painfully deep breath and hurried on before she could change her mind. "When the guard tore off your mask, I saw you. And I am willing to guess that you have a fresh bullet wound, on your left arm, from our encounter on Hounslow Heath two weeks ago. You are the Night Raider, and you are much more valuable than I."

She had expected outrage at her revelation. Instead, he laughed, a humorless, mocking sound. "What an absurd accusation. If you think to save yourself with that tale, think again."

"It's the truth."

"Even if you were right—which you are not—you have no evidence. I, on the other hand, have your pistol, your disguise—"

"I could claim I never saw them before." She swallowed hard, trying to think quickly despite the ache and dizziness that assailed her. "I could say you shot me and concocted the whole tale to get the four hundred pounds reward. I have witnesses who would attest to my good character. Who would stand up for *you*?"

Elizabeth saw a flash of the most dangerous sort of anger in his eyes. She hurried on before he could interrupt, desperate to make him see the consequences of turning her in. "No one will believe a woman could possibly be Blackerby Swift. But with your reputation, I think the authorities would be quick to accept that you are the Night Raider. Even if they don't, do you really want that question raised in public? Think of how quickly the gossips would spread such a rumor."

"You, madam," he said flatly, "are in no position to tell anyone anything."

Pierce glared down at her, feeling a maddening combination of fury and admiration at the way she had so neatly removed the teeth from this threat. Why the bloody hell hadn't he thought of this? A girl quick-witted enough to be a successful highwayman would of course be smart enough to puzzle out his identity. He should have left her on that blasted hillside. What idiocy had ever possessed him to pick her up and carry her to his home?

Christ, he didn't need this. He wasn't going to let her have Charles Montaigne's money, and he wasn't going to split it with her. He needed every shilling to buy back the Wolverton estates.

On the other hand, he couldn't afford to have a reckless little fool with a pistol in her petticoats blathering his identity all over London. She was like a burr he couldn't shake loose, and she was getting more irritating every minute.

For perhaps the first time in years, he wasn't at all sure what his next step should be. It was an unsettling feeling, one he disliked intensely.

Her violet eyes sparkled with defiance despite her precarious situation. "Well, my lord? You know who *I* am. I know who *you* are. What do you propose we do about one another?"

Setting his teeth, he leaned over her and placed the candle on the bedside table. Then he planted one hand on either side of her head and gave her his most threatening glare. Her already pale cheeks whitened. She was clearly tired, and terrified, yet she returned his gaze steadily. His chest was only inches away from coming into contact with her breasts, yet she didn't whimper or plead as other women might. She didn't even flinch.

Her bravery was almost as impressive as her beauty. The latter—or was it the former?—was doing strange things to his heartbeat. The fresh, forest scent that clung to her hair bewitched him. The open neck of the shirt she wore, his shirt, revealed the hollow of her throat. He imagined her skin would feel petal-soft beneath his lips if he kissed her there.

He chased such thoughts from his mind and tried to focus on the problem at hand. He had stopped Blackerby

Swift's raids, temporarily. But what was he to do with her now?

He noticed lines of fatigue around her eyes, and a sallowness to her skin, that revealed deep exhaustion. She was suffering from much more than being shot. Her wound had bled badly, but it was not serious enough to kill her; some other strain had obviously been taking a toll on her.

She needed rest, not more interrogation from him. He turned his head away, sighing in disgust at his own weakness. Since when did he care a fig about a woman's delicate feelings?

"So, my lord?" she asked in a meek whisper. "Shall we keep quiet about one another's identities?"

His gaze snapped back to hers. Pierce knew he was at a stalemate, and resented her for it. "I am certain the magistrate will find your tales very amusing," he said, sitting up at last, "but other business requires my attention at the moment, *Mr.* Swift."

He intended to stand, but couldn't bring himself to move away. She kept staring at him with those infinite amethyst eyes. "What the devil is your real name anyway?" he asked impulsively. "Is the Lady Elizabeth Barnes-Finchley part at least true?"

She looked away and remained stubbornly silent.

"What harm is there in revealing your name?"

" 'Mr. Swift' will do quite well," she said tartly.

He stood at last, irritated by her defiance. "I shall give you time to consider the wisdom of ceasing your raids. Rest assured, if you do not agree, I will turn you in without hesitation." He turned to leave.

"Wait," she called after him. "My friends will be worried about me. Could I send them a note?"

"No."

"I don't have to reveal my location," she said wearily. "I only wish to relieve their concern. You could have your butler deliver the note to . . ." She chewed at her bottom lip for a second, her expression guarded. "To a shop on the Strand called Osgood's. The people there will see that it is passed along to my friends."

Pierce hesitated, his hand on the door latch. Friends. It had been a very long time since he had used that word, since *he* had cared about anyone's feelings. It was even more difficult to remember a time when someone had been concerned about him. He supposed it would be safe to send Quinn with a verbal message.

He shook off the sympathetic feeling. What the devil did he care? She had better learn, starting now, that he was not kindhearted, not gentle, not a man she could twist about her finger.

"No," he repeated. And with that, Pierce left the room.

"Don't ye give up yet, now Georgi. We'll find Bess, we will." Nell paced restlessly up and down along the rows of fabrics in her shop. She had just convinced Georgiana to sit down, but found herself unable to sit still.

"But it's been two days." Georgiana dabbed at the tears on her cheeks, then blew her nose on her lace-edged handkerchief. "It's our fault, Nell. We should have insisted she not go out. I had a—"

"I know, I know. Ye 'ad a feelin'. We should 'ave listened to ye." Nell went to the front room and looked out at the gray, rainy afternoon. When Elizabeth hadn't returned at her regular hour, they had gone out looking for her. It had begun to rain, turning the roads into impassable mud, but they continued to search, checking back at the shop every few hours, hoping to find Elizabeth waiting, laughing that they had been so worried.

It had been two days now, and still there was no sign of her.

"What if she's . . . she's . . ." Georgiana's sniffle broke into a sob.

Nell quickly returned to her friend. She paused a moment, then awkwardly leaned down and hugged her. She knew Georgiana was especially fond of Bess, and understood why: the viscountess had never been able to have children of her own, and that sorrow clung to her heart despite her cheery exterior. Elizabeth was the closest thing she had ever had to a daughter.

"There, now, Georgi. Don't ye be thinkin' she's gone. Our Bess is a strong one, an' more wily than a fox. She'll be fine." Nell wished she could believe her own words of comfort; she knew all the strength and intelligence in the world wouldn't stop a bullet.

She picked up her still-sodden cloak from where it lay drying over a counter. "Ye stay 'ere an' rest, Georgi. I'm goin' t' go back out one more time. We never really checked the part of the road way up north—"

A knock at the back door interrupted her.

"It must be her!" Georgiana leaped up and was hustling toward the rear of the shop before Nell could even turn around. They ran to the back door and opened it to find a blond man standing in the alley.

His broad shoulders nearly filled the doorway; he surveyed them with an almost regal disdain that instantly sparked resentment in Nell. From the fine fabric and tailoring of his nut-brown frock coat and breeches she guessed him to be a member of the upper class. He dismissed her with a glance that lasted less than a second, and his gray eyes settled on Georgiana.

"I have a message," he stated in a clipped, polished tone, addressing Georgiana. "Your friend has been injured. But she is being cared for and is expected to recover completely."

"Who the blast are ye?" Nell snapped.

The man turned toward her. His expression, filled with annoyance at first, changed as his gaze traveled from her blond hair to the hem of her gown and back. An unmistakable appreciation came into his eyes. "And who would *you* be, Miss . . . ?"

"Never mind who we be. Who the devil are ye, and where's Bess?" Nell demanded, so irritated at his manner she didn't even bother to correct the "Miss."

"I cannot reveal her whereabouts. You will have to trust me when I say she is well."

"I don't 'ave t' do nothin' ye say, ye dandiprat."

He looked bemused. "True enough." He turned to leave.

"But who are you, sir?" Georgiana called after him.

He turned back toward them, pulling up the collar of his coat against the rain. His eyes lingered over Nell. "I am afraid I cannot reveal that, either."

"Well, whoever ye are," Nell spat, feeling a blush warm her cheeks as he looked at her, "ye 'ear me, now. If anythin' 'appens to that girl, ye'll answer to me."

Her tirade didn't appear to bother him in the least. He smiled at her. "Then I give you my word of honor that nothing shall *'appen* to her."

Nell cursed him, frustrated by his abrupt manner and angry at the way he made fun of her. They watched him walk off until he was swallowed up by the rain.

"Cor, Georgi, what the devil has Bess gotten 'erself into now?"

Chapter 5

It was foolish to keep falling asleep, Elizabeth admonished herself as she yawned and came awake. In the past two days, she had slept longer and more deeply than at any time within recent memory, despite the fact that she should be on guard with her wits about her.

She attributed it to total exhaustion. Or perhaps it was the fact that she had no identity to conceal here, no role to play, since Lord Darkridge already knew she was Blackerby Swift.

Whatever the reason, it was time to come to her senses and plan her escape. Darkridge hadn't killed her or turned her in yet, but he could change his mind at any time. She barely knew the man, and he could indeed be a murderer and lunatic as everyone said.

She opened one eye and peeked at the door. Quinn had just left, taking her supper tray with him. He had checked on her several times but said very little. The butler appeared to be even more stingy with his words than his master, if that were possible.

Elizabeth thought it strange that she had seen only Quinn and no one else. Most aristocrats found it impossible to run a household without troops of servants, from a valet and cook to footmen and maids by the dozen. But she had heard no sounds of anyone cleaning, or speaking, or moving about. She hadn't even seen Lord Darkridge since that first time.

She should be relieved about that, but instead wondered nervously why he hadn't returned for two days. She found herself listening for his voice in the house, and feeling uneasy when she did not hear him.

She sat up and slowly moved to the edge of the bed, taking care not to jostle her wounded side. She had already discovered she couldn't walk far without having to sit down, but she was strong enough at least to explore the house a bit, and it would be wise to plot her escape route.

She doubted she could simply walk out the front door unnoticed, but perhaps she could find a back stair or other exit. There was time enough for a quick look around before Quinn checked on her again.

She slipped out of bed, pausing to catch her breath at the ache in her side, and crossed to the corner of the room. The thick Oriental rug felt bristly beneath her bare toes. Opening the mahogany wardrobe, she found a variety of finely tailored coats, waistcoats and breeches inside, all in black, navy and charcoal gray. It was a somber wardrobe for a nobleman, but it certainly suited him, Elizabeth decided with a frown.

She pulled out a silk robe done in an oriental pattern of dark blues, browns and golds. She had to roll back the sleeves, and the hem dragged behind her like a train, but it was better than walking about clad only in his shirt.

She took a candle and peeked out the door, deciding she could act delirious if she happened upon someone. To her relief, she saw no sign of Quinn, or anyone else. The entire place was silent as a . . .

The word "tomb" was accurate, but it gave her a little frisson between her shoulder blades. Forcing the image from her mind, she slipped into the darkened hallway.

Lord Darkridge's town house appeared to follow the traditional pattern of rooms arranged around a central staircase. She seemed to be on the middle floor. The hall was decorated in deep green damask, an eerie hue in the candle's glow. She stepped as quietly as possible into the room next door, and was surprised at what she found.

It held no furniture. It was, in fact, empty—no fire on the hearth, no candles, no pictures, no bric-a-brac on the mantel, no rugs, not even any wallpaper. She went down the hall to the next room, and the next. They were all in the same state, well-kept and clean, but abandoned. No, not abandoned exactly. Just . . . empty.

Utterly perplexed, she sat down on the stairs to rest a few minutes, then tiptoed up to the third floor and discovered it to be the same as the second. There was no indication that a wealthy man lived here at all.

Elizabeth came to the end of the hall on the third floor, chagrined that there seemed to be no back stair. She opened the last door, and discovered a room so different from the others it stole her breath away.

This one was brightly lit by an enormous crystal chandelier, the walls decorated with pictures: hunting and historical scenes, landscapes, and, above the hearth, a portrait of an older woman, an attractive brown-eyed blond dressed in black. Most striking of all were the bookshelves, floor to ceiling, crammed with leather-bound volumes of every description. She had never in her life imagined a library of this size.

Elizabeth knew she should be looking for a way out of the house, a way to escape when her strength returned, but she couldn't tear herself from the astounding array. To someone who had grown up with only borrowed books, this was a dream beyond belief. Drawn like metal to a magnet, she stepped closer to admire them. There were histories, novels, treatises on mathematics, chemistry, music, boxing—and a score of identical small blue volumes with no lettering on the spine.

She pulled one of them down and flipped through the pages. It contained poems, all hand-written, and all apparently by the same writer. It seemed odd that Pierce Wolverton should be a man of letters, but odder still that he collected poetry. She looked at another of the little books, then another. He appeared to have bought the poet's entire collection.

She had to admire his taste, for the verses were captivating. Each was like a portrait in words and ink, describing a lady of Covent Garden or a gambler or a Thames dockworker. The images fairly leaped from the paper, each conveying a captured spark of personality.

Curious, she flipped to the first page to note the writer's name. She could find nothing but the owner's signature, *Pierce Wolverton,* in bold black lettering. There was no mention anywhere of who had written the poems.

Elizabeth replaced the book with a shrug and turned away from the shelf. She walked about the room, but the only other item of interest was a desk, and it held nothing useful, only a pen and inkwell, and another of the little blue volumes, this one lying open. She started to move away, then froze and turned back.

Leaning closer to the book, she blinked, stared, and still couldn't believe what she saw: a half-finished poem, in the same handwriting as all the others.

Pierce Wolverton was not a poetry collector; he was the *poet*! She could not have been more shocked if she had found a session of Parliament meeting in his house. It seemed utterly out of place with what she knew of Lord Darkridge.

Then she remembered he had mentioned being "something of a poet" that night at the Rowlands' party. He hadn't been telling her a tale; he *was* a poet, and tremendously talented.

She had barely recovered from that surprise when she recognized the subject of his half-finished piece. It was her!

He had only written a few lines, but it was unmistakably about her, for the opening described her lavender Watteau gown and the gazebo at the Rowlands' party. The rest depicted an Elizabeth she had never seen in a mirror: parted lips, flowing night-touched hair, a seductive challenge in her gaze.

A blush warmed her cheeks when she read of her bounteous—

"What the bloody hell do you think you are doing in here?"

The angry demand so startled Elizabeth she actually jumped. Pressing one hand to her aching side, she turned and saw Lord Darkridge behind her, dressed in traveling clothes. She had no difficulty gauging his mood this time. She was familiar enough with male rage to recognize it easily.

"Th . . . the door wasn't locked."

"I have never had cause to lock it." He threw his cloak to the floor with a snap of his arm. "Had I guessed you were well enough to wander about my house, I would have."

Elizabeth resisted the urge to shrink from him. Hard experience with her late husband taught her that showing fear was the worst mistake she could make in this situation. The only way to handle an angry man was to stand her ground. "I was restless," she explained. "I've grown used to keeping late hours."

His anger seemed to subside, just a bit. Though his expression remained hard, a cynical grin tugged at one corner of his mouth for a fleeting moment. "It does become something of a habit, doesn't it?"

Then he appeared to notice her state of undress for the first time, for his gaze suddenly skimmed downward. Elizabeth felt a strange tightening sensation in her midsection, along with an unsettling heat that washed over her entire body.

The direction of his thoughts became clear—as if she needed any clarification after reading that poem. A much more familiar feeling quickly undermined her determination to face him without flinching: fear.

She folded her arms over her breasts, the sleeves of his robe flapping. "You've a very strange house, my lord," she said sharply, trying to redirect his attention and hide how vulnerable his perusal made her feel. "Why don't any of the rooms have furniture? Why aren't there any guest rooms?"

"Because there aren't any guests." He advanced toward her, his voice dropping to a slightly deeper tone, his gaze rising to lock with hers. His eyes had darkened.

Elizabeth didn't move, couldn't move. She felt a powerful urge to run, but his eyes conveyed an equally powerful command to stay. She struggled to think of another question to keep him talking. "Then where . . . where have you been staying since I've been here?"

Damnation, that was a foolish choice of topic.

As if sensing her unease, he grinned, and this time

the expression actually reflected a touch of humor. "There's a couch in my study downstairs."

He stopped a couple of feet away, so close that Elizabeth's every rapid breath was filled with the spicy, masculine scent of him. Her heart began to pound. Even as she feared what he might do next, she felt a twinge of sympathy and understanding; he lived without friends, without servants but for Quinn, because he couldn't trust anyone with his identity.

She also understood now why he had put her in his own bedroom. There weren't any others. It seemed an oddly kind gesture for a man purported to be an utter blackguard.

"And w . . . what about Quinn?" she asked, trying to keep her voice steady. "Is that his last name or his first? I called him Mr. Quinn and he said to simply call him Quinn."

Lord Darkridge's broad shoulders moved upward, then down in a slow shrug. "I keep his secrets. He keeps mine."

Elizabeth swallowed hard. She couldn't help but wonder whether Lord Darkridge's secrets included the murder of his father. She edged away from him a pace and tried again to change the subject.

"I was under the impression you spent all your money on gambling and debauchery, but you haven't, have you? You've spent it on books." She nodded toward the open volume on his desk. "You're very talented."

"My work is not meant for public viewing," he snapped, his anger returning. "Or public comment."

"But your poems are good, really," she insisted honestly. "That description is . . . it's very . . . flattering. Though my hair isn't long or flowing at all. I think you exaggerated a bit there, and on the part about my—"

She stopped herself, blushing furiously. Confound it, she kept turning the conversation in a direction she didn't want to go!

As if he knew her thoughts, his eyes narrowed and an appreciative expression curved his mouth. "No." He looked pointedly at her bosom. "I assure you that is quite accurate."

He gave her an insolent stare, as if daring her to slap him, curse him, to stamp her foot in feminine outrage. Elizabeth, to her surprise, didn't feel like doing any of those things; she only knew a lingering heat, deep inside, that grew more intense each moment she stayed near him.

She found it difficult to breathe, and couldn't think of a response. The silence between them stretched until it was taut as a string on a violin. Elizabeth began to feel light-headed; her side ached, and she wished fervently for a drink of water to cool her suddenly dry throat.

Finally she turned and moved past him, unable to bear his regard any longer. She walked toward the portrait of the attractive blond woman. "Is this your mother?" she asked lightly.

"Yes."

The word had a rough, harsh edge to it. Elizabeth couldn't tell if it was because he, too, was affected by what had just passed between them, or if the emotion had to do with his mother. As usual, he didn't seem inclined to comment further.

She glanced at the other paintings in the room. "But there doesn't seem to be one of your father."

"No."

This terse reply was uttered without any emotion at all. It disturbed Elizabeth, but before she could question him further, he turned the tables on her.

"As long as we're asking questions, why the devil *do* you wear your hair so short?"

He slowly moved closer again, until he was so near she could sense the heat of his body at her back. Elizabeth did her best to imitate the careless shrug he had given her earlier. "It makes it easier to pass as a lad."

He chuckled, the sound filled with mockery. "Then you may grow it long again, because your highwayman days are over."

Elizabeth's fear and confusion dissipated in a blaze of anger at his confident statement. She turned to face him, not caring that she had to look up to do so. "You are wrong, my lord. I have no intention of quitting, and you cannot make me stop unless you kill me."

"*I* won't have to," he growled. "If you don't quit, someone else is going to kill you. You've a big enough price on your head to attract every addlepated clod with a pistol to take a shot at you. And you're giving them plenty of opportunities."

"They'll never catch me."

"Christ, you can't be that naive. You can't even defend yourself properly. I checked your pistol. It wasn't loaded. What kind of fool are you, raiding with an empty gun?"

She dropped her gaze from his. "I don't want to hurt anyone."

"Really?" he scoffed. "You shot me easily enough."

She looked at his arm and her stomach twisted painfully. Somehow, the memory of having wounded him was even more vexing than before. "I'm sorry," she said honestly. "It was an accident. I haven't carried a loaded pistol since."

When he didn't comment, she glanced up. He was looking at her with a perplexed frown, as if she were nattering in a foreign language he didn't understand.

He finally spoke, his tone low and insulting. "How in the name of God did a little tender-heart like you ever end up behind a black mask?"

"I'm not a tender-heart," she retorted. "I know exactly what I'm doing—"

"You don't know a damn thing. Guns and gold rule the world, madam, and if you can't accept that, you'd better get out of the game now. Before someone forces you out."

"I am not going to quit," she insisted stubbornly. "And the thief-takers will never catch me, for the simple reason that the *man* they are seeking is a woman. No one would ever believe a woman could possibly do the things I have done."

"I did," he pointed out. "I tracked you down, I caught you, and I could have turned you in right then. How long do you think it will be before someone else does the same?''

"*You* only found me because I let you get close enough to see my face that night on Hounslow Heath," Elizabeth argued. "I made a mistake. I won't make it again."

"You've already made too many. Like naming yourself after the Blackerby Arms. Someone might make the connection between you and a certain Elizabeth Blackerby."

Elizabeth could feel the color draining from her cheeks. "I . . . I don't know what you mean—"

"Don't bother denying it. I've been to Northampton."

Elizabeth gaped at him in stunned silence.

" 'Know thy enemy,' " he said tightly. "It's the basic rule of any battle."

"Is that what we are?" she asked breathlessly, feeling angry and inexplicably hurt. "Enemies? In a battle?"

"Enemies, rivals, it's all the same. Words don't make any difference," he snapped. "What I can't figure out is what happened between the time you left there and your first raids here. The last thing anyone in Northampton remembered was that you left for London with your new husband. No one remembered much about him except that he was a stranger who wore fine clothes, his name was Geoffrey Thornhill, and he was a handsome young devil."

Elizabeth numbly listened to her carefully-woven cover unraveling strand by strand. She gave Lord Darkridge an icy stare. If he considered them enemies, so be it. She wasn't going to give her enemy any potentially helpful information.

He kept prodding for details. "What was he, some lord up from London who visited your father's inn and got you in the family way? Whisked you off to the Continent and kept the fact that he was Lord Barnes-Finchley quiet to avoid scandal? I'll bet Thornhill wasn't even his real name, was it?"

Elizabeth felt a tiny measure of relief which she managed to keep hidden. At least part of her story was intact; Darkridge still believed she was Lady Barnes-Finchley.

"I don't suppose it matters," he said when she remained silent. "What does matter is that you don't seem to care if you get killed, and that makes you damned dangerous. The only reason you've succeeded thus far is that you're so bloody reckless. What is it, *Mr.* Swift? Do you *want* to die?"

She didn't respond.

"My God, you honestly don't care, do you?" He gave her a look of utter disbelief. "And they call *me* a lunatic."

His accusation stung. Elizabeth feared it was because he had struck painfully close to the truth. Why the deuce was he so insistent on knowing all about her? Why did he seem so angry at her one moment, so curious the next?

And why did she feel the same about him?

She felt another wave of dizziness and wanted desperately to get away from him before she crumpled at his feet. "I don't owe you or anyone an explanation!"

She turned, but before she could take a step, he reached out and stopped her. His arm curved about her back and shoulders and he pulled her against his chest, his hand closing about the nape of her neck, his fingers threading through her hair. His other arm remained at his side, as if he were confident he could hold her still with one hand, as if he knew she would not fight him.

She should. She wanted to.

She didn't.

He lowered his head, until his lips were only inches from hers. "When I brought you here, when I undressed you," he said roughly, his breath hot on her cheek, "I saw marks on your skin, on your belly. I would say you've had a child, Elizabeth. Does that have something to do with this?"

She tried to pull away, but his fingers were tangled in her hair, and she discovered he was indeed strong enough to hold her still with one arm. "Let me go!"

"What kind of woman leaves her child with her husband on the Continent while she gallivants around London as a *highwayman*?"

She stopped struggling and glared at him. "What kind of man makes advances at another man's *wife*?"

"You haven't answered my question. What happened to your child?"

Elizabeth stiffened. "Go to hell."

"I am quite sure I will," he growled. "Someday."

Elizabeth managed to utter only a single sound of protest before his mouth covered hers. His lips captured hers with an aggressiveness that sent her mind reeling. The prickly roughness of his unshaven chin sent shivers dancing down her back. He tasted of salt and dark ale and he made a low sound, deep in his throat, holding her tighter, making her even more vividly aware of the barely-leashed power in his arms, the flat, rock-hard planes of his chest.

Yet even as he held her in that unyielding embrace, he seemed to be taking care not to hurt her wounded side. To Elizabeth's amazement, her fear and outrage gradually melted in a consuming heat that flamed through her entire body as he kissed her thoroughly.

Her breasts felt tingly and full, crushed against him, covered only by the skimpy silk robe and cotton shirt. Her husband had never kissed her this way; Geoffrey had rarely kissed her at all. Her entire experience of kissing encompassed only the briefest, cold touching of male lips to hers. Never had she imagined such a hot, consuming joining as this. Lord Darkridge's lips moved over hers, demanding, urging her toward some end she didn't understand.

Pierce groaned as her lips at last opened beneath his and her tongue hesitantly, timidly allowed his touch. He boldly claimed her mouth and the tightness in his lower body became almost unbearable. His every muscle and nerve ending felt fire-hot.

He realized too late he had made an error, a dangerous error, by giving in to the desire to kiss her. One kiss would never, *never* be enough. Instead of slaking his overpowering longing for her, it only strengthened his desire. He would not be satisfied until he had tasted every inch of her, discovered her every passion, experienced the full pleasure of her deepest response.

She began to go limp, actually swooning in his arms, and Pierce suddenly realized how very weak she still was. It was difficult to reconcile the obstinate, strong-willed Elizabeth she allowed the world to see with the much more delicate, feminine Elizabeth she kept so carefully hidden. God help him, he found the combination enchanting.

He broke the kiss at last and picked her up. The silk of his own robe, wrapped about her curves, felt more exquisite than he had ever known it to be.

"No," she pleaded, her eyes dusky with exactly the expression he had captured on paper, then suddenly widening in alarm. "God, no, don't."

Pierce didn't respond, carrying her from the room with fast, determined steps until he reached his bedchamber on the floor below.

Without a word, he shouldered the door open, stalked across the room and laid her carefully on the bed. Then he turned on his heel and walked out. It took more will than he had ever needed to summon in his life, but he left her there, untouched. He knew if he lingered even a second more, he would be in the bed beside her, and he wouldn't leave until morning.

And that was a mistake he had no intention of making.

Chapter 6

Pierce stood at the window in his study, holding the heavy wine-colored curtains to one side, scowling out at the deserted streets below. He was still fully dressed, though it was almost two in the morning.

He swirled the brandy in his glass, took a sip, and paced back to the couch. His study didn't contain the traditional desk, papers and books; those were in his garret. This room he reserved for liquor and lounging and leaving the day behind.

Except that tonight he couldn't seem to relax. Everything grated on his nerves, even the snap of the fire on the hearth. He barely noticed the smooth taste of his favorite brandy. Normally it soothed him, but not tonight.

It was strange, this tension he felt. He knew part of it was desire, foolishly aroused by kissing Elizabeth, but there was another element mingled in, unfamiliar and elusive. All in all, this restlessness was similar to the way he felt after a night of raiding. But that usually faded after an hour or so; this seemed to be growing more intense.

He kept thinking he should have stayed in Northampton, tried to find out more about Elizabeth's husband. As soon as he had heard the man described as a handsome young devil, he had stopped asking questions. Filled with something that felt annoyingly like jealousy, he had wanted only to get back to London.

Back to her.

Pierce shoved a hand through his hair. Still holding the brandy, he stalked out of the room, pulling the door shut behind him. He crossed the marble-floored entry hall to the stairway and took the steps two at a time. Working in his garret usually wore him out when nothing else could.

He stopped on the second floor, his eyes drawn inexorably to his bedroom door. Almost without thinking, he walked toward it and stood there, staring at the latch. He started to reach for it, then clenched his hand into a fist.

Why the devil not? He wanted her. Elizabeth was attracted to him. He had seen it in her eyes, felt it when she trembled in his arms.

Why shouldn't he just go in and take her, right now, all night if he wanted to?

He finished the rest of his brandy in one gulp and let the glass goblet fall to the floor. It hit the thick Axminster carpet with a thump and rolled away. He wiped the back of his hand across his mouth. Why in hellfire not? Why should he treat her differently from any other woman?

She was in his room, in his bed, wearing bloody little of his clothes. He pictured her lying there, her long, pale legs tangled in the navy satin of his bedcovers, her eyes closed and lips slightly parted, his shirt perhaps rumpled just so, one of her perfect breasts peeking through the deep neckline.

"Christ," he muttered under his breath. He could feel his body responding to the image, swiftly and urgently. He could never remember feeling such forceful desire for any woman, and he had certainly known his share.

London's ladies of quality feared him, but the city's less aristocratic haunts held more than enough willing beauties—single and married—to keep him from living a celibate life. That suited him quite well. Always he had maintained a certain cool detachment. Always he had been able to walk away when and if he chose.

This feeling was entirely new. It had struck him as unexpectedly as lightning out of a cloudless sky, and the stronger it became, the more he resented it.

He braced his hands against the doorjamb and glared down at the latch. He had always preferred experienced women, practical types like himself who harbored no ridiculous illusions about what took place between a man and woman. He willingly gave and accepted pleasure, and expected nothing more.

So why was he torturing himself? Elizabeth was no virgin; it was obvious from the marks on her abdomen that she had borne a child. She had more or less left her husband; she didn't even wear her wedding band, except when it suited her. He had noticed its absence when he undressed her. All the signals cried out to him that she was ripe for the plucking.

But why, then, had there been a sweetness, almost an innocence, in her response to his kiss? Why had there been a virgin's panic in her eyes when she thought he meant to ravish her?

He straightened and forced himself to turn away from her door. He had made one mistake in bringing her here, another in kissing her. He seemed to have made nothing *but* mistakes from the moment he met her. Getting physically involved with her would be reckless beyond reason—especially since he couldn't seem to get this overpowering desire under control.

No. She was an obstacle to his revenge against Montaigne, and he couldn't afford to see her as anything but an enemy. He had spent fifteen years hating and planning; both were too deeply ingrained in him now to be tossed aside for the sake of mere physical pleasure.

He tore himself away from her door, strode to the stairs and went up to the third floor. A wry grin tugged at the corner of his mouth; he could understand how a visitor such as Elizabeth might find the empty rooms in his house strange, but it made perfect sense to him. This wasn't home.

Home was Wolverton Manor, and soon he would reclaim it. Once he had driven Montaigne to ruin, he would force the bastard to tell the truth about Thomas Wolverton's death; his "peers" would finally have to admit they had been wrong all these years. He had thought about killing Montaigne after that, but it was much more satisfying to think of him living in utter misery in debtors' prison. The Wolverton estates would be sold, and Pierce would be the highest bidder, using Montaigne's own money.

Everything would be restored to the way it was. He would live as an earl was meant to live, marry a blue-blooded girl with ancestry as elite as a queen's, and have a houseful of heirs to carry on the Wolverton name.

He felt somewhat better at that thought. Opening the door to his garret, however, he frowned. He couldn't help but feel that his sanctuary was somehow changed, now that Elizabeth had been in it. Feeling a renewed spark of anger at her boldness, he crossed to his desk and sat down, staring at the poem he had started.

He suddenly tore it from the book, crumpled it into a ball and flung it aside. None of the images satisfied him. Picking up a pen, he dipped it in the inkwell and started over. He wrote furiously, determined to capture the woman on paper.

Words like *alluring, maddening, naive* and *defiant* filled the page, and slowly the tension he had felt all night began to fade.

When he tried to describe Elizabeth's eyes, though, he found himself at a loss. No language he knew could hope to capture the combination of brash spirit and the haunted look that intertwined in her deep violet gaze. He settled for calling her eyes "twin amethysts royally dusted with gold"—then crossed the words out with a black stroke of ink.

An hour later he was still not satisfied, but he put his pen down. Yawning, he checked his silver pocket watch. It was five in the morning. He leaned back in his chair, studying the half-finished poem and mulling over the woman it depicted.

What the hell was he going to do about her?

He couldn't turn her in, lest she reveal his identity. And if she stayed in his house much longer, he was going to seduce her, which would only complicate matters further.

But perhaps not, he thought, the germ of an idea growing into a plan. Indeed, there might be a way both to satisfy his desire *and* convince Elizabeth to follow his orders.

A seduction might be exactly what was called for in this situation.

Women were an odd lot; they never failed to associate sex with love. And he had never met a woman yet who didn't become absolutely pliable once she fell in love with a man. Elizabeth had been apart from her husband for some time; if Pierce knew the female of the species—and he did—it would take only a well-placed nudge to ease her into an affair.

If he could seduce her quickly yet thoroughly, make her fall in love with him, he could make her do what he wanted. Between his reputation and her obvious fear, it would be no easy task, but it would be worth the work. Once he had her under his control, he would order her to give up her raids, and she would do so willingly. In the meantime, he would keep her occupied and off the roads.

He smiled, feeling like himself again, for the first time since he had encountered his rival on Hounslow Heath.

Yes, a thorough seduction was definitely in order. He would begin first thing in the morning.

Elizabeth tossed and turned, unable to sleep. She felt chilled and dizzy, and couldn't stop thinking about Lord Darkridge's rough kiss, the terror she felt when he carried her to his bed—and her amazement when he left her alone.

At one point she thought she heard a noise in the hall-way outside, like a thump, and sat upright, her heart pounding. Hearing nothing more after a few minutes, she tried again to sleep, but to no avail.

One thing became clear as she collected her scattered thoughts. She should have run away as soon as she had the strength to stand. Lord Darkridge was her enemy—as he had so coolly pointed out—and wounded or not, she was a fool to linger in his very strange house. The man was dangerous, and she doubted he ever granted his enemies any quarter.

Worse, she could not trust herself. She had never had trouble fending off unwanted advances before, but that was because she never had such trouble controlling her own responses. Tonight she had not only allowed Darkridge's kiss, she had *enjoyed* it.

There was no telling what might happen if he tried it again, or if he tried something more. Men were like that; she had given in once, and now he would think himself entitled to all kinds of liberties. Her invented "husband" offered only the flimsiest protection against a man of so few morals.

Well, she wasn't going to let Pierce Wolverton or any man take such liberties with her. And she certainly wasn't going to allow anyone to end her plans for Charles Montaigne's money. To the devil with Lord Darkridge if he thought otherwise! Besides, the costume ball given by Montaigne's solicitor was to be held in a few days, and she *had* to be there; it was her best chance to find out about the huge transaction he was planning for this summer.

Elizabeth took a deep breath, summoned all her strength and got out of bed. Fighting a wave of dizziness and nausea, she moved to the wardrobe. She donned a pair of Lord Darkridge's breeches and a coat. Both were ridiculously large on her, but she couldn't stand the thought of fastening a belt over her wounded side. Holding the pants up with one hand, she tiptoed from the room.

She wished she had her boots; it would be impossible to walk in a pair of his. She also hated to leave her pistol behind, but she had no idea where he had hidden her things. Better to face the streets of London barefoot and unarmed than to face Pierce Wolverton in the morning.

She crept out into the hall. All was dark. Not a sound reached her ears from below. She swallowed hard; she would have to pass directly in front of his study to reach the front entrance. Praying that he was asleep, she descended the wide staircase, her eyes on his door. Firelight from the other side flickered shadows across the marble floor.

He obviously thought her too weakened to attempt escape; actually he wasn't entirely wrong, she thought, biting her lip against the pain. But even if she had to crawl home, she wasn't going to spend another minute in his presence. Elizabeth slowly walked across the clammy marble to the front door.

Nothing would make her happier, she thought as she stepped into the London streets, than never to lay eyes on Lord Darkridge again.

Charles Montaigne leaned back in his plushly upholstered chair and fingered the silver coin in his palm, smiling, waiting for the man who stood on the other side of his desk to speak.

"Zis coin is counterfeit," the man said at last. "Ze staff of Britannia on zis side is too short."

"Very good, Monsieur Rochambeau," Montaigne said, nodding. "And it only took you five minutes."

The Frenchman tossed the coin in the air and caught it. "Zat is why Jean-Pascal Rochambeau is a very busy man, monsieur." A smile curved his thin lips. "I have a sharp eye and a mind zat can match ze criminal's step for step."

"Precisely why I have hired you." Montaigne stood and passed the man a handful of counterfeit shillings and guineas. "Once I heard that you caught the infamous killer Maurice Delieu in less than a fortnight, I knew you were exactly the detective I needed to bring in Blackerby Swift."

Rochambeau studied the coins. "You zay he has taken on a partner?"

"So it would seem," Montaigne said sourly. "Swift and another highwayman attacked one of my coaches on Hounslow Heath three weeks ago. He apparently didn't discover that I had substituted these counterfeit coins for the real silver. Scores of them have been spent already."

"Yet none of your men have been able to track him down?"

"No." Montaigne grimaced. He hated working with foreigners, but he had no choice. Unlike the other civilized countries of the world, England had no police force. It was one of the reasons bastardly gullions like Swift were so rampant. "I haven't many men left, actually. Several more quit last week after two of my guards were shot."

"*Quel dommage,* monsieur. I am sorry to hear zat."

"There was no real harm done."

"I thought one of ze guards was killed."

"Yes, but Swift and his new partner didn't get any of my money that time," Montaigne pointed out. "The problem is, I can't hire enough men now to take the risk of accompanying my coaches, no matter how much I pay them."

"But ze coins, monsieur. Where did Swift spend ze coins?"

"Oddly enough, several of them surfaced at one of my own gin shops. They were used to pay the debt of an impoverished woman. I personally interrogated her. It took a bit of beating, but she finally revealed everything. A new trust fund at the London Bank has been giving money away. Insolvent debtors forward their bills to the bank, and the debts are paid anonymously."

Rochambeau picked up his heavy brocade redingote and gold-trimmed tricorne. "Zen I would say my first step is to call on ze bank."

"Yes. I'll have a servant bring a coach around for you at ten."

"And I will find out from zis bank how Blackerby Swift's stolen silver got into zeir accounts. And before you know it, Monsieur Montaigne, your Monsieur Swift *and* his new partner will be swinging from—where is it you English do ze hangings?"

"Tyburn," Montaigne said, smiling in anticipation. "They will be executed at Tyburn."

Chapter 7

Elizabeth could barely hear the nattering of her dancing partner over the loud music, and the heat in the crowded ballroom was even worse than the noise. Could no one in London find other entertainment this night, she wondered irritably. It seemed that half the city's gentry had packed into this one country house, to celebrate the birthday of Sir John Fairfax, a minor baronet and solicitor to Charles Montaigne.

She grew dizzy watching the swirling costumes; the light from a dozen crystal chandeliers reflected off the jewels and brocades of Turkish sultans, knights and their ladies, cavaliers, and bird and animal masks of every description. The air was thick with the scents of French perfumes and waxy hair pomatum. The ache in her wounded side and stiffness in her leg didn't improve Elizabeth's disposition, either.

After sneaking out of Lord Darkridge's town house four nights ago, she had slowly and painfully made her way home through the streets and alleys. She spent the next few days resting and trying to convince Georgiana and Nell that she would be well enough to attend tonight's masquerade ball. She was still tired and weak, and so far the night was a complete failure. It was after midnight and she had yet to find out a single clue about the transaction Montaigne was planning for this summer. He hadn't attended, hadn't even responded to the invitation, the hostess had mentioned in a miffed tone. Apparently his business didn't leave time for either frivolity or social niceties.

Elizabeth had managed to get one dance with the host,

but Sir John talked so fast and so endlessly about the most trivial topics, she couldn't squeeze in any useful questions.

She wasn't sure how much longer she could hold up. The elaborate headdress of her swan costume threw her off balance, and the feathers on the *pâpier-maché* beak that covered her eyes and nose kept making her sneeze. The heavy beadwork on her white gown and the imitation wings attached to the sleeves didn't improve her dancing ability, either. She forgot to pay attention to the rhythm of the music, and stepped on her partner's foot for the second time.

She quickly removed her toe from the satin slipper he wore. "I am so sorry, Lord . . . er—"

"Lord Mortimer, Lady Barnes-Finchley." He appeared understandably miffed that she could not remember his name after dancing with him twice this evening and stepping on him an equal number of times. He frowned at her from beneath the turban of his sultan's costume.

Just then the music ended and Lord Mortimer escorted her back toward her companions. Elizabeth felt relieved, certain one more dance would finish her. "Thank you, my lord," she remembered to say.

"No, thank *you*, madam," he said politely, bowing over her hand before he limped away.

Elizabeth sank onto a velvet-upholstered bench beside two of Lady Kimble's friends, one dressed as a hummingbird, the other as the hunting goddess Diana. Elizabeth didn't know which was worse: the throb in her left side, the boring chatter of her handsome dancing partners, or being stuck with Lady Kimble and her gossiping flock of friends for the evening.

Georgiana, after searching so long in the rain when Elizabeth disappeared, had taken to bed with a cold; however, she had refused to allow Elizabeth to attend this party alone. She insisted it would be improper for a young woman, "married" or not, to appear in society alone.

Elizabeth sighed in chagrin. She felt terrible about

Georgiana's being ill, but sometimes the rules of the aristocracy could be deucedly inconvenient.

The women were so engrossed in their conversation they barely noticed Elizabeth. "Can you believe the vanity of the man?" the hunting goddess was saying. "To take a mistress is one thing, but to flaunt her so brazenly. Bringing her to his own house, right under his wife's nose!"

"Indeed," the hummingbird replied. "Look at them dancing together. Does he think no one knows it's her in that gypsy costume?"

Elizabeth had had enough of hearing the other guests' private lives picked apart. She thought of excusing herself, but she was too tired and sore even to move.

"Well, now we know why Fairfax insisted on a masquerade ball for his birthday celebration." Lady Kimble giggled, the sound muffled by the blue-and-green mask of her butterfly costume. "But, my dears, this latest liaison of his is not new. Not at all. It has been going on for quite some time. Why, I heard that months ago—simply months and months—one of the chambermaids was dusting in his study, and a packet of love notes from his paramour fell out of a secret slot behind one of the paintings."

"Fairfax is quite fortunate his wife never bothers with his business affairs," the hummingbird smirked. "Who knows what sort of nasty surprises she might find if ever she spent a bit of time in his study?"

Elizabeth was covering a yawn with the fan of white feathers attached to her sleeve. She stopped in mid-flutter, feeling a tingle of curiosity at the woman's comment. If Montaigne's solicitor kept his mistress's love notes behind his paintings, what other sort of correspondence might one find there?

"Do excuse me, ladies." She snapped her fan shut and stood up. "I think I see one of my Aunt Georgiana's old friends. I must say hello to her." The chattering women didn't acknowledge her departure any more than they had her arrival. Pleased that she might yet make something of this miserable evening, Elizabeth threaded her way through the crowded hall, heading for the stairs that led to the rooms above.

She was at the edge of the dance floor when a gloved hand caught her wrist.

"Nay, my lovely swan, do not fly 'til I have had my turn with you."

Startled, Elizabeth spun about and tried to pull away, but it was too late. A tall, broad-shouldered stranger was leading her onto the dance floor. From the back, it might have been anyone, dressed all in black, from his tricorne to his cape to his boots. But when he turned about and pulled her into his arms, a strange feeling thrilled through her limbs: a spark of fear, a surge of anger, then a flame of some wild emotion she could not name.

It was Pierce, dressed in his highwayman garb.

"Do not gape at me, Elizabeth. You look as if you think I might beat you." Holding her close—a bit too close for propriety's sake and much too close for Elizabeth's peace of mind—he moved effortlessly into the steps of a minuet. "Or is it my costume you dislike? Not imaginative, perhaps, but it was all I had on hand."

"I would not call it a costume at all, since you are, in fact, a brigand." Elizabeth forced her fear and the ache in her side and the unfamiliar, tingly feeling to the back of her mind, clinging to her anger. She had enough problems without Darkridge dogging her steps at every turn! "What are you doing here? And how did you recognize me?"

"I am here, I would imagine, for the same reasons you are. As to how I knew you, I asked some of the gentlemen if any had danced with Lady Barnes-Finchley this evening. It seems you made quite an impression. Mainly on their toes."

"I have already had my fill of dancing, my lord. Let me go."

He smiled, a lazy grin of masculine pleasure that she had never seen him use before. "Nay, sweet swan, I let you fly once. I'll not make that mistake a second time."

"You did not *let* me fly at all, my lord," she corrected. "Which brings to mind a question I've been wondering about. Why did you send Quinn with a message for my friends after you said you would not?''

He shrugged slightly. ''Perhaps I had a weak moment.''

''I doubt that, Lord Darkridge,'' she said dryly. ''I can't believe you've had one in your entire life.''

A bit of the humor left his expression, and he didn't reply. Elizabeth knew him well enough by now to realize he wasn't going to offer any further explanation.

She also couldn't get over the feeling that he *did* seem different tonight, his words and manner as blunt and insistent as ever but somehow gentler, almost . . . charming. She didn't detect any of the anger or outrage she would expect after the way she had escaped from his town house. It made her feel confused—and suspicious.

''If you are so kindhearted, my lord,'' she whispered, ''I suppose you might give back my pistol?''

''No.''

She grit her teeth. ''I'll have to buy another, then.''

''You're not going to need one.''

He spoke with an irritating air of utter confidence. Before Elizabeth could correct him, he began moving faster about the floor and she was forced to hold tight to his well-muscled arm, trying to ignore a wave of dizziness that assailed her. She could feel a blush warm her cheeks as the other dancers looked their way, nodding slightly and smiling as if the swan and the black-garbed brigand made a handsome couple.

She also noticed Pierce wasn't holding her correctly—the position was backwards, his hand on the right side of her waist rather than her wounded left side. He was being thoughtful, which only irritated her. The man was making it deucedly difficult for her to hate him. He had saved her life, given up his own room and bed for her, had not ravished her when he had the chance, and now he was taking care not to hurt her.

Each bit of kindness he showed made her wonder whether Georgiana and everyone else were indeed wrong about him. Each moment she spent with him made her fear fade a bit more, gradually replaced by another, softer feeling that warmed her right down to her toes.

She tried to shake it off, reminding herself that Lord Darkridge had declared himself her enemy in no uncertain terms.

"Ouch," he muttered as she accidently stepped on his foot. "Has anyone told you that you are a terrible dancer?"

"No, no one has yet been rude enough to point that out."

"I suppose your other partners were too busy watching out for their toes to carry on a conversation."

"Their conversation was quite enchanting," she lied. "It was refreshing to spend some time with men who know how to talk to a lady."

"And how surprised they would be to discover that this lady is in truth a highwa—ouch."

Elizabeth took small satisfaction in treading purposely on his toe this time. "May I remind you, my lord, that if you attempt to clip the wings of this particular swan, she will sing quite loudly and long about the true identity of a certain highwayman."

"How fortunate for me that you, lady swan, are much better at keeping your beak shut than you are at dancing."

She tried unsuccessfully to get her hand out of his. He held her firmly, the leather of his glove warm against her fingers. Elizabeth struggled against another rush of dizziness. "Your critique of my abilities is all very interesting, Lord Darkridge, but I've a better use for my time," she said quickly. "I have squandered enough of it with you."

"Hmmm," he murmured. "I take that to mean you've found out something about Montaigne's business transaction this summer?"

Elizabeth couldn't stifle an exclamation of surprise. "How did you—" she stopped herself and carefully adopted a neutral expression. "I have no idea what you mean."

"Please, don't be tedious. I've known for some time

that Montaigne means to purchase an enormous shipment of gin this summer. That's why I want you to stop your incessant raids. If you make him nervous, he'll never risk transporting a large amount of gold all at once.''

Elizabeth almost groaned in frustration and annoyance. Why did this blackguard always seem to be one step ahead of her or one step right behind? The worst of it was that she could see the logic in his argument. She might have thought of it herself, if grief and vengeance hadn't been clouding her reason.

''So?'' he prompted. ''What have you discovered?''

''Nothing that I care to discuss with you,'' she ground out.

''From the way you were heading for the steps, I would say you were on your way upstairs—perhaps to an assignation?'' He held her hand tighter, drawing it between their bodies, his thumb toying with the wedding band on her finger. ''Tsk, madam. You *are* a married woman.''

The idea that Pierce Wolverton would dare to lecture her on morality struck Elizabeth speechless for a moment. ''Yes, I *am* married,'' she said hotly. ''A fact which you seem to forget at your convenience.''

''True enough,'' he admitted, his voice low and velvety. ''Would now be convenient?''

Elizabeth might have slapped him, if he hadn't been holding her so tightly. But even as she felt outraged at his boldness, she realized it was playing havoc with her heartbeat. ''Let us be clear on one point, my lord,'' she said, her voice shaking. ''I have no desire for any sort of assignation, with *any* man, ever.''

He swept her closer as the tempo of the music quickened. ''That's not true.'' He raised her hand to his lips. ''And I think we both know it.''

Elizabeth thought she would lose her mind as he surreptitiously nibbled at her fingertips, the tip of his tongue just grazing the sensitive pads. She trembled, knowing he could feel it and hating that he knew, despising the way he could make her respond against her will. ''Go to hell.''

"As you wish." He chuckled at her ire and recaptured her hand when she managed to snatch it away. "I'll likely burn for eternity. God knows I've broken enough commandments. 'Thou shalt not steal. Thou shalt not kill . . . Thou shalt not covet thy neighbor's wife.' " His voice shifted to a more serious tone. "Though with your husband in Italy, I could hardly consider him a neighbor, could I?"

Elizabeth was grateful when the music ended; she desperately wanted to sit down—and just as desperately wanted to get away from her dancing partner. "I'm quite sure my husband wouldn't approve of your line of thinking, my lord."

"Enough about him," Darkridge said abruptly. The musicians struck up a new tune. Still holding her, he smoothly moved into the steps of a gavotte. "If you were not on your way to a tête-à-tête upstairs, then you must have been meaning to have a look about. What were you going to search for, Elizabeth?"

She bestowed a silent glare on him.

"Very well. I shall be happy to keep you occupied until you decide to tell me. I've only just arrived, and I could spend the entire night dancing. You, on the other hand—Elizabeth!"

She went limp suddenly and would have fallen, had he not been holding her so tight. With one arm about her waist, he immediately led her from the dance floor and found her a seat in an alcove away from the crush of party guests.

"You are obviously not strong enough to be here at all tonight," he growled. Kneeling beside her, he started rubbing her hands vigorously. "Why the devil didn't you tell me you weren't feeling well?"

"You might have asked *before* you started spinning me about like a top." She snatched her hands out of his, feeling better now that she was away from the stuffy, perfume-choked dance floor. She was half angry at him and half upset with herself for swooning in his arms, like some silly miss with no more backbone than a daffodil.

"None of your other dancing partners seemed to have

had such an effect on you.'' He looked up at her, his brown eyes smoky with an expression that made her stomach give an odd little jump. ''Do I make you nervous, Elizabeth?''

''Absolutely not. It's the lack of air in here.'' She opened her fan with a snap and started fanning herself furiously. She told herself she had almost fainted from simple exhaustion, but a secret voice in her mind whispered that there *was* something about him; whenever he held her close, she felt all weak and melting inside. She had to get away from the rogue and get on about her search. ''Thank you *so* much for the dance and your entertaining observations, my lord. Now, please leave.''

Darkridge ignored her request and sat beside her on the little bench, leaning close, his voice low and intent when he spoke. ''Listen to me. Whatever it is you are searching for, we could find it more quickly if we were to work together.''

''I have no need for a partner. I've done quite well on my own up to now.''

''You've a strange idea of doing well if you think getting shot off your horse qualifies,'' he snapped. ''If ever there were someone who needed help, madam, it is you.''

Startled at his sudden vehemence, Elizabeth held up her feathered fan as if it could ward him off. Why was he so different tonight? Was he actually worried about her, or was all of this an act? ''I do *not* need help. And even if I did, you are the last person I would ask.''

''Sorry, but I do seem to be the only one making the offer.''

''And I am refusing your offer.''

''I insist.''

''You are forgetting one thing.''

''Which is?''

''*You* are the one who declared us enemies.''

He grinned at her. ''Perhaps I spoke too hastily. May not a man change his mind, or is that exclusively the right of women?''

"You may change your mind all you like. I'll not change mine." She started to rise.

He grabbed her arm and pulled her back down beside him, exerting just enough pressure to hold her still. "Tell me, my light-fingered little swan, how are you at picking locks and moving heavy objects? Whatever it is you are searching for, I'm sure our host will have it well hidden and well protected."

Elizabeth frowned. "I'll manage, just as I have up to now."

"No, more likely you'll leave here empty-handed to-night—unless you accept my help."

Elizabeth chewed the inside of her cheek. He was right, though it irked her to have to admit it. No doubt he was much more adept at thievery than she was. But after the way he kept changing his mood from one moment to the next, she was not about to trust him. Still . . . perhaps she *could* use his help, provided she kept her eyes open and took care not to turn her back on him for a second.

He seemed to sense her change of heart before she said a word. He smiled and shifted his grip from her arm to her hand. "Truce?"

She eyed him warily. "Only temporarily."

"Good enough." He helped her to her feet and escorted her along the edge of the crowd to the foot of the stairs. "Wait for me upstairs."

"Where are you going?"

Pierce disappeared into the crowd without giving Elizabeth an answer. As he walked away, he indulged in a satisfied smile. His seduction plan was working perfectly. He knew he had her thoroughly confused; a few more kind words, and a gentle kiss or two, and he would have her in the palm of his hand.

Elizabeth ascended the stair and waited in the shadows at the top, fuming at the way Lord Darkridge had taken charge. He joined her a few minutes later.

"Where did you go?" she demanded.

"I wanted to assure that everyone will be kept entertained.'' He took her elbow. "Now tell me what it is we're looking for.''

Elizabeth jerked her elbow out of his grip. "First, my lord, let us understand one another. I agreed to a temporary truce only, and I am *not* going to follow your orders. We work as partners or we don't work together at all.''

He smiled at her outburst, but didn't try to take her arm again. "Very well, *partner.* We will share whatever information we discover, but then it is every highwayman for himself.'' His gaze flicked from her face to her bodice and back up. "Or herself.''

Turning so that he wouldn't see her blush, Elizabeth moved down the corridor. "Then let us see if we can locate our host's study. I believe we might find some useful correspondence there.'' She went from one door to the next, peeking in the rooms. Pierce did the same on the other side of the hallway.

"What will we say,'' she whispered, "if someone finds the two of us sneaking about up here?''

Pierce responded with a low, throaty chuckle. "Let them think we are looking for an empty bedroom.''

"You are disgusting.''

"You didn't seem to think so the other night.''

Elizabeth spun about, a denial on her tongue, only to find that Pierce had swiftly and silently moved up behind her. Before she could say a word, he reached up and placed a finger on her lips, then touched her cheek.

"Take that damned beak off,'' he muttered, whisking her mask away. The next instant his arm was about her shoulders and he was kissing her, a different sort of kiss, softer, sweeter than before. He was not being demanding and forceful this time, but warm and gentle. Instead of feeling outraged, Elizabeth found herself melting into the hard, lean lines of his body, her objections and wariness floating away with every fluttering beat of her heart.

"You see,'' he released her mouth at last and nuzzled her cheek, his breath hot and moist on her skin. "I am not so disgusting after all.''

Before she could come to her senses and chastise him,

he placed the mask in her hand and turned away, apparently unaffected. She was still standing there, feeling confused and slightly light-headed, when he called to her.

"Elizabeth," he repeated. "Come here. I've found it."

He was holding open a door. Elizabeth blinked at him for a second then slipped her mask back on, trying to act as if she weren't affected either, silently cursing her shaking fingers. Chin high, she walked past him without a word and entered the room.

Sir John Fairfax's study contained a large desk, writing tables and chairs, a bookshelf with latticework doors, and an impressive collection of paintings. A pair of tall French windows opened onto a small, decorative balcony. Pierce paused in the doorway for a second, head cocked as if he were listening for something. With a frown, he shut the door and quickly crossed toward the desk. Elizabeth started to follow, but he stopped her. "Stay at the door and warn me if anyone comes."

"I told you, I am not going to take your orders," she reminded him, crossing to stand at his side. "It will be faster if we both search. There may be some important letters behind one of these paintings."

Ignoring her, he glanced about the room. "Our search will be to no avail if someone finds us. I don't think anyone would believe we're here to make love on the desk."

Elizabeth started to utter a retort when she noticed he was staring at the desk, his expression suddenly hard and angry. She followed his gaze and saw a small wooden box, etched with gold on the top, obviously very old and very valuable. "What is it?" she asked. "Is it a clue? Does it mean something?"

He stepped forward and ran a finger over the box. "No," he replied after a moment. His next words were so soft she barely heard them. "If I took it with me, they would know someone had been in here." Clenching his hand into a fist, he moved to the paintings behind the desk. "Stay at the door," he ordered gruffly.

Elizabeth gritted her teeth, muttered a few unladylike words about overbearing, impossible men, then gave in and did as he told her. Opening the door just the tiniest crack, she tried to keep an eye on Pierce while watching the hallway.

The first time she glanced his way, he was using a small metal instrument to pick the lock on a secret compartment behind one of the paintings. Next she saw him with a sheaf of papers in his hand. He skimmed over them and started to return them to their hiding place.

"Wait a moment!" Elizabeth objected. "How do I know you haven't found something useful and are keeping it from me?"

"Would you like me to read them aloud?" He gave her a devilish look and proceeded to read from one of the letters. " 'My darling John, I love your touch, I love your kisses, I especially love it when you lie down beside me and put your tongue in my—' "

"Stop," Elizabeth interrupted, her face awash with heat. "Very well, I believe you."

"But I was just getting to the interesting part."

Elizabeth bit her bottom lip to stop an oath and returned her attention to the corridor. Seeming to enjoy himself thoroughly, Darkridge worked his way from one painting to the next, finding correspondence from a variety of women and reading aloud the most erotic passages.

Elizabeth almost clapped her hands over her ears, certain she must be blushing from head to heels. Finally he fell silent for a moment. She glanced over her shoulder to see him reading to himself, his features cast into a frown.

"Is that one about Montaigne? What does it say?"

He didn't look up. "He means to conduct his transaction in August."

"Where?"

Pierce ignored her question and cocked his head again as if he were listening for something.

"My lord?" Elizabeth couldn't hear anything but the

noisy hum of the party downstairs. "What the devil are you—"

"It seems my diversion has been delayed," Pierce said abruptly, folding the letter. "We shouldn't linger in here."

"Oh, no you don't." Elizabeth hurried to his side. "We had an agreement. This letter I would read for myself."

She grabbed for it but he held it out of her reach. "I've already told you what it says. Stop being difficult and let's get out of here."

"Damn you, you blackguard—"

Both of them froze. There were voices coming down the hall.

Standing on tiptoe, Elizabeth snatched the letter from his hand and ran to the other side of the desk, reading quickly before he could grab it away. Her underhanded "partner" had told her only some of the truth. The letter was an invitation, sent by Montaigne's solicitor to the distillers in the north. They were to bring all their best gin to St. Bartholomew's Fair in August. Fairfax verified that there would be enough gold on hand to cover the purchase of an entire year's supply.

"Hellfire!" Pierce growled, catching her. He grabbed Elizabeth's arm in a painful grip and took the letter from her hand. He stuffed the missive back into its hiding place just as the voices in the hall came to a stop outside the door.

"Hazard, *messieurs*?" a man was saying, speaking with a French accent. "No wager less zan five pounds?"

Elizabeth looked frantically about the room. She started to dive under the desk, but Pierce caught her about the waist and half carried her to the tall windows that opened onto the tiny balcony outside.

"Ten, Monsieur Rochambeau," one of the others replied. "You will find that we Englishmen take our gambling most seriously."

Pierce had just managed to throw the window open when the study door slowly swung inward.

Chapter 8

Pierce shoved Elizabeth over the sill and leaped out after her as the group of men entered the room. He flattened her against the wall, pressing his body against hers. She uttered an angry protest, which he cut off with a hand over her mouth. His black clothes would hide him in the darkness, but Elizabeth's white costume shone like a flag of surrender; he tried to cover her with his cloak. He could feel the pounding of her heart against his chest. The window was still open.

"You are certain your wife won't come up here looking for you, Fairfax?" one of the men said.

"No, the bitch is busy showing off that damned Queen Elizabeth costume that cost me a thousand pounds," the solicitor replied. "I'll have one of the servants send up some brandy."

"Whiskey too," another man requested.

"And some more of zees fine cigars of yours," the Frenchman added.

Pierce swore under his breath. It sounded as if they were going to be there for hours. What the devil had happened to the diversion he had paid for? Hoping to keep the party guests occupied *out*side, he had bribed one of the footmen to start Fairfax's birthday fireworks early. Perhaps he should have offered a timepiece as well as money, he thought sourly.

He looked down at Elizabeth's pale face. She struggled a bit and tried to free her mouth. Keeping her pinned against the wall with his weight, he gave her a warning look and slowly removed his hand. The idea of being stranded on a balcony with her for the night had a certain appeal, but he doubted she would share his enthusiasm, even though her responses so far tonight had been even better than he'd hoped.

Curiously, he found he was actually enjoying himself, more than at any time within recent memory. Elizabeth's wit charmed him, her stubbornness challenged him, and God, her kiss. . . . He kept having to remind himself that this was only part of a larger scheme meant to win him the Wolverton estates.

The thought of his home brought a tightness to Pierce's throat as he remembered his father's tobacco box sitting on Fairfax's desk. That box had been in the Wolverton family for more than a century. Montaigne, the bastard, had cast it off to one of his underlings as if it were nothing.

Pierce looked down at Elizabeth. Her eyes were wide, her breathing fast, her breasts rising and falling against his chest in a tantalizing rhythm.

No, he couldn't stay out here all night. Before he left this party, he meant to have her thoroughly under his spell. A hard stone balcony didn't lend itself to what he had in mind.

He could hear the man named Rochambeau drawing near the open window. ''Are your English servants so careless, zat zey leave windows open like zis?''

The man stood so close Pierce could smell his cigar smoke and hear him taking a deep breath of the night air. Pierce bent his head over Elizabeth's, trying to hide her completely and almost sneezing on the feathers in her headdress. She started to tremble—whether from fear or his nearness, he couldn't tell. Suddenly his own body responded, desire curling in his gut and tightening his every muscle. *Hellfire,* he thought. Why couldn't he control his responses to her? *Easy, Darkridge. Take this slowly or you'll scare her off again.*

''Leave it open, monsieur. It's warm in here,'' one of the men called. ''Let's start the game.''

The instant the Frenchman left the window, Pierce edged toward the balcony railing, pulling Elizabeth with him. There was grass below; he judged the distance to be about ten feet.

Elizabeth gaped at him. "Have you lost your—mmphh."

Pierce firmly silenced her protest with his mouth, swallowing her cry of alarm. Before she could recover, he released her and lifted himself up onto the balustrade, then grasped her chin in his fingers. "No arguments," he whispered. "You're going to learn to fly tonight, little swan."

Not giving her a chance to reply, he swung his legs over the railing and lowered himself down the side of the balcony. Clinging to one of the slim stone pillars with both hands, he shifted his weight and let his legs dangle. He heard Elizabeth gasp when he let go.

Landing with a jolt that must have permanently flattened his heels, Pierce stumbled backward, but regained his balance in a heartbeat. Reaching up, he motioned for Elizabeth to jump.

Wide-eyed, she shook her head vigorously.

He glared at her and held out his arms, indicating he could catch her easily. She didn't budge.

At that moment, the diversion he had arranged finally began. He heard a loud crack as a sparkling sea of bright jewel tones exploded over the gardens on the west side of the house.

"By Jove!" one of the card players exclaimed. "What was that?"

Pierce cursed vividly. Elizabeth was going to be caught if she didn't move right now.

With a gulp and a quick glance over her shoulder, Elizabeth apparently came to the same conclusion. She suddenly leaped up onto the railing, stared down at Pierce for just a second, closed her eyes, and jumped.

Pierce saw a dazzling image of sheer silk and white wings fluttering against the night sky, and then he caught her, pulling her against his chest as he half-fell into the shadows beneath the balcony.

The group of men all came to the window this time.

''Eh what?'' one of them said. ''Did you hear something else out here?''

Pierce, his back against the wall, held Elizabeth in his arms and didn't even breathe for fear of making a sound. Another round of colorful shells exploded.

Fairfax spoke from directly over their heads. ''It's just the old bitch starting my birthday fireworks without me.''

There was silence above for a few minutes, and Pierce couldn't tell if the men were still up there or not. Then Fairfax spoke again. ''To hell with her, then.''

After watching the spectacle for a moment more, the card players closed the windows and returned to their game.

Exhaling, Pierce lowered Elizabeth to her feet. ''Are you all right?'' He had done his best to be careful of her wounded side, but knew it must hurt anyway; he rubbed it soothingly.

''I'm fine,'' she said shakily, pushing his hand away. ''You could have broken both our necks!''

''In another second they would have seen us.'' Pierce kept one arm about her waist as if to steady her, holding her much more tightly than was necessary.

''You always think you are doing exactly the right thing, don't you, my lord? It is a most irritating habit.''

Her words were angry, but as another shell exploded in the night sky, he could see a different feeling sparkling in her eyes: excitement. Her hands were pressed against his chest as if to push him away, but she did not.

Feeling as satisfied as a cat presented with a bowl of sweet cream, Pierce smiled and lowered his head to hers. His tricorne, knocked askew when he caught her, slid down over his forehead.

Elizabeth reached up as if to fix it and instead pulled it down even farther over his face. ''There,'' she declared. ''That is an improvement.''

''Take the deuced thing off,'' Pierce growled through the brim. When she only laughed, he flung the hat off with a shake of his head and turned about, pushing her back against the wall. She gave a little gasp of surprise and struggled in his arms, but she still wasn't putting up what he considered serious resistance. The fireworks high above crackled and filled the air with the biting scent of smoke and cascades of glowing color.

Before he could kiss her again, a man's voice interrupted, coming from a balcony to their left. "Come, Margaret," the man was pleading huskily. "I promise you, you shall have a much better view from out here."

"*Certainly* she will," Elizabeth muttered. "Men."

Pierce snatched up his hat, took Elizabeth's hand and led her along the edge of the house. He didn't want to give her a chance to ponder too long on the evils of his sex.

Most of the party guests had gathered at the west side of the estate to watch the fireworks. Pierce went in the opposite direction, Elizabeth hurrying to keep up with his stride.

"What the devil are you running from?" She puffed, one hand pressed to her side. "Slow down. I can't . . . go any . . . f . . . further."

Pierce swept her up in his arms and carried her. "I wanted to get away from the house before someone saw us and started asking questions," he said smoothly. "I know how you hate answering questions."

She either believed him or was too tired to reply, because for once she didn't argue. He moved through the gardens until he spotted a site that suited his purposes: a little gazebo, surrounded by shrubbery, similar to the one at the Rowlands' party. It was isolated. Romantic. Perfect.

He didn't release her until they were inside. He gently lowered her to her feet, walked about casually admiring the interior for a bit, then sat on an oriental-style cane bench that had been placed along the rail. She remained standing, breathing hard.

Pierce felt the unfamiliar twinge of a feeling that might have been guilt. She was still weak from her wound; that was probably why she hadn't put up much of a fight against his advances. It was contemptible to prey upon her when she was so vulnerable. If he were any kind of a gentleman, he would—

No, he thought savagely. This was too important. If she kept up her raids, Montaigne would cancel his plans for the transaction in August, and Pierce's chance to reclaim the Wolverton estates would disappear like a puff of smoke in a strong wind. Force had failed, and logic would be useless with a woman; seduction was his best alternative.

Besides, he reminded himself, no one would ever mistake Pierce Wolverton for a gentleman.

"Elizabeth, sit down before you fall down."

"I . . . can't," she puffed, half bent over.

He smiled. "So I do make you nervous after all."

"It's not that," she retorted, removing her mask. "Nell made this costume from some of her most expensive Macclesfield silk. She'll have my head if I get it soiled."

Pierce removed his cloak and spread it over the bench beside him so she could sit. At her look of surprise, he mustered his most charming smile. "I was *raised* a gentleman, you know. I can still behave like one when I have to."

The sympathetic look in her eyes told Pierce that his comment had hit the target squarely. Good, he thought, slouching lower into his seat. This was going exceedingly well.

Elizabeth stood up straight as her breathing slowed, and cautiously inched toward the bench, her eyes never leaving Lord Darkridge. She found his words oddly touching. What *had* his boyhood been like? How could he have started life as a member of the privileged aristocracy, only to become a criminal with a price on his head?

Another small explosion echoed on the night wind and Elizabeth looked out at the sparkling bits of red and green fire that drifted down through the darkness. A shell sizzled up through the air, then burst, cascading out into the shape of a bird with wings of silver sparks, like shooting stars. She couldn't suppress a soft cry of wonder.

''Have you never seen fireworks before?'' Pierce asked softly.

''Only once,'' Elizabeth said, her attention still on the brilliant display. ''Just after I arrived in London. On St. Michael's Eve, with Geoffrey.'' Hardly realizing what she was doing, she sat on the bench and leaned out over the gazebo railing to get a better view.

''So his name really is Geoffrey,'' Pierce murmured. ''And when was this? Before the two of you left for the Continent?''

He had to repeat the question before Elizabeth realized what she had said. She turned about, and discovered that Pierce had moved very close beside her. He removed his mask, and as he looked down at her, she couldn't help but notice how handsome he was, with the wind ruffling his hair and the fireworks dancing in his coffee-dark eyes. His snug black waistcoat rose and fell with his every slow breath, drawing her gaze to the lean, powerfully muscled form beneath.

''Yes,'' she said quickly. ''My husband and I spent a few days in London before our ship sailed.''

''A honeymoon at sea. It sounds as if you were happy together.''

There was an obvious note of jealousy in Pierce's voice that didn't escape Elizabeth's attention. She didn't know why, but she suddenly wanted to tell him the truth: that she was not a wife, but a widow. That Geoffrey had never been ''Lord'' anybody, and she wasn't ''Lady'' anybody. That her husband was dead, and when he had been alive, he'd brought her nothing but pain and sadness.

In that moment, she realized just how desperately tired she was of hiding behind lies and disguises. They pressed down on her like iron weights. She had an impulse, so strong it frightened her, to throw them off, admit everything, and curl up against Pierce's strong side and have him hold her, comfort her, protect her.

Instead she stuck to the mixture of truth and falsehood she had told him before. ''We . . . we never were happy, not really. Because Geoffrey drank too much. When he started spending most of his time away on business affairs, I didn't mind."

Pierce lowered his eyes. She could feel his finger tracing along her hand. "Do you love him?"

A shiver ran up Elizabeth's arm, but by the time it reached her shoulder it had somehow turned into a tingling heat that warmed her entire body. She almost couldn't believe her ears. Lord Darkridge was acting as if . . . as if he were smitten with her. "He would not have been my choice for a husband."

Pierce raised his head, his eyes intent. "But do you love him?"

"No," she blurted, not knowing why she said that when it would have been just as easy, and eminently more sensible, to say yes.

Pierce edged even closer to her. "And does he know what you are doing here in London, the risks you're taking?"

Elizabeth wasn't sure which risks he was referring to: raiding, or being alone in a gazebo with him. "N . . . no." She changed the subject quickly before he could pose another question. "What was that box on Fairfax's desk?"

"It belonged to my family."

"But how did it—" Before she could finish her question Pierce was kissing her again, one of those wonderful, sweet kisses that made her turn to melting honey in his hands.

"I don't want to talk about it, Elizabeth." His words, much more of a vulnerable plea than a command, took Elizabeth by surprise. He wrapped his arms about her, gently arching her backward.

"No, I . . . I musn't."

The protest sounded weak even to her ears, and when his lips came down on hers again, the sensations that rioted through her body scattered any thought of a struggle. Her fists came up to press against his chest, but she could not make herself push him away. She should be acting outraged. She should be trying to convince him she was a faithful wife—God knew she had done a poor job of it up to now. She should be clinging to that shield for all it was worth.

Instead she found herself willingly giving in to his kiss, then tentatively responding. She heard him make a sound, deep in his throat, like distress and pleasure both mixed together.

She had a fleeting, frightening image of Geoffrey, of how he had hurt her when he came to her at night, tasting of liquor, rough in his eagerness to claim what he called his "husbandly rights." She had endured his advances, because everyone—Geoffrey included—had always called it her duty.

This feeling, though, was entirely different. Even as Pierce held her in an unyielding embrace, she somehow felt he would not hurt her. She knew she *shouldn't* be enjoying his kisses, but she did.

This was not something to be afraid of, something to be endured; this was . . . this was hot and sparkling and wondrous, like the fireworks exploding in the darkness of the night sky.

"Pierce," she sighed his name then opened her lips under his gentle, insistent pressure. Her fingers relaxed, then grasped his lapels to pull him closer.

"God, Elizabeth," Pierce groaned against her mouth. Suddenly his hands were on her rib cage, just below her breasts. He stood and lifted her up onto the railing, kicking the bench out of the way. She would have fallen backwards, but he held on to her, leaning into her, kissing her harder. The muscles of his arms trembled and his lips suddenly left hers, tracing along her jaw, down her neck, lower.

She moaned and tangled her fingers in his hair, intending to stop him—and instead holding him closer. His lips and teeth nibbled at the edge of her bodice until she felt the touch of the wind on her skin, quickly followed by the hotter touch of his tongue on one breast, just touching the sensitive peak, then laving it, then suckling it before he turned his attention to the other.

His hands moved down her back, sliding over her waist to cup her hips. His head came up suddenly and he kissed her again, his tongue in her mouth, thrusting, claiming. The urgency in him brought a moan from deep in her throat. Her breasts were wet and sensitive from his kisses and the soft material covering his chest felt rougher than sandpaper against her taut nipples.

One of his hands moved to her leg, sliding the silky material of her white skirt up, over her knee, her thigh, higher. He pressed his hips against her, and she could feel that he was heavy with desire.

Elizabeth's eyes flew open as reality burst through the sensual haze he had woven around her. She pushed her fists against his shoulders and tore her lips from his. "No," she gasped. "No, stop. I cannot."

He raised his head and looked down at her, surprise and passion warring in his eyes. "I want you," he said roughly. "You've no need to act like a silly virgin. I'll not hurt you."

"Stop it. Let me go."

He held her still, his head dipping to nuzzle the bared curve of her shoulder. "You are a married woman, Elizabeth. You cannot be unknowledgeable of desire."

"And that gives you the right to . . . to do this? No!"

"You said your husband was a drunkard. I'm not. Let me show you, Elizabeth. Let me show you how special it can be between a man and woman."

"No!" She angrily shoved him away and this time he released her. She scrambled off the railing, rearranging her disarrayed bodice, shame and fear hot on her cheeks. How could she have let him go so far? She should have realized his intentions from the first time he kissed her tonight. He wasn't concerned about her in the least; he only wanted to bed her. He felt nothing for her but lust.

Never, Elizabeth vowed, never would she risk losing her heart to a man as deceptive and underhanded as Pierce Wolverton.

"Elizabeth—" he stepped toward her.

"No!" She backed away, trying to think. She must get him out of her life; if he kept kissing her and caressing her like that, she would give in despite herself. She could not let that happen. She could not let him distract her from her plans for Montaigne.

She could certainly not risk getting pregnant.

It took only seconds to decide what she had to do. He was right about ceasing her raids; she could see the logic in not scaring off Montaigne, and she had enough money in the Trust to last until the Fair, precisely because she had been driving herself so relentlessly. ''I shall do what you asked.''

''What?'' he exclaimed. ''You just said—''

''No, not *that*. I will stop my raids, at least until St. Bartholomew's Fair.''

A wary look came into his eyes. ''You expect me to believe you would stop, just like that?''

''No, I have one condition.''

''Which is?''

''That you leave me alone. Stop pursuing me. If you will agree not to follow me anymore, I will stop my raids on Montaigne's coaches.'' Elizabeth felt a stab of hurt at the obvious pleasure her words gave him.

He raised an eyebrow. ''And what about St. Bartholomew's Fair?''

''I'll not agree to that. At the Fair it will be every man for himself.''

He smiled, the more familiar predatory smile, and Elizabeth knew in that moment that she had been wrong to think his ultimate goal was bedding her.

This was what he really wanted!

Force had failed, so he thought to seduce her into stopping her raids. The rest was an act: his charm, his thoughtfulness, his kisses. To think he had nearly convinced her that she . . . no, that *everyone* . . . had been wrong about him.

Before her stood the real Pierce Wolverton: ruthless, single-minded and utterly unscrupulous. He had been a complete fraud, and she had almost fallen for it! Humiliation washed over her; she had just proven herself to be exactly the naive, foolish little tender-heart he had accused her of being.

''Well?'' she said sharply. ''Have we an agreement?''

He nodded. "Agreed."

Elizabeth raised her chin. She felt tears burning her eyes and hated him for it. He had almost made her believe that he cared for her. The fake. The devil. "Then I shall not see you until the Fair, my lord."

She turned and stalked from the gazebo, wanting to run from him, glad that her aching side and leg made that impossible. She moved away stiffly, and hoped he interpreted it as dignity rather than pain. She told herself this was all for the best. Far better to see him for what he was now, before she let him . . .

The thought of what she had nearly let him do made her tears start to fall. She bit her bottom lip to keep from sobbing and hurried toward the house as fast as she could.

Pierce watched her go, trying to ignore the pain in his gut that had started the instant he saw the hurt in her eyes. He told himself this was what he wanted all along— an end to Blackerby Swift's raids. His seduction plan hadn't come off exactly right, but he had what he wanted . . . didn't he?

Yes, of course he did. She had even saved him a great deal of trouble. A tiresome, drawn-out wooing, complete with idiotic words he didn't mean and silly gestures of affection, hadn't even been necessary.

But why did none of those thoughts ease the pain in the pit of his stomach? Worse, his body was still heavy and tight with need for her. She had seared him with a desire that he sensed only her amethyst eyes and achingly sweet kisses could quench. The memory of her softly moaning his name actually made him tremble.

He shook his head as if by doing so he could shake off the hold she had over him. Snatching up his cloak, he strode out of the gazebo. Hellfire, staying away from Elizabeth for the next two months was the most sensible thing he could do.

But even as he told himself that, he knew that staying away from Elizabeth was going to be a damn difficult agreement to keep.

Chapter 9

Sprawled behind one of the massive trestle tables in the Black Stag Tavern, Pierce stretched his legs and inhaled deeply of air that was thick with the smells of tobacco, sweat and ale spilled on the dirt floor. It was a supremely masculine scent, almost strong enough to blot out the memory of a softly feminine perfume and a pair of violet eyes shining with hurt. Almost.

He gnawed on a piece of cold salt pork that the serving girl had brought with his fourth pewter tankard of ale. For three weeks now, thoughts of Elizabeth had haunted him; the more he tried not to think of her, the more she occupied his mind. He saw the color of her eyes in the midsummer flowers, the movement of her hips in the undulations of sheets drying on the breeze. He heard the sound of her voice in the husky rhythm of the Thames. Damn the woman. What had she done to him?

It had gotten worse rather than better with time. In the past week he had wandered among his favorite pubs, played billiards at the coffee houses, taken in a boxing match, and downed much more liquor than was prudent. He had even gone to the races, though he did not gamble; gambling was the most impractical of all pursuits, and Pierce was a practical man.

The *practical* thing to do in this situation, he thought sourly, was to forget Elizabeth. He finished the salt pork and lit a cigar, the match flaring red in the darkened room, the smoke swirling about his unshaven chin as he exhaled. It was senseless to keep wanting a woman who was beyond his grasp; he had sworn not to see her, and he wasn't going to break their agreement and give her a reason to start her raids again.

Why, then, could he not still these tantalizing thoughts? Even Quinn had noticed his restlessness; the ever-loyal, ever-discreet butler hadn't said a word, but Pierce knew he had noticed. It only added to his irritation.

The serving girl brought a heaping plate of bubble and squeak, the favorite meal of many a British peasant and very few earls. Pierce ground out his cigar and dug into the boiled beef, fried cabbage and sizzling onions with gusto. He supposed many lordly types would frown on his dreadfully pedestrian tastes in food. Even as he thought that, he caught himself wondering whether Elizabeth was the kind of woman who would turn up her adorable nose, or pull up a chair and join him.

He suddenly stopped eating and shoved the plate away, scowling that even his favorite food offered no refuge from thoughts of her. Tossing a few coins on the table top, he stood. Perhaps he would try to work in his garret again tonight, start a new poem. The one about Elizabeth should be finished by now; instead it was still little more than a collection of half-satisfying images. It eluded him somehow, and he could never bring himself to begin a new work until the last was done. The prospect of staring at that page over the rim of a brandy glass for yet another night was less than appealing.

Damn the woman.

He was heading for the door when a low growl of conversation caught his ear.

"Swift got away with more'n a 'undred pounds, 'e did," a man was saying. "Right up 'ere on the Bedford Road last week. 'E was in an' out so fast, they never knew what 'it 'em."

Pierce stopped, disbelief firing through his mind, so stunning he couldn't move for a moment. "Excuse me, friend." He turned slowly around and stepped toward a table where a pair of shabbily-dressed men sat. "That wouldn't be *Blackerby* Swift you're speaking of? The highwayman?"

One of the men turned toward Pierce, his expression wary. "Might be, guv."

"What's it worth to ye?" his companion added.

Greed made the world go round, Pierce thought cynically. He tossed a few coppers on the man's empty plate. "It's worth more, if you are telling the truth."

"God's truth, guv," the man said, scooping the coins into his soiled shirtfront. "I 'eard it from a mate o' mine who be an odd job man at the Two Oaks Inn, up there on the Bedford. Mr. Charles Montaigne's guards came in right after it 'appened, they did, and they were bloody upset. Thought they'd 'eard the last of Swift, then 'e struck 'em again on Tuesday last. Got away with two fat sacks full o' gold, 'e did."

Pierce gave the man a penetrating glare. "And how did they know it was Swift?" Elizabeth's telltale silver-plated pistol was still at his town house.

"Oh, it 'ad to be 'im, all right," the man insisted. "What other 'ighwayman 'ave ye 'eard of what's got a taste for Montaigne's gold and guts enough to go up 'gainst so many guards?"

Pierce ground his teeth. "Indeed."

The little man's companion tapped on his empty plate. "If that's no' a story worth more 'n sixpence, guv, what is?"

Pierce flipped the man a silver half-guinea, spun on his heel and stormed out of the tavern without another word. Fury seethed in his veins, hotter than liquid flame. He fought to control it, telling himself the highwayman might have been anyone, reminding himself London thrived on gossip and rumor, half of it untrue.

But by God, if Elizabeth had broken their agreement already, he'd break her beautiful neck.

"Oh!" Georgiana exclaimed, reaching for her neck so fast she dropped her gilded etui.

"What is it?" Elizabeth bent to retrieve her friend's evening bag. "Is your throat still bothering you?"

"Can't be," Nell interjected. "She finished up 'er

'ackin' days ago. Now let's get movin' er we'll miss the start of the play.''

"Thank you for your concern, *Elizabeth,*" Georgiana said with a frown, "but I assure you I am fully recovered." She gingerly felt the high neck of her deep emerald gown. "I just had the strangest sensation, as if . . . as if someone were choking me."

"Hmph. More'n likely ye should've listened t' me when I said that gown was a size too small." Nell held the door open. "Ye sure ye don't want t' come wi' us, Bess?"

"No thank you, I've had my fill of evenings on the town. I thought I would catch up on my reading."

"The *Crusoe*?" Georgiana asked. "It's the most marvelous tale."

"No, actually, I finished that last week. Since Blackerby Swift is in retirement for a while, I've so much time on my hands I don't know what to do with myself." Elizabeth gave Nell a conspiratorial wink. "I've been reading the book Nell gave me for my birthday—*The Lives and Adventures of the Most Famous Highwaymen.*"

"Oh, goodness," Georgiana fanned herself. "Really, Elizabeth, that's not suitable at all for a lady."

"Dod-rot. It's perfect fer 'er," Nell countered. "Ye stay 'ere and enjoy yer quiet evenin', Bess. Ye've got yer color back and ye look prettier'n a bloomin' rose, now that ye've been takin' care o' yerself."

"Thank you, Nell." Elizabeth smiled. "Now, you two enjoy the play."

"I am not sitting in the pit again." Georgiana wagged a finger at Nell as they stepped out into the street. "The last time I spent most of the evening dodging overripe apples."

"Then you can pay the extra four shillings fer a box. I *like* the pit."

Elizabeth shut the door behind them, smiling. She was indeed feeling much better—they all were—since she had stopped her raids. She hadn't been out for three weeks.

Except for that one brief time last Tuesday.

Chewing the inside of her cheek, Elizabeth crossed the

entry hall of their small town house, climbed the stairs and went up to her bedroom. She hoped Lord Darkridge hadn't found out about that night. He would never understand that she had had no choice.

She consoled herself with the fact that she had been very careful not to speak during the raid, or give any clues as to her identity. Besides, she couldn't believe one isolated attack would make Montaigne so nervous as to cancel his plans for the Fair.

In any event, she truly had had no choice.

She sighed in chagrin as she opened the door to her room, trying to banish her worry about Lord Darkridge's reaction. She must cease thinking about that self-interested, unscrupulous, underhanded blackguard. If he were angry, she certainly would have heard from him by now. She cursed herself for the hundredth time for ever giving him the location of Nell's shop.

Elizabeth thrust her nervousness aside. If he intended to chastise her, he would have already done so. He was not the sort of man to keep his anger to himself. Other emotions, yes—but not anger.

Slipping off her shoes, she left them on the diamond-patterned floorcloth beside her bed and opened her small armoire. Once and for all, Pierce Wolverton was out of her life. "And good riddance," she added under her breath.

Part of her, though—a very small part that she was doing her best to ignore—perversely missed spending time with him, missed their verbal duels and his bold demands, that unnerving gaze and his arms pulling her near. . . .

Elizabeth choked off that thought. He had only been acting, she reminded herself, only interested in edging her out of the gold. Lord Darkridge had proven he would do *anything* to get that money—including seducing a woman whom he believed to be married. The man had the morals of a snake, and she was infinitely better off without him around.

Infinitely.

Focusing her attention on her modest wardrobe, Elizabeth unlaced her gown, selected a comfortable deshabille and took her time dressing in the silky, long-sleeved white chemise and matching wrapper. Since her "retirement," she had had time to enjoy such frivolities.

She had even had time to sew a new satin spread for her bed and keep her floor swept with a sweet-scented mixture of lavender and tea. What luxury to linger over such trifling matters, instead of racing from one raid to the next. Relaxing at last, she crossed to her writing desk and picked up the volume Nell had given her.

What bliss to have nothing more dangerous than a book to occupy her evening.

She went downstairs with a smile, to the salon, and opened one of the windows for a breeze. Curling up in her favorite chair, she began to read. Not only was *The Lives and Adventures of the Most Famous Highwaymen* entertaining, it was full of ideas that might prove useful at St. Bartholomew's Fair in August. She was soon engrossed in the tale of reckless and daring John Cottington.

So engrossed she didn't notice when she was no longer alone.

"You really should lock your front door. No telling what sort off rabble might wander in."

Elizabeth jerked upright, her heart pounding. "What are you doing here? We had an agreement—"

"Yes, indeed we did," Pierce snapped, striding across the room. "And from what I have heard, you, madam, haven't honored it."

Before Elizabeth could stand, he blocked her movement, caging her with a hand on either side of her chair. Only now did she notice the fury in his eyes, the barely-controlled anger in every taut line of his body. The book slipped from her fingers. Her throat went dry. God help her, he had found out.

She knew she couldn't hope to explain. "I . . . I have no idea what you are talking about. I want you to leave—"

"Not until you give me an answer." His hands grasped the sides of the chair, so hard Elizabeth could feel it shake. "Did you attack one of Montaigne's coaches last week?"

She could smell liquor on his breath. Together with the sensation of being trapped, it brought an image of Geoffrey flashing to mind and sent cold fear shivering through her body. "You've been drinking—"

"Yes, too bloody much. Now answer the bloody question!"

"Georgiana and Nell are coming back. You—"

"You are not a very good liar, madam. I've been watching the house. I heard them tell the hackney driver to take them to Haymarket. Now give me an answer, God damn it. Did you or did you not rob one of Montaigne's coaches last week?"

Elizabeth swallowed hard, her heart hammering. It was a measure of either his anger or his drunkenness that he hadn't yet noticed her state of deshabille; his gaze was locked on her face. There was no telling what he might do in this mood. The truth would enrage him, but a lie might be worse.

"Yes!" she admitted at last. "Yes, I did. There is your answer. Are you satisfied?"

She tried to stand up. He shoved her back down into the chair, so hard it brought tears to her eyes.

His expression had turned murderous. "You lying little—"

"If you'd care to listen, I can explain," she said hoarsely. "I *had* to break our agreement, just this one time—"

"Why, because you needed a new ball gown?"

"No, you insufferable lout," she yelled back, her own temper flaring beneath her desperation to make him listen. "To get enough money to help a young woman who was going to be sent to the gaol."

He frowned in an expression of utter disbelief. "What the deuce does that have to do with anything?"

"That's what I have been doing with Montaigne's money. My friends and I have established a charitable trust. We pay the debts of women and children who are faced with prison and have nowhere else to turn."

"You must be joking." Taking her by the shoulders, he pulled her to her feet and looked down at her as if she had just claimed to be Queen Caroline herself. "You mean to tell me you're some sort of addlepated Robin Hood in a skirt, robbing Montaigne to help the *poor*?"

"It's not quite all that noble, but yes," she said quickly. "Essentially, that is where the money goes."

His face was so close now she could see the stubble on his chin and name the liquor he had been drinking: whiskey and ale. His fingers felt hot, as if they were searing right through the flimsy silk of her wrapper and chemise. Terror and anger and uncertainty paralyzed her. She fought to keep her knees from shaking.

"You're risking your life to help the *poor*?" he repeated as if he still could not comprehend.

"You say that as if it were offensive."

"Not offensive, just stupid." Pierce's fingers dug into her shoulders, so hard Elizabeth knew he was leaving marks. "Do you really think your pitiful efforts are going to make any difference? For every poor wretch you give a handout, there will be ten more standing in line. The wealth of a thousand Montaignes couldn't cover all their debts."

"I knew you wouldn't understand." She struggled to break free, but he held her fast. "At least I'm *trying* to help. At least I'm not a selfish, dishonorable, contemptible—"

"I don't give half a damn what you think of me." He snarled at her, his voice low and sharp. "You're missing the point. What you did could have ended everything."

"I *know* I took a chance. I know I broke our agreement, and I'm sorry. But I didn't do it on a whim. I . . ." Elizabeth pressed her fists against his chest. How could she possibly make him grasp what this meant to her? "This woman was going to be sent to Fleet Prison—"

"Happens all the time," he said flatly. "You should have given her whatever money you had or sent her on her way. Instead, you acted like a reckless little idiot!"

He shoved her away from him, and for the first time,

his eyes dropped from her face to her barely-clad bosom. Something changed in his gaze, but Elizabeth was too angry now to pay heed. "How can you—I knew you didn't have a heart, but you don't even have a scrap of a soul! I couldn't just send her on her way. Her debt was so large it would have wiped out all the money in the Trust, and she—"

"Better that than risk wiping out the August gold shipment!"

"But she was *pregnant*!"

He shook his head, a sardonic twist to his lips. "That happens all the time, too."

Elizabeth was stunned speechless at the depth of his cynicism. How could he be so uncaring about something so vital and meaningful? Trembling with outrage, she placed her hands on her hips, not realizing that this pulled the neckline of her wrapper lower still. She had to swallow several times before she managed to form coherent words. "Why am I even trying to explain this to you? You couldn't possibly understand. Get out!"

He spoke through gritted teeth. "Not until I make myself clear. I am not going to let you ruin my plans any more than you already have—"

"Your plans! That's all that matters to you, isn't it? Your plans, your orders, your*self*!"

"What matters," he said, his hands clenching into fists, "is that you broke our agreement, Elizabeth. It is important that you never do so again. If you dare—"

"If *I* dare? Who are *you* to dare dictate to me?" Her fury boiled over and she gave in to the impulse to tell him exactly what she thought of him. "You, who are so utterly without redeeming qualities that no man in London calls you friend. Even mongrels wouldn't find you fit company!"

In response, Pierce smiled—a taut, humorless grin that Elizabeth should have recognized as a warning. His eyes turned cold, his voice steely. "Say one more word, Elizabeth, and I'll show you exactly how I earned that reputation."

"Stop threatening me," she replied boldly. "Get out

of my house. You'll have no need to chastise me further for my behavior. Other than that one time, I have honored our agreement—''

"Then it seems you need a lesson in honor!"

"Well I'm not bloody likely to get one from a murdering lunatic capable of killing his own father!"

Too late, Elizabeth realized her words were a mistake. A hasty, thoughtless, terrible mistake. "Oh, God," she gasped. "I didn't mean that. I'm sorry. I—"

She tried to say more, but the expression on Pierce's face choked the breath from her throat.

His sudden silence was a thousand times more frightening than any words he could have uttered. His eyes darkened with an emotion that might have been pain—or homicidal fury.

She could hear Georgiana's voice in her memory . . . *"Killed his father in a drunken rage . . ."*

Pierce was certainly drunk.

And enraged.

He took one step toward her and Elizabeth fled the room.

She ran up the stairs, shaking by the time she reached her bedroom door, slamming and locking it behind her without pausing to see if he had followed her. Perhaps he would leave. Perhaps he would take out his anger on the breakables downstairs and then just leave. Per—

"Elizabeth." His voice sounded from the other side of her door, soft and ominous. He said nothing more, as if that one word should be enough to make her obey.

"Get out of my house!" She backed across the room, putting out a hand to steady herself, accidently knocking a small vase of flowers off the writing desk beside her bed. It smashed to the floor, unnoticed.

Her gaze flew to the window. There was a cobbled street below. Too far below. She looked frantically about for a weapon, something to protect herself.

Then she felt water soaking the floorcloth beneath her bare feet.

She looked down, knelt quickly. Her fingers closed about a shard of the broken vase.

The door crashed inward.

Their eyes locked, his ablaze with emotions so strong and so savage Elizabeth couldn't begin to name them. One was something fierce and mysterious that set her heart beating wildly. She stood and stepped back, gasping as bits of glass pricked her foot and drew blood.

He moved toward her. She raised the jagged piece of the vase. He was either fearless or too drunk to care, for he kept coming, with slow, prowling steps, until he was but inches away.

His eyes locked on her makeshift weapon. "Go ahead."

"W . . . what?"

"Stab me," he mocked.

Elizabeth didn't move, but didn't drop it. *God help her, she couldn't hurt him.* "G . . . get out or I'll—"

"You'll what?" he said softly, derisively. "Send your husband after me? I don't believe there *is* a husband, Elizabeth." He knocked the glass from her hand and grabbed her wrist. "I think that was a lie, too."

He yanked her against his chest. His face was cast in hard lines. She braced herself for his punishment. She expected him to strike her, hurt her. He didn't.

His whole body shook with the force of some inner battle.

Looking down at her, he groaned, then whispered, "You don't kiss like a wife."

Suddenly his mouth came down on hers. It was a bruising kiss, thick with the taste of whiskey and ale and mindless desire. His arms slipped about her waist, locking her to him, holding her helpless. She struggled and made a frightened sound of protest, deep in her throat, but he only kissed her harder, held her tighter until her feet left the floor and she was suspended against the hard length of his body.

His beard raked her tender skin as he deepened the kiss. His sensual onslaught was utterly devoid of the caring and gentleness he had shown her before; he was taking, punishing, conquering, as if she were nothing more than a convenient outlet for his lust. He was treating her as Geoffrey always had. Elizabeth fought with the strength of stark terror, but he subdued her effortlessly.

He tore his lips from hers and pushed her backward into the bedpost. "Not like a wife at all," he said roughly, trailing a path down her neck, nuzzling and nipping.

"Don't," she rasped, twisting in his arms, trying to escape his questing mouth. Anger and fear clashed with sparks of fire-hot sensation that tingled wherever he kissed. His lips were igniting her entire body. She could feel her reason spinning away beyond reach.

"You kiss like a woman who hasn't been kissed often enough."

"Let me go!"

"Like a woman who has much to learn."

His mouth closed over her breast, dampening her nightgown until the silk was wet and transparent, the pebble-hard nipple thrusting forward to meet every darting touch of his tongue. An icy-hot rain of sensation swept to the center of her belly, pure and terrifying in its power.

"Pierce!" His name was a raw cry on her lips. Elizabeth panicked, pleading now—with him, *with herself.* She didn't care how desperate she sounded, only that this stop. Now. "You don't know what you're doing. You're drunk—"

"Yes," he replied, his voice as hot as his touch. "Drunk as a piper. Utterly foxed." His mouth moved to her other breast. "On a sweet liquor by the name of Elizabeth."

"Pierce, don't." There were tears in her eyes now, tears of confusion and hurt and heart-stopping fear. "I didn't mean what I said. I'm sorry. I *do* know how important our agreement is. I won't break it again—"

"No." His head came up and he tangled his fingers in her hair to hold her still. "You won't." The coldness in his eyes, the fury, were gone, replaced by a searing desire that branded her with its intensity. His other hand slipped inside her wrapper to unfasten the laces of her chemise.

Elizabeth squeezed her eyes shut, unable to bear the agonizing tangle of emotions she felt. She grasped at whatever straws might make him see reason, desperate to make him understand her fear. "Don't do this! You were right—I'm not married. I'm a widow. We concocted a husband as part of my Lady Barnes-Finchley disguise because I—"

"So it was a lie." He growled, between rough, arousing kisses. "I take back what I said before. You are a good liar."

"But you don't understand! I'm *afraid*. I can't risk—"

"I don't care."

"But I—"

"I don't *care*," he said harshly. "Don't you know that by now? I'm a murderer and a lunatic and a heartless bastard. You've made up your mind on that score. Just like everyone else. You said it yourself." Pierce slipped her white silk garments off her shoulders. Without a sound, they whisked down her body and pooled on the floor at her feet. His eyes raked her nakedness. *"I don't have a scrap of a soul."*

"I didn't mean it," she repeated, a tear slipping down her cheek. "I was wrong—"

"No," he bit out. "You weren't."

He pushed her down on the bed, pinning her with his weight before she could scramble away. He kissed her again, hot and hard and demanding. His lips slanted across hers, then caught her chin, her neck, her earlobe.

He used whisper-sweet words to tell her of the most unspeakably erotic things he was going to do to her, the places he would touch, the places he would kiss. He lavished attention on her body, ignoring her protests, pleas, and tears. His palm found her breast, feathered over the nipple, and she stiffened beneath him.

"Stop it," she sobbed, tensing as his fingers traced over her ribs, the curve of her waist, lower. "You don't understand—"

"I understand you better than you understand yourself. Let me show you."

She cried out as he touched her thigh, his fingers hot and rough on her soft, vulnerable skin. Having known his tenderness once, she despised him for the coldness he was showing her now. He didn't have to be such a ruthless, uncaring brute—he *chose* to be. Fury and resentment overwhelmed even her fear. "You're not listening," she shouted. "You have to let me explain—"

"Be still!" he said thickly, his mouth coming down on hers again. With one hand he caught her wrists, while his tongue played at her lips, seeking entry. His weight, heavy and solid, pressed her into the satin coverlet. His fingertips grazed her most intimate, most feminine softness, finding the moistness there. He uttered a low, masculine sound of approval. He nudged her thighs apart.

Elizabeth started to scream but his mouth captured the sound, smothering it. He reached down to strip away his breeches. She bit his lip and freed her mouth. "This is rape!"

Pierce stilled, suspended above her. *Rape.* That word, that one horrible word, lanced through the whiskey and ale that clouded his reason, through his anger and hurt, and found his lust-ravaged mind. *What in the name of God was he doing?*

Blinking, he looked down into Elizabeth's eyes, saw her terror and pain for the first time—and knew he was the source of both. It made him feel repulsive. He thought he would be ill. He was drunk, but not so drunk that he hadn't heard her when she said she was afraid. How could he have shoved all thought of her feelings aside?

Was he that intent on his own satisfaction, that much of a selfish bastard? He had lashed out at her in the worst possible way, purposely driven to reinforce her low opinion of him. In trying to prove to her that he was completely heartless, he had instead proven it to himself.

Slowly, gently, he moved off of Elizabeth's naked form. The instant he let her go, she rolled away from him, turning her back and curling into a ball. She made small, muffled sounds that rained down on him like steel blades.

He sat on the edge of the bed, knowing he should just

leave her alone, instead feeling a powerful urge to offer comfort. He battled with himself to keep from touching her, certain she wouldn't be able to bear it after the way he had just humiliated her.

Unable to reach out, unable to move away and leave her in her pain, he sat there and listened to her cry. Each tear told him he had sunk to the lowest ranks of all that was vile and loathsome. Never had he done such a thing before. He had actually tried to force a woman—and not just any woman, but Elizabeth. Soft-hearted, sweet Elizabeth, who had tantalized his thoughts day and night for weeks.

With that thoughtless, despicable act, he had lost something. The realization filled him with a sickening certainty that was like a rope tightening around his neck. He had lost something he could not name or even begin to grasp, knowing only that its absence left a black, ragged void inside him.

It was as if the last bit of goodness or kindness he possessed had just been burned away, leaving behind only smoke and ashes.

. . . As if he had just become the souless son of a bitch everyone believed him to be.

"Elizabeth." His voice raw, he began tentatively, not knowing how to even begin to ask her forgiveness, only that he must have it. "I—"

"I hate you!" She flung it at him like a blow, then buried her face in her satin coverlet, refusing even to look at him. "I hate you. I'll hate you until the day I die!"

Shaking, Pierce stood and stepped back from the bed, caught in the grip of some emotion he didn't understand. Her outburst was more than justified, but inexplicably, he felt hurt—no, not just hurt.

Empty.

Cursing himself as a fool, he turned away and stalked to the door. She didn't want his apologies, his comfort or his presence. The logical, practical thing to do was comply. He could give her at least that dignity.

He stopped with his hand on the latch, struggling for

a moment with the remorse, pain and self-loathing that roiled inside him. Only with the greatest effort did he manage to keep them all out of his voice.

"Do not make any more trouble with Montaigne, Elizabeth," he said evenly. "If you do, I shall hear of it."

With that, he shut the door behind him and left.

Chapter 10

Elizabeth sobbed until her throat was raw. The fact that Pierce had stopped in mid-assault didn't change the way she felt—humiliated and helpless. Worst of all was the shame: even now, even after the way he had treated her so horribly and walked out so coldly, part of her ached for him to come back and hold her and comfort her. Anguished at her own weakness, she gave herself over to her tears.

An hour later, her crying had finally subsided and she was able to think, to sort through the unfamiliar feelings that plagued her and get straight to the heart of the truth. The truth, however, left her more troubled and uncertain than ever.

She did not hate Pierce Wolverton.

Despite what she had yelled at him in anger, she had to admit to herself that it wasn't true. She couldn't fathom it. She despised his behavior tonight, realized now more than ever that he was arrogant and self-centered and capable of the most thoughtless, dishonorable acts . . .

Yet some part of her saw beyond that, caught just a glimpse of the vulnerable side that he kept so well hidden—the sensitive poet who could create great beauty, the brave, caring man who had saved her life and could touch her with aching gentleness. He could be all that and more . . . when he wanted to be.

"Fool," she chastised herself, shoving the coverlet aside and getting out of bed. He would never give in to that side of himself. He had proven as much tonight. True, he had stopped—but only because she had pointed out that he was about to commit a rape. He had terrorized her while remaining every bit as cool, unaffected, and completely aloof as he always was; in the end he had walked out with nothing more than a terse warning about her raids.

Elizabeth snatched up her wrapper from the floor. Her raids. The gold. He always came back to that. The money was the only thing that had any meaning for him.

He didn't care about anyone's needs or feelings but his own. She might as well wish that the moon and the stars would fall to earth as wish that Pierce Wolverton would change. It was impossible. He saw her as nothing more than a rival and an object of lust.

She paced her bedroom, all her emotions dancing so dangerously close to the surface she thought she would go mad. What if he had completed the act? He might have gotten her with child. The thought terrified her so, she had to sit down again before her legs gave way.

One thing became clear: It was useless to trust that Darkridge would leave her alone. And next time, she might not be able to stop him.

She must get away from him, from London. It was the only way she could be safe from his attentions, and plan her strategy for St. Bartholomew's Fair without interference.

There was no need for her to stay in the city; the Fair was still four weeks away. Sitting at her desk, she scribbled a note to Georgiana and Nell. She supposed it was cowardly to flee from him this way, but she was beyond caring. She could go to the seaside, or to Bath, or . . .

Home.

The word filled her with a sense of longing she had not felt in a very long time. Since coming to London she had known only pain and unhappiness; Northampton was a place of security and comfort. There she wouldn't have to feel like a hunted animal. There she could concentrate on all of Darkridge's despicable traits and forget his miniscule good qualities.

She finished the note, telling her friends only that she felt well enough to take a short holiday in Northampton. They would know something was amiss, with her leaving in the middle of the night this way, but there was no helping that.

She quickly cleaned up her room and dressed in a sapphire blue traveling habit, trying to ignore that all of her body's most sensitive places were still tingling from Pierce's attentions.

She briefly considered walking the two blocks to Nell's shop to dress in her more comfortable men's garments, then discarded the idea. She did not want to chance running into Nell and Georgiana and having to explain face to face; they would prod and cajole until she revealed her real reason for leaving, and the thought of telling them what had happened here tonight made her cheeks burn with shame and embarrassment. She paused only long enough to pack a valise, then crossed to the door.

She caught her reflection in the mirror over her dressing table. She quickly looked away and swept from the room, angrily dabbing at her reddened eyes.

She would waste no more tears on Pierce Wolverton.

Jean-Pascal Rochambeau stared out the window of one of the Strand's most fashionable coffeehouses, sipping at his fourth insipid cup and wondering how long he could survive on England's dismally bland food and drink.

Another part of his ever-active mind was going over every detail of his meeting that morning with the head of the London Bank. Surely he had missed something. . . .

"I am sorry that I cannot help you, sir. The Women and Children's Trust is a private account," the bank officer had insisted, eyeing him with the look of distaste that Rochambeau was getting used to, the look that said that while the English admired French fashion, French colognes, and French cuisine, they detested the French.

"But a crime has been committed, Monsieur Mulready," Rochambeau countered. "Ze coins your bank accepted were counterfeit. Surely you would wish to know ze name of ze criminal?"

The banker shrugged and got to his feet. "I am certain the matter of the counterfeit coins was a mistake. You may be assured it will not happen again. We now carefully check all moneys deposited to ensure that they are genuine." He extended his hand. "Good day, sir."

Keeping his frustration hidden, Jean-Pascal stood and politely accepted the man's dismissal, leaning forward to shake his hand. The many layers of lace ruffles edging his sleeve brushed a stack of papers off Mulready's desk.

"*Pardon,* monsieur." Rochambeau knelt to gather up the mess, fighting a grin that the Englishman had left himself open to such an old trick. "We French, you know, our fashion can be so clumsy."

"Quite all right," Mulready blustered through gritted teeth, nudging him out of the way.

The man was so caught up in his irritation, he didn't even notice when Jean-Pascal extended a nimble finger toward one of the scraps of paper. It was in his pocket before the Englishman could blink an eye. "My apologies for ze trouble, monsieur."

They shook hands and Rochambeau left, waiting until he was in his carriage before reading the slip of paper. He had grabbed for it upon seeing the words "Women's and Children's Trust" across the top. Once he had a chance for a closer look, however, he was disappointed to find that it offered only that notation and an amount, written in a neat, perhaps feminine hand. There were no names.

He flipped it over. On the back was part of a sentence, barely scratched into the surface, as if someone had written a note on another sheet of paper with this one underneath. Rochambeau held it up to the light. The notation ran off the edge of the page, but there was just enough to make out the words *Receipt to Osgo,* and below that, *twenty-first May.*

Jean-Pascal felt a tingling excitement, which he tried to keep in check. It was likely nothing. It might even concern an entirely different account.

On the other hand, it might be a clue, the name of some place where Swift might be found.

After a few hours of asking about, he discovered that there was no tavern, gaming establishment, or bawdy house with a name that began with the letters O–S–G–O. But there was, he quickly learned, a popular ladies' shop on the Strand by the name of Osgood's. . . .

Which had brought him to this coffeehouse. The past few weeks he had searched for other clues and come up with blessed little, so he had taken to spending his afternoons here. He watched the fabric shop across the street while enduring the weak brew the English tried to pass off as coffee.

Surely this was a mistake, he thought again. What would a lowbred criminal like Swift have to do with a shop that purveyed laces and velvets and feminine frippery?

He had thought of going inside and asking questions, but if the store *was* connected with Swift in some way, he didn't wish to arouse suspicion. So he patiently watched and waited for a clue to present itself.

Did Swift have a paramour here? Some woman with whom he kept assignations? Or perhaps a sister who took care of his bank deposits for him?

Rochambeau had seen few men so far, all footmen or coach drivers. None looked the least bit like a dangerous, elusive highwayman. Mostly he had seen a steady stream of women. Tall women, petite women, beautiful and plain, elegant and average, fat women and women who— were he not already married—he might have persuaded to make his afternoon a bit more pleasant.

Nothing but women.

Sighing in resignation, Jean-Pascal ordered another cup of coffee. Something would come to him.

If not, he would wait until dark tonight, sneak in and finally see for himself what secrets Osgood's held.

Chapter 11

Georgiana stumbled down the darkened hallway toward Nell's room, clutching a single candle as if it were a weapon against the fear that gripped her heart. The pain in her head was so sharp she thought she might faint.

"Nell!" She pounded on the door. Her voice was tremulous, her hand shaking so hard the candlelight danced nightmarish shadows along the golden flocked wallpaper. "Nell, wake up!"

The door was wrenched open before Georgiana could knock again. "What the devil d' ye want at this time o' the mornin'? It's still dark out—"

"It's Elizabeth." Georgiana pushed past Nell into the room, barely making it to the thickly upholstered chair by the window before she collapsed into tears. "She's . . . She's—"

"She's on 'oliday in Northampton." Nell said in irritation, tying the belt of her green cotton robe. "We found 'er note when we got 'ome las' night. Don' ye remember?"

"Yes." Georgiana shook her head, unable to speak for a moment. "But I . . . I just had the most horrible premonition." She squeezed her eyes shut. "Horrible. Horrible!"

Nell grabbed the candle from Georgiana's hand just as it was about to fall to the carpet. "Now, now, Georgi. Don' go gettin' yerself all flusterpated." She set the candle on her writing table and knelt beside the chair. "Ye just 'ad a nightmare—"

"Would that it were!" Georgiana reached out and

grasped Nell's arm. "I was wide awake, Nell. As awake as I am right now. I was reading and suddenly I . . . I could see a . . . a *vision*. It was Elizabeth. She was oddly dressed, and there were men with her, strangers, beastly-looking. Two of them. They were pointing pistols at her—"

"Yer sure this wasn't a nightmare?"

"No, Nell it was not. And do not look at me as if I were a half-wit!" Georgiana shouted in indignation, only to regret it immediately as it made her headache worse. Her heart pounding, she tried to put the horror she had seen into words. "The men were yelling at her. One of them put the gun to her head. And—and then . . ."

"What?" Nell urged.

"This was the strangest part. Lord Darkridge was there. He hit the man's arm just as the gun went off."

"Darkridge?"

"Yes, I know that sounds odd. He saved Elizabeth from being shot. B . . . but then the other man . . ." She released Nell's arm and put a hand to her forehead, trying to ignore the pain. "He came at her with a knife. I could see the blade, Nell." Georgiana's voice began to quiver again. "It was like a bolt of lightning, so silvery and bright and moving toward her so fast. I heard Elizabeth scream." Her other hand gripped the chair arm. "Oh, Nell, that scream! I can still hear it. And I don't know what happened to her next. The vision ended there. But she was screaming as if she were . . . she were—"

"Dyin'?" Nell whispered, her face utterly serious now.

Georgiana could only nod, hiccuping on a sob. "I've never experienced anything like it before. I've had odd feelings about things, but this was like . . . like a play, right before my eyes." She massaged her temples, her fingers trembling. "Please, Nell. You must believe me."

"I know ye well enough to know ye wouldn't make this up. We 'ave t' do somethin'." Nell stood. "We 'ave to go t' Bess an' warn 'er."

Georgiana shook her head dejectedly. "I doubt that would do any good. Remember the last time we warned her about one of my premonitions? She's so confounded stubborn.''

''We'll make 'er listen.''

''And what if she doesn't? I can't stop thinking about what happened before. She ignored us and ended up very badly hurt, Nell. And that time I had only an uneasy feeling. This—this was like . . . *like seeing the future*.'' She began to cry again and covered her face with her hands.

''There, there now, Georgi.'' Nell patted her shoulder. ''We'll think of somethin'.''

Georgiana let her hands fall to her lap, feeling helpless and determined all at once. ''The only thing I can think of . . . Nell, I know this is going to sound insane. But *we* weren't in the vision. It was Lord Darkridge protecting her.''

''What are ye suggestin'? That we send 'im after 'er? Bess would kill us.''

''I *know* she dislikes him.'' Georgiana stood and began to pace, fretting over her dilemma.

''Dislikes 'im? She refused t' talk about 'im after she came 'ome from 'is town 'ouse. And she didn' even want t' 'ear 'is name mentioned after that party a few weeks ago, when she decided t' go int' retirement.''

Georgiana nodded, trying to think past the ache in her head. ''I'm well aware of Elizabeth's animosity toward Lord Darkridge.''

Nell folded her arms. ''In fact, yer the one what warned Bess t' stay away from 'im in the first place!''

Georgiana sighed. It was true. Lord Darkridge had the most nefarious reputation . . . But on the other hand, he had saved Elizabeth once before, when he could have turned her over to the authorities.

It took only a moment to decide she must stick with her feeling. She was not about to play games with Elizabeth's life; the girl was the closest thing she had—or ever would have—to a daughter. ''Elizabeth is in danger, Nell. Deadly danger,'' Georgiana said with sudden vehemence. ''She might never forgive us, but could we live with ourselves if we *didn't* send him to save her, and something awful happened?''

Nell gave her a look of pure exasperation. ''An' 'ow would we go about this? Walk up t' 'is town 'ouse an' say, ' 'Scuse me, my lord, but Georgi 'ad this real odd vision and we want ye t' go save Bess?' ''

''That's true.'' Georgiana stopped her pacing as she wrestled with the problem, then brightened. ''You might relay the message through Mr. Quinn.''

Nell made a face. ''I am not gettin' within five miles of *'im.*''

''Nell, this is no time to be stubborn. He seemed nice enough, and I do believe he fancies you.''

''Hmph.'' Nell's scowl deepened.

''He does. After all, he sent you that pretty little bracelet to make up for his brusque behavior that night at the shop.''

''And if I 'ad 'alf a shillin's worth o' sense, I would 'ave sent it right back.'' Nell grumbled, though she was blushing. ''Besides, 'e's not goin' t' believe in yer premonitions any more than 'is master would.''

''You don't have to mention anything about my vision,'' Georgiana insisted. ''Just let him know where Elizabeth has gone. I'm sure he'll tell Lord Darkridge, and Darkridge will . . . He'll go to her. I know he will.''

''And 'ow am I supposed t' bring 'er 'oliday up in the conversation?''

''You'll think of something.'' Georgiana was already feeling better, now that they had a plan of action. ''Just let Mr. Quinn know where she's gone. But don't let him know that you're letting him know. You'll have to be subtle.''

''Subtle?'' Nell blinked, realization dawning on her pretty features. ''Georgi, I am not goin' t' let that popinjay of a dandiprat kiss me.''

''Now, Nell,'' Georgiana admonished. ''You must think of Elizabeth.''

''I *am* thinkin' o' Bess. But I'm not goin' t' kiss no coxcomb who acts like I'm somethin' 'e should be scrapin' off 'is shoe.''

Georgiana winced at her friend's vehemence—and her volume. "If you wish to argue over this further, please let's go down to the kitchen so I can make myself something for my headache."

Nell folded her arms stubbornly as she followed Georgiana from the room. "I am *not* goin' t' kiss 'im."

This was a mistake. Elizabeth had decided that before the public stage even left London, when her traveling companions exhibited an intense curiosity about what a young woman was doing traveling alone.

She had held some vague idea of seeking solace among her old neighbors and acquaintances in Northampton; now she realized she did not wish to answer the questions they would naturally ask. She could not discuss what she had been doing since going to London.

When the coach stopped at an inn for the night, she purchased some masculine clothing from the innkeeper, who seemed to care more about the offered coin than her reasons for wanting the clothes.

The next morning, she donned the plain dun-colored garments, which were all a bit big on her, then tied her hair in a queue and topped off the outfit with a hat so large it kept slipping down over her forehead. Satisfied that no one would recognize her, she took a different coach and continued her journey home.

Now, after three days in Northampton, she realized it did not offer the refuge she had thought to find. She could not even think, much less find solace here. Wandering among her favorite places only filled her with oppressive sadness, loneliness, and grief. She felt every inch the criminal she was, skulking about trying to avoid familiar faces. Worst of all, the small, rather shabby inn where she stayed brought tearful memories of the more spacious, charming establishment her father had run. She took out her ill mood by cursing the name of Pierce Wolverton for driving her out of London.

Finally Elizabeth decided to leave. She ensconced herself in a dark corner of one of the town's taverns, trying to decide where she should go. Thinking to perhaps drown her sorrows—which, after all, was what men did, and she *was* dressed as a man—she ordered a tankard of ale, only to find the stuff tasted bitter and musty. She could not imagine what men found to recommend it. Perhaps one had to grow accustomed to the taste, she thought, taking a few more sips.

By the time she had finished only a fraction of the tankard, a muzzy feeling descended on her head, leaving her feeling sleepy and slightly disoriented. She neglected to keep a careful watch for familiar faces.

"Do you think it wise to frequent such a place at this hour of the night, *sir*?"

Blinking, Elizabeth looked up at the person addressing her. The walls tilted in a thoroughly nauseating motion, and it took a moment for her to focus on the tall, dark-garbed man who stood beside her seat.

Because this was the last person in the world she expected to see, it took another moment to recognize him. "What in the blue blazes are you doing here?" she slurred.

Before she could get to her feet, Pierce sat beside her on the bench, squeezing her between his large frame and the wall. "I've already looked for you in all the reputable places in town." He raised one eyebrow. "I do believe you are in your cups."

Elizabeth wanted to slap him, but didn't have adequate space to do so. The feeling of his body pressed against hers brought a hot rush of color to her face, and a painful torrent of memories to mind. "Don't touch me! Lay one hand on me and I *swear* I will kill you." She shoved her hand into the pocket of her frock coat, grabbing the small pistol she carried and pressing it against his ribs.

He didn't even flinch. His expression remained completely unperturbed and after a second he grinned—that sardonic, humorless grin. "You forget, I know that's not loaded."

She kept her gaze locked on his. "How do you know I haven't learned my lesson and changed my ways?"

His smiled fled, replaced by a hard-edged look that reminded Elizabeth he could overpower her in a heartbeat and knock the gun from her hand. He didn't. He only stared down at her, something intense and mysterious swirling in his dark brown eyes. "No," he said slowly. "I don't think you would."

Gritting her teeth in helpless frustration, Elizabeth let the pistol slide to the bottom of her pocket. She had *bought* some ammunition, but that was as close as she'd come to changing her ways; she carried the little powder flask and lead balls in her other pocket, unable to make herself load the deuced gun.

Pierce knew her far too well, and she found it a most unsettling feeling. "*Why* must you keep following me?" she demanded. "Where must I go to be free of you? A desert island? The Far East perhaps? Name the place and I shall go there!"

"I thought you were rather fond of Italy."

His cool sarcasm stung, forcing Elizabeth to remember her lie about having a husband; it hadn't ever been much of a shield against him—but now it was entirely gone. She tried to edge away from him, to no avail. His dark presence, his hard-muscled form, even his scent surrounded and unnerved her.

She tried to imitate his air of unruffled aloofness. "H . . . have you nothing better to do than bother me? Surely you have some friends *somewhere* who could occupy your time."

He shook his head. "I've never found much of a use for friends."

"Perhaps that's your entire problem—"

"I'm not here to discuss my life," he interrupted, his tone stern. "I'm here to ensure that you stay away from a certain gentleman's coaches."

"I could not be further away, if you would notice! I'm not even in the same city as his bloody coaches." She frowned. "How the devil did you even find me in the first place?"

"That's not important," he said with a dismissing

wave of his hand. ''What is important is that someone has to keep you from causing any more trouble.''

Elizabeth was speechless. How dare he appoint himself her warder after the way he had treated her! He hadn't even bothered to apologize. From his attitude it was obvious he felt not the least bit of guilt or regret for it, either. That made her even more furious. ''You . . . You conniving cur! I would be better off under the watchful eye of a vulture!'' She tried to wriggle away under the table.

He grabbed her wrist. ''I suggest you keep your voice down, Elizabeth, lest some of the noble patrons of this impeccable establishment start to wonder whether there is a female in their midst.''

Elizabeth shuddered at Pierce's touch, remembering all too well how easily he could make her respond to him. ''Let go of me. I am tired of being manhandled and I do not need *anyone* to watch over me. I am not going to let you bully me any longer.''

''You shall have to grow used to it,'' he said sharply. ''I intend to stick to you like a handbill to a wall until the Fair.''

She gave him a contemptuous smile. ''I wish you luck, my lord.''

With that, she brought her heel back to catch him in the shin. He didn't even wince. Instead of winning her freedom, it earned her a dangerous-looking glower. Worse, he moved one of his legs over hers to keep her still. Elizabeth stiffened. She thought of screaming for help, but knew that would only make matters worse.

''Keep making this difficult, Elizabeth, and you and I are going to have a very unpleasant time the next three weeks.''

''You are hateful.'' She struggled, knowing it would be useless. ''I am tired of your threats and I am tired of *you*. The very sight of you sickens me!''

Though she hadn't meant it literally, Elizabeth felt her stomach lurch, and suddenly realized that the ale she had downed did not want to stay down. It gave her an idea.

She stopped fighting Pierce and said in a small voice, "I do think I am going to be sick."

"Really?" He leaned closer, his eyes smoldering in the glow of the stubby candle that offered the only light at the table. "You don't look the least bit green. In fact, you look as if you're blushing."

Elizabeth glared at him. "Unless you allow me to go outside, I shall be forced to demonstrate all over your lap."

Giving her a probing look, Pierce tried to discern whether she was telling the truth, and wondered for the tenth time that day what lunacy had brought him here. He had taken to his horse as soon as Quinn had said Elizabeth was in Northampton.

He had managed to convince himself he had a perfectly sensible reason to continue his pursuit of her. He was only ensuring she didn't cause him any more trouble. After all, he had badly botched his seduction plan, the agreement they had made was in shreds, and she had proven that he couldn't trust her.

There was only one way left to make sure she didn't ruin his plans for Montaigne: He wasn't going to let her out of his sight. Entirely practical.

Some part of him, though, also wanted to make up for his reprehensible treatment of her. He wanted her forgiveness and he meant to have it.

He slid to the edge of the bench. "Let's leave, then. Where are your lodgings?"

Elizabeth's cheeks were aflame. "If you think I am going to share my room with you—"

"Don't be tiresome, Elizabeth. As I have already explained, you may consider me your shadow for the next three weeks."

He thought he caught a whispered curse as she edged past him and walked, somewhat unsteadily, toward the tavern entrance. He stayed right at her heels.

"Here now, me lad." The serving wench stepped in front of Elizabeth before they reached the door. "Ye haven't paid fer yer ale yet!"

Elizabeth stopped. "Do you mean this establishment doesn't extend credit?'' she slurred, searching through her pockets. ''I didn't realize. I haven't any money.''

Pierce thought he caught the slightest hint of a smile on Elizabeth's face.

The tavern owner, a burly man with onion breath and a nose that had apparently been broken on more than one occasion, stepped up beside them. ''We got plenty of work in the kitchen for them what ain't got money.''

Elizabeth turned toward him and smiled up at Pierce. ''But that won't be necessary. My friend here will gladly pay you.''

Sensing her game, Pierce took a firm grasp of her shoulder, already digging in his coat with his other hand. Unfortunately the tavern owner seemed to think he was reaching for a pistol.

''No ye don't, guv.'' The man grabbed Pierce's arm. ''Just pay up.''

Elizabeth took advantage of the momentary confusion to wrest herself free. She made a fast—if somewhat tipsy—departure out the door. ''I shall wait for you outside, *friend*,'' she called back over her shoulder.

''Hellfire and bloody damnation,'' Pierce growled, shaking off the tavernkeeper's hand. He slapped a silver half-guinea into the outstretched palm. It seemed to more than satisfy the man.

''Sorry fer the trouble, guv. Be sure an' come back—''

As he was already out the door, Pierce missed the rest of the invitation. But Elizabeth had disappeared into the darkness. He ran around the corner of the tavern. She couldn't have gotten far in only seconds.

''Elizabeth,'' he called out softly. ''Stop playing games. I promise that I mean you no harm.''

From the shadows of a pewter shop a bit further down the street, Elizabeth heard his assurance and had to bite her tongue to stop a scathing retort. She edged along the building, moving away from the sound of his voice as quickly and quietly as possible. He called after her again, then fell silent, as if realizing she was using his voice to guess his position.

She felt her way along the street, wanting to run but not daring, for fear she would trip and give herself away. She could see blessed little. All the shops were long since closed for the night, and the only light was that which occasionally spilled out the tavern door. With the ale clouding her senses, she couldn't make out much of anything.

She pulled the small pistol from her pocket and loaded it this time, her hand shaking. She didn't want to hurt Pierce, but she wasn't going anywhere with him, either. If a show of force was the only thing that would convince him of that, so be it.

Elizabeth told herself the odds were in her favor; she knew the area, while Pierce did not. Her foot splashed in a puddle and she cursed under her breath, then froze in place. Was that a footfall behind her? Peering into the darkness, she paused only the span of a heartbeat before continuing forward. At the end of the row of shops, she darted around the corner—

—and almost collided with a pair of well-armed men, apparently in the midst of a robbery! She jerked to a halt, unable to choke back an exclamation. A third man, finely dressed and groomed, was up against the wall, his hands in the air.

Pierce ran around the corner the next instant. "God damn it, Eli—" Her name died on his lips and he stopped a few inches behind her.

"What be this, now?" One of the armed men demanded. "Eh, mate, ye didn't tell us there was others of yer knot in the area."

His partner turned his twin flintlock pistols on Elizabeth. "Drop it, boy."

Realizing only then that she still held her gun, Elizabeth hesitated. The man raised his weapons so that one was aimed at each of her eyes. Staring down those two cold, black barrels, she reluctantly let the little pistol slip from her fingers.

''Looks like the three of 'em were plannin' an ambush.'' The man said as he knelt to pick it up.

''You're barmy-brained.'' The one with his hands in the air snarled at them. ''I've never seen neither of them before.''

The first man gave a short burst of laughter. ''That proves it. He's tryin' to protect 'em. Well, Mick, with the Crown payin' thirty a piece for footpads an' such, I'd say we just made ourselves ninety pounds.''

''Not a bad night's work.'' The one named Mick moved closer to Elizabeth, his pistols now aimed at her chest. ''Who are ye? Are ye in with Lowe or nay?''

''I . . . I . . .'' Elizabeth's heart was hammering against her ribs. She had the situation all wrong! It seemed the man against the wall was a criminal, and these two were *bounty hunters*. Unable to think of a way to explain her identity, her garb, or her gun, she opted for silence.

She wished Pierce would do something. He would likely be happy to see her arrested, but surely he wanted to save himself!

The object of her thoughts finally spoke up. ''I assure you we are no criminals, sir,'' Pierce said, sounding like a thoroughly insulted London lord. ''My nephew here has simply imbibed too much. I'll be taking him home now.'' He stepped up beside Elizabeth and nudged her behind him. ''So sorry to interrupt—''

''Not so fast, guv.'' Mick raised one pistol so it was aimed squarely at Pierce's chest. ''Yer fancy talk don't convince me you ain't part o' Lowe's knot. They're known for takin' on the manners an' dress o' their betters.''

''If it's a matter of money,'' Pierce replied smoothly, ''I am willing to pay you much more than thirty pounds each for our release.''

''Wait a minute, Mick,'' the other bounty hunter insisted. ''If he's tryin' to bribe us, and they ain't willin' to tell us their names, they can't be up t' no good, even if they ain't part o' Lowe's gang. These two might be worth *lots* more than thirty apiece.''

"Yer right, John. I think we best let the circuit justice sort all this out when he gets here Tuesday next. Hands in the air, if ye please," Mick ordered, taking in both Pierce and Elizabeth with a wave of his pistols. "I hereby place ye under arrest in the name of the Crown."

Chapter 12

The gaol sat on a hill at the north end of town. Elizabeth shivered as they drew near the gates. After holding her hands in the air for so long, she could barely feel her fingers; they weren't even tingling anymore.

She remembered the awful tales she had heard of this place. *Be good or you'll be sent up the hill* was a threat often used to frighten ill-behaved Northampton children.

Calling it a "gaol" was overly generous; it was little more than a dungeon, deep in the ruins of a castle that had protected the town in centuries past. The thought of being imprisoned again made Elizabeth's heart beat erratically. She cast nervous looks at Pierce as they walked, hoping he would do something to get them out of this.

He gave her no signal, no sign that he was planning anything at all. He just kept walking, gazing straight ahead. If he had any thoughts of escape, he kept them to himself. Did he think they would have any chance to get away once inside? Perhaps he didn't know how it felt to be locked in a cell, Elizabeth thought. Well she did, and she had no wish to repeat the experience.

Sweat broke out on her brow as the gaoler opened the gates. The man ushered them inside with an enthusiastic greeting.

"Damn me eyes, Mick, John." He nodded to each of the bounty hunters in turn. "I can't keep up wi' the two of ye! Before ye know it, yer goin' t' be the richest thieftakers in all o' England."

"If anyone can do it, it's us," Mick declared, motioning Pierce, Elizabeth and the third prisoner inside with a wave of his pistols.

''Ye know, I've still got the other three o'`Lowe's bloody gang ye brought in last week,'' the gaoler complained. ''And I ain't got but me and Wilton t' watch 'em all.''

They crossed a small courtyard and he unlocked a tall, ancient-looking door, reinforced with iron hinges that groaned as he pushed it open. Inside, he lifted a lantern from a hook. Elizabeth couldn't seem to catch her breath, and her legs started to tremble. In the flickering light, she could make out a cramped passageway, its walls and ceiling of stone.

''The justice'll clear 'em all out for ye on Tuesday,'' John said, his voice echoing eerily. ''Likely he'll have 'em all carted down to the square for a public hangin'.''

The bounty hunter shoved Elizabeth forward. Shaking, she stumbled after the gaoler, down a staircase of slippery steps that had been hollowed out by centuries of reluctant feet. Pierce and the other prisoner were sent down after her, and she heard the bounty hunters bringing up the rear.

''You remember t' tell us when the circuit justice gets here,'' Mick said sternly. ''We want t' be sure he knows it was us what brought all these coves in.''

''Right, mates, right. Just as long as I gets my cut, is all. And a bit fer Wilton.''

Elizabeth was horrified to be treated as an object of casual commerce. The phrases ''carted down to the square'' and ''public hanging'' gave her chills.

She felt a rising sense of panic as they descended the curving stone staircase. The underground prison bore a stark resemblance to a place she had hoped to put out of her mind forever, a place where she had endured the most horrifying experience of her life. *Fleet*. She felt as if she were suffocating.

As they moved deeper and deeper into the earth, the walls and ceilings seemed to close in on her, the stone only inches from crushing her completely. Her heartbeat rose to a deafening roar in her ears.

A torrent of memories that she had held back for

months assailed her, one after the other, each more vivid than the last: the stench of chamber pots and unwashed bodies, the cold, the moans and sobs, the men and women and children pressed together, scrambling over one another to get their morning gruel . . . the children . . . *Oh, God, the babies.*

The men around her shimmered in her vision, changing into Montaigne's footmen. She could feel their hands upon her, dragging her forward. She could feel the awkwardness of her body, the weight of her belly, the movement of the child within her. In her mind each step carried her, not into the bounty hunters' dungeon, but deeper into the bowels of Fleet. She must stop. She must. If she allowed them to put her in a cell, her baby would die.

They had reached the bottom of the stairs.

A thin young man came forward, lifting a heavy ring of iron keys at his waist.

"Three more fer us, Wilton," the gaoler said cheerfully.

Elizabeth breathed in short, shallow gasps. Her legs felt so weak she could barely stand. A tide of sheer terror held her powerless. She watched the young man open the door to an empty cell. A pistol jabbed into the small of her back.

"Inside, lad."

"I'm not going in there," she said, in a deep, angry voice. The swirl of memories made her dizzy. "I've done nothing wrong. I'm not going in there," she repeated more firmly.

A man stepped in front of her, brandishing two pistols, shouting at her in a gutteral voice. Elizabeth looked right through him, the last of her reason shredded by a fear more powerful than any feeling she had ever known. She saw nothing but a throng of milling prisoners, heard nothing but the cries and sobs and shouts of Fleet. She started to back up. She had to get away. For the sake of her baby, she had to run.

Rough hands on her shoulders stopped her. One of the men spun her about, grabbed the front of her coat and shoved her up against the wall. She threw up her arms to protect herself, but not quickly enough to ward off the stinging blow that landed on her cheek. She cried out and was vaguely aware of a shout and a sudden, brief scuffle to one side, the sound of someone being hit, hard.

"Lock these other two up!" a man growled. Elizabeth heard the voice as if from far away. "I'll take care of this one."

The other prisoners were gone and she felt hands on her shoulders again. She struck out at her tormentor with a hoarse cry of rage, so frightened now she was beyond words. She must not let him put her in that cell!

The man held her by the arms and wrestled her toward the dark chamber. "Stop makin' trouble er I'll bash ye good, kid."

To prove his point he landed another blow to her face. Momentarily dazed, Elizabeth kept fighting, but her weak struggles weren't enough to save her. The man threw her inside and shut the heavy wooden door behind her.

"If yer lucky," he snarled as he locked it, "ye might get some food an' water before the justice arrives. Then again," he added with a laugh. "Ye might not."

Elizabeth ignored his taunt, lying still where he had thrown her, not even feeling the pain in her cheek and jaw, so great was the turmoil in her mind. She looked up at the dank stone above, seeing instead the earthen ceiling of Fleet that she had stared at for so many hours. She could hear murmurs of men and women and children, all around her. Tossing her head wildly, she peered into every corner of the cell. She could see no one, but she knew they were there. The sounds grew louder, pressing down upon her like a crushing, killing weight.

Then, high above the noise, came the cry of a baby.

Another joined in, then a third, and on and on until the entire cell seemed to explode with the sounds of infants desperate for their mothers.

Elizabeth jerked upright. She had to get out. If she didn't, her baby would die. She would do anything to prevent that. Anything.

She crawled on her hands and knees toward the door,

shoving aside the grasping hands of her cellmates. She knew what they wanted: to steal her cloak, her shoes, her gown. She wouldn't let them. She had to stay warm, for her baby's sake. Here in Fleet, the only rule was survival. She made it to the door and began clawing at it with her bare hands.

She must get out. She clung to that one thought, for it was her baby's only hope. He would be born soon, and there would be no physician, no midwife to help her through it. She must get help. She dug at the wood until she had splinters in her fingers, and kept on digging.

"Let me out," she begged softly. "My baby, my baby. Let me out. Let me out let me out let me out let me out let me out . . ."

Long after her fingers were bloody, she kept on digging.

"I ain't goin' t' torture nobody," Wilton said, keeping his pistol aimed at Pierce's chest as he escorted him out of his cell. "They said not t' give 'im food nor water, but I ain't goin t' torture nobody. Funny thing is, I been sneakin' it through the door fer three days now, but I noticed t'night he ain't been eatin' nor drinkin' none of it."

Tense and silent, Pierce followed him toward Elizabeth's cell. Ever since the girl's foolishness had gotten them into this mess three days ago, he had been looking for just such an opportunity as this. The gaoler had gone home for the night; Pierce was alone with the boy, who had only the one pistol for protection. He was sure he could take Wilton with minimal damage to himself. Only one foolish thought, stuck stubbornly in his mind, stayed his hand: he wasn't leaving without Elizabeth.

"Ye seemed t' be a friend o' his." Wilton unlocked her door and pushed it open. "So I thought ye might know what's wrong wit' him."

Pierce was ready to make a move for the gun, but he froze, shocked at the sight that met his eyes.

Elizabeth lay beside the door, curled into a ball, her

hands, battered and bloody, over her ears. Her expression was blank, her eyes wide with horror.

"The circuit justice is comin' tomorrow," the boy continued. "And he'll want t' talk t' yer friend here, so ye better rouse him, if ye can. Has he done this before?"

"No." His heart beating strangely, Pierce knelt beside Elizabeth. He touched her shoulder. She didn't respond, didn't seem to recognize him, didn't even blink. What in the name of all that was holy had happened to her?

"If y' ask me, I'd say he's gone 'round the bend. And lunatics don' fetch no thirty pounds," Wilton said, a note of profound irritation in his voice. "So get him talkin'."

Pierce looked up to see that the boy had stepped out of the cell and was already closing the door. He silently cursed himself; in his concern for Elizabeth, he had forgotten about their escape. "Wait—"

"Do whatever ye have to." Wilton ordered as he turned the key in the lock. "Ye just better get him talkin'. The justice'll be here in the mornin'."

"Bloody blazing hellfire," Pierce hissed under his breath as he heard the lad moving away. He doubted another opportunity to get out of here would present itself in the next few hours. How the devil was he going to explain himself to the justice—and get away with his skin and his identity intact?

Thoughts of himself evaporated when he again looked at Elizabeth. He felt an uncomfortable, unfamiliar emotion that he could only describe as fear. What had she done to herself? He leaned over her, reaching out to brush her matted hair from her forehead. "Elizabeth?" he whispered.

She kept staring straight ahead. He picked up one of the cups of water that sat untouched by her side and, using a corner of his shirt, cleaned the dried blood from her injured fingers. She didn't flinch, didn't acknowledge his presence at all. His fear deepened. Had she truly slipped into madness?

He tried unsuccessfully to ease her hands away from

her ears. "Elizabeth, it's me." He shook her gently. "Tell me what's wrong."

When she still made no sound, he splashed some of the water over her face. She blinked and uttered a moan so weak he wasn't sure he heard it at first.

"Elizabeth, talk to me," he commanded, his voice growing more forceful. He didn't know how or why she had worked herself into this unnatural trance, but he wasn't going to let her remain in it. It was almost as if she were willing herself to die. That thought flooded him with a sense of loss that left him surprised and shaken.

A desperate, urgent need gripped him. He must bring her back from this abyss. "Elizabeth, I'm not going to let you do this to yourself." He grasped her wrists and forced her hands away from her head. "Elizabeth—"

"No!" She awakened suddenly, clawing at him.

"It's all right—"

"No! Can't you hear him? He's crying."

"Who's crying?" Pierce tried to pull her into his arms but she fought him with inhuman strength, trying to break away and throw herself toward the door.

"Edward," she cried in a hoarse, dry voice. "Edward is crying. He's *not* dead. I can hear him! He's still alive and I have to get help because he's so small and he's crying and no one's coming and he's going to—"

"Calm down." Pierce refused to let her go. "We'll get out. It's all right."

She flailed at him. "And what about Edward? Who will save him?" She was hysterical, striking out mindlessly. "I can't help him. He's crying and I can't help him and if I can't . . . If I can't get out—oh, God, *Edward.*"

She stiffened again, her whole body braced as if against a hurricane force wind. Pierce took her in his arms, trying to soothe her, but her every muscle remained rigid as iron. Her eyes widened and her mouth opened and closed silently, as if she were watching a scene so hellish it robbed her of her voice, of reason, of her very soul. Just when Pierce thought she had surely surrendered to madness, her body began to shake like a fragile branch caught in a storm.

"Let it go, Elizabeth," he commanded. He held her against his chest and rocked her gently. "Just let it go."

"I . . . I . . . I can't! I can't let him go. I can't. I can't. I know he's still alive. He's all I have left." She shut her eyes tight, tighter, shaking her head. "He's still alive . . . he's still . . . he's . . . he's—"

Her lower lip began to tremble, then suddenly her resolve and her body seemed to crumple at the same time. A pair of silent tears slipped from beneath her lashes. For a minute, she cried silently, then a low groan of pain choked out of her throat. She took a deep, heaving breath of air, still fighting whatever force it was that wracked her.

Pierce wrapped his arms around her, holding her closer, pressing her head into his shoulder. "Let it go."

His whispered words seemed to release her at last.

"Oh, God, he's gone," she moaned against his coat. "He's *gone*."

She started sobbing, suddenly, with the force of a wave crashing on the shore. The sounds tore out of her, echoing from deep within her chest, filled with such desolate, anguished power Pierce thought they would tear her in two. She went limp against him and wept.

He was stunned at the depth of her sorrow. He had no idea who Edward was, or what had triggered her attack, but he thanked whatever gods there might be above that she had turned away from the brink of insanity. The sounds of her crying were so heartrending, he felt utterly helpless. All he could do was slowly stroke her hair, her shoulders, her back. Under normal circumstances, he would be the last person she would turn to for comfort, but he wasn't sure she even knew who he was at the moment. Her arms went around him, clinging with desperate strength, and still her tears didn't subside.

It was almost an hour before she lapsed into exhaustion; her sobbing ebbed to harsh breathing, then, slowly, silence.

"It's all right now," he whispered, still stroking her

hair. He didn't know what other words he could say, what he could possibly do to comfort her. He wasn't sure there *was* any comfort for a pain as deep as what she obviously felt. She didn't respond, but made no effort to pull away from him. After a while, he thought she might be asleep.

"I wanted to be such a good mother to my son," she said softly, after lying quietly in his arms for a time. "He took that away from me, forever."

At the words "mother" and "son," Pierce began to guess the truth. "Who? Who took it away?"

"Montaigne." She said it without malice, without any emotion at all.

Pierce kept moving his hand over her back. He felt a fresh surge of anger and hatred at his longtime enemy, knowing it was him who had caused Elizabeth this anguish. "Tell me what he did to you, Elizabeth."

She didn't say anything for a moment. When she finally spoke, she sounded weary, resigned, her voice worn thin from crying. "He had me committed to Fleet. I owed him seven shillings and he had me imprisoned because I couldn't pay."

The scraps of truth Pierce already knew about Elizabeth slowly began to fit together in his mind. He understood now why she had been so terrified of going into the cell, and why she had suffered so after being alone in it for three days. Yet he sensed there was much more to the story than that, and it was somehow important to him to know all of it. "How did you come to owe Montaigne money?"

"It was my husband's debt. He owed money to everyone." Elizabeth spoke hesitantly at first, then her voice began to pick up speed, almost as if she were eager to rid herself of the tale and the feelings that accompanied it. "Geoffrey wasn't a London lord, he was a tailor from Coventry, a friend of my family. My father thought Geoffrey would use my marriage portion to set up his own shop, but Geoffrey wanted to live in London. We used all of my money to get to the city and find a place to live, but he couldn't find a position because there were so many tailors already and the guild wouldn't admit an outsider. He started drinking. And then I . . . then I . . ."

"You what?" Pierce urged softly.

"I found out I was pregnant." Elizabeth started crying again. "We had only been married such a short time, and we were so poor. Geoffrey was furious. I *begged* him to return to Northampton, but he said he would rather die than return home a failure. He wouldn't let me go alone, because he said it would make him look as if he couldn't take care of his wife."

Pierce thought of a few appropriate epithets for such a "man," but kept them to himself. He prodded Elizabeth to keep talking, for it seemed to be helping her. "But how did you come to be imprisoned?"

Disgust crept into her tone, edging out even her grief. "Geoffrey was killed in a brawl at a gin-house in St. Giles. By then it was too late for me to go home. It was November, and the roads were in such a terrible state, and I was so far along, I didn't dare travel. I didn't realize how bad things were until Geoffrey's creditors began knocking at the door. I sold everything I had to pay them: my wedding ring, my clothes—"

"Your hair?" Pierce asked softly, threading his fingers into the black tresses that barely reached her shoulders. When she nodded into his coat, he felt a burning surge of anger at her husband, and a deep sense of satisfaction that the idiot had gotten the ignominious death he deserved.

"Montaigne was the last of Geoffrey's creditors," Elizabeth continued hoarsely. "And it was only seven shillings. But he didn't want to hear about my hardship. He didn't care about anything but his money. He sent me to Fleet and . . . and . . ."

Pierce fit the last puzzle piece into place. "Your child was born in prison."

It was a long time before Elizabeth could answer. She nodded, crying again, though more softly than before. "Edward never even lived to see the end of his first day," she whispered. "I'll never be able to know him. He was gone before I even had the chance to hold him in my arms.''

She uttered another faint sob, then simply held on to Pierce, breathing shakily, as if she didn't even have the strength to cry anymore. Pierce could tell she was completely, mentally, physically exhausted. He cradled her against his chest, engulfed by a storm of emotions: anger at such senseless tragedy, rage at Montaigne, and above it all, a fierce, tender protectiveness for Elizabeth, like nothing he had ever felt in his life. His arms tightened around her. He wished there was some way he could will his own strength into her shivering form.

''Don't think about it anymore,'' he commanded softly. ''Put it out of your mind, Elizabeth. All of it.''

''No,'' she said weakly. ''Not until I make Montaigne pay—''

''Shh.'' Pierce eased her away from him, cupping her face in hands, his fingers looking large and dark against her pale skin. ''You don't have to. I'll take care of Montaigne.''

She closed her eyes, a fresh tear trickling down one cheek to land on his thumb. Gently, carefully, Pierce brushed it away and lowered her to the floor, pillowing her head in his lap. A renewed tempest of fury and tenderness struck him at the sight of her battered, bloodied fingers.

''I'll take care of Montaigne,'' he repeated more forcefully. Tearing a strip of cloth from his shirt, he started to tend her injured hands.

''You can't,'' she insisted, as if it should be obvious. ''I have to do it. I want every last bit of gold he has and I'm going to take it.'' She laughed at that point, a bit hysterically. ''Except for seven shillings. I'm going to leave him exactly seven shillings.'' With her free hand, she made a trembling motion as if counting out the coins. ''Lined up across the bottom of his fine coach.''

Pierce didn't like the frenzied tone of her voice or the gleam in her eyes. Both suggested she was not entirely safe from the madness that had almost claimed her. He must make her see reason, but he had to be very careful how he went about it. Silently, he cleansed her fingers as best he could and wrapped them in bits of his shirt linen.

The minute he was finished, she sat up and edged away from him until she was beside the door again. This time he didn't try to pull her back. "Elizabeth," he said soothingly, "there's no need for you to keep risking your life. I'll do what needs to be done."

She folded her arms across her chest and stared off into a corner of the cell. She seemed to be gathering strength—not from his comforting words, but from the idea of vengeance. "I am going to take all of that gold," she said with soft vehemence, "and put it to good use and *no one* is going to stop me. Not Montaigne. Not you." She glared at him, as if daring him to contradict her.

He did, but subtly. "All you have to do is trust me—"

"No," she said hotly. "The last time I depended on a man, it cost me my baby's life." Tears shone in her eyes again and she wiped at them angrily. "I should have left Geoffrey when I had a chance, but I didn't. I did what he told me to do. I stayed with him." Her voice was fraught with guilt and bitterness. "I wasn't able to save my son, but I can save other women and other children and I'm going to do it. And this time I won't depend on anyone but myself."

She started trembling again. Pierce knew he had to calm her down, but commands and reason weren't working, and he didn't know what else to use. He reached out to her, but she flinched away. The best he could do, he decided, was to keep her talking, keep her from withdrawing again into silence.

"Why," he asked carefully, "do you help only women and children with this charity of yours? Are not men in need as well?"

"Men," Elizabeth said tightly, "always seem to find their way out of trouble on their own. Or they disappear and leave it in the lap of some poor woman."

"The way your husband did?"

"Exactly," she said with bitter ire. "If Geoffrey had cared a fig about me, if he had returned to Northampton when we had the chance, things would have been all right. But he insisted on staying in London, because of his ridiculous male pride. His bloody pride meant more to him than his wife or his child."

"He was a fool."

"Well, I'm not. Not anymore. I'm better off without him. At least I don't have to put up with his . . . his *attentions*."

The full impact of what she was saying finally hit Pierce, like a fist in the gut. The abusive, drunken Geoffrey obviously hadn't been the kindest of lovers. God, was it any wonder she resisted lovemaking? It wasn't innocence that made her pull away, it was terror.

An image flashed into his mind: that night at her town house, the look in Elizabeth's eyes, the way he had treated her. It must have been a nightmare for her. The thought of hurting her filled him with self-loathing. "Elizabeth," he began haltingly. "That night in your room—I never meant to hurt you. I wasn't in my right mind. If I had known how you felt, I never would have—"

"But you didn't bother to ask, did you? You didn't think of me at all. You were only thinking of yourself."

He closed his eyes in self-disgust. He deserved that. His next words were some of the most difficult he had ever spoken, and the most true. "I'm sorry."

"Save your apology. I don't *want* it. All I want is that you never touch me like that again. Ever! I . . . I couldn't risk . . ." She put her head in her hands. "If I lost another baby, I couldn't bear it. I think it would kill me."

Pierce ached to reach out to her, to clasp her trembling form against him and kiss her fears and sorrow away. But that was obviously the last thing she wanted.

He fought with himself, wrestling with the desire he felt for her—and the other, less familiar feelings that he could not define. "I'm not like your husband, Elizabeth,'' he insisted in a low, purposely hypnotic tone. ''And there are ways to avoid the risk. You don't know how it might be, between us.''

''I don't *want* to know,'' she cried, refusing to look at him.

Pierce knew that wasn't entirely true; he had felt her tentative response to him, more than once. She wasn't ready to let go of her fears yet—but the day would come. He was sure of it. Elizabeth could only suppress her natural sensuality for so long. Eventually it would overpower her. Only when she was willing to let that happen would her painful memories start to heal.

For now, he knew he shouldn't force the issue. ''I give you my word, Elizabeth,'' he said slowly. ''I won't touch you . . .''

She raised her head, surprise and hope in her eyes.

He finished his sentence. ''Until you come to me.''

Her expression turned to one of reproach, but she lowered her head to her knees, apparently confident in her own power to resist him, and thus satisfied with his answer.

It was a long time before either of them spoke again.

When he finally heard her voice again, she at least seemed calmer than before. ''How many days have we been here?''

''It's almost Tuesday morning,'' Pierce replied. ''And we'd best start thinking about how we're going to get out of here.''

Elizabeth raised her head. ''Before the justice arrives.''

''Yes,'' he agreed, pleased that she appeared to be thinking rationally. ''We're a very long way underground, but we might try—''

He never completed his thought. A gunshot just outside their cell brought them both to their feet.

The door was unlocked and yanked open the next instant. Pierce squinted in the sudden brightness and Elizabeth gasped.

Young Wilton lay on the floor, a neat bullet hole between his eyes.

A half dozen men stood about the body, all impeccably dressed, brandishing pistols and muskets and blunderbusses. A man with a neatly trimmed beard and cold, blue eyes stood at their door, a saber in his left hand and the iron circle of keys in his right.

"Who be this likely-looking pair, now?" he asked.

"They were arrested when I was, Lowe," a voice from the back of the group said.

"Who are you?" the bearded man demanded again.

Before either had a chance to reply, another man raised his twin flintlock pistols, aiming one at Pierce and one at Elizabeth. "I don't care who they are. We've already taken too many risks to free our mates here." He cocked the weapons. "We'd best not leave any witnesses."

Chapter 13

"Wait there, Sikes," the bearded man said, holding up his saber to stop the imminent execution. "Let's not be hasty. We've lost a few men this past month. These two look like they might make able enough replacements." He turned toward Pierce. "What sort are you? Footpad? Pickpocket? Highwayman?"

Elizabeth, her heart pounding so hard it hurt, felt grateful he hadn't addressed her. She looked steadily at the ground. From the others' obedience, she realized that this man must be their leader. She thought she had heard one of them call him Lowe, the same name the bounty hunters had mentioned. Somehow the name Gideon Lowe tickled her mind. It set off alarm bells in her head, but she couldn't remember why. Did she know him from somewhere? Did he know her? Would he recognize her?

She tried to stay out of the light and keep her head bowed.

"Come, now, mate," Lowe demanded when Pierce didn't respond. "What are you in for?"

"I assure you, we wouldn't be the least bit useful to you," Pierce replied at last. "But we thank you for our freedom. My nephew and I have pressing business in London."

Elizabeth felt his hand on her shoulder, urging her toward the stairs that led out of the prison. She resisted; two of the men held lanterns, and moving toward the steps would mean passing through the light. Pierce increased the pressure on her shoulder. She took one hesitant step when Lowe's saber sliced upward to block her path. The sharp side of the blade hovered an inch away from her midsection.

"I didn't say I was just going to let you go, now did I?" he said smoothly. "I could leave you here for the justice. Or," he purred, "I could take you along with us, turn you in tomorrow and collect thirty pounds apiece."

Elizabeth held her breath, eyes locked on the shining blade that was close to slicing her through. She knew his threat was serious. Many criminals made a living by hunting down and turning in their fellow criminals—or blackmailing them into further crimes, making them virtual slaves. All that was needed was a warrant, and that could be bought or forged for a very low price.

"On the other hand, mates," Lowe continued. "I'm offering you a chance to join one of the best knots in all of England—if you're good enough for us."

"Thank you for the kind offer," Pierce said silkily. "But we really can't accept."

Lowe didn't reply. Instead, he raised his weapon until the flat of the blade touched Elizabeth's chin. She stifled a shiver at the feel of the cold metal against her skin. He pressed upward, forcing her to raise her head. A bead of sweat trickled down her temple. She took in every inch of his expensive garb as she slowly, reluctantly looked up. He wore shoes with jeweled buckles, breeches and coat of sapphire satin, a richly embroidered waistcoat studded with gold buttons, and a cravat edged with ruffles and lace.

The minute she looked into his steel-blue eyes, she knew why his name was familiar.

Dandy Gideon Lowe, scourge of the north country, terror of women everywhere—she had read about him in the book Nell had given her! This was the highwayman who had once posed as a messenger to gain entry to a rich squire's home; once inside, he tied the aristocrat up, gagged the servants and raped the lady of the house and her daughter before riding off with a sack of plunder.

His eyes perused her face, and Elizabeth felt as if her heart were pumping pure ice through her veins. She swallowed hard, silently thankful for her matted hair and the dirt and blood on her face that had resulted from her ordeal in the cell. Pray God it was enough to conceal her sex. If Lowe and his band realized she was a woman, she would be subjected to a fate much worse than a hangman's noose.

"This one'll need some cleaning up before he's fit for our company," Lowe said at last, drawing a round of laughter from his men. "What's your name, lad?"

Elizabeth gulped. The sharp edge of the saber grazed her Adam's apple. "E . . . Eli," she choked out, trying to keep her voice at a low growl.

"Well, Eli, tell your uncle here he should tell us what we want to know." He pressed the sword into her skin. "Because you don't want to get your head lopped off."

Elizabeth couldn't speak. She knew if she moved an inch, if she even took a deep breath, he'd cut her throat.

"All right," Pierce snarled. "Let him go."

"Tell us about yourself first, mate. Gideon Lowe doesn't take just any calf-lolly cull into his knot."

A heartbeat passed before Elizabeth heard Pierce's voice, low and sharp. "I've made my living in London for fifteen years. Picking pockets, burglary, highway robbery, all of it."

This brought a murmur of interest from Lowe's men.

"Have you, now?" Lowe asked, not moving the saber away from Elizabeth's throat. "Handy with a pistol are you?"

"The best," Pierce replied without a hint of boasting. "All I ask is—"

"I'll be asking the questions here, mate. What's your name? Are you someone I've heard of, perhaps?"

"Not likely. I do my best to stay out of the papers. Name's Jonathan Webster," Pierce lied smoothly. "Friends call me Black Jack. Enemies don't live long enough to call me anything."

There were more mutters and nods of approval from the men surrounding them. Elizabeth exhaled as the blade moved ever so slightly away from her neck. Lowe turned to look at Pierce.

''And what brings you all the way up from London, Black Jack?''

''I came to visit relatives,'' Pierce replied with a shrug. ''I was getting my nephew here out of a spot of trouble when we ran into a pair of bounty hunters.''

Elizabeth hoped she was the only one who caught the irony in his tone when he spoke of getting her out of trouble. She almost sank to her knees in relief when Lowe finally lowered his sword.

''And sure as taxes you didn't let them know about your activities in London.'' He laughed. ''Else they would have trussed you up and carted you down to the city to cash you in proper.''

''Exactly.''

''Well, mates,'' the highwayman turned toward his men, smiling. ''Looks like we just added one of London's best gullions to our little group.'' He turned his grin on Pierce. ''Come with us, Black Jack. We could use a good man, and you'll make more money than a Kensington Square duke. What say you?''

Though it was cordially phrased, Elizabeth knew the man would accept only one answer—and he would just as soon turn them in or kill them if he didn't get it. Pierce looked at her across the short distance that separated them. She thought she saw a flicker of some unfamiliar emotion in his gaze, like concern, but somehow deeper.

''I'll go with you,'' he agreed, still looking at her. ''*If* you let my nephew go. He's only a boy, lazy at that, and wouldn't know one end of a pistol from the other. He's of no use to you.''

Elizabeth choked back a cry of alarm. Did he have any idea who these savages were? He couldn't go with them. He couldn't! Even as she thought that, it struck her that Pierce was doing all this to protect her. It gave her an odd melting feeling in her stomach to realize he was willing to sacrifice himself to save her.

''I disagree,'' Lowe said. ''I think he'll be very useful.''

Pierce shook his head. ''He's always been a sickly lad.''

Elizabeth coughed to reinforce this line of thinking.

"He *is* a skinny one," one of the men muttered, poking at Elizabeth with the butt of his flintlock.

Unfortunately, Lowe seemed determined. "I think we'll just hang onto the lad to make sure Black Jack here doesn't get any ideas about leaving."

"Trust me," Pierce urged tightly.

Lowe nodded. "Long as I have little Eli for insurance." He sheathed his saber in the ornately jeweled and embroidered leather scabbard attached to his belt. "You sound like a smart one, Black Jack, and I hope you stay that way. Just remember, I can turn you *and* your nephew in any time for sixty quid."

With that cheerful thought, he motioned for his men to climb the stairs. As he turned, his cold blue gaze settled on Elizabeth, and she found herself unable to move, terror-stricken that he might realize she was not a boy at all.

One of the men stepped over the dead body on the floor and slapped her on the back. "You're part of Gideon Lowe's knot now, boy." He pushed her toward the exit. "Loyalty or death, that's our motto."

"Here, here," several of the others shouted. "Loyalty or death!"

Death, Elizabeth thought, might be preferable to the state of steadily increasing anxiety she was under. Lowe's men promptly relieved them of all their money, calling it an "initiation fee." Pierce objected when one of the knot took a fancy to his silver pocket watch, effectively holding everyone's attention while Elizabeth handed over her coin purse and did her best to stay far from the lantern light. Before the two men could come to blows, Lowe ordered his henchman to let Pierce keep the watch.

It was still dark as they left the gaol, but Elizabeth knew it was only a matter of time until the ruthless band discovered the woman in their midst. She prayed that Lowe had been joking about cleaning her up.

Unfortunately, they had no sooner reached the criminals' camp, deep in the forest beyond the town, when he reopened the subject of her appearance.

Their hideaway was a cave, the entrance hidden by a deep copse of bushes and underbrush. The sentries who had been left behind greeted them, and the men moved inside. When Elizabeth started to follow, Lowe stopped her with a shove.

"Not you, lad," he growled. "Not 'til you've cleaned yourself up proper. There's a stream through those trees, there." He pointed to the left. "Gill, you go along with him. Make sure he doesn't get any ideas about wandering off."

One of the men came forward to escort her, a tall, bulky sort armed with a flintlock and a wicked-looking knife that he wore in a fancy belt about his waist.

Too frightened to object, afraid she would give herself away if she but spoke a word, Elizabeth glanced at Pierce, silently asking for help.

"Mind if I accompany them, Lowe?" Pierce asked casually. He ran a hand over the dark stubble on his chin. "I could use a bit of cleaning up myself."

Lowe studied him for a moment, then nodded toward another of his men. This one looked even bigger and more dangerous than the first, Elizabeth noted with chagrin. "Go ahead, Black Jack. But I'm sending Sikes here with you. Try anything and you're a dead man."

"Understood." Pierce nodded. "Don't suppose I could borrow a razor?"

Lowe looked at him through narrowed eyes. "Gill will lend you his, won't you Gill?"

Grumbling, the burly man disappeared into the cave, then reappeared a moment later with a folded razor in one hand. He and Sikes each took a lantern, then pushed their charges none too gently toward the trees. Elizabeth kept close beside Pierce, painfully aware of the watchful eyes—and guns—trained on her back.

Thankfully, as soon as they reached the stream, the two men sat on the grass and lit a cigar to share. Gill tossed the razor to Pierce.

"Thanks, mate," Pierce said with a friendly smile.

Crossing the short distance to the edge of the water, he crouched down and started splashing more than was necessary. Elizabeth followed his example.

"We've only a minute here," Pierce whispered. "So listen to me and pay attention—"

"You never should have agreed to join them so easily," she hissed. "Now we're really in the soup."

"Pardon me, *Eli*. I was *trying* to get you out of there. And who landed us in the soup in the first place?"

Elizabeth winced, knowing he was right. It wasn't fair to blame him; he had been trying to protect her. "I'm sorry," she said in a shaky voice. "It's just that I've read all about Gideon Lowe. His knot has committed the most hideous crimes. They attack homes. They've been known to hold a victim over the flames of his own hearth until he reveals where his valuables are. Lowe himself once poured a kettle of boiling water over an old man to make him talk—"

"Trust me, I am well aware of our new comrades' reputations," Pierce snapped. "And I am also aware that Lowe never considers a job complete until he has raped every woman within reach."

Elizabeth shuddered at hearing that fact spoken aloud. She almost broke into very un-boylike tears. "What are we going to do?"

"Well, we can't just take on the whole bloody gang." Pierce started shaving. "I doubt either of us would survive that."

"But if we could just get our hands on a couple of their guns—"

"No, it's a safe wager they won't let us anywhere near a weapon. Lowe isn't going to trust me at first, and he certainly won't trust a good-for-nothing lad. Besides, you're not the world's best shot." His tone softened. "And with your hands injured, I doubt you could even hold a gun at the moment."

Elizabeth knew he was right about that as well, and felt desperation taking hold. "But we've got to try something! If I wash my face, they'll all know I'm a woman as soon as I walk back into camp!"

"Now is not the time to go senseless on me," Pierce said sternly. "If we can't rely on dirt for a disguise, we'll have to rely on something else."

"But *what*?"

One of their guards called out. "Hurry up, there, mates. Don't be taking all night."

Pierce cast a glance back at the two men, smiled and waved. "As I see it, we've got one hope," he whispered. "It's still dark. They lie low during the day and do most of their work at night. All we have to do is get them to stay away from you when it's light out."

"But Lowe is going to want to inspect me personally when we get back, to see if I'm suitably cleaned up—"

"Be quiet and stop arguing! We've already told them you're a sickly lad. We'll just have to do a better job of convincing them."

"How?"

"Just do what I tell you." He finished his less-than-perfect shave and folded the razor. "And when we get back to the cave, keep your mouth shut and don't get more than a few inches away from me. I'll do my damndest to protect you Elizabeth, but—"

"But if it comes down to fighting the whole gang, you'll look out for yourself first."

"I was going to say," he glowered at her, "that if a chance to slip away presents itself, take it and don't look back."

Elizabeth instantly regretted her quick tongue, realizing she was being unfair to him again. It was just that she was so used to men looking out for themselves first, and so frightened she couldn't think straight. Her mind conjured up nightmarish images of what Lowe and his men would do if they discovered her in their midst. "What about you?" she asked meekly.

"I'll manage. Now cough."

"What?"

"Cough. And make it convincing."

Elizabeth complied with a throaty sound.

"Louder," he urged.

She coughed her deepest.

"Better. Now as you stand up, let your knees buckle as though you're going to fall."

Elizabeth finally understood what he was about. He rose. She started to stand as well, then fell forward with a moan. Pierce caught her and lifted her over his shoulder. Hanging upside down, she lost her hat, but she was facing his back and her hair was just long enough to cover her cheeks.

"Sorry to take so long, mates." Pierce picked up her tricorne and carried her back toward their guards. "My nephew here has taken ill again."

He punctuated the last word with a gentle slap to Elizabeth's bottom. Her heart was beating so fast she had forgotten her coughing. A fresh volley of phlegmatic sounds made the two men back away.

"What is it he's got?" one of them asked warily.

"I'm not sure, but he recently returned from his Grand Tour in Italy. I heard they've had a nasty outbreak of the spotted fever there."

He patted Elizabeth's behind again and she outdid herself with a storm of wheezing, interspersed by gasps and hiccups.

Gill's next words were muffled by a hand over his mouth. "Keep the little bugger away from me." He quickly followed Sikes, who was already hastening back through the trees toward their camp.

"Well done," Pierce whispered as he followed them at a healthy distance.

As soon as they came within sight of the cave, Lowe's voice rang out. "Let's have a look at him, now. See if he's fit company without the dirt."

Elizabeth's breath caught in her throat and the choking sound she made was real.

"No, cap'n, I wouldn't get too close to him," Gill warned. "He's got some sort of Italian sickness."

"Might be spotted fever," Pierce supplied.

Elizabeth managed a small moan.

"I don't care what he's got. If you think I'm letting him go, you're wrong." Lowe's voice was taut with suspicion; however, the words "spotted fever" seemed enough to make him cautious. To Elizabeth's great relief, he let them pass. ''Just put him well in the back of the cave, away from the rest of us.''

Elizabeth's heart finally resumed its normal pace as Pierce complied with Lowe's order. He carried her through the underbrush at the mouth of the cave, past the campfires the men had lit, past the sacks of supplies and casks and crates of booty, and deposited her in the darkness at the back. She curled up facing the wall.

Pierce doffed his coat and covered her with it. ''You can rest here, Eli,'' he said in a voice loud enough to carry to the men at the entrance. Leaning over her, he tucked the black garment closer about her face. In a gesture that none of the others could see, he brushed his knuckles over her cheek, whispering for her ears only, ''And remember what I told you.''

When he turned away, Elizabeth had to stifle a mad urge to grab his hand and hold on for dear life. A single ridiculous thought flashed through her mind: Pierce had just broken his promise to avoid touching her in such an intimate fashion.

But as she lay there listening to his fading footsteps and the much louder pounding of her own heart, she realized something else.

She didn't mind. Not one bit.

Chapter 14

S nug in the darkness of the cave, the gang of thieves slept as morning awakened the rest of the countryside. Snores echoed off the walls and ceiling, but Elizabeth, huddled against the wall, didn't even close her eyes. She kept her back to the men, trying to conceal herself deep within Pierce's coat.

Every so often she coughed or sneezed or cleared her throat to keep up her guise of illness, but each minute seemed to last an hour, and each hour she felt more desperate. If any one of Lowe's men looked at her closely she would be lost. She longed to make a mad dash for safety, but didn't dare.

Her stomach began to growl as morning wore into afternoon and Elizabeth wished that she had eaten some of the bread offered to her in the prison; it had been days since her last meal. Finally, weak from hunger and dazed from being on edge for too many hours, she slipped into a fitful doze.

A rough hand on her shoulder brought her back to reality all too soon.

"You're staying here with us, lad."

"Mmm?" she mumbled, peering at the man over the collar of Pierce's coat.

"The others are going out." The man backed away as she stirred. "Lowe says you're to stay here, as insurance."

Looking toward the front of the cave, Elizabeth saw that night had fallen. The men were gathering up their weapons and filing out one by one. They were going on a raid—and taking Pierce with them! Unarmed, he followed the others into the brush that concealed the entrance.

He turned toward her and flashed the briefest flicker of a smile. "Be a good lad, now, Eli," he called out. "I'll be back before long." His gaze held hers a moment more, then he was gone.

The thought of being separated from him made panic well up in Elizabeth's throat. "Wait!" She raised herself on one elbow.

The man who had awakened her backed away. "You stay where you are, boy," he said with a snarl. "I ain't going to catch whatever it is you've got."

He hastily retreated toward the small fire at the entrance. He and two other men left behind arranged their bedrolls around the bonfire and seemed to be settling in for the night. One took out a deck of cards while another uncorked a bottle of wine.

In moments the thieves' lair was empty but for Elizabeth and her guards. *Damnation,* she thought, lying down again. Lowe obviously wasn't taking any chance of her getting away, not if he thought it necessary to leave three men to watch one sickly lad. There was no way she would be able to slip past them. Still, this would likely be her best opportunity to escape—perhaps her only one. She would have to think of something.

She willed herself not to worry about Pierce. He had ordered her to slip away if she had the chance, and the man was certainly able to take care of himself. Nevertheless, the thought of him being out with Lowe's cutthroats sent a frisson of fear through her. She offered up a quick, silent prayer for his safety and tried to focus her attention on her own predicament.

Curled up with her back to the sentries, she wondered if she could somehow get one of their pistols. But if she did, could she even hold the deuced thing? She experimentally flexed her fingers; they were still stiff and painful. Fumbling with a gun wouldn't make her look like very much of a threat.

And what if it came down to a choice between her life and actually having to shoot one of them? She had never been forced to face that situation. Elizabeth wasn't sure she could purposely harm another human being, cutthroat or not.

No, she decided, weapons weren't the answer. She would have to think of something else. She kept up a steady stream of unpleasant coughs and wheezes and other sickly noises while her mind whirled.

"Shut up, there, will ye?" one of the men shouted at her.

"Here," one of the others growled. "Have a drink and quiet down."

Elizabeth heard a bottle rolling across the dirt floor, and a second later it thumped into her back. They obviously didn't even want to get close enough to hand it to her. Muttering a thank-you, she reached behind her and picked it up, uncorked the bottle and took a sip. It was rum, strong and hot as it seared down her throat. She choked, her eyes watering, and set the bottle aside. On an empty stomach, one drink might hit her with the strength of a whole tankard. She kept her coughing to a minimum, concentrating instead on listening to the men's conversation.

"He'll have a nasty surprise, all right," one of them was saying with a chuckle.

"Just as long as I get my cut." A second grumbled. "This is the third time this month I been left on sentry."

"Quit your yawping. You still get one-tenth of a share," the third man pointed out. "And it beats the bloody hell out of getting shot at."

"But I don't get one-tenth of the women." The complainer insisted. "And I hear Hibbert's got himself a pair of pretty little daughters."

Elizabeth shivered as she realized what he meant, and who he was speaking of. She knew the Hibberts; they had occasionally stopped at her family's inn when they came to town. The two girls were several years younger than she. Their father was a squire with a modest house and a great deal of acreage, the perfect target for Lowe and his crew. A sudden flicker of rage overcame her fear.

She couldn't lie here worrying about herself when she knew such a heinous crime was about to be committed.

But what could she hope to do against these men, without getting herself killed?

Filled with a renewed sense of determination, she surveyed the items at her disposal: a bottle of rum, Pierce's coat, and her own wits.

Slowly, a plan started to form in her mind.

Pierce crouched in the shadows of a modest country home that, he had gathered, belonged to someone named Hibbert. Two of Lowe's five men had been keeping a close eye on him since they left the cave, but now their attention was focused on the door of the mansion, where their leader was politely addressing a footman.

Pierce itched to call out and warn their intended victim, and only the thought of Elizabeth kept him from doing so. He knew that if he interfered with Lowe's men in any way, or if he somehow managed to escape, her life would be forfeit.

"I know the hour is late," Lowe said in the perfectly refined tones of a London dandy. "But my employer insisted I deliver this personally."

"The squire is taking his chocolate in the library and does not wish to be disturbed," the man replied. "If you would come back in the morning—"

"Very well." Lowe waved a sealed envelope under the servant's nose. "But I'm sure you recognize the seal of the House of Commons. Since you refuse to admit me, I shall let *you* explain to your master why he received it too late." He turned as if to leave.

Pierce could hardly believe Lowe would go to the trouble of making a quiet entrance rather than simply smashing his way in through the windows. "Why doesn't he just get on with it?" Pierce ground out under his breath.

The man beside him clapped him on the shoulder. "Don't be impatient, mate," he whispered. "This is the sport of it. If we make too much noise right at the start, some of the ladies inside might have time t' get away."

Pierce found the man's logic revolting. He almost

groaned in frustration when the footman called after Lowe.

"Wait, sir. Perhaps you could give the letter to me."

"No," Lowe replied, turning slowly around. "For a matter of this importance, Squire Hibbert would wish to meet with me himself. I must deliver it personally."

"I see." The servant hesitated, then opened the door wider.

Lowe, grinning, gave the signal his men had been waiting for. They slunk out of the bushes and sped toward the entrance like a silent horde of rats. Pierce felt sickened at the look of sudden horror on the servant's face. The poor devil never even got a chance to scream; one of the gang slit his throat and he fell like a stone onto the porch, the shocked expression frozen on his features.

The thieves leaped over the body in their eagerness to get inside. Lowe led the charge as they rushed into the hall.

Pierce followed at the rear of the group. The scene inside made his stomach turn. Hibbert's house was small by London standards, but it offered quite a prize to Lowe's gutter filth. They dispersed like a well-trained army regiment, sweeping valuables and trinkets and whatever else they could get their hands on into the sacks they had brought with them. Mirrors, copper candlesticks, porcelain figurines, pewter plates, silverware and whatever furniture they could carry disappeared like ripe wheat under a swarm of ravenous insects.

They had been inside only minutes when the first screams reached his ears. A shrill cry split the silence of the night, then all pretense at a quiet attack disappeared; the thieves swiftly turned the rooms into chaos, whooping and yelling, shooting off their pistols. The male servants' lives were quickly snuffed out; the women were not so lucky. Lowe's men were on them like wild dogs.

Pierce could only thank God that he had managed to save Elizabeth from a similar fate—for now. Someone thrust a bag into his hands and shouted at him to get to work. Numbed with a sense of helpless frustration, he moved away, toward the back of the house. The parlor he passed had already been picked clean.

He stepped into the dining room to see two girls, no more than sixteen, cowering in a corner, clinging to each other, screaming and sobbing as one of Lowe's men stood over them brandishing a gun.

"Say there, Gill," Pierce called from the door, recognizing the man and thinking quickly. "You wouldn't believe what's in Hibbert's study. They're saying he's got himself a safe full of gold."

Gill's head swung around, greed replacing the lust in his eyes. "Anyone opened it yet?"

"Opened it? Damnation, they haven't found it yet. I sure as hellfire couldn't. But I'll wager whoever does isn't going to be splitting it ten ways." He looked down at the dazed girls and gave them a wolfish grin. "I'll keep the ladies entertained for you if you want to try your hand."

Pierce could almost see the man's pea-sized brain weighing a moment's sadistic pleasure against pocketsful of gold. After only a second, Gill turned and hurried from the room. "I owe you one, Black Jack," he called over his shoulder.

The minute he was gone, Pierce ran toward the girls. They huddled together, screaming, only to fall silent when he went past them to a window on the far wall. He pushed it open and gestured impatiently.

"Come on, damn it. Don't just sit there."

Still in a stupor, they only blinked at him. Pierce crossed the room in three strides, yanked them to their feet and shoved them in the direction of the window. "Go on. Run!"

"Y . . . you're letting us go?" one gasped.

"Yes." He pushed her up onto the sill. "Get the hell out of here!"

The girls snapped out of their stupor and scrambled out onto the lawn. One of them turned back toward him. "Thank you," she said with breathless wonder.

"Don't stand there thanking me," he growled. "Run for your bloody lives and don't look back."

As soon as they followed his order, Pierce turned and stalked from the room, heading for the kitchen. There had to be some way to stop this insanity—if he could just get his hands on a knife, some kind of weapon, *anything*.

Inside, he found only more brutality. Lowe was just lifting himself off the bruised, naked body of a young maid; fastening his breeches, he turned toward Pierce and smiled.

"Come on, missy." Lowe hauled the girl to her feet. "Say hello to a gentleman from London." He shoved her toward Pierce. "Help yourself, Black Jack."

Pierce held the trembling girl at arm's length and glared at Lowe over her head. "I do not rape children," he said, unable to keep the disgust from his voice.

"Well, pardon me," Lowe replied with a sneer. "Maybe one of the ladies of the house might be more to your taste." He jerked his head in the direction of an adjoining hallway. "Let's see what we can find."

Elizabeth knew this was a rash plan, but after thinking it over for several heart-pounding minutes, she couldn't devise a better one.

She picked up the bottle of rum. Moaning and groaning more piteously than before, she raised herself to her knees, carefully adjusting her collar to hide her face. She lurched to her feet. Half bent over, the bottle held loosely in one hand, she swayed a minute, then shuffled toward the three sentries.

"Don't come any closer, boy," one of them snapped.

"I'm t . . . too cold," she mumbled as if delirious, keeping her head bowed as she cautiously stumbled forward.

"Keep away," another man said, his voice rising.

She kept going until she felt the heat of the fire. "B . . . better up here." She stepped into the circle of light, raising her arms as if to warm her hands, purposely shivering as she did so. Some of the rum sloshed out of the bottle and onto the blankets the men sat on.

"Watch it there, you cull!"

"Hmm?" Elizabeth muttered, turning toward the man

in a jerky movement that spilled more of the liquor on their belongings. Some of it splashed his breeches and he leaped to his feet.

"Get back to your place!" he shouted, shoving her away.

Elizabeth fell backward, arms flailing, rum liberally dousing everything around her. She almost lost her balance for real this time, but recovered quickly enough to land a hard kick at the fire. Sparks and burning bits of wood showered across the cave floor, igniting every bit of alcohol-soaked fabric they touched.

The sentry screamed, beating at the flames that sprang to life on his leg. The man beside him grabbed a blanket to help but it too was afire. Sparks cascaded from the burning wool onto one of their pistols. It exploded with a roar. The impact knocked Elizabeth to the ground. Her ears ringing, she lay dazed for a second, the flames drawing perilously close, before she managed to half roll and half scramble away toward the cave opening.

In seconds, the fire spread to the sacks and barrels of supplies and booty, and then to the bushes that concealed the entrance. The third sentry suddenly abandoned his fellows and ran for his life.

Elizabeth, coughing on smoke that seared her throat and stung her eyes, staggered to her feet. She snatched up the closest weapons, a pistol and a flintlock, then pushed her way through the blazing underbrush.

The guard who had escaped ahead of her obviously cared more for his own skin than his duty; he was long gone. Elizabeth stumbled away from the cave, driven back by the heat. She expected the other two to be right at her heels, but when she turned, she realized they were still inside!

She gasped, horrified, realizing they were trapped. She hadn't meant to kill anyone! She had only thought to distract them so she could get away.

The men never even screamed. Their silence rang in her ears. She tried to tell herself they were ruthless criminals, murderers, rapists. But none of that excused the fact that she had just taken two lives; it was like a knife slicing through her heart.

She turned and ran into the forest, gulping in great, sobbing gasps of the night air, fighting her way through thickets and underbrush. Branches scraped her skin and tore at her hair and clothes and still she ran, heedless of where she was going until she reached the road. There she finally stopped.

She heard nothing in the cool night air but the heaving rasp of her own breathing and the hammering of her pulse in her ears.

Looking down, she realized she was still holding the pistol and the flintlock. She almost dropped them then, but an image of Pierce leaped into her mind. She thought of the way he had tried to protect her, that brief flash of a smile he had given her before going off with Lowe's men. He had known that she would have a chance to escape; he was trying to tell her to follow his orders . . . and leave him to manage on his own.

Holding the weapons in her trembling, painful hands, she looked up and down the deserted road. To the south lay Northampton; to the north, if she remembered correctly, she would find the Hibberts' house.

It would be such a relief to leave all this terror and violence behind. Elizabeth actually considered obeying Pierce's order, but the thought lasted less than a second.

Swallowing hard and mustering her resolve, Elizabeth shoved the smaller gun into the pocket of Pierce's coat. She told herself it was concern for the Hibbert girls that made her turn north.

But it was that smile she was thinking of as she hurried up the road at a ground-eating pace, the flintlock grasped in her swollen fingers.

Pierce thought he had seen the worst, the absolute lowest, of human behavior this night. He realized as they entered the library that he had not.

To the left, the French doors were open. Outside on the grass lay the body of a maid who had obviously tried and failed to escape. In the center of the room, a balding man, his few strands of white hair pasted to his forehead with sweat, sat on the floor. One of Lowe's knot, the burly cove by the name of Sikes, loomed over him. Before the hearth, half hidden by a pair of wing chairs, the body of a gray-haired woman lay unmoving.

Sikes was shouting. "Choose!"

The balding man looked up as Pierce and Lowe entered, his expression almost feral. "I . . . I . . ." his eyes beseeched them for help. "I . . . I . . . I—"

"Shut up and choose," Sikes insisted. "One's loaded and one's empty. Pick the right one and I'll let you go."

"Bloody bastard." Pierce stepped forward despite his resolve not to do anything to hinder them. He could not believe they could torture a human being and treat it as a game.

Lowe's saber swept up in front of him.

Pierce saw that the highwayman was watching the scene with a grin, his icy blue eyes alight with sadistic pleasure.

The man on the floor, trembling so hard the tasseled sash on his night robe danced, looked from one pistol to the other. "I . . . I . . . I . . ." It seemed the only word he was now capable of.

"Choose," Sikes insisted.

"Choose!" Lowe echoed from beside Pierce.

Suddenly Hibbert snapped. As if he could stand no more, he closed his eyes and grabbed one of the guns. He put it to his head.

"Christ, *no*!" Pierce yelled, lunging forward.

The sound of his voice hung on the air for one horrible instant before it was drowned out by the roar of the gun. He recoiled, one arm still reaching out, distantly aware of the sound of laughter over the ringing in his ears.

"Sorry, Hibbert, wrong one," Sikes chuckled.

Pierce stood frozen in shock, staring at the blood on the floorboards, his breeches . . . his hand.

"Come on," Lowe said, sheathing his saber. "There must be more women hiding here somewhere. We can't have found them all yet."

Sikes retrieved the pistols, wrenching the one from

Hibbert's lifeless fingers. Pierce didn't move, still staring at his bloody palm as the others moved toward the hall.

"Let's go, Black Jack," Lowe said, his voice edged with derision. "What? Have you no stomach for it?"

Pierce turned, slowly, his vision clouded with hate, his blood simmering with a rage that was as pure and anguished as it had been in another room in another house, fifteen years before.

Except this time he didn't give a single word of warning. He launched himself at Lowe's throat.

He slammed into the other highwayman and the two fell to the floor. Lowe grabbed at Pierce's wrists in a frenzied attempt to break the death grip on his neck, gurgling and choking.

"Get him off me!" He sputtered at Sikes. "Shoot him. Shoot him!"

Elizabeth knew she was too late. Before she had even come within sight of the Hibberts' house, she heard a feminine scream drift to her on the night wind. She shuddered, filled with dread at thoughts of what was happening inside the elegant, loving home. Still determined to do something, she skirted the house and crept around to the back.

To her horror, she found the bodies of two footmen, sprawled on the perfectly manicured lawn, apparently killed as they tried to flee. Elizabeth closed her eyes and choked back the nausea that rose in her throat.

She could hear the thieves inside, sounding for all the world like a band of Christmas revelers, but for the occasional scream or plea or pistol shot that rent the air. Where was Pierce?

She heard a shout of alarm, coming from an open pair of French doors a few yards away. At least someone inside was still able to put up a fight. Gripping the flintlock, Elizabeth hurried toward the noise, keeping to the shadows.

At the edge of the light, she darted a glance inside. At first she couldn't tear her gaze from the shocking sight of Squire Hibbert's body, lying twisted across the floor.

Then she looked up, and at last saw Pierce. He was grappling with Lowe, apparently bent on killing him with his bare hands. Lowe choked out a curse at his henchman, who raised a pistol to shoot Pierce in the back.

"No!" Elizabeth screamed.

Sikes spun toward her. "Jesus!" he exclaimed. "It's his nephew—but that's no lad's voice!"

Elizabeth, staring down the barrel of his gun, didn't remember her own weapon until it was too late. She raised the flintlock, but the huge man was upon her before she could even take aim. He knocked it from her numb hands and grabbed her, half choking her with one burly arm around her throat. With his other hand, he raised his pistol to finish off Pierce.

Pierce rolled onto his back, using Lowe as a shield, just as Sikes pulled the trigger. The gun went off, the sound so loud and so close that Elizabeth thought for a moment she had gone deaf. She could see everything that was happening in the room in terrible detail, but could hear nothing.

The bullet struck Lowe in the back just below his ribs, and he choked out a cry, his body stiffening. Pierce let him fall to the floor and launched himself at Sikes. Suddenly Elizabeth found herself released and she fell to her knees, coughing.

Then, from the corner of her eye, she saw Lowe struggling to his feet. He turned toward her, the look in his eyes vicious, and unsheathed his saber. Elizabeth fumbled for the pistol in her pocket as he came at her. She pulled out the gun, but her stiff fingers couldn't reach the trigger fast enough. The sword flashed toward her, as bright and fast as a bolt of lightning. She heard a high-pitched shriek of pure terror and realized the voice was her own.

The next sound she heard was a grunt of pain, but it came from Pierce. He had knocked the blade aside, taking a nasty slash on his arm as he threw himself at Lowe. Both tumbled to the floor.

Pierce rolled and came up in a crouch, holding his wounded arm. Lowe looked for his henchman, but Sikes lay moaning on the far side of the room. Cornered, Lowe snarled in pure rage. Grasping the sword, he launched himself at Pierce.

Elizabeth felt the gun jump in her shaking hands, heard a roar and opened her eyes, realizing only then that she had squeezed them shut and fired the pistol. She hadn't had time to take aim or even think about what she was doing. Lowe fell to his knees, screaming, his hands covering his face.

Shaking uncontrollably, Elizabeth let the smoking gun slip from her numb fingers. She felt as though she were going to faint, but suddenly Pierce was beside her, pushing her toward the French doors.

"Run!" he yelled. "Run!"

He grabbed her hand, pulled her outside, and the two of them ran toward the trees.

Chapter 15

They had been walking for more than an hour, Elizabeth guessed, and before that they had been running almost as long. She was so numbed by the horror they had just been through, and so weak from hunger and exhaustion, she was sure each step would be her last. The urge to just fall down in the dusty road and lie there was almost overpowering. Pierce, however, insisted they keep moving.

He walked several feet in front of her, his straight back and stiff shoulders dappled by moonlight that spilled through the trees. Elizabeth had tried to talk to him several times, needing comfort and relief from the awful, violent images that kept slashing through her memory. Though he hadn't asked, she explained how she had escaped from the guards at the cave.

He had only grunted in response. After a while, she realized she was babbling, and fell silent. She was still too dazed herself to wonder about his lack of reaction.

Pierce hadn't spoken half a dozen words to her since, except for a gruff command to keep going whenever she slowed down. He kept trudging down this road—if one could truly call this weed-choked trail a road—heading south. Elizabeth couldn't see the point in driving themselves so hard. There had been no pursuit after they ran from the Hibberts' house, and Pierce had frequently changed directions in the forest, occasionally doubling back on their own trail.

She was exhausted, and hungry, and thirsty, and ready to drop, and knew Pierce must be as well. He might appear to have the stamina of a war horse, but he needed rest, and he needed to have that arm tended. The man was only human, much as he might hate to admit it.

One of them had to be concerned about such practical matters, Elizabeth thought with a weary sigh, and for once it was obviously going to have to be her. She stopped walking.

Pierce kept going for several paces before he discovered she had lagged behind. He turned about and eyed her with annoyance. "What is it?"

"What *is* it?" Elizabeth echoed incredulously. "Do you plan to walk all the way back to London tonight?"

He moved toward her, a darker shadow among the shifting forest shades of black and midnight blue. "I'm sorry, madam, that we haven't the funds to rent you a fine hackney coach. Why don't you wait here and I'll go fetch you one?"

Elizabeth ignored his sarcasm, too tired to even feel its sting. "We can't go any further tonight," she said calmly. "We need food, and water, and you should have your wound tended. Besides, it will be light soon, and you're bound to draw a great deal of attention looking like that." She gestured to his blood-spattered clothes.

"I have a better idea," he snapped. "Why don't you just get the hell away from me? You have been nothing but trouble from the moment I met you, and I have bloody well had enough. I'm not going to live much longer if I keep getting thrown in the gaol or shot at every time you land yourself in another disaster with someone like Gideon God-damn Lowe!"

Elizabeth flinched and backed away a step, startled and hurt by his outburst. "I'm sorry that I got us involved with Lowe's knot. I certainly didn't do it on purpose," she replied defensively.

"Of course not. You never do anything on purpose. That's because you don't have a single ounce of logic in your entire empty head. Trouble is just drawn to you like a magnet. Well, I don't exist for the purpose of saving your reckless little arse! I'm not going to keep chasing after you. If you want to get killed, do it alone!"

He turned to stalk away and Elizabeth's temper flared.

"I never *asked* you to keep chasing after me! In fact, if you'll recall, I asked you to leave me alone!"

He stopped but he didn't respond. After a second, he turned around and just stood there, looking down at her as if she were a bug, a pest he wanted to brush out of his way. "True enough," he said derisively. "I only wish to God that I had."

Elizabeth suddenly felt tears pooling in her eyes. Did Pierce hate her so much? He had seemed genuinely concerned for her while they were with Lowe's gang. Had she misinterpreted his words, and that gentle brush of his fingers on her cheek?

Ever since then, he had been by turns oblivious, indifferent, and now furious. He seemed more like the man he had been in London, aloof and distant and concerned only for himself. It hurt to be the object of such a cold glare, after he had been kind to her. She blinked rapidly, telling herself it didn't matter that he had changed back, or what he felt for her.

But as she looked up at him, at his hard features illuminated by moonlight, shadowed by the stubble of a beard and smudged with dirt, she felt an almost painful flip-flopping sensation in the pit of her stomach—and it wasn't hunger. She realized to her dismay that she *did* care what he felt for her.

But she wasn't about to let him know that.

"I thought I saw some lights off to the left a little way back," she said, trying to keep her voice steady, appealing to his practical side. "Perhaps we could find some lodging. We have to get some rest before we both collapse."

"And how do you suggest we might pay for this lodging?"

Elizabeth bent down and wiggled a finger under the buckles on her shoes. From each, she produced a silver shilling. "My mother always taught me to be prepared for any inconvenience."

"That won't buy us more than a heel of bread to share between us."

''Well at least it's something!'' She was rapidly losing patience with his foul mood.

Pierce didn't reply. With a shrug and a muttered oath, he walked past her, heading toward the lights, apparently unconcerned whether she followed or not.

Elizabeth almost didn't. She folded her arms over her chest and frowned at his departing back. Why the devil should she stay with him? Why not just do what he wanted and let him keep going until he dropped?

And why did that thought give her a sudden, twisting pain inside?

She ignored it concentrating on the fact that he was being unfair, placing *all* the blame for the events of the past days at her feet. She never would have had to flee London in the first place if Pierce hadn't been foisting his attentions on her.

Perhaps she *had* been nothing but trouble since the moment they met, but his thoughtless behavior at least equaled hers. He had made advances on a woman he believed married; had almost raped her in her own house; had, in short, been doing everything in his power to trick, force or seduce her into giving up her plans for the Trust! And all for the sole purpose of his own personal financial gain!

On the other hand, she thought, her frown fading as his form grew dim in the darkness, he had tenderly comforted her in the Northampton gaol, when she had been lost in a black void of grief and pain. He had also protected her from Lowe's gang when he could have escaped and saved his own skin. And tonight, he had saved her life—again—and gotten wounded in the process.

Feeling abashed and frustrated, she plodded after him. Perhaps it was time for them both to call things equal and wipe the slates clean. In any event, she couldn't leave him until he had his arm tended. She *was* responsible for that, and it made her feel obligated to him— though she wasn't comfortable feeling obligated, not when he was in this mood.

Elizabeth caught up with him then tagged along behind, studying the rigid lines of his broad back. She fished through her pockets, and the pockets of Pierce's coat, which she still wore. To her pleasure, she came up with a gold guinea that had worked itself into the lining of her waistcoat.

They snuck into the town, cautious not to be seen, though the residents had long since taken to their beds. It was a fairly large village, with well-kept homes and cottages clustered around a grand church at the center, and row after row of shops, their windows crammed full of furniture and pewterware and shoes and the latest London fashions.

"I doubt we'll find inexpensive lodging here," Pierce muttered.

Elizabeth held up the gold coin with a determined smile. "Have faith."

"In this town, that coin and your faith won't buy us more than a bottle of cheap wine to go with the heel of bread."

Elizabeth gave up trying to improve his humor. If all he could offer were mean-spirited barbs, she didn't want to talk to him anyway.

At the east side of the town, they came upon what appeared to be an inn: a timber frame structure crouched behind a thick hedge, its roof newly rethatched, its windows hidden behind freshly-painted shutters. A sign hung by a chain from the eaves, along with a lantern. By the light, Elizabeth could make out the words, "The Coach-and-Six."

She thought it looked so civilized, so heavenly she could almost cry. Here was a place where she could remind herself that the world wasn't made up entirely of savagery and violence. She turned to Pierce.

"I think I should handle this," she suggested. "If the occupants get a look at the blood on you, they'll run screaming out of the place."

"Certainly," he agreed with a mocking twist to his lips. He clearly didn't think she had a chance in the world of securing a room. "I'll wait for you at the back. It shouldn't take more than a few seconds for the proprietor to boot you out on your back end."

Elizabeth took off his coat and handed it to him, refusing to be drawn into another argument. "May I borrow your pocket watch?"

He started to object, then apparently changed his mind. Shaking his head as if none of it mattered to him in the least, he took out his watch, dropped it into her upraised palm, then turned and walked away.

Elizabeth pocketed the prize, then rifled through her frock coat one more time. She came up with her empty, worn leather coin purse that Lowe's men hadn't bothered to keep. She supposed it would do for her purpose.

Crouching down, she filled it with pebbles, placed her three coins on top, then attached it to the belt at her waist. She also dirtied her face and mussed up her hair to better conceal her femininity. Taking a deep breath, she walked up to the inn door and tried to open it. It was locked for the night.

She had to knock several times before a bleary-eyed man appeared, squinting at her from beneath his nightcap. He glanced from her dusty face to her disheveled clothing to her scuffed shoes. "Go away, boy. I don't hearken to peddlers at this hour." He started to close the door.

"Wait, my good sir." Elizabeth stuck her foot over the threshold before he could shut her out. "I am on a mission of the utmost importance. For a *personage* of the utmost importance."

"What are you blathering about?" He looked at her suspiciously.

"I require a room, for only a day," she said in a secretive tone. "Not for myself, mind you, but for my employer." She slipped the man one of the silver coins.

He raised an eyebrow at the ponderous size of her purse, but didn't seem any more eager to open the door. "And where might your employer be?"

"Waiting for me, off there." She waved in no particular direction. "He cannot risk being seen. His name would be known to you, could I reveal it."

She casually took Pierce's watch from her pocket and

flipped it open. The back, decorated with three ostrich feathers, symbol of the Prince of Wales, flashed ever so briefly in the lantern light.

She pocketed the watch with a sigh. "Good God, it's been seven hours. We've been lost in the forest for seven hours and it's all my fault. You see, we became separated from our hunting party, and then the Pr—my employer's horse came up lame."

The innkeeper's eyes, large as a pair of serving platters, were still locked on the pocket where she had placed Pierce's watch.

"Ah, I see you don't believe me." She shrugged. "Well, I can hardly blame you, viewing my present condition. I suppose we shall have to sleep in the woods, then, since we daren't risk approaching another inn and being seen."

She looked left and right, then leaned toward him and lowered her voice to a conspiratorial whisper. "Were the Ki—my employer's father, rather, to discover that his son has been off hunting again instead of attending to business, there would be quite a row back at St. James. Quite a row."

The innkeeper's face brightened. He pushed his cap out of his eyes. "You truly mean to say—"

"Oh, now I see that I've said too much." Elizabeth stepped back from the door. "He simply *can't* have anyone know he was here. Forget that you saw me. Keep the silver for your trouble. I'm sorry."

"No, wait." The innkeeper came out after her. "We can't have the Prince of Wales sleeping on the ground, now can we?"

"I *have* said too much." Elizabeth groaned. "He'll be furious with me. I must go, really. Goodbye."

The man grabbed her arm to restrain her. "I assure you, I shall have the utmost discretion. No one will know that either of you is here."

"No, I must leave." Elizabeth made a small show of trying to pull away.

"At least allow me to show you the room. We've only

just finished redecorating the inn. Please." He bobbed a quick little bow.

"Well . . ." She paused dramatically. "I suppose that would be all right."

He ushered her inside with alacrity. From what Elizabeth could make out in the darkness, the inn was indeed one of the finest she had ever visited. She could feel a carpet beneath her feet in the entry hall, and caught the scent of wax polish and the lingering aromas of roast beef and fresh bread that must have been served for dinner. Her stomach growled.

At the end of the hall upstairs, the offered room dazzled her weary eyes. A four-poster draped in amber damask filled much of the chamber, with a small table beside it. On the opposite wall, arranged about the grate, sat a pair of wing chairs upholstered in blue brocade, a washstand, and even a writing desk. The innkeeper crossed to the window, threw back the heavy curtains and opened the shutters to let in some fresh air.

"Will this do?" he asked nervously.

"Yes," Elizabeth said slowly, adding a grave nod. "I think it will be adequate. We shall only need it until His Highness is rested and ready to return to his party." She fought the urge to take off her shoes and stockings right then and wiggle her bare toes in the thick Wilton rug.

"We call it the Paragon Room."

"How charming." She offered him the other silver shilling from her fat purse. "Might we also obtain something to eat and drink? And some water and towels for washing as well."

"Yes, certainly. Ask for anything and you shall have it." The man took the coin and bobbed a pair of quick bows.

"Thank you. You are most kind. I shall certainly have to relate to the Prince how very hospitable you have been."

"Bacon. The name's Nicholas Bacon." The innkeeper beamed at her. "Let us go and fetch him."

"Well—of course, yes." Elizabeth swallowed hard and

thought quickly. "Though, after having been about in the woods all day, he's somewhat unkempt, and he usually doesn't wish to have his subjects see him at anything less than his best—you know how these royals can be. But . . . Well, I'm sure he could make an exception."

"Oh, no, quite all right," Bacon insisted, though he looked crestfallen. "I wouldn't wish to inconvenience him in the least. I shall have the items you requested brought up while you go and fetch him. You may be assured of my utmost discretion."

Elizabeth gave him a warm smile. "I shall most definitely tell the Prince what an excellent host you are, sir."

Following him down the stairs, she hurried out the door and around the inn, trying to make up her mind which she wanted first, food or sleep.

She found Pierce slouched, still glowering, beneath a tree. He didn't rise as she approached.

"Well?" She waved impatiently. "Are you coming or not?"

He gave her a look of utter disbelief. "You're joking."

"Not at all. In fact, I've not only secured a room"—she flashed a victorious grin—"I've secured a promotion in rank for you as well. You're no longer an earl, but a prince."

He got to his feet and walked over to her. "What the devil do you mean?"

"Come and see," Elizabeth said mysteriously. Turning, she led him inside and up the stairs to the Paragon Room.

A steaming pitcher of water, a porcelain basin, and towels and linens had already been placed on the washstand. Elizabeth closed the door behind them and watched as Pierce moved about the room, running his fingers over the expensive furnishings, grimacing as he caught his reflection in the mirror over the grate. "How did you manage all this?"

Elizabeth walked over and handed him his watch. "It's not how much money one has," she said softly. "It's what one does with it."

Before he could reply there was a knock on their door.

"It's me, sir. Bacon."

"Quick," Elizabeth whispered. "Sit in that chair and face the window. You're supposed to be the Prince of Wales."

"I'm supposed to be the bleeding *what*?"

"*Sit,*" she hissed, pushing him toward one of the tall wing chairs.

He dragged it around so its back faced the door, settling his large frame just as the door creaked open.

The innkeeper peeked in. "I'm not interrupting, am I?"

"Not at all, Mr. Bacon." Elizabeth eagerly reached out to take the tray of food and drinks he carried. She set it on the table beside the bed. "Not at all."

"Sir." Bacon bowed toward the chair. "The Coach-and-Six is deeply, deeply honored by your presence."

Pierce raised a hand and gave him an airy wave.

The innkeeper became so red-faced and flustered, one would think he had just been knighted. "Thank you, Your Highness." He bowed a second and third time as he backed toward the door, doffing his nightcap nervously, grinning until he giggled. "Thank you!"

Elizabeth followed him and gave him the last coin she had, the gold guinea. "No, it is we who thank you, Mr. Bacon." She hefted the heavy purse at her waist. "Do you wish me to pay for the room now?"

"Oh, no, not at all," he said with a firm shake of his head. "I wouldn't think of it. We can discuss such routine matters upon your departure."

"Good evening to you, then."

"Shall I come fetch the trays in, perhaps, an hour?" he asked eagerly.

"Actually, the prince needs his rest," Elizabeth said in a low tone. "He won't wish to be disturbed. I'm sure you understand."

"Oh, yes. Yes, of course. He'll not be bothered by anyone, you have my word." Bacon bobbed his way out. "Good evening."

Elizabeth leaned against the door a moment after she closed it, inwardly offering up a relieved prayer of gratitude. She had no idea what she would have said if he requested payment.

"And how *are* we to pay for all this?" Pierce demanded, rising from his chair.

"I've asked for the room for the day. We'll just have to slip away tomorrow without him seeing us."

"Like thieves in the night."

"Not at all." She sniffed. "I shall send him the money as soon as we return to London."

"Of course. Accompanied by a note on the royal stationery, no doubt."

She rounded on him. "I would be grateful if you would keep your remarks to yourself!"

"Fine." He turned to the window and leaned on the sill.

Elizabeth felt confused by the change in him. She had expected him to blow up at her again; instead he remained tense and silent. The silver glow of the moon highlighted his profile, and she could see that his face was set in hard lines, his shoulders, his back, his every muscle taut with strain.

She felt as if she were watching the sparking fuse on a bomb, but had no idea how to avert the imminent explosion.

"What the devil *is* it?" She pushed away from the door and came to stand in the middle of the room. "If you're still angry with me for getting us mixed up with Lowe's knot, go ahead and rant and rave and have done—"

"I don't care about that." He didn't look at her.

"Then why have you been snapping at me since we left the . . ." Her voice faltered. "The house."

"It has nothing to do with you."

Puzzled, she took a step closer. "Then why have you been acting this way?" she said more gently.

It was a long time before he spoke, and when he did his voice was as sharp and cold as newly-forged steel. "Didn't you see him?"

"Who?"

"Hibbert. On the floor. Blasted his brains out."

Elizabeth chewed the inside of her cheek, shuddering. Yes, she had seen Mr. Hibbert. She would never forget that sight, knew it would haunt her in a thousand nightmares. But she didn't understand why Pierce, a man who was more than familiar with death and violence, would be so affected by it. "Yes," she said softly. "It was horrible."

"Horrible?" He shoved himself away from the window, his movements uncharacteristically jerky, his face a mask of rigid control. "Horrible doesn't begin to describe it. They drove him to it."

He crossed the room in three strides and came to stand in front of her, his fists clenching and unclenching as if he wanted to strike out—or reach out—but couldn't. "They drove him to it. Tortured him until he couldn't stand any more." Pierce's eyes turned icy. "He blew his own head off and they laughed about it. *Laughed* about it."

He stared up at the ceiling, then down at his boots, which were still covered with blood and dirt in a muddy mess. His arms were so tense they were shaking. "He could have shot one of *them*. Why didn't he see that? Why didn't the blasted idiotic coward see that?"

"Y . . . you can't blame yourself," Elizabeth soothed, sensing the barely-leashed violence in him and struggling with an instinctive urge to back away.

"I don't," he said flatly. Suddenly he stalked away across the room. "He knew what he was doing."

"Then what do you mean?" Elizabeth stayed where she was, bewildered and trembling. "What are you talking about?"

Pierce reached for one of the goblets on the tray, tossed off a long gulp, then wiped his mouth. He regarded her with a frozen smile. "You want to hear the whole 'horrible' thing? Fine. I suppose it's only fair. I know all about you, don't I?" He drank again. "What the hell. Why not?"

Elizabeth tried to move out of his way this time, but wasn't fast enough to elude him. Still holding the cup in one hand, he caught her by the arm and walked her three quick steps backwards. She came up against the wall with a gasp.

He leaned close until his face was only inches from hers, his expression cool and distant and ominous. "Let me tell you the whole 'horrible' story."

Chapter 16

A little stab of fear leaped wildly in Elizabeth's chest. Only one thought, firm in her mind, kept her from using her fists or her nails or a knee to try and break away: he wouldn't hurt her. She saw it beneath the frostiness in his eyes. *He* was in pain, somehow, and only wanted it to stop.

"I don't understand," she whispered.

Pierce raised his eyebrows in a mocking expression. "Then allow me to explain it for you, miss goodness and light. I was fifteen when my father blew his head off. Our house was so big he shot himself one night and we never heard it. I was the one who found him the next morning." His voice was a cool monotone, as if he were merely reciting a passage memorized from a lesson book long ago. "He was lying there, with his blood and his brains all over the floor and the wallpaper and his expensive furniture—and his pistol."

The rapid rising and falling of Pierce's chest was the only sign that he was feeling anything beyond casual interest in the story he was relating. "Montaigne and his men came to throw us out at dawn and I was sitting there holding that gun, screaming that I knew what he had done. That I was going to report him."

Elizabeth felt so anguished at the image of a young boy, young Pierce, kneeling over his father's body, she had to close her eyes. "Report him for what?" she whispered, not wanting to know the answer, yet needing to hear all of it. "What had he done?"

"Montaigne," Pierce said in the same deceptively soft, absolutely controlled tone, "was one of four good *friends*

189

who lured my father into the South Seas madness back in 'nineteen. They talked him into investing all he could. He made huge profits at first, more money than both the Darkridge earls before him. He was mad for more cash to buy more shares, and Montaigne offered to loan it to him. All my father had to do was sign a note putting up all the Wolverton estates against the loan. Then the crash came.''

Pierce stated the rest of it in staccato sentences, like bursts of fire from a pistol. ''My father found out that his friends had been involved in the company's management all along. They knew the end was coming and used him to get out. His investment allowed them to unload their own shares at a rich profit. They were all fat and happy. We lost everything. That night my father sat down and told my mother and me the whole sordid story. He told us everything was going to be all right.''

Pierce fell silent, and Elizabeth opened her eyes to find that he had closed his. A single muscle jerked spasmodically in his cheek. She ached to reach up and soothe it with a touch; she started to raise her hand but he opened his eyes, and his expression told her she didn't dare.

''The next morning,'' he continued calmly, ''when Montaigne and his men came, I tried to attack him. He grabbed the pistol and hit me across the face with it. Then he tossed us out, threw the empty gun after us. Said if we tried to make any trouble, he would say that he and his witnesses had seen *me* kill my father.''

Pierce finally let Elizabeth go and moved away, still holding the goblet in one hand, his back rigid. He drained the cup in a single long drink, then dropped it on the tray. It landed with a clatter. ''They had him buried in a pauper's grave. Wouldn't even pay for a headstone out of the money they had stolen from him.''

Elizabeth hung her head, taking a deep, shaking breath, stunned by the force of what he had said—and the absolutely detached, unemotional way he had said it. She felt bruised inside, as if she had just been pummeled by dozens of cruel blows; she could only imagine what it had been like for Pierce all these years, carrying that pain around and never letting it out.

She raised her head, gazing at him in empathy, noticing the scar on his cheek as if for the first time. She felt a chill, realizing the mark must have come from Montaigne, from the gun that Pierce's father had used to commit suicide.

"Oh, Pierce," she whispered, her throat dry. "Oh, I'm so sorry—"

"Save it," he said curtly. "I've lived with it for fifteen years. I don't need anybody's sympathy."

She came away from the wall, stepping tentatively toward him. "Is it all right if I just say . . . I understand?"

He stiffened as if she had struck him. "I am not one of your charity cases. I don't need anything from you. Hate is the only thing I need to do what I have to do."

Elizabeth felt as if another invisible blow had just hit her, and this one brought tears to her eyes. It sounded as though he welcomed hate, thrived on it. She took another step toward him. "You've every reason to hate Montaigne, but—"

"Not him." Pierce's eyes glittered unnaturally dark in the half-light. "My father. My God-damned coward father."

Elizabeth was taken aback, the idea of despising a parent utterly foreign to her. "You can't mean that."

"It's the truth. He deserted us. Took the coward's way out. We went from one relative and friend to another. No one would take us in. Most of them had been ruined in the South Seas Company, and even the ones who had anything left turned us away. Montaigne had started a rumor that I killed my father. None of them wanted to be touched by the *scandal* of Thomas Wolverton's suspicious death."

He sat on the bed and choked out a sarcastic bark of bitter laughter. "One day we had all the friends money could buy. The next day, when we were penniless, we were outcasts."

Elizabeth blinked back the tears that stung her eyes as she imagined the rest: a fifteen-year-old boy who needed to take care of his mother, with nothing more than a pistol and his own cunning to live by, hatred burning in his heart. He had probably been scared witless the first time he robbed someone, but it became easier the next night, and the next.

Now, after so many years, it was all he knew. The road and the gun. Darkness and danger and death.

He had no softness in his life, no friends or family to blunt the sharp edges of vengeance and solitude. She knew how that felt, and the feeling was not a pleasant one. It gave her chills to think Pierce had lived that way so long.

And to think that here was a mirror of what she herself might someday become.

"Pierce," she whispered, "I know—"

He cut her off with a single contemptuous glare.

Elizabeth lowered her eyes, realizing that he wasn't going to accept even the smallest overture of sympathy. He wanted to be left alone in his hate.

Unable to bear that thought, and not knowing what else to do, she turned away and walked to the writing desk. She poured some water from the pitcher into the porcelain basin. He might not let her comfort him, but he would at least have to let her tend his wound.

It pained Elizabeth to realize that the only emotions Pierce had allowed himself for years were anger and resentment and hatred for his father and Montaigne. All else he mocked or ignored or shoved aside before it could distract him from his goal. Just as he had been mocking and ignoring and shoving her aside all day.

Was there no capacity for caring left in him, buried beneath those rocky, treacherous layers of cold cynicism? He seemed determined to convince her there wasn't, but Elizabeth couldn't believe it, not after the way he had been kind and tender and protective with her before.

That tiny grain of an idea bloomed into hope inside her. Perhaps she had already begun to chip away at those layers without even knowing it. Was that the real reason he had been so surly with her today? Was it possible that he had started to have some feelings for her, feelings that disturbed him?

Still turning the idea over in her head, she picked up the basin, along with some linens. Slowly, she turned toward Pierce.

He looked up, watching her, his face still cast in hard lines, that muscle twitching in his tanned cheek.

Before she could change her mind, she walked over and set the basin on the rug.

"Let me see your arm," she said softly.

Without saying a word, without ever looking away from her face, he took off his frock coat and tossed it to the floor. His waistcoat followed. His fingers moved to the buttons on his shirt. He unfastened them with fast, sharp movements.

Elizabeth held his gaze, refusing to let him stare her down. His entire demeanor was aggressive and angry. Perhaps he had thought he could push her away completely with his revelations, that she would be disgusted or reviled by his hatred for his father. Elizabeth wouldn't be pushed. She wouldn't leave him alone with the demons that plagued him.

He peeled off the shirt, wincing only slightly when it stuck to the cut on his arm for an instant. With a flick of his hand, he sent it sailing after his other garments. It floated to the floor, glimmering briefly in a beam of moonlight before it landed.

Elizabeth thought the sound of her breathing had become far too loud in the room. Pierce, now naked to the waist, looked like one of the mythic warriors of ancient Greece come to life and ready to do battle anew.

Only the bleeding cut on his right arm marred his perfection. He was all smooth, muscular magnificence, from the contours of his shoulders and chest to the sculpted steel of his ribs and the tapered line of his waist. A whorl of dark hair began just below his flat belly and disappeared at the waist of his breeches.

She swallowed on a parched throat, knelt, and wet a length of linen in the basin. When she stood, his gaze was there again, capturing hers with a challenge, a dare.

Trying to keep her hand steady, she stepped closer, leaned over him and gently dabbed at the cut with a wet cloth. His scent enveloped her, dark and spicy, playing on her nerves like warm fingers over cool harpsichord keys.

Elizabeth decided she'd best put her mind to something other than Pierce's physical attributes. A bit of conversation was most definitely in order. "Did your mother know about it?" she asked suddenly.

"About what?"

Though he spoke quietly, his voice sounded inordinately loud, so close to her ear.

"How you earned your money."

"I told her I'd found work as a hackney coachman," he stated. "It explained why I was always out at night."

"And she never questioned you?"

He didn't reply for a time, and Elizabeth thought he might not. Then he spoke again, so quietly she had to lean closer to hear him. "Only once. A coach driver shot me in the leg. I told her I had gotten caught in a disagreement between two drunken customers. She didn't believe it for a minute, but she didn't try to stop me. Every night after that, though, when I left, she would say, 'Do be careful, Pierce. Please do.' "

Elizabeth felt a lump in her throat and had to make an effort to speak past it. "What became of her?"

"She wore nothing but black and talked of nothing but returning to Wolverton Manor until the day she died. A fever took her when I was about twenty. She never got over my father's death." Pierce's voice suddenly became louder and clearer and turned cold again, as if he realized he had just revealed more than he'd intended. "My coward father killed her too, that night."

Along with all the kindness and love and hope in you as well, Elizabeth thought. *I could almost hate your father for that myself.*

Caught off guard by that last stray bit of feeling, Elizabeth forced herself to dismiss it as an overreaction to Pierce's story, and put it out of her mind.

"I'm going to get it all back," Pierce said icily. "All

of it. Every brick, every blade of grass, every blessed trapping of the aristocratic life a Darkridge earl is supposed to have.''

Elizabeth didn't reply. She finished cleaning his wound and wrapped a clean strip of linen around it, tying the ends. It took a bit of effort, for her two hands together couldn't span his arm. As she worked, she noticed that his skin felt soft, an odd contrast to the granite-hard muscles flexing beneath her fingers.

She pulled away the instant she was done. ''There,'' she said a bit too brightly. ''It's not so bad as it looks.''

''Speaking as the man who's been bleeding all night,'' he retorted, ''I have to disagree. It's damned painful.''

Elizabeth ignored his sarcastic complaint. It was transparently clear that he was trying to cover up for his brief moment of vulnerability by turning irascible again. She was not going to be goaded into another argument. She smiled sweetly. ''It will feel better by the morrow.''

''God, you are an optimistic little tender-heart.'' He said it like an insult.

''So sorry I don't measure up,'' she replied, gently mocking him. ''It's not easy for everyone to be so ruthless and blackhearted as you. I shall have to try harder.''

Stepping around his clothes on the floor, she carried the basin to the window, and emptied it into the dark alley below. She heard the creak of bed ropes as Pierce, apparently weary of trying to spark her temper, let himself fall back on the mattress.

He remained silent, but Elizabeth could feel his gaze on her back. She leaned against the sill a moment. ''I suppose,'' she said, ''that it would look rather odd for the Prince of Wales and his man to be sharing the same room. I think I should ask the innkeeper for another.''

''You probably could talk him into giving you the entire inn,'' Pierce said caustically. ''But don't feel you have to leave on my account.''

''I don't.''

''Then don't go.''

He said it casually, as if he were trying to be flippant,

but Elizabeth thought she heard the most distant note of request in his words.

She reminded herself that his wound was tended, her obligation to him done; there was no reason to stay in his room. Returning to the writing desk, she set the basin down and lifted the pitcher to pour some fresh water. She could just walk out the door and leave him to stew in his own peevishness until it was time to leave tomorrow. It might do him some good.

But it wasn't what she wanted.

The thought flitted through her head and almost made her drop the pitcher. She set it down with a thump, her hand trembling. Why did the idea of being separated from Pierce for even a short time give her such an odd, twisting feeling inside?

Her heart supplied the answer before her mind even completed the question.

She was falling in love with him.

Elizabeth stood very still for a minute, reason scattering while her heart thudded in her chest. The next instant, she busied herself wetting a length of fresh linen, trying to chase the feeling away.

How could she possibly be in love with Pierce Wolverton? She had met any number of suitable, kindhearted, upstanding men in London, and had never felt the slightest stirring of feeling for any of them.

What was wrong with her that she should feel this way about such a brooding, aloof, cynical rogue as Lord Darkridge? He was determined to live a life apart, rejecting even so basic a human emotion as sympathy. He didn't want to be redeemed. He didn't want to change.

Elizabeth tried to rein in her bolting emotions. With her back carefully turned to Pierce, she concentrated on keeping her hand steady as she washed her face and neck and arms—as much of her as she dared without unbuttoning too many buttons. When she refastened her collar and cuffs, it seemed to take forever, her fingers tingling, the buttons suddenly slippery.

Doing her best to think logically, she reasoned that it was almost morning, and she hated to risk her luck with

Mr. Bacon by rousing the innkeeper from his bed a second time. She supposed she could wait until later in the day to request separate accommodations.

Besides, what was there to fear? Back in the gaol in Northampton—it seemed like ages ago, but it had only been days—Pierce had promised not to touch her. He hadn't made any sexually suggestive overtures since then.

For now, she would stay, but only for her own comfort—not for Pierce or any fleeting, outlandish feelings she might have. She was starving and thirsty, and she wasn't going to leave that entire platter of food and drink for the Earl of Irritable.

She crossed to the tray beside the bed, not letting herself look at him, and picked up one of the goblets. A sniff told her it was some sort of tavern punch, a heady mixture of wine, juice, spices, and sugar. Frowning, she poured half her cup into Pierce's empty one, then moved back to the pitcher and thinned her drink with water.

She sipped at it as she turned to survey the little banquet. There were cold veal cutlets and chicken legs, thick slices of roast beef, cheese, dark bread, and apple tarts. The thoughtful innkeeper had even provided pewter plates. Taking a large portion of everything on the tray, Elizabeth went and sat in the chair by the window.

When she finally got the courage to cast a sideways glance at Pierce, she found that he was watching her with an odd look in his eyes.

It was a decidedly hungry expression—and it wasn't directed at the chicken leg in her hand.

His gaze still on her, he reached for his goblet and tossed off its entire contents in one gulp. Elizabeth thought of commenting on his drinking overmuch, or reminding him of his promise, then thought the better of it.

She wouldn't want him to think she was nervous.

Turning back to the window, she tried to concentrate on the taste of her food. Instead she found herself listening to the sound of Pierce eating as he reclined on the bed.

She tried to get comfortable in the chair, and found

herself wondering if he had put his shirt back on yet. She didn't want to look to find out. Finishing her meal, she set the cup and plate beside her chair.

After a while, she could hear that he had finished eating as well. They sat in silence.

Finally Elizabeth's nerves couldn't stand it a second longer. She turned his way. "Listen, perhaps it *would* be best if I . . ."

Her words trailed off as she frowned at the bed. He had fallen asleep, one hand across his bare chest, the other flung out over the edge of the mattress.

She slouched down in the chair and scowled at him, half relieved and half annoyed. His chest rose and fell rhythmically. A snore rippled out of him.

She chided herself for her foolishness, for misinterpreting his glance and his mood. Perhaps she had been mistaken about everything else as well. What made her think she could see through his words and actions and understand his true feelings?

How could she ignore the evidence before her own eyes? He was exactly what he wanted to be: cold and distant. The man had been working at thinking only of himself for fifteen years. It was his way of life.

There was no chance, she thought sadly, that Pierce Wolverton could pass as a prince by any leap of the imagination; he was barely a gentleman, except when it suited him for some nefarious purpose. True, he had a few admirable qualities. He was strong and single-minded and didn't let anything stand in the way of what he wanted.

But she wasn't what he wanted. She was in the way.

And if he were to discover that she was falling in love with him, he would only use that love to manipulate her.

Elizabeth curled up in the chair and closed her eyes. She wasn't going to cry, she vowed, and she wasn't going to leave, either. He didn't care about her? Her presence wasn't disquieting to him in the least? Fine. She wouldn't care, either.

He had promised not to touch her unless she came to him, and she'd be damned before she would *ever* give him that satisfaction. She was exhausted, and she needed some sleep. And she was going to have it, difficult as it might be in this deuced chair.

Tomorrow, she would go back to London without him. Just walk away. Every highwayman for himself. Pierce was definitely right as far as that idea was concerned.

She blinked away the burning sensation in her eyes. Definitely.

Pierce came awake with a start. Sitting up, he rubbed a hand over his face, squinting in the bright light. Warm summer air and the full sun of late afternoon drifted together in the open window. God, had he slept that long?

He pushed off the blanket, then wondered how he had come to be covered with a blanket. His boots were off as well.

He slanted a look at Elizabeth. She was sprawled in the chair, asleep, her legs slung over one side, her head lolled back over the other. She was going to have the devil of a kink in her neck when she awakened, he thought with a wince.

He moved to the edge of the bed, scowling. The boots and blanket were just one more act of kindness on her part; it seemed nothing could squelch that quality in Elizabeth. Not even all the snarling and snapping he had done.

Well, he could hardly be blamed for that, he decided sullenly. God help him, he was only a man. How much was he supposed to withstand? She was constantly within arm's length, yet beyond his reach because of that idiotic promise he had made.

He rubbed his sore shoulder as he studied her sleeping form. She looked so young in repose, so pale and sweet it made him ache, right in the center of his chest.

Nothing a quick tumble wouldn't cure, he assured himself.

No, he swore softly, looking away. Much as it irked him to admit it, that wasn't true. From the start, this slip of a girl had wreaked havoc with his reason and made him feel things he didn't want to feel. He vividly remembered the fear that had gripped him when she suddenly appeared at the Hibberts' house, a fear so cold it was like an icicle jammed into his heart. He had wanted to rail at her for the supreme stupidity of coming after him. It made no sense, that she should be willing to risk her own neck for him.

It showed that she cared about him.

That had filled him with an unsettling maelstrom of emotions. One minute, he wanted to take her in his arms and kiss her breathless, the next he exploded at her, then before he knew it, he was spilling his guts about every agonizing detail of his family history.

He couldn't fathom it. What was wrong with him? What was this power she had over him? He settled his gaze on her again.

He wasn't the only one transfixed by her magic, he consoled himself, thinking of the way Elizabeth had talked her way into the innkeeper's finest room, bold as brass, with nothing more than a bag of pebbles and a borrowed watch to her credit.

Given enough time and the right props, the girl could likely talk the moon and the stars into falling from the sky.

The idea of her sending the money upon returning to London was almost enough to make him laugh, except that he had no doubt she would do it. She was that soft-hearted. Didn't want to hurt anyone. How naive.

Elizabeth uttered a slight moan in her sleep, her body shifting in a way that suddenly rekindled the desire in him, the smoldering embers he had been trying to douse. Damn her, she set his senses afire without even trying. He itched to walk over and scoop her into his arms and carry her back to the bed.

He didn't want to think anymore; he had done too bloody much of that. He wanted to kiss her, caress her, lose himself in that sweetness and the soft, hot passion that he knew simmered just beneath her surface.

He had glimpsed it, tasted it ever so briefly. God, their last kiss seemed like a century ago.

He rose from the bed. Why fight it? *Why?*

Because he had promised not to touch her, not until she came to him.

He turned away from her, bracing his arms against the wall, wanting to put his fist through it. He struggled to get his breathing and himself under control—and cursed for the thousandth time the impulse that had made him say those words. Wrestling with that blasted vow was rapidly turning him into a lunatic with Satan's own temper.

He had almost lost it completely while she tended his wound, when she had leaned over him, her hair innocently tickling his shoulder, her breasts beckoning to be cupped in his hands. Jesus, he'd felt as if he would shatter and fall in splinters to the floor.

Then, when she had touched him, oh, God, when she had touched him . . . her fingers sliding along his bare arm, light and warm and tantalizing. He had come within a hairbreadth of taking her, rolling her on the bed beneath him—and promises be damned.

He glanced over his shoulder and glared at her. Did she truly have no idea of the way she affected him?

The worst part was that she was so close to surrendering, to herself and to him. He had felt it. She had trembled at the sensation of his skin against hers. He had deliberately flexed the muscles of his arm—despite the pain from the cut—teasing her, trying to draw her in and let him surround her with the passion they both felt.

As before, she pulled away. He swore under his breath. Always she withdrew. Always gave in to the ghosts that still danced in the depths of her eyes—the husband who had abused her, the baby she had lost.

Hellfire and damnation. He turned and took a step toward the chair.

It was time for her to stop flinching at phantoms. They were no more than memories, illusions; he was solid and real, and strong enough for them both. If only she would let him, he could chase the shadows away. He could show her that there was nothing to fear, not with him.

She needed him.

From a distant corner of his being, barely acknowledged, came an answering thought: *he needed her.*

He moved toward the chair, hesitation and questions falling away like a tattered cloak that was no longer needed. He stole across the floor, his heart pumping, his entire body alive with longing.

He reached out to touch the glossy glory of Elizabeth's black tresses.

It was time.

Chapter 17

Elizabeth awakened to what she thought was the breeze caressing her cheek.

She kept her eyes shut and turned her head away, murmuring sleepily. A cramping pain in her neck brought her fully awake. She sat up with an oath, rubbing·at the stiffness and wondering how long she had been asleep.

It was then that she saw him.

Pierce stood beside her chair, still bare to the waist, looking down at her with an expression that was at once gentle and scorching.

Elizabeth blinked, one hand still on her throat, half expecting him to shimmer and disappear with the rest of her drowsy dreams. He remained as solid and real as the thick-hewn chair beneath her. The glow from the late afternoon sun that spilled in the window bathed the tense muscles of his arms with flickering fire. He didn't move.

The flat planes of his chest rose and fell rapidly and the sound of his breathing was harsh in the stillness of the room. Elizabeth's heart began to pound. Her skin tingled. Why, oh why, *why* hadn't she left when she had the chance? She was a thousand times a fool for believing a mere promise would make him honorable.

A warning ready on her lips, she started to rise.

She wasn't even fully on her feet when Pierce reached out, wordlessly, slipping an arm about her waist. She didn't have time to utter a syllable before he pulled her up against the solid wall of his chest and kissed her, his mouth capturing hers with breath-stealing swiftness.

Elizabeth tried to arch away, but he crushed her to him, one of his hands splayed across her shoulders, the other tangling in her hair. His tongue traced her lips, opened them, darted inside then out again, forceful, demanding. He tasted of the wine punch, spicy and exotic and potent.

She made a sound of protest deep in her throat, yet she trembled at the fierceness of his desire for her, so blatant she didn't know how she could possibly have doubted its presence earlier. Fiery heat raced through her body at his touch, at the feeling of his fingers caressing her, flexing and curving around her shoulders, kneading.

His lips began to move more slowly, in a long, deep, wet kiss that left Elizabeth dizzy. Her knees went weak but he held her clasped to him. Damnation, he had promised! He wasn't supposed to make her feel this way, shivering and hot and aching with a feeling she couldn't name.

It *wasn't* love. It couldn't be. She had known love all her life; it was pure and honest and reassuring. This was wild and reckless and terrifying in its intensity, all wrapped up with wanting and fear and the anger that always flared between them and, yes, desire. *Yes.*

Pierce deepened the kiss even more, his tongue exploring her mouth, tasting, claiming. She uttered a soft whimper, but even she couldn't tell if it meant protest or pleasure anymore. God help her, she had been right about the physical need he had for her, more than right. Had she been right about the rest—the tenderness she had glimpsed in him, the caring she hoped he might have for her?

Did he feel only forceful passion . . . or something more?

She had just begun to wonder about it when Pierce's hands slid down her spine, coming to rest at the small of her back. It was almost as if he had sensed her thoughts and offered an answer. He had no other hold on her now save that feather-light touch. The message was clear, the choice hers. He was giving her the chance to break the kiss, pull away, rail at him, remind him of his promise.

Reason and rationality swirled from her mind like bits of paper swept away by a windstorm. She could no longer deny that this man awakened some secret part of her, an ancient, undiscovered magic that met and mingled with his own to form a bond, a feeling unlike any she had ever experienced.

She had tasted it briefly, the few times Pierce had kissed her, touched her, held her. Now it bloomed and filled every sinew of her being, like the sun, but hotter, like melting honey, but sweeter. It was rare and delicious and she wanted it to go on forever.

Unable to resist the heady sensation, she leaned against him, her tongue stroking and playing with his.

He groaned and opened his mouth to her gentle invasion, his fingers kneading the muscles of her back. Her fists, still pressed against his chest to push him away, slowly relaxed and moved upward in a tentative exploration of his broad, muscular angles and warm skin. One hand found his pounding heartbeat and lingered there.

His fingers played along her back, pressing her forward, fitting her body to his.

The instant their hips came together Elizabeth stiffened. She felt his hardness straining in his breeches, thrusting against her belly. An icy bolt of fear shot through her, frosting the warm sensuality in her muscles.

"No!" She tore her mouth from his on a sob. "No, I can't!"

Before she could pull away, Pierce took her face between his hands, holding her still. "Tell me to stop," he murmured, his voice deep and strong like thunder amid hot summer rain. "Tell me you *want* me to stop and I will."

Elizabeth, shivering, closed her eyes to shut out the intensity of his passionate gaze. Another second and the heat in those fathomless dark brown eyes would wrest sensual whispers of longing from her lips. Her mind scrambled to collect all the reasons she should demand he unhand her with haste. She *must* resist the wild impulses he sparked in her, must ignore her racing heart and languid limbs—and the emotion in his voice.

That, more than anything else, almost made her forget what she knew of lovemaking: the pain, the frightening possibility of pregnancy. No, it was too much to risk! She thought the word *stop,* willed it to her tongue, but failed to force it past her lips.

She couldn't, not when every fiber of her body and soul were sighing, singing, crying, clamoring *yes.*

Her lower lip quivered. She couldn't bring herself to speak, or open her eyes, or move toward him or away. Fear and confusion and helpless longing twined in her. She bit her lip to still its trembling. A tear slipped from beneath her lashes.

She felt Pierce's breath, warm and moist on her cheek as he leaned closer. He kissed away the tear, then dropped light kisses over her eyelids, her nose, her temple, her jaw.

His voice was infinitely soft when he whispered, ''There are as many ways to make love, Elizabeth, as there are days in the year. Probably more.'' He brushed his lips across her hair, tracing a path to her other cheek. ''Not all of them will get you with child.''

Elizabeth hadn't realized until that moment that she'd been holding her breath. She exhaled and it came out as a trembly sigh. Was it true? Could it be possible to know fully this indefinable magic they seemed to share, without pain or risk? The idea made her shiver with apprehension—and anticipation.

She tried again to think of all the reasons she should resist, but couldn't find a single one. The tenderness in his words and his touch stole the hesitation from her heart.

She took a deep breath and opened her eyes. The fire in his gaze seared the rest of her objections to cinders.

He ran his thumb over her mouth. ''Let me show you.''

Unable to voice her answer, Elizabeth tilted her chin up to welcome his kiss.

With a groan, Pierce caught her about the waist and lifted her against him. He kissed her thoroughly before he let her feet return to the floor, sliding her body down his.

Elizabeth rested her cheek against his bare chest, speaking on swollen, tingling lips. "I . . . I'm afraid."

"I know," he said gently, his voice thick with desire. "I'll not hurt you. Trust me." Taking her hand in his, he stepped toward the bed.

Elizabeth held back, unable to overcome her ingrained resistance. She couldn't quell a memory of Geoffrey and his idea of lovemaking, the way he used to push her down on the bed, lift her nightdress and have his way with her.

Pierce gave her a rueful look and didn't try to tug her forward. "All right then, no bed. We'll not go anywhere near the bed."

His gaze flicked about the room and settled on the other blue brocade wing chair, the one that sat beside the grate. Raising an eyebrow, he looked down at Elizabeth and smiled.

The tenderness in his expression sailed straight to her heart, swift and true as an arrow, loosening—at least a little—the fear that had gripped her for so long. That all-too-rare smile reminded her that Pierce wasn't like Geoffrey, not at all. He wasn't filled with some boorish need to assert his physical superiority; Pierce knew how to use his strength gently, how to share it with her.

She drew courage from him, and felt a bit more of her old anxiety slip away.

He led her over to the chair and settled himself comfortably, legs wide.

Elizabeth, still holding his hand, looked down at him in confusion. He pulled her closer until she was standing between his thighs.

"Take this off," he murmured, tugging at her frock coat.

Elizabeth still felt reticent, yet she was mesmerized by his caressing tone, by the promise of being gently enveloped by his strength and power. Surrendering to his hypnotic command, she shrugged the garment from her shoulders and let it slip to the floor.

Pierce's gaze never left her face. "This too." He ran a finger over her waistcoat.

Elizabeth trembled, and her mouth and throat suddenly felt dry. She realized with a little jolt of surprise that the feeling came not from fear, but from excitement, a heart-quickening sense of approaching the unknown.

She unfastened the buttons on her waistcoat and let it fall.

Pierce's wandering hand strayed downward and came to rest on the waistband of her breeches. His eyes had darkened to a shade deeper than warm spiced wine. His lashes half-lowered, he looked up at her in unspoken request.

Elizabeth's heart gave one little skip, then took up a new and reckless pace. The heat radiating from his fingertips held her captive. She unlaced the oversized pants and stepped out of them before she realized just how little she now wore—a white shirt that fell to her knees, no more, not even the briefest camisole or pantaloons underneath.

The air in the room seemed hot and hard to breathe, despite the open window. Her very blood seemed to be afire, surging toward the center of her being. Pierce wasn't even touching her at the moment, yet she felt a warm moistness between her legs that brought a flush of color to her cheeks.

He smiled, slow and sensual, as if sensing her innocent response. Rather than asking her to remove the shirt as she had expected, he eased her down onto his lap, moving his legs so she sat crosswise on his thighs.

She tentatively rested one arm on his bronzed shoulder for balance. He felt very muscular beneath her, all his strength and power held in check, like a stallion on a very short rein. He wanted to go much more quickly, she could tell, but he was holding himself back.

It gave her a feeling akin to wonderment as she looked down at his smoldering gaze, his sharp-winged brows, the boyish tangle of dark hair over his forehead. She hadn't thought him capable of putting anyone's needs ahead of his own; his thoughtfulness touched her, and made her realize she had judged him too hastily.

Pierce Wolverton was a man of many facets. She would

be wise to remember that. It would be impossible to truly know him until she had discovered them all.

At the moment, however, she only wanted to explore one facet, in all its dizzying glory, and to her amazement she found herself becoming the impatient one. When he reached up to touch her hair, she closed her eyes, turning her face into his hand, kissing his fingers. A low groan reverberated through his chest, and he quickly moved to unfasten the top button of her shirt.

He worked it loose, then the one below it, then the next until the white fabric, her last bit of covering, opened to reveal her bare skin. Elizabeth squeezed her eyes shut, breathing hard.

"Shh," he said, kissing the soft place behind her ear. "You'll be all right, I promise."

She gulped and nodded, trying to force away the fear that hovered at the back of her mind.

He shifted so that she was leaning backward, supported only by his arm. The shirt parted and Pierce slipped the garment down over her shoulders, exposing her completely to his gaze. Elizabeth felt a flush over her entire body.

"You are so beautiful," he murmured, his fingers moving over the curve of her breast, caressing, stroking. He cupped the soft swell in his palm, and his thumb flicked at the nipple. Her harsh breathing deepened into a moan. He placed a damp kiss at the hollow of her throat, then teased her with little touches of his tongue along her collarbone. She tossed her head, feeling helplessly vulnerable in this position—and helplessly eager for more of the icy-hot sensations he lavished on her body.

His mouth lingered along the arching column of her neck then, suddenly, shifted to her breast, nipping and laving her delicate skin. His tongue played in circles about the tip, then he nibbled it ever so gently. Elizabeth's breath caught in her throat, turning her moan into a gasp of pleasure. She dug her fingers into his leg. With a growl, he turned his attentions to her other breast, kissing and teasing and suckling.

Elizabeth's lips parted as an intense, unfamiliar feeling began, deep in the center of her belly, a curling, tightening sensation. Pierce's fingers again touched her breast, trailing the moistness from his kiss downward, over her ribs and belly in a damp, tingling path. When he touched the dark triangle between her legs Elizabeth cried out and sat up suddenly, grasping his wrist.

He gazed into her eyes, silent, until she slowly, hesitantly released his hand. Frightened and excited and breathless all at once, she leaned into his chest, laying her head against the solid, sculpted curve of his shoulder. She touched her mouth to his skin, tasting the salt of his own excitement. To her amazement, the little kiss of acceptance made him shudder.

With one hand he held her close, and with the other began a slow, erotic game unlike anything Elizabeth had ever experienced. Never had she been touched so intimately; his caress and the feelings it aroused were all utterly, breathtakingly new.

Pierce's fingers swirled and played over her downy curls before slipping lower, to the damp cleft between her thighs. He parted her, opened her to his touch. His thumb found an almost unbearably sensitive spot and he rubbed it gently. Elizabeth gasped in quick gulps of air between soft, sharp cries of surprise and pleasure. She pressed her face against his throat, feeling his pulse throbbing beneath her cheek.

His chest rose and fell as rapidly as her own. His thumb moved faster as one finger traced the damp outline of her feminine channel. The trembling sensation in her belly built to a feverish intensity, like icicles and sparks clashing and raining through her body in a sensual storm. She was shaking, her hips lifting to meet his touch, her fingers digging into the muscles of his shoulder and his thigh.

She closed her lips on the slick skin of his throat, kissing him hard, nipping him. His thumb slowed, pressing against her swollen nubbin in a lazy circling motion, and the tension deep within her spun so tight she thought she would go mad. She could barely breathe, couldn't utter anything more coherent than a soft, pleading moan.

She needed some sort of release, and sensed that he knew exactly how to give it to her, but was deliberately prolonging this sweet torture. Need overwhelmed her, but she bit her lip to keep from begging him.

He slid one finger inside her, withdrew it, then pushed forward again with merciless slowness. *"Pierce,"* she gasped, arching shamelessly against his hand.

He nudged her head up with his shoulder, taking her mouth as he slipped a second finger inside her, stretching, moving deeper and faster. Elizabeth groaned against his mouth, opening her lips beneath his. His tongue swept her mouth, thrusting into her moist recess just as his fingers moved in her dampness below.

The dual onslaught proved her undoing. The storm in her belly broke suddenly, crashing over her with stunning force. Fire and ice swept through her body, leaving her undulating and shuddering in his arms, crying out into his mouth with an astonished groan of ecstasy. When the waves ebbed into little tremors she lay limp in his arms, spent, mind and body floating on a cloud of exquisite sensation.

Pierce kissed her closed eyes, wrapping his arms around her. As she lay against his chest, her breath tickling his neck in little sighs, he could never remember feeling such pleasure at giving pleasure. He sensed that he had been the first to bring her to release, and it filled him with a purely masculine sense of satisfaction.

He indulged in a smile and stroked her back, consumed by possessiveness, and something more—a feeling much stronger, yet elusive, mingled with passion, protectiveness and tenderness.

She shifted in his lap, bringing a groan from his lips and his mind back to his physical predicament. He was still aching with his own need. After drawing on every ounce of his self-restraint, his control was nearly depleted. Elizabeth's wildly sensual response, her small cries of pleasure, and the instinctive thrusting of her hips all beckoned him to drive himself into her. For her sake,

he could not. Not because of the chance of pregnancy—
he knew of ways to avoid that—but because of her fear.
She wasn't completely ready, not yet.

She raised her head to look at him, her eyes sparkling
like lavender gemstones, her cheeks flushed and glisten-
ing with the glow of her release. "Isn't there more?"
she whispered.

"More?" He grinned wryly, taking hold of her hips
to still her agonizingly arousing movements. "Have I an
insatiable little vixen on my hands?"

"No. I . . ." Her lashes drifted shyly downward. "I
meant, for you."

Her hand slid over his shoulder to rest at the center of
his chest, then slipped lower, to his ribs.

"God, Elizabeth." He closed his eyes and swallowed
hard, gripped by an excitement unlike any he had ever
known. He found the merest brush of her hand a hundred
times more exciting than the most skilled caress of a
courtesan. "You're going to be the death of me."

"I think not," she said mischievously. Her fingers
came to rest on the waistband of his breeches. "I should
think you able to withstand at least as much as I."

His eyes flew open and he saw her regarding him with
an innocent little smile that filled him with more heat
than her touch. "Elizabeth," he choked out in soft warning, unsure how long he could last without utterly losing
control. The urge to thrust into the very depths of her
femininity seared him, body and soul.

She started to unfasten his breeches, trying unsuccessfully to change her expression to complete seriousness.
"I only wish to be fair." She moved her leg a bit, just
enough to allow her access to that part of him that so
ached for her attentions. The laces weren't even completely undone when his shaft spilled into her hand.

He sucked in a ragged breath as she hesitantly, lightly
ran her nails along his length. When she rubbed her fingertips over the swollen tip, his entire body jerked in
response, nearly landing them both on the floor.

"*Elizabeth!*" he ground out.

Her hand moved away. She gazed at him, her eyes

liquid and languorous and filled with feminine curiosity. "But there must be a way I can please you without . . . without risk."

"There is, but I—" He lost the rest in a groan as her fingers returned to stroke him.

"Then you must let me try," she whispered. "I want to give you pleasure as you gave me."

He stopped objecting, helpless against the white-hot flashes of ecstasy that arced through him. With one hand he gripped the arm of the chair while his other arm supported her back.

She held him more firmly now, moving her hand up and down his length slowly, experimentally. Her gaze, at first fascinated by his pulsing manhood, now lifted to his face. Her eyes had darkened with desire to a truly royal shade of purple. She kept watching him, smiling at his reaction.

With her hair tumbling about her shoulders, her lips wet and swollen and her pale curves framed by the rumpled shirt, she looked the very image of every man's ultimate fantasy, a woman at once sweetly innocent and wildly sensual. Pierce's breath choked out in harsh bursts as he struggled against the urgent desire to lower her to the rug and sheath himself in her moist heat.

He wanted to make her his, he thought fiercely, wholly and completely and forever.

He never got the chance to even wonder where that extraordinary idea had come from; in the next heartbeat all reason fled as Elizabeth's fingers took up a new and playful position, rubbing his thickness against her bare thigh.

"God." He squeezed his eyes shut. "Oh God."

Leaning forward, she kissed his temple, his cheek, then teased him with her tongue—exactly as he had done to her—darting a damp path along his collarbone. He struggled for breath, for sanity.

Suddenly he felt her lips on his in an open-mouthed kiss, her tongue thrusting forward. Her fingers closed tightly about his manhood.

The sun and all the stars in the universe exploded inside him in that single second. A hoarse shout rolled up from deep in his chest and she swallowed it hungrily. A spasm shook his body and with a liquid rush, he found release, his seed flowing over her hand and her skin. The sensation was so intense and lasted so long he thought for a moment he might pass out.

When reason returned and his eyes opened, he was looking up into her smiling face. She dropped another light kiss on his lips, her expression one of almost feline satisfaction, like a cat who had just conquered a very large canary.

Still breathing heavily, he enfolded her against him. "Oh, sweet Elizabeth." He wrapped his hands in her hair and tilted her head back. "My sweet, sweet Elizabeth."

He kissed her, deep and long and hard. Then he lifted her in his arms, shirt and all. Rising from the chair, he strode toward the bed. She shivered against him but made no protest.

He threw back the blankets and laid her on the sheets.

She didn't try to draw away as he settled himself beside her, but looked up at him, her eyes wide and shining with newfound wonder. "Isn't there . . ." Her voice was a soft, unsteady whisper, "more?"

He laughed, a genuine, full laugh unlike any he had enjoyed in a very long time. "I've created a tyrant."

She ducked her head, a blush dusting her cheeks.

Pierce pulled the sheet over them. He tipped her head up and ran his thumb over the delicate curve of her jawline. Even as he reveled in her newfound enthusiasm, he heard the note of reticence that still lingered in her voice. She wasn't ready yet . . . but soon. He would give her time. He wanted to be careful of her feelings.

That was a novel sensation for him, and it bewildered him. He didn't know how it had come about, but this girl had come to mean a great deal to him. It made him uneasy to discover just how much.

He had been quite comfortable thinking of Elizabeth Blackerby Thornhill as enemy, thorn in his side, infuriating rival, beautiful object of desire, or bewitching obsession. Now he didn't know how to think of her, and it made him deucedly uncomfortable.

Just as she needed time to get used to the idea of lovemaking, he needed time to get used to the idea of her fitting into his life in some new and different way.

But he wasn't sure how long that would take—and he knew that time was a commodity in short supply and dwindling rapidly. They had to leave the inn, and soon. London awaited, and St. Bartholomew's Fair and Montaigne and his gold.

Pierce forced those thoughts away. Pulling Elizabeth into his arms, he finally answered her question. "Yes, there's more," he whispered, stroking her back. "There's this."

He kneaded and caressed her muscles until she closed her eyes on a sigh. Even after her breathing relaxed into the slow, even patterns of sleep, Pierce still held her close. And wondered how much time with her would ever be enough.

Chapter 18

Elizabeth wasn't sure how long she had slept when she felt Pierce nudging her awake, but her body still tingled in all her most sensitive places. Opening one eye, she saw that it was dark out, the room illuminated only by moonlight.

"Wake up," Pierce murmured. "It's time for us to go."

"Mmm," she replied sleepily, letting her lashes drift downward. Her reasonable side realized he was right; they had taken an awful chance staying as long as they had. But another part of her was reluctant to leave. Once she had feared sharing a bed with Pierce, but now, with him beside her, it didn't seem so frightening. He filled up those dark, haunted hollows of her memory where Geoffrey had lurked so long.

Pierce placed a kiss at the small of her back. "Up, my laze-abed lady, before the innkeeper stops thinking about the joys of hosting royalty and starts thinking of cold hard cash."

She felt the mattress move as he got up.

"Before we go," he continued. "We have matters of importance to discuss."

"Which matters?" she mumbled.

"London," he stated in a clipped, serious tone. "And the Fair."

This drew her full attention and made her sit up. His gaze lingered over her nakedness before she belatedly thought to cover herself with the sheet. "What about the Fair?" she asked suspiciously.

He had already donned his breeches. Sitting on the

bed beside her, he started to button his shirt. Elizabeth caught a glimpse of some strong emotion in his eyes, just for a second. She didn't know what to call it, only that it seemed very determined and aimed utterly at her.

"I've decided that you shouldn't go. To the Fair, that is."

"You've decided *what*?" she cried indignantly.

"Try to be logical, Elizabeth," he said patiently, as if he had given the matter a great deal of thought. "You are a disaster with a gun, and that shipment is going to have more guards than an heir apparent on Coronation Day. You'll never succeed."

"I'll never—you've—oh!" Speechless with fury, Elizabeth started to leap to her feet, and instead wound up wrestling with the sheet as she tried to get out of the bed. "If you think that . . . that one time together is going to make me bow out of my plans for Montaigne, you've got a lot more thinking to do!"

"Before you explode at me, I think you should hear me out." He straightened, speaking in a commanding tone that Elizabeth found infuriating. "I'm willing to take the gold alone . . . and share some of it with you."

"Share?" she spluttered, still trying to cover herself with the sheet. "Share! I'm not about to settle for your leavings and I don't want your help. I've done fine on my own—"

"No." He shook his head. "You haven't. We've already had that discussion."

"That's right! We . . . have." Her eyes widened. "And this is just one more of your schemes, isn't it? All you care about is keeping me away from Montaigne's gold." Her gaze stabbed the blue wing chair. "Maybe all of this—"

She never got to finish that thought. He grabbed her about the waist and yanked her up against him, hard. His kiss was slow and endless and it sent objections and angry words spinning from her mind.

"Last night," he said tightly once he released her mouth, "had nothing to do with Montaigne."

It was a moment before Elizabeth could gather her

wits enough to answer. "Th . . . then why?" she asked, her heart pounding. "Why is it so important that I not go to the Fair?"

He released her and moved away, his shoulders rising in a slight shrug. He finished buttoning his shirt. "I only thought to save you the trouble. There's no sense in both of us trying to take that coach when I can do it alone."

She regarded him with pursed lips, sensing that there was more to it than that. She wasn't quite sure, didn't dare hope, that he was actually so concerned about her that he was trying to protect her . . . that he cared for her.

Did he? Or was she only inferring what she wanted to hear? It was much more likely that his offer was part of some scheme. She knew he was capable of *acting* infatuated with her—she had fallen for it once before, the night of that awful masquerade party. It made her hurt, sharply, right in the center of her chest, to think this might be just another ruse.

"So?" he said impatiently. "Are you going to do the practical thing for once? I'll take the gold alone and give you, say, a third. Invest it wisely and it should be enough to take care of your widows and orphans for years."

Elizabeth chewed at the inside of her cheek, trying to decide whether he was telling the truth. It would be so tempting to let Pierce take over as he wanted to do, to turn to his strength and let him take the risks.

But he might be lying. And even if he wasn't, she had a hard time believing he had changed so much that he would share the gold. He might *think* he meant it, especially after the magical afternoon they had just spent together. But once he had that gold in his hands, he would keep it all for his own plans. She shook her head. Pierce Wolverton had lived alone too long to change so quickly.

"No," she said flatly. "I can't accept."

"Why the devil not?"

"Because I don't trust you."

He stood silent for a minute, eyes glittering with affront. Then his expression darkened and he turned away. "Honest to a bloody God-damned fault, aren't you?"

He snatched up his coat and waistcoat from the floor. "I suppose I should be grateful for your frankness."

Elizabeth felt a clenching sensation in her stomach. He almost sounded hurt—or was it all part of an act? "I—"

"How can you say you don't trust me?" he demanded. "After what just happened between us?"

"That was different." She struggled to come up with the right words. "It was . . . physical."

"Don't give me that, madam," he said hotly, pointing at the chair. "*That* wasn't just lust and you damn well know it."

Elizabeth's cheeks colored and she bowed her head, her eyes on the sheet that tangled about her body. "This isn't coming out right at all," she said helplessly. "I *do* trust you, at least that way. What I meant was—"

"What you meant was that you still believe I'm a self-interested, black-hearted bastard, except perhaps in bed."

"No—"

"Forget it. It doesn't matter." He picked up her clothes and tossed them to her. "Get dressed. We have to leave. Consider my offer rescinded."

He stalked to the door and left without giving her another glance.

Elizabeth felt lower than the heel on a worn-out boot. His reaction made her wonder whether his motives were true after all. Perhaps he *was* trying to protect her, and just couldn't admit that he cared for her. Perhaps she was wrong to doubt him, after the tenderness they had shared, and the . . . magic. God, she had to call it magic; there just wasn't any other word.

Maybe he was *starting* to change. He was at least making some effort, and she had just deflected his good intentions as coldly and sharply as a sword blade.

She dressed quickly and slipped into the darkened hall. The inn was quiet but for a few guests in the public room below. She tiptoed down the stairs, looked about to make sure the innkeeper wasn't nearby, and made a quick, stealthy exit out the front door.

Pierce was waiting for her in the shadows outside, the glower on his face.

"Let's find ourselves a change of clothes." He strode off without waiting for her reply.

"Damnation," Elizabeth said under her breath. She really *had* hurt him. Only days ago, she wouldn't have believed it possible. She tried to think of some way to make amends as they snuck through the darkened streets.

A brief perusal of the town's well-kept homes brought them to a line of laundry left out by a careless housemaid. Pierce helped himself to a shirt and breeches. Elizabeth chose a simple gown and slipped around the corner to change. She made a mental note of the house's location, planning to send payment once she returned to London.

Pierce remained stonily silent when she rejoined him. He led the way out of town, taking the road south toward London, not sparing her a single glance. As she hurried to keep up with his long-legged stride, Elizabeth thought about his offer to share the stolen gold. It was still hard to believe he would do so. But, she had to admit, she could very likely end up with no gold at all, if forced to rely on her own meager skill with a pistol.

But could she trust him?

"I suppose," she said softly, just louder than the rustle of the summer leaves, "that we might work something out about the Fair, if you would still be agreeable."

"I've already rescinded the offer."

"Then perhaps I might make an offer of my own. It's true that you're better with a pistol than I. But I believe I might be better at another aspect of our plan."

"And what precisely is *our* plan?" he scoffed.

"Well, to start with, we don't know enough about how and where and when the gold is to be brought in. I could find out."

"How?"

"I could meet with Montaigne."

"It would never work," he said derisively. "He knows you."

"He knew me as Elizabeth Thornhill, not as Lady

Barnes-Finchley. I could wear heavy cosmetics and a wig. Nell could help me. Montaigne would never recognize me as the poor bedraggled woman he condemned to Fleet.''

Pierce didn't reply for a time. He kept walking, looking straight ahead. ''And once you have the information we need, how do I know you won't keep it to yourself? Or tell me something completely false?''

''You'll have to trust me.''

''Oh, *that's* a pretty request, coming from you.''

Elizabeth ignored his cutting sarcasm and kept her voice calm. ''I shall convey the information to you, and you can carry out the actual robbery. I shall arrange a second assignation with Montaigne to keep him occupied while you're stealing the gold.''

Pierce stopped and swung toward her. ''I don't like it.''

''Why not?'' she asked in exasperation. ''I'm agreeing to stay away from the Fair. Isn't that what you wanted?''

''It's . . .'' He paused. ''It's still too dangerous.''

''How so? You'll have a much better chance if I act as a decoy and distract Montaigne.''

''Not for me, you little fool. For you.''

Elizabeth felt a warm wave of pleasure unfurl within her. Pierce *did* care for her! He was changing despite himself, the stubborn rogue. She looked down at her shoes, hoping he couldn't make out her smile in the darkness. ''Montaigne will never know I'm me,'' she said with quiet determination. ''And would you rather have me involved in drawing room conversation or gunfire?''

Pierce made a low sound of frustration. ''And what do you propose, my little plan-maker, *after* I have fetched the gold? How do you know I won't ride off into the sunset with the whole bloody lot?''

''I shall have to trust you.''

His only response was a pained grimace.

''But I want half, not a third.''

''Greedy as well as insistent.'' He frowned, then turned and resumed walking.

Miffed at his description, she thought of pointing out

his own greed, then changed her mind. There had been too much name-calling and too many accusations between them already. If they were to make any progress at all, she would have to keep this arrangement on a calm and rational level. "Shall I take that as an acceptance?"

"Let me see if I understand this completely. You get the information, I fetch the gold, and we each take half and go our separate ways."

Elizabeth felt a bit hurt by the words "separate ways"—and the sudden coldness in his voice. He seemed eager to be done with her as soon as this business was over.

Of course, he had never said one word to her about any sort of future together. She was a fool for even thinking about it. How could she forget his ultimate goal? He wanted to reclaim not only his estates, but his life as a member of the nobility. An innkeeper's daughter from a small village would never fit into that life, whether he cared for her or not.

He seemed to accept that fact. Why couldn't she? She was good enough for a little companionship, a smattering of affection, a brief tumble now and again—but no more.

"Yes," she said harshly. "We each take half and go our separate ways."

"Fine." He shot back. "Then consider our agreement sealed."

Elizabeth had to swallow past a lump in her throat. "Fine."

She gave up trying to keep pace with him and fell into step behind, struggling with the unhappy feeling that this solution was no solution at all.

Worse, she sensed with a sinking feeling in the pit of her stomach that this truce of theirs was doomed to failure.

Chapter 19

"**N**ow don't ye misunderstand me, Bess," Nell intoned as she stabbed one last pin into Elizabeth's tall white wig. "It's not that I think Montaigne'll remember ye. I just don't like sendin' ye into the lion's den lookin' like such an appetizin' morsel."

Elizabeth sighed and placed a paper cone over her face as her friend dusted the wig with white powder. She'd had an entire week now to go over every detail of this day; nonetheless, she had a frantic flock of butterflies in her stomach as the hour approached.

"Nell," she said patiently, her voice muffled by the paper contraption. "It's the perfect disguise and the perfect plan. I've explained this fifteen times."

Georgiana, sitting on the other side of Elizabeth's bedroom to supervise the preparations, clucked her tongue. "You can explain it to me fifteen more times and I'll still say it's far from perfect. All the rouge and silk in the world won't hide those eyes of yours, Elizabeth, or your voice. He could very well remember you."

"Jus' get in an' out fast as ye can," Nell advised.

"But I have to spend a certain amount of time with him." Elizabeth discarded the cone as soon as Nell set aside the little hand bellows. A cloud of white drifted around her shoulders before settling on her dressing table. "I can't just burst in and start asking questions."

Georgiana's only response to that was a rather frustrated grumble. Trying to bolster her own confidence, Elizabeth leaned forward and surveyed her appearance in the mirror. Never had she worn such an outrageous amount of paint. Her entire face had been artificially paled, her cheeks brightened with rouge and highlighted with a diamond-shaped patch just to one side of her mouth. Nell had dabbed a great deal of carmine on Elizabeth's lips, a thick coating of lead pencil on her brows, and had tried to play down the color of her eyes with brown and sand-hued powders.

"Really, Georgiana," Elizabeth insisted, tucking a stray ringlet from her wig behind her ear. "My own mother, God rest her soul, would never know me." She rose from her seat as Nell began capping the various bottles and jars.

"Hmph," Georgiana replied. "Perhaps, perhaps not. But I suppose no *man* will pay much attention to your eyes once he sees that gown Nell made." Relenting at last, she came over to help Elizabeth don corset, pannier and petticoats while Nell hurried to collect the gown from the bed.

Elizabeth held her breath as they lifted the gown over her head and laced it tight. London's elite might call this outfit stylish, but to her eyes it bordered on garish. The gown was of a shade Nell called "ravish-me red," and perilously low-cut. To Georgiana's dismay, Elizabeth had refused a modesty piece, the better to distract Montaigne.

Georgiana stepped back to look at her with a decidedly worried frown. "I do wish you'd allow one of us to accompany you, Elizabeth."

"Or both o' us," Nell added. "Ye could've just as easily explained in yer note that you *and* two o' yer friends needed advice on investin'."

Elizabeth wanted to dismiss their concern as overprotectiveness, but found herself surreptitiously drying sweaty palms on her skirt. "It was hard enough to get an appointment on such short notice. And I'll have a much better chance of achieving my ends if I'm alone with him."

Trying to convince herself as well as her friends, she picked up her red fan from the dressing table, opened it with a snap, fluttered it artfully and dropped into a low curtsy that exposed a great deal of her bosom. "My *dear*

Mr. Montaigne,'' she said in a practiced, husky tone. ''I do *so* hope you'll assist me in deciding what to do with all my millions.''

Nell nodded at the performance. ''You'll 'ave 'is complete attention all right, Bess, me girl.''

''Yes, but how *much* attention?'' Georgiana asked with an exasperated gesture.

''Please, both of you. I've made up my mind.'' Elizabeth hung the fan by its cord from her wrist, then opened the center drawer of her dressing table. ''I'll be safe enough, I promise.''

She picked up the small dueling pistol she had purchased just for this occasion, and slipped it into her deep skirt pocket. She hadn't loaded it, but her friends didn't know that. As before, she intended to use it only as a threat, if the need arose.

Elizabeth hated to think herself capable of murder, but she didn't trust herself to face Montaigne with a loaded gun.

Georgiana watched her pocket the weapon. ''*That* at least makes me feel a bit better.''

''Good,'' Elizabeth said. ''Because it is either this, or you may fetch my breeches and tricorne and I ride as Blackerby Swift once more.''

''Ye mean, *if* our mysterious visitor 'asn't come back t' take 'em,'' Nell muttered as she handed Elizabeth a flacon of perfume.

Elizabeth dabbed a bit of the scent on her wrists and earlobes and tried unsuccessfully to subdue a shiver; she knew precisely what her friend was referring to. Georgiana and Nell had explained that there had been an intruder in the shop while she was away.

Nothing had been stolen, but some items—including her pistol and disguise—were rearranged, as if someone had picked them up and put them back not quite in place. But the door to the upstairs was locked, and there was no sign that it had been opened. It would have taken a sophisticated thief to have pulled that off.

Or a sophisticated thief-*taker*.

She handed back the bottle of perfume and tried to

shake off her uneasiness with a joke. "I would say you were visited by a ghost, Nell, not an intruder. Perhaps your late husband has been floating about to check up on you."

Nell chuckled but Georgiana rolled her eyes. "Elizabeth, it is not amusing in the least. What if someone has noticed our comings and goings and gotten suspicious?" She folded her arms over her ample bosom. "I'm sure if we told Lord Darkridge, he would take it quite seriously."

"There is no need to involve him." Elizabeth's head snapped up and her gaze locked with Georgiana's. She still hadn't quite forgiven her friend for sending Pierce after her to Northampton, despite any good intentions. Georgiana had explained about her vision, and Elizabeth had told them everything—well, *almost* everything—about how she had been imprisoned and forced into Lowe's gang, and how Pierce had saved her life and accompanied her back to London.

She had also made it abundantly clear that she and the earl had a business arrangement now, nothing more. With Pierce taking the riskier job of raiding the coach, Elizabeth had thought her friends would be happy; instead, they fussed over her more than ever.

It irked her that every person in her life seemed determined to take her under his or her wing and decide what was best for her. Since the day she left Fleet Prison, Elizabeth had been doing her best to stand on her own two feet, and she wanted to stay there, no matter how difficult it might be. Never again would she let someone else make her choices for her, the way Geoffrey had. It had brought her too much sadness and pain.

With a resolute set to her chin, Elizabeth turned to pick up her silk-lined black cloak from the bed. "Nell's intruder has nothing to do with Lord Darkridge's end of the bargain, so there's no need to bother him with it."

"No need a' all," Nell interjected with a smile. "Maybe we'll just mention it the next time 'e drops by."

"He won't *be* dropping by again." Elizabeth felt warmth rush to her cheeks. Pierce had been to see her every day since their return. She had refused to spend any time with him, but he had seemed quite content to visit with Nell and Georgiana before taking his leave. The three of them were growing downright chummy, Elizabeth thought sourly. Georgiana had even said she might have been wrong in her previous opinion of the Earl.

"He has been quite a frequent guest, hasn't he?" Georgiana smiled, lifting a burnished red eyebrow. "One would almost think the man smitten."

"He's very good at making people believe what he wants them to believe," Elizabeth insisted. "His visits were only to make sure of my whereabouts. I'm a link to the gold he's after, and if I disappear on him again, he might be inconvenienced. After today, he'll have the information he needs. There won't be any reason for him to visit me again."

Georgiana didn't reply, but simply held Elizabeth's gaze. Elizabeth had the eerie feeling her friend could see right through to her very soul.

And if she could, what would she see there? Elizabeth wasn't certain herself. She didn't want to think about it. Once Pierce had his half of the gold, he would forget about her in a trice. Better she should chase every bit of feeling for him out of her heart now than suffer later.

Elizabeth fumbled with her fan, purposely dropping it when she could stand Georgiana's uncanny look no longer. She bent over to pick it up. "He doesn't think of me that way," she said softly as she rose. "He really wouldn't know how."

"Who's t' know what a man thinks?" Nell replied. "Most men don't put a whole lot o' their time into thinkin'. They act first and wait fer their brains t' catch up later."

"*I'll* be the one playing catch-up, if I don't leave for my appointment right now," Elizabeth declared in a desperate attempt to change the subject. With an exasperated glance at her friends, she led the way out the door.

With each step, she felt the pistol bump against her leg, and prayed she wouldn't need it.

* * *

The late afternoon sunlight warmed Pierce's shoulders as he strolled about Cavendish Square, keeping Montaigne's town house within sight. The streets were busy at this time of day, as servants bustled about their duties, peddlers ranging from milkmaids to knife-grinders sold their wares, and gentlemen and their ladies enjoyed the summer air. Elizabeth hadn't yet arrived.

Pierce told himself he had come here only to provide Elizabeth his protection, in case something went wrong, but part of him knew that wasn't true.

He wanted to see her again. Something inside him ached to have even a glimpse of her. It irritated him beyond all reason that she had refused to see him this week. Elizabeth Blackerby Thornhill knew more about him than anyone in all of England, yet she still wouldn't trust him.

She was so softhearted, so eager to believe in the essential goodness of mankind. Except for one particular specimen: him.

Her attitude cut him—and sparked his temper to new heights. He was used to seducing, cajoling or otherwise bending women to his will; none of those tactics worked with Elizabeth. She was the first woman he'd met who seemed beyond his control.

As he kept an eye on the passing coaches, a grudging smile tugged at one corner of his mouth. He supposed that challenge was one of the reasons he was so attracted to her.

Elizabeth's beauty, her sweetness, her kind heart drew him in—but it was the constant test of wills, the almost sensual battle for dominance, that kept him awake at night, wishing she lay beside him, held close in the circle of his arms. He sensed the battle would never end between them, and with a jolt of surprise, he realized he didn't want it to.

His feelings for her grew stronger every day, and it was getting damn difficult to keep them inside. They tested the very limits of his control. He didn't like needing her so much, especially not when she rebuffed him at every turn.

A cold determination settled over Pierce's heart, and even the August heat couldn't thaw it. She was going to have to change her low opinion of him. That was simply that. One way or another, he was going to bring her around.

As she stepped down from the hackney coach into the rich, sunlit splendor of Cavendish Square, Elizabeth's heart seemed to be in her throat.

Montaigne's town house looked exactly as it had the first time she was here. The beige brick, gleaming windows, and polished door with brass fittings were still perfect. There wasn't a nick in the black paint on the iron fence, nor a petal out of place in the carefully-arranged flowers that bordered the walk. She felt her legs start to tremble, and had to fight an urge to get right back in the coach.

She had stood in this very spot when Montaigne's footmen had forced her into the carriage bound for Fleet. His words echoed in her memory: *"Until you drop the brat you are of no use to me."*

The memory sent a cold trickle of anger shivering down her spine. Her life had been utterly, irreversibly changed, yet his comfortable existence had gone on without a single mote of dust out of place.

Not for long, she vowed.

Clinging to that thought, she paid the driver, giving him a generous tip, and asked him to return for her in an hour. As the coach pulled away, Elizabeth checked the little watch attached to her fan. Three o'clock. Her appointment wasn't until three-thirty.

She stared up at the house, then turned away, unable to stand the sight of it a second longer. It would be rude to appear so early, she told herself, and a stroll about the square might fortify her nerves. She walked down the street, nodding polite greetings to the passing gentlefolk.

At the corner, she almost tripped over a man's walking stick. The ladylike apology on her lips quickly turned into an oath as she turned toward him. "This was not part of our arrangement!"

Pierce, dressed in dove gray brocade and a white wig, bowed and doffed his feathered chapeau. "Pardon, madam. I thought it wise to be in the neighborhood should you find yourself in need of assistance."

"I don't *want* your assistance." Elizabeth tried to keep her voice level but found it an impossible task. He wasn't even touching her, but her heart fluttered in her chest, her every emotion careened to the surface, and every part of her that could tingle was tingling.

The truth knifed through her, swift and undeniable. She *was* in love. Hopelessly, heedlessly in love.

It wasn't fair, she cried inwardly, that he should have such a devastating impact on her while he remained so aloof, so unaffected. He couldn't accept her love; his heart was already overcrowded: with hate and resentment for his father, murderous rage for Montaigne, and the obsessive need to reclaim all those bricks and blades of grass and his aristocratic life.

"I don't need you here," she said hotly. "I am supposed to be alone."

He took her elbow and walked around the corner. "I hardly recommend your going anywhere alone looking like that." His sideways glance flicked over her face and rested on her cloak. "What exactly *are* you wearing under there?"

"My disguise." She fought the sensations that danced through her body at his touch. "And I would thank you to leave me alone so I can get on with putting it to good use."

"Am I so bothersome?"

"When you insist on checking up on me at every turn, I find your company insufferable!"

His voice turned cold and sharp and his grip on her elbow tightened. "I am only ensuring you see fit to keep your end of our agreement."

It hurt to hear him confirm her own thoughts. He wasn't concerned about her; he only cared about the gold.

His feelings hadn't changed during their week apart—but unfortunately, neither had hers.

Get used to him being gone, she warned herself, *because that's what he'll be after the Fair.* "I fully intend to keep my end of the agreement, my lord," she said coolly. "When *I* make a promise, I keep it."

"Not always, madam."

"More often than you."

He spun her about suddenly, taking her by both arms. "Listen to me, Elizabeth. This is not a game and Montaigne is not a man to toy with. Exactly how far do you plan to go in wheedling this information out of him?"

Elizabeth could hardly believe he was jealous—but she couldn't stop herself from purposely goading him. "A kiss, perhaps more."

"More?" he said darkly.

She still couldn't gauge Pierce's feelings from his stony expression. He looked more angry than anything else. "I'm not afraid of doing what I have to do," she insisted.

His jaw clenched and his expression took on a fierceness that made Elizabeth fear she had pushed him too far. "You'd *better* be afraid, madam."

To her astonishment, he yanked her up against his chest. He was going to kiss her. Right there in broad daylight on the open street in front of a half-dozen passersby! His eyes held hers and his expression softened, just a bit.

Could he tell? she wondered wildly. Did it shine through like a beacon, like the sun? Was it obvious that she had fallen in love with him?

"Don't." She turned her head away, determined not to let herself give in to him anymore, and afraid one kiss might prove her undoing. "Y . . . you'll smear my rouge."

He suddenly released her and stepped back. "No, we couldn't have that, could we?" He jerked his head in the direction of Montaigne's town house. "Don't let me keep you."

Elizabeth glared at him. What did he have to be so

angry about? He was the one interfering; she was only doing what they had agreed upon!

"Good day, sir," she said coolly, struggling to calm her ruffled emotions. She turned and willed herself to walk away without giving him another glance.

She checked her watch. Her appointment wasn't for twenty minutes yet, and it wasn't socially acceptable to arrive this early, but she didn't care. The desire to get this awful business over with seized her, and she hurried down the street.

"I'll be right here," Pierce called after her.

Elizabeth didn't bother to insist that she could handle this by herself.

Besides, even if things turned ugly, what could Pierce alone do against Montaigne's army of footmen?

Chapter 20

A cold, flip-flopping sensation began in Elizabeth's stomach as she approached the front door. Her throat felt tight and her legs were shaking as she climbed the steps, lifted the gold-plated knocker and let it fall.

A footman clad in burgundy-and-gray livery opened the huge portal and ushered her inside. Before the servant could take her cape, the study doors opened and Montaigne himself strolled out, his attention on a man beside him who carried a stack of ledger books and papers.

"They will arrive here the day before the Fair, sir," the man was saying, "disguised as deliveries from various shops. Ten trunks in all—"

Montaigne, noticing Elizabeth, held up a hand to interrupt. "Ah, this would be the beautiful Lady Barnes-Finchley?"

His voice scraped over her nerves like a sharp-tined fork. His sallow features, paled by a particularly bad shade of scented powder, looked just as she had seen them in eight months of nightmares: the frosty blue gaze, perfectly coiffed tie wig and lecherous smile were all the same. A dizzying sense of time repeating itself swept over her.

She stood rooted where she was and managed to force a smile to her face and a greeting past her carmined lips. "G . . . good afternoon, Mr. Montaigne."

He looked at her silently for what felt like an hour, his gaze lingering over her face.

Panic gripped Elizabeth, and she almost turned and ran out the door. Then the moment passed, and he was waving the footman away and turning to the man beside him.

"That will be all for now, Roberts. We can review the rest of our plans later."

The word *plans* lanced into Elizabeth's consciousness and forced her to remember her purpose in being here.

Hadn't the man with the ledgers mentioned the Fair? They had been discussing Montaigne's plans for St. Bartholomew's Fair! She scrambled to remember all Roberts had said: the day before . . . ten trunks . . . disguised as deliveries from various shops.

Relief bubbled up inside her. She hadn't been here five minutes and she already knew a great deal about the gold. Perhaps she could claim a headache and depart right now—

That impulse dissipated when Roberts bobbed a bow to her and left her alone with Montaigne.

She couldn't leave yet. She had to find out much more: what time the coach would be leaving for the Fair, how many men would be guarding it, what route they would take. Pierce would need all the information she could get.

Mustering every ounce of courage she possessed, she kept the smile pasted to her face. "I'm sorry to have arrived so early, Mr. Montaigne. I didn't mean to interrupt your meeting."

"Think nothing of it," he said, stepping behind her to remove her cape himself. "I've a very busy schedule, but I am always willing to make time for a lovely woman in need."

Elizabeth almost choked on his double entendre and prayed it had been unintentional. She had been a woman in need the last time she was here.

His liver-spotted fingers "accidentally" brushed her bosom—and she knew in that second just how much a lie her declaration of courage to Georgiana and Nell had been.

She *was* afraid. Oh, God, she was so very afraid—of the stark, black hatred that drained every last bit of kindness and light from her soul and threatened to fill her forever.

Thank God she hadn't brought a loaded pistol. With a numbing flash of self-insight, she knew she wouldn't have thought twice about shooting him dead.

"I . . . I appreciate your generosity, Mr. Montaigne," she choked out.

"Please, you must call me Charles," he purred. "I have heard so much about you, I feel as if I've known you a long time."

"Truly?" Elizabeth's mind spun out all sorts of possible sources of his comment. His gaze locked on her decolletage, and she had the sick feeling that he was mentally peeling the red dress from her body. She hoped her voice sounded stronger than it felt. "I do hope our mutual acquaintances have been kind."

He smiled and motioned for her to proceed him into his study. Her legs felt wooden, but she managed to make it across the large entry hall. As she stepped inside the well-remembered room, she felt all the breath leave her body.

"My solicitor spoke quite well of you," Montaigne continued. "I understand you attended a party of his a few weeks past. Everyone was quite taken with you."

"Oh, yes. I remember now." Elizabeth struggled to inhale just one mouthful of air as wave after wave of memories assaulted her. The Queen Anne desk, spindle-legged chairs, ledger books and silver inkwell were all there. The scent of wax and lemons assailed her. All was exactly as it had been on that frigid November day when she had come here seeking mercy and found none.

She summoned a bored sigh. "All the parties run together in one's mind after a while."

"I've little time to attend such frivolities myself," he replied. "My businesses require my complete attention."

Instead of seating her before his desk this time, he escorted her to a plush pea-green settee before the window. A title and money, Elizabeth thought bitterly, apparently made all the difference necessary between being tossed into prison and treated like an honored guest.

Montaigne went to a three-tiered corner table that sported a variety of bottles and glasses, pouring a generous measure of claret for each of them. As he walked toward her, the cut crystal goblets gleamed like diamonds in the sunlight that streamed through the tall sash windows.

What was wrong with the world, she thought with a flash of despair, that this ruthless, calculating viper should enjoy such splendor while others suffered? Perhaps Pierce was right: guns and gold and men like Montaigne ruled England and always would. Perhaps she was a fool for risking her life to try and change that in even a small way.

She accepted the glass he handed her. "It sounds as if you are indeed a busy man . . . Charles."

Montaigne sat beside her. "Busy, yes. But I can always find time to advise a charming lady like yourself. It's so rare I am able to host a member of the fairer sex in my own home."

His tongue seemed to linger over the word "sex."

Elizabeth thrust her doubts aside. She *must* keep her mind on her role, she scolded herself. She had a great deal to accomplish and despair and this polite chitchat weren't going to get her anywhere.

She arranged herself in a pose that was proper but verging on provocative. Nell had spent the entire week teaching it to her. Forcing a smile to her lips, she set about obtaining the information that would erase Montaigne and his greed forever from her memory.

And the bitterness from her soul.

"Charles," she said sweetly. "I understand how very valuable your time is, so I won't waste it."

"My time is yours." He took a long drink. "How may I be of service?"

Elizabeth took the tiniest sip of her claret. The last thing she needed to be at the moment was intoxicated. "As I mentioned, I am in need of advice in the area of investments. Everyone who is anyone says you are the most successful investor in all of London.''

"Flattery." He grinned.

"Not at all, I'm sure. I shall be coming into a bit of money soon, and I wish to find some way of increasing it. My husband, you see, has had some success with his recent business ventures on the Continent, and has instructed me to begin work on an estate.''

"A younger son, is he, not inheriting the family home?" Montaigne nodded knowingly. "I have consulted with many people in your situation, Lady Barnes-Finchley. May I call you Elizabeth?''

"Please do," she said smoothly, holding his gaze. Would he remember another Elizabeth on another day in this room?

"Well, Elizabeth." He leaned toward her. "There are any number of choices that would keep your money quite safe and provide a modest profit. The East India Company is doing splendidly in China. And the Spitalfields silk trade has been particularly good this year. Or perhaps—''

"Yes, of course." Elizabeth inched closer to him. "But I am not interested in a *modest* profit.''

His smile widened and his eyes dropped to her bodice again. "A woman after my own heart.''

She returned his smile and lowered her voice to a conspiratorial level. "I am told that there is a much faster way to make a very large amount of money.''

He glanced up with a sly look, then his expression changed to one of intense interest. "You have the most beautiful eyes, Elizabeth. Such a lovely shade.''

Elizabeth nearly bolted from her seat. Only by the greatest effort of will did she remain frozen in place.

His brows came together in puzzlement. "I've seen that color before . . ." He shook his head. "But for the life of me I cannot remember where.''

Elizabeth wanted to strike him. *It was me!* she nearly shouted. *A poor pregnant woman whom you condemned without a thought! Was I so insignificant that I didn't even rate a speck of memory?*

She knew she should be grateful, but instead wanted to drop the entire charade right now and tell him exactly who she was and what she thought of him.

It horrified her to realize that if she'd had ammunition in the little pistol in her pocket, she might have done it— and the gold be damned!

As it was, she managed to hold onto her smile and tilt her head to one side in a coquettish gesture. ''Thank you, sir, for the compliment. I must tell you''—her voice dropped to a husky, lulling tone—''with my husband away so long, it's been quite a while since I've been able to enjoy a gentleman's . . . compliments.'' She purposely ran her tongue over her lips. ''I've been so dreadfully lonely.''

He lifted his arm and slid it along the back of the settee. His fingertips brushed her bare shoulder, and Elizabeth felt bile rising in her throat.

''And it's been a very long time,'' he said, putting his empty glass on the floor. ''Since I've had the company of such a charming and beautiful young woman.''

She looked at him boldly from beneath her kohl-blackened lashes. ''A pity for us both to suffer so,'' she replied slowly.

Before she had time to consider the wisdom of what she was doing, he was on her. Pressing her back into the padded seat, he started kissing her. Elizabeth felt a scream rising in her chest, and forced herself to turn it into a moan. His lips felt wet and rubbery on hers. Filled with disgust and self-loathing, she returned his kiss and focused her attention on trying not to throw up.

His hand dove into her bodice, grabbing her breast.

''Charles, please!''

''Anything, my sweet. Anything.''

He apparently thought she was begging for more. Elizabeth felt tears stinging her eyes and struggled to bring him back to the topic she had in mind—now, while lust made him vulnerable.

''W . . . we were speaking of my money.''

''Yes, yes.'' He took her claret from her hand, tipped the glass and spilled it over her decolletage. ''Well . . .''

He slobbered over her as he slurped up the wine. ". . . For fast profits, the gin trade is best."

"The gin trade?" she asked innocently, barely keeping her hands from clawing at his face.

"Cursed highwaymen have been giving me trouble, but it's still the fastest way to easy money." He raised his head at last, his eyes sparkling with lust and greed. "I can tell you everything you need to know."

"Wonderful," she whispered. Suddenly she extricated herself from his embrace and stood up. "But I'm sure we'll not have time to discuss it all today. When may I see you again?"

"B . . . but . . ." he babbled, surprise and disappointment on his face. "But . . ."

"Really, Charles," she reprimanded. She felt eminently better out of his arms, but knew a day-long bath wouldn't be enough to make her feel clean after his pawing. "A tumble in your study would be so *common*."

His expression brightened. "Of course. You're right. I was carried away by your beauty. Let us go upstairs."

She sashayed out of reach as he rose from the settee. "With your servants all about? Think of my reputation."

"But what do you suggest?" he squeaked.

"Let us meet again in a more . . . exciting place." She took a deep breath and launched her salvo, hoping his lust-crazed mind would loosen his tongue. "My home, perhaps? On Sunday next?" She purposely chose the day of St. Bartholomew's Fair.

"Sunday next? My sweet, I would love to, but I am to meet with my coachmen here in the morning—" He stopped himself suddenly.

"Coachmen, pooh!" She pouted, dropping her fan. She bent over to pick it up, exactly as she had practiced. "We could meet early, if you like. Before church. Think of it!"

His gaze was glued to her decolletage and the immoral idea apparently excited him beyond his power of reason, for he replied quickly. "Yes. I'm to meet them at seven, but after . . ." He shook his head, frowning. "No that won't do at all. It's the day of St. Bartholomew's Fair, you know.''

''Oh, the Fair. I had forgotten. Simply everyone will be there, won't they? How disappointing. We won't be able to''—she fluttered her lashes—''get together after all.''

He took her arm. ''You must see me before then. I won't last!''

Elizabeth hesitated. The more time she spent with him, the more likely it was he would eventually figure out where he had seen her violet eyes before. But she still knew only some of his plan for the Fair. Another tête-à-tête might reveal more.

Or it might land her in a situation beyond her control.

She decided that an event with a larger number of people might solve both problems. ''Charles, I've so little time and so *many* social engagements.''

''Make time,'' he begged.

''Perhaps . . . I recall that Lady Beauclerk is having an assembly on Wednesday. It's an all-day affair, with dinner in the gardens and cards and then dancing and supper.'' Elizabeth had already declined an invitation from Lady Kimble, Georgiana's annoying acquaintance, to accompany her and her lady friends. She supposed she could change her mind. ''Meet me there?''

''Yes. Anything. They've a large house, haven't they? With many bedrooms?''

''Dozens,'' Elizabeth said huskily. She had no idea, having never been in Lady Beauclerk's house.

She had to withstand another kiss before he would let her go. It was all she could do not to wipe her mouth and run for the exit.

He flashed that lecherous grin. ''I've never met a—''

The sounds of yelling in the entry hall interrupted him. A second later the study doors crashed inward. Elizabeth leaped back with a gasp as a strapping young man, fending off two footmen, tried to throw himself at Montaigne.

''Bastard!'' he cried, sobbing. ''You killed them, you bastard!''

Montaigne moved so that he was partially shielded behind Elizabeth. "Underwood! Apsley! Remove this riffraff!"

The two servants wrestled the man to the ground but they couldn't keep him quiet.

"They were only children!" he shouted. "My little girls, my babies! You let your filthy friends use them until they died of it!"

Elizabeth, shocked to the depths of her heart, couldn't speak, couldn't move.

Montaigne came out from behind her now that his attacker had been subdued. "You offered their services as payment for your debts," he said with annoyance, signaling to his servants to take the man away.

"You said you would have them work in the kitchens! Liar! Murderer!" He kicked and bit at the footmen. "I'll kill you. I swear on the lives of my children I'll kill you!"

"Apsley!" Montaigne called after his servant. "Take that piece of filth to the magistrate and have a charge sworn out against him for breaking into my home and attacking my person. Tell them I won't settle for anything less than a hanging, and I want it soon. None of their thumb-twiddling this time!"

The servant nodded. The study doors closed with a thump of finality.

Not sparing the poor man another thought, Montaigne turned toward Elizabeth. "Are you quite all right, my dear?"

Her mind reeling with the horror of what he had done, Elizabeth looked at him with a blank stare.

"There, there. I know it's frightening, the way these lower class types intrude on our lives these days." He put an arm around her shoulders. "But rest assured, I've sent dozens like that one to a well-deserved end. Disgusting rabble. The world would be a better place if we just exterminated them all. Don't you agree?"

Elizabeth desperately tried to remember her role and find her voice. "Y . . . yes."

Montaigne escorted her to the front door. He helped

her into her cape himself, taking a long time about it and fondling her all over. Elizabeth shuddered, but the egotistical slime took it for arousal.

"I've never met a woman like you!" He smiled broadly, finally letting her go and holding the door for her.

Elizabeth forced herself to return his smile. *Yes, yes you have, you bastard.* "Good day, Charles. It's been a most . . . delightful afternoon."

She wouldn't remember later how she got out the door and down the steps to the hackney coach that—thank God—was waiting by the curb. The driver had to half-lift her inside. She barely managed to choke out a direction before she clapped her hands over her eyes to conceal her tears. He closed the door and she collapsed into the seat.

"How did it go?" a deep voice rumbled from the seat across from her.

Her head came up, but she didn't even care that Pierce had taken it upon himself to wait inside her coach. She didn't care about anything right now. "How do you think it went? Smashing. Absolutely smashing!"

To her dismay, she proceeded to break down in tears. She flung herself into a corner of the coach and hid her face in the crook of her arm. She felt drained, wrung out. Pierce touched her shoulder but she shrugged him off.

"Don't touch me!" she cried, raising her head to glare at him. "I'm sick of this wretched plan and these lies and deceptions and . . ." She wiped at the smeared powder and rouge on her lips and face, trying to get it off. "And frauds and things and people that aren't what they seem! Including myself!"

This last came out as a sob. Pierce moved to her seat, taking her by the shoulders despite her objections. "What did he do to you?" he demanded. "Elizabeth—"

"Nothing! He kissed me, and that was all."

Pierce tried to pull her into his arms but she jerked away. "Stop it!"

"Stop what?"

"Acting as if you care about me," she accused through her tears. "Montaigne's cursed gold is all that matters to you and we both know it."

"Do we?"

She ignored his angry tone. "Let me relieve your concern. I found out a good deal. The gold is arriving at his house Saturday, in ten trunks, disguised as deliveries from different shops. He's meeting with his coachmen at seven the morning of the Fair. I'm not sure what route they mean to take, or how many guards there will be, but I'll find out. Don't worry that I won't."

"What do you mean, you'll find out? You're not meeting with him again!"

"I have to. I didn't want to ask too many questions all at once or he would have started to suspect. As it is, he just thinks I'm a lonely wife in need of a little company. We're meeting at Lady Beauclerk's assembly Wednesday afternoon."

Pierce's hold on her tightened. "You are not meeting with him again. Not alone."

"I won't *be* alone. I'll be going with Lady Kimble and her friends. I'll just go off with him for a bit."

"Absolutely not," he growled. His fingers bit into her shoulders and she could tell he wanted to shake her. "We know all we need to know. There's no reason for you to see him again."

"We do *not* know enough yet," she insisted, twisting away from him. He sounded more than worried or even jealous now; he sounded deeply concerned for her. It was all too much to think about, after what she had just been through. Her feelings were in a hopeless jumble.

"Your part is done, Elizabeth. I'll take it from here."

His tone was flat and unyielding and full of emotions that Elizabeth couldn't sort out at the moment. She felt fresh tears well in her eyes. "I have to keep this second assignation with him. If I don't, he'll definitely be suspicious, after the performance I just put on."

"Exactly what kind of performance do you mean?"

Elizabeth remained stubbornly silent, pulling a handkerchief from her pocket to try and wipe off the rest of her face paint. The hackney coach came to a halt, in front of Nell's shop.

"Elizabeth—"

"I don't want to discuss it anymore!"

The driver hadn't even opened the door yet but she got out on her own, wanting to put this entire dreadful day behind her. Pierce was right at her heels. She ignored him and started toward the shop.

A man she had never seen before stepped forward from where he had been leaning against the wall. He blocked her path. "*Pardonnez-moi madame,* but may I ask you some questions?"

Pierce was at her side instantly. "What's this about?"

"Beg your pardon, *monsieur.* I should introduce myself." He bowed. "I am Monsieur Jean-Pascal Rochambeau."

Chapter 21

"**P**leased to make your acquaintance, *monsieur*," Elizabeth said quickly, trying to move around the Frenchman and get to the door. She took him for some sort of *haute monde* peddler. "You really must excuse me. I'm in something of a hurry."

The man blocked her way again, speaking in a low voice. "*Oui,* I have seen you here before, madame. Hurrying in and out at all hours."

Elizabeth stopped and stared at him, feeling all the color drain from her cheeks. Her mind went blank. Was he only trying to make conversation, or did that comment mean something more? She started to stutter a response when Pierce cut in.

"See here, friend," he said, taking Elizabeth's elbow. "The lady has had a terrible fright, as I'm sure you can tell by her appearance. We don't wish to be rude, but we haven't time to chat."

"A fright?" the Frenchman asked softly, not moving an inch.

"Footpads caught us down at the park," Pierce said irritably. "She wishes to go inside and refresh herself."

"Yes," Elizabeth added quickly. "The shopkeeper's a friend of mine."

"*Vraiment?* So sorry to hear of your misfortune, madame." He kept looking her up and down, subtly, as if trying to measure her size. His gaze locked on her face. "All of England is overrun with criminals, *n'est-ce pas?*"

Elizabeth suddenly felt light-headed. The air around her shimmered silver-gray and she might have fainted if

Pierce hadn't increased the pressure on her arm. "I . . . I'm not sure what you mean, sir."

The man moved out of her way at last. "Only zat you English, you are so resistant to having any policemen, you must rely on ze thief-takers." He smiled, a friendly, charming grin that Elizabeth found not the least bit warm. "And most of zem are not so successful, eh?"

"Good day, *monsieur*." Pierce urged Elizabeth forward and opened the door for her.

"Au revoir," he said cheerily.

Elizabeth couldn't speak a word, but felt her gaze drawn back to the stranger. He looked at her with that unnerving, direct stare again. "I am sure, madame, zat we will meet again."

With that, he turned and strolled away.

Only when the door had swung shut behind them did Elizabeth allow herself to lean fully on Pierce. He helped her to a seat in one of Nell's striped satin chairs. A tea cart had been pulled in for the afternoon, and Elizabeth reached for the china pot, but quickly changed her mind. She was trembling so badly, she was afraid she might drop it. Clasping her hands in her lap, she tried to calm herself, but the mysterious Frenchman and his questions—on top of everything else she had been through today—had left her deeply shaken.

Nell was engaged at the counter, where it looked as if half the fabrics in the shop had been pulled out for the customer she was waiting on.

"This, Lady Rogers, is wonderful charmin'." Nell gave Elizabeth a worried glance as she unwrapped a bolt of yellow kerseymere for the woman. "Would that I 'ad a thousand yards o' it."

Elizabeth shook her head in response to Nell's concerned look, trying to convey that she wasn't hurt. *No, only terrified out of my wits,* she thought. Pierce thrust a cup of tea into her hand and she drank it in one gulp.

Nell was doing her best to get rid of her fussy client. "Really, yer ladyship. It suits yer face so well." She held up the fabric to the portly woman's cheek.

Lady Rogers rubbed her fingers over it, then looked at

the pile of rejected silks, cambrics, chintzes, German serges and Manchester velvets on the counter. She nodded. "I'll give you twelve shillings a yard."

Nell was still looking at Elizabeth with a furrowed brow, but her gaze suddenly snapped back to her customer. "Twelve shillin's! Beggin' yer pardon, but the weavers would come riot in me shop if I was t' let it go at that price. Twenty."

The woman gave the kerseymere another shrewd appraisal, pursing her lips. "Seventeen. But I shall have the whole bolt."

Nell's face lit up with relief. "Always a pleasure doin' business with a person o' yer fine taste, Lady Rogers. I'll 'ave it sent round t' yer mantua-maker in the mornin'."

"Excellent," the woman declared. She barely had time for a polite nod in Elizabeth's and Pierce's direction before Nell hustled her toward the door.

"Good day t' yer ladyship, and do be sure t' tell all yer friends that ye got it at Osgood's when they tell ye how charmin' ye look."

She paused only to close and lock the door and pull the shades before she hurried to Elizabeth's side. "Are ye all right, Bess? Look at ye! What did 'e do?"

"I'm fine, Nell. He didn't do anything, really. I found out what I went there to find out." She looked up at Pierce, who had been standing beside her chair in foreboding silence since they came in. "Or some of it."

"You found out all you're going to find out," he said flatly.

Nell appeared relieved. "I'm glad t' 'ear yer not 'urt. But 'ow did ye end up lookin' all wrecked?" She went to the back of the shop and returned a few seconds later carrying a wet cloth.

Elizabeth accepted it gratefully. "I smeared my own rouge and powder, Nell. I was upset." She eagerly started to clean away all traces of Montaigne's touch, then turned to Pierce, tingling with awareness that he was watching her every move. "If you wouldn't mind?"

He slowly turned his back, but his expression brought a flush of color to her cheeks.

"But what did Montaigne do t' upset ye so much?" Nell shot an accusing look in Pierce's direction. "Ye were supposed to be protectin' 'er."

"Nell, really, there's nothing to—wait a minute." Elizabeth had washed up as best she could and was about to put the cloth down, but suddenly her fingers tightened around it. "What do you mean *he* was supposed to be protecting me? You *knew* he was going to be there?"

Nell looked sheepish and discovered an urgent need to tidy up the empty cups and saucers on the tea cart. "Well . . . 'e . . . er, 'e mighta' mentioned it—"

"You and Georgiana have been putting your heads together again, haven't you?" Flooded with indignation, Elizabeth got to her feet. "I would greatly appreciate it if the three of you would stop conspiring behind my back!"

Pierce spun toward her. "Calm down, Elizabeth. If we've been 'conspiring,' as you put it, it's only been in your best interests."

"Ye do 'ave the most awful 'abit of gettin' int' trouble, Bess."

"Thank you for pointing out my shortcomings, but let me remind you"—Elizabeth scowled at each in turn—"*both* of you that I managed Montaigne quite well on my own. I didn't *need* protecting and I can look to my own best interests!"

"And what about our French friend out there?" Pierce inclined his head in the direction of the door. "How do you plan to protect yourself from him?"

Elizabeth felt as if her legs had turned to jelly. She sank back into her chair. "Who the devil *was* he?" Twisting the cloth in her hands, she looked up at Nell. "Have you seen him around before?"

"Who?"

"The Frenchman outside, expensively dressed and rather forward. By the name of Ro-sham-something-or-other. I thought he was a peddler, but now I . . . I don't think so."

Nell looked perplexed. "I've never seen any French-man like that 'round me shop. Nor 'eard of 'im."

"You may not have noticed him, but he seemed to know all about Elizabeth's comings and goings." Pierce fixed a somber, commanding stare on Elizabeth. "The only thing for you to do is lie low, starting right now. You can forget about your party on Wednesday."

"I certainly will not." She glared up at him mutinous-ly. "I am going to carry out my half of our agreement. I have to meet with Montaigne again to do so."

"And what if you meet up with this Frenchman in-stead? It's too dangerous, Elizabeth. This whole facade of yours is close to coming down around your ears."

"That man could have been a lunatic for all we know, just babbling." Elizabeth looked to Nell for support, but found none. To her chagrin, her friend was nodding at everything Pierce said.

"Or he could have been a thief-taker." Pierce's voice had an unusually hard edge. "He mentioned that, if you'll recall."

"Well, if he *were* a thief-taker," Elizabeth said in ex-asperation, "why the devil would he let me know I'm being followed? Wouldn't it be better to stalk me from afar without revealing himself?"

"Perhaps he's been stalking you for some time. Per-haps he's getting frustrated and thinks to scare you into doing something stupid." Pierce bent over and braced his hands on the arms of her chair. "Fortunately for *him,* that isn't particularly difficult."

"I 'ave t' warn ye, guv," Nell put in. "Our Bess, she doesn't listen t' reason real well."

"Well, she's going to bloody well start!"

"*She* knows what's she's doing," Elizabeth replied silkily. "And *she's* getting tired of everyone else making decisions for her." Her glare encompassed Nell.

Shifting uncomfortably, Nell turned away and pushed the tea cart against the wall. The cups and saucers rattled in the tense silence. "Bess," she said tentatively, "what if 'is lordship 'ere 'as a point? What if this Frenchie 'as somethin' to do with our intruder?"

"What intruder?" Pierce demanded.

"Nell!"

"What intruder?" Pierce repeated more loudly. He didn't loosen his grip on Elizabeth's chair, ~~but~~ turned his seething gaze on Nell.

Nell gulped and looked down at her hands. "I . . . Well, ye see . . ." She threw an apologetic glance Elizabeth's way and proceeded to spill the whole tale. "While ye was away, someone was in 'ere, in the shop. Everythin' was a bit out a' place—even Bess's things, 'er highwaymen outfit and 'er pistol, even though we keep 'em locked away, upstairs. It was like someone was . . . lookin' for somethin'."

Elizabeth grimaced and closed her eyes. Now she was well and truly in the soup.

"Speakin' of upstairs," Nell continued quickly, her voice rising. "I almost fergot, I 'aven't cleaned me . . . uh, me rugs this week, so I'll leave ye two t' agree on what yer goin' t' do about this." As she made a hasty retreat, she called back over her shoulder. "Just let me know what ye decide, Bess. I wouldn't want ye t' think I was interferin'."

A fine time to get a conscience, Elizabeth thought. The door to the upstairs apartments shut with a bang.

"Look at me, Elizabeth."

Pierce's voice sent a shiver down her spine. That deceptively soft tone, so deep and compelling, left her unnerved in a way his loudest shout never did.

Reluctantly, she opened her eyes, first one, then the other.

His gaze had darkened to a shade just short of black. "Why the hell didn't you tell me about this?"

She chose to answer honestly. "I didn't think it was worth mentioning."

"You still don't trust me." His voice snapped with anger.

"I didn't see that Nell's intruder had anything to do with your end of our agreement, that's all."

"*My* end, *your* end." He shoved himself away from

her. "Why do you insist on keeping everything so bloody neat and separate?"

"It's better that way," she said calmly.

"Well, this intruder of yours really ties it," he replied just as coolly. "Consider 'your end' finished. You are not going out this week, Elizabeth. You are going to stay home and hope to God this Rochambeau doesn't have enough evidence to prove anything."

"No, I won't." Her fingers closed around the padded arms of her chair. For Pierce's sake, she had to get more information. The raid would be too dangerous for him otherwise. But he wouldn't listen to that argument. "Can't you understand?" she begged softly. "*I* have to finish it."

"And what if you finish it by swinging at Tyburn?"

His staccato question echoed the path Elizabeth's own thoughts had been taking; hearing it spoken aloud scattered the last of her composure. Her fear and hurt came out all in a rush. "And what if I did? Why would that matter to you? I should think you would find it a relief!"

He looked at her as if she'd gone completely around the bend. "Is that what you really think?"

"What else am I supposed to think?" She fought the tears that suddenly welled in her eyes. "You told me before I'm nothing but trouble. If I were out of the way, you wouldn't have to share the gold. You could have everything you want—your estates, your aristocratic life—"

"You, madam, obviously don't have the most distant notion what it is I want."

"Yes, I do," she accused. "*You* were the one who said you wanted us to go our separate ways!"

His eyes widened in a look of astonishment and one corner of his mouth quirked with what was almost a grin. "My God. You women are absolutely the most unreasonable, illogical creatures—"

"Really?" she snapped, wounded that he found humor in this when she was becoming more miserable by the second. "As if men are always so sensible. When was the last time you saw two *women* fighting a duel?"

''Don't try to change the subject. I never said I wanted us to go our separate ways.''

Elizabeth thrust herself out of the chair, incensed that he could lie so blatantly. ''You did! You said those words exactly.''

''I was attempting to sum up,'' he growled, ''what I thought it was that *you* wanted.''

Elizabeth had already taken a breath to voice a vivid response, but his statement stole the angry words from her lips. She just stood there with her mouth open, feeling like a fool, and resenting him for making her feel that way. How the devil was she supposed to have known that was what he meant? The confounded man never expressed himself very clearly—and he'd never said a single word about wanting them to stay together.

When she didn't speak, he looked at her through narrowed eyes for a moment, then turned his back and walked to the counter. ''What *do* you plan to do, once you've filled up the coffers of this Trust of yours? Have you given any thought to that at all?''

The way he said it, the question sounded more like an interrogation than an indication of interest. Confusion and irritation made Elizabeth answer in an equally surly tone. ''As a matter of fact, I have. Lady Barnes-Finchley is going to have a sudden religious conversion. She'll donate all her wordly goods to the Trust and retire to the country. Blackerby Swift will become just another legend, never to be heard from again.''

Pierce turned to face her, leaning back against the counter, his fingers resting lightly on the fabrics that spilled over the edge. When he finally spoke, it was in that low, compelling tone. ''I don't care half a damn about either one of them.'' He formed each word distinctly, as if he wanted to emblazon them on her memory. ''What about you? What about Elizabeth Thornhill?''

The word *care* rang in Elizabeth's ears. He hadn't applied it directly to her—but it was as close to a declaration of affection as she had yet heard from him. Perhaps it was as close as he would ever get.

His question gave her an opening, an opportunity to say, *I want to be with you. More than anything else, I want to find out who you really are, without all the masks and disguises. I want it not to matter that you're an earl and I'm an innkeeper's daughter. I want to run to you right now, and have you hold me and kiss me and call me your sweet Elizabeth and never let me go.*

"I . . ." She swallowed, finding her mouth too dry to speak. "I . . . I want . . ."

In that moment, his expression took on a hopefulness she had never seen before. She very nearly ran to him and whispered the words she knew were her heart's own truth.

Shaken by the impulse, she threaded her fingers together and looked down at the floor. The gentle, loving phrases suddenly choked up in the back of her throat.

Her "ravish-me red" dress seemed to mock her, reminding her of Montaigne, reflecting every bit of rivalry and distrust and scheming and hurt that had passed between her and Pierce.

There was so much of that between them.

And so much gold.

The gown stood out like a signal flag, a warning not to reveal herself to him. Pierce Wolverton was a loner, a man who had turned against a world that had turned against him, a man who couldn't bring himself to trust, to love—or to accept love.

Elizabeth's heart throbbed painfully. If he rejected her, it would be more than she could bear. She couldn't withstand another blow, not after the way she had lost her family and her son.

Her emotions in a hopeless tangle, she closed her eyes and told him what used to be the truth, weeks ago. "I want to stay here in London with Georgiana and Nell. Someone has to manage the Trust and invest the funds. I understand the East India Company is doing splendidly in China—"

"Is that what you really want?" he said tightly.

"Yes. I . . ." She glanced up and caught his coal-black gaze—and the vulnerability he couldn't quite mask quickly enough. The lie died on her lips. "I . . . I mean, no . . . I . . ." She spun away from him and covered her face with her hands. "Oh, I don't know! Why do you keep asking? Why do you have to confuse me like this?"

There was a long pause. "Elizabeth, you may be naive and reckless and a bit too soft in the heart," he said quietly, "but one thing you are not is stupid."

She could hear him moving away from the counter, coming toward her. "What is that supposed to mean?" she cried.

"I think you know." He was directly behind her.

"I don't. I don't know anything. I don't understand anything anymore."

"Yes, you do."

She flinched when he touched her shoulder, his fingers hotter than a brand on her bare skin.

"What?" she asked stiffly, hoping that he couldn't feel her trembling. "Th . . . that you care about me? I don't believe it."

"Don't?" he whispered. "Or won't?"

"I can't!"

"I came to see you every day for a week," he reminded her. "You were the one who refused to see me."

She couldn't catch her breath. "B . . . because you were only trying to verify that I hadn't left town."

"No." He started to knead her tense muscles, just as he had that night at Mr. Bacon's inn.

His caress and his simple, one-word denial touched off a riot of feelings inside Elizabeth. God, how she wanted to believe him. If only he could feel for her a fraction of the feelings she had for him—if only it could be *true*.

"Let yourself believe, Elizabeth." Pierce's voice was very close to her ear, and more gentle than the touch of a falling autumn leaf. "Let yourself believe in me."

For a second, just one second, she closed her eyes and let a little breath of longing slip out.

His other hand came up and touched her left shoulder. She broke free and whirled to face him. "I can't! I can't believe in you! The moment I do, you'll change back again!''

He glared at her and started to rake his fingers through his hair, then suddenly clenched his fist and thrust it into his pocket. "Elizabeth," he said through gritted teeth. "What I am standing here like a moonstruck cowherd trying to say . . . What I am trying to tell you is that—''

"I've heard it before, my lord earl, that night at the costume party." She was breathing hard, blinking at him through unshed tears. "After we searched Fairfax's study together. You used sweet words then, too. You kissed me and you made me believe in your affections, and it was all just a ploy—''

"This is different, damn it." His gaze and voice were sizzling.

"Is it? You've lived by yourself for fifteen years. You've hated so long, you probably don't even remember what it's like to feel anything else."

"Elizabeth," he growled, stepping toward her.

She backed away, a tear spilling onto her cheek. "You can't even feel friendship for anyone, except the people you keep in your notebooks—''

"Stop it—''

"It's all very convenient, isn't it? You write them down as *you* want them to be, not as they are. Then you put them on a shelf to gather dust. You only take them out when it suits you. Well I won't *be* one of those people in your notebooks, Pierce. You can't just toy with me and file me away!''

He grabbed her, taking a painful grip on her arms. "I am not toying, Elizabeth, and I have no intention of filing you away." He pulled her against him so that his face was only inches from hers, his breath hot against her mouth. "What I want is for you to trust me, that's all. Trust me, damn it. None of this has anything to do with that blasted gold. I don't want you going to that assembly on Wednesday because I don't want you to be hurt. Because I—''

''Don't! Please don't,'' she sobbed, turning her head away. ''I don't want to hear it. It isn't true—''

''It is true, you little fool. I don't understand this any more than you do, but I'm not going to keep denying it. I'm not going to let you deny it either. There's something between us, something I've never felt before. Whatever the deuce it is, it makes me feel like throwing out this entire idiotic plan!''

''Pierce,'' she whispered. ''You don't—''

''Shut up. I'm not going to argue about it anymore.'' He locked his arms around her in an unyielding embrace. ''I want you, Elizabeth. I want to be with you, and inside you, and all around you, and I don't want to stop. Ever. *That's* what the truth is, and if you don't believe me, then, God-damn it . . .'' He expelled a harsh breath. ''Oh, to hell with it.''

His mouth captured hers, hard and hot and passionately. He put every sinew of his body and every breath of his being into that kiss—and swept away the lingering doubts she had about the truth of his words.

This wasn't a lie or a trick or part of any plan; he *did* want her and care for her, with all the honesty and depth of feeling he possessed. She could feel it in the tense muscles of his arms, crushing her close. She could taste it in his kiss, sweeter and more deeply satisfying than any food or drink that had ever touched her tongue.

His feelings for her were even stronger than she'd dared hope. Elizabeth felt resistance melting from her limbs. Tingling weakness and exhilarating feminine strength washed over her by turns. He arched her backward and she clung to him, feeling as though she were spiraling toward the heavens on a tempest of summer winds.

The fever that had simmered between them for weeks at last ran wild and engulfed them both. She stopped questioning and wondering and fighting and gave herself over to it.

He clasped her against his lean form as if he wanted to lock her there forever. Pierce used his body so eloquently, more expressively than he ever used words. Need and tenderness and an all-consuming longing radiated from him like light from the sun, and Elizabeth responded with a fervor she hadn't known she possessed. She returned the kiss in full measure, her tongue meeting and dancing with his, her arms wrapping about his shoulders, her fingers digging into the fabric of his coat.

She shivered and moaned into his mouth when his hands slid down her back, shaping her buttocks, molding her soft curves against his hardness. Elizabeth couldn't help but tense as a sudden, anxious memory of Geoffrey leaped to mind.

"No," Pierce said raggedly against her mouth. "Don't think of him. Think of me. Think of *us*."

The emotion in his voice overpowered Elizabeth's reluctance. *Us*. Two letters joined in a word that was at once simple and infinitely strong—strong enough, she knew, to put an end to her old fears, once and for all.

Her hands closed around Pierce's thick-hewn arms. She relaxed into his embrace. It was time.

With a groan, he made a quick turn and took two steps backward, lifting her onto the fabric-strewn counter. He broke the kiss to push the materials aside, shifting her onto a length of peacock-colored silk.

"W . . . what are you doing?" she asked breathlessly.

His eyes flashed a scorching, silent message, just before his head dipped toward her neck, lips and tongue hungrily playing along the column of her throat. She arched her head back, closing her eyes at the searing intensity of his kisses. The next second, she felt her skirt and petticoats pushed up around her thighs.

"Pierce, not here!" She managed to gasp. "Not on Nell's best silk!"

Without diverting his attentions from her, he growled a wordless reply, snagged a coin purse from his frock coat, and tossed it on the counter. His hands came up to unfasten her wig, sending hairpins flying. The carefully coiffed piece tumbled unceremoniously to the floor. His fingers tangled in her real, black tresses, then pulled her bodice lower. It was as if he wanted to touch her everywhere, all at once.

Elizabeth gasped at feeling his hot breath on her breast

a second before his tongue. When he took the sensitive tip between his teeth, she groaned and made one last, wild bid for sanity. "But Nell is upstairs and Georgiana might come any—"

He dragged her head down to his and silenced her with his mouth, holding her still with one hand. His tongue parted her lips, thrusting forward aggressively. Thoughts of anything and anyone else fled Elizabeth's mind. The absolutely scandalous suddenly seemed utterly irresistible.

She had the briefest flash of insight that Pierce always seemed to affect her that way. He alone seemed to have this power to chase fears and doubts from her mind, filling her instead with strength and hope . . . and love.

Love. There it was again, that word she had been dancing around for days—and the only one that made sense when she tried to put a name to these feelings. With a moan, she stopped resisting it, let it wash over her like a shower of sparkling stars from the night sky. She *loved* him. It wasn't the kind of love she had ever expected, but nothing about Pierce was what she expected. How could her love for him be a safe, predictable emotion?

His kiss took on a new urgency, and suddenly all thought became impossible, buried under an avalanche of feeling . . . glorious, dizzying feeling. With one steely arm about her waist, he pulled her toward him until she was just perched on the edge of the counter. He lifted her, pushing her skirts out of the way. She felt the coolness of the peacock-colored silk beneath her, then the hot pressure of Pierce's hardness throbbing against the naked juncture of her thighs.

A shock of desire flared inside Elizabeth. The fabric of his breeches was all that separated them, but to her amazement she felt only a shiver of fear this time, and it lasted only a second before she was consumed by a trembling, aching need to feel filled and complete—as she instinctively knew she would feel with Pierce. She threaded her fingers into his hair, and broke their kiss just long enough to whisper one word.

"Yes."

The sound of her voice hung in the silence for a second. Pierce's whole body went taut and still. Then he was tearing at his breeches. A moment later she felt his shaft throbbing against her thigh, his heat only an inch from melding with her own. She caught his scent, strong and tangy and infinitely masculine, mingling with the lighter, more delicate muskiness of her own arousal. The combination seemed to unleash some ancient, primitive impulse deep within her, and she instinctively moved her hips toward him.

Suddenly his hand was there, touching her downy triangle. She whimpered softly when his blunt fingers brushed against her wetness, slipping inside her for one tantalizing second. Then he was seeking the swollen nub of her desire, finding it with a rough, urgent caress, giving her pleasure as never before.

He aroused her mercilessly, bringing her to the very peak without giving her release. One moment, his thumb and fingers stroked with a fast, forceful motion that left her gasping; the next he only grazed her with the very tip of one finger, flicking with a touch lighter than that of a butterfly's wing.

Elizabeth felt wild, spiraling tension coiling within her belly and bit her bottom lip to keep from crying out. At last he stopped, wrenching a low sound of protest from deep in her throat.

Her objection instantly turned into an aching moan when the velvety steel of his manhood moved into the position his hand had just deserted. He rubbed against her in a way that was more gentle, yet more intimate and intense. Wrapping a hand about her neck, he took her mouth in a deep, probing kiss, moving his hips in small, deliberate circles that moistened his swollen tip in her dampness.

Then his hands were on her hips and he was pressing forward. She held onto Pierce's shoulders, crying out softly as he became part of her. With a single thrust he was deep inside, groaning with the pleasure of it, his hard maleness smoothly blending into her soft femininity.

Elizabeth felt filled and stretched—and astonished. She couldn't suppress a low cry of surprise at how exquisite it felt to have him within her. They were one, as completely and surely as if heaven and all the angels had created them exclusively for each other. He was large and hot and solid as steel, but she felt no pain, only the delicious little pulsations that came from her body's accommodating and holding his.

Nothing had ever matched this, not his kiss or his touch or his most intimate caress. She wanted to savor the sensation, learning the feel of him, but he withdrew a bit, breathing raggedly. Then he moved his hips in a rhythm that thrilled her even more, it was so fierce and exquisitely sweet.

She abandoned herself to a feeling of closeness and mutual possession unlike any she had ever known, letting go of her fearful memories, letting them become part of the past.

For she knew in that moment she would never, never again have reason to think of another.

Pierce held her body close as he thrust inside her, deeper, harder, caught up in a tide of desire beyond his most fevered dreams. Elizabeth's tiny gasps and cries were like music, filling him with a joy he had never experienced. Her small, soft hands clutched his shoulders with a feminine strength that was at once delicate and infinite, the same way her body clasped his rigid shaft.

His breath came in harsh gulps, but even breathing didn't seem important anymore. He would die happily, later, so long as he could absorb every bit of this feeling now. The touch of cool silk each time he withdrew was a tantalizing contrast to the tight heat of Elizabeth's sheath. They surged together, each driving the other higher, harder, faster toward the pinnacle of release.

The sensations rippling up and down his body magnified, blazing through blood and bone and sinew, mind and heart and soul. For the first time in his life he found himself losing control. He drove into her, heedlessly, mindlessly, giving himself to her completely. He heard his voice, low and caressing, whispering her name, whispering words of love he didn't even know he remembered.

Then there were no words at all, only her high, soft sounds of bliss echoing his fierce, deep groans in a symphony of mingling passion. He felt her body quivering, tightening, suddenly arching in a spasm of tension. He managed to lift his head, wanting to watch her face as she found release. She looked down and their gazes met just as her every muscle began to shimmer in a wave of pleasure.

In that brief second, her eyes were darker than the rarest amethysts, filled with wonder and bliss—and an emotion that was as startling as it was unmistakable: love.

Before it could even register completely in Pierce's mind, Elizabeth's lips parted, a flush of color lit her cheeks, and she squeezed her eyes shut, surrendering to the climax that shuddered through her. The throbbing pressure of her sheath around Pierce's hardness sent pure, almost painful ecstasy ripping through his body. He just managed to pull out before his climax flowed forth, spilling over the peacock-blue silk as he grated out a last, low moan.

Elizabeth went limp against him and he held her close, listening to the sweet sighs of her breathing and the thunder of his own heartbeat. "I shouldn't have waited so long," he apologized between breaths. "There's still a danger—"

She placed a finger on his lips. "I don't care about danger," she whispered, lifting her head to look down at him with drowsy eyes. "Not when I'm with you."

The tenderness, the *trust* in her voice stunned him into silence. He felt a gripping, tightening ache in his chest. In that instant, reason and practicality and logic existed only at the very fringes of his being, and he found himself totally lost in emotion. The feeling was utterly new, and deeply unnerving. It left him off balance, as if he might fall to the floor if he didn't hold on to her.

Everything between them had shifted, in some unalterable way. He suddenly felt awkward as a schoolboy. It wasn't an unpleasant feeling, but it wasn't reassuring either. He didn't know how he should react, what he should say or do.

He settled for giving her a smile and a little kiss as he lifted her from the counter. He lowered her gently to the floor, still silent, then straightened her disarrayed gown before seeing to his own clothes.

To his chagrin, the awkwardness didn't dissipate; in fact, it grew worse. Frowning at his own uncertainty, he fell back on more familiar behavior.

Catching her chin in one hand, he spoke in his most commanding voice. "There is absolutely no way you are going to that assembly on Wednesday, Elizabeth."

She blinked up at him, the languor in her eyes replaced by confusion and hurt. "I thought we settled that. I'm not going to leave my part of—"

"We did settle it. I'm not listening to any more about 'mine' and 'yours' and who's carrying out which part. You're not going."

Her entire body went rigid, her eyes sparkling with fury. "And what makes you think you can stop me?"

"Don't test me, Elizabeth," he warned.

"You can't keep an eye on me all the time." Her beautifully sculpted lips curved into a determined smile. "I *will* be at that party Wednesday. One way or another."

Pierce let her go, clenching his hand into a fist. He had heard that tone before; she hated being pushed, so much so that she would end up doing something reckless and foolish just to thwart him.

Something that might land her lovely little neck in a noose.

He growled a frustrated oath. Compromise was utterly foreign to his nature, but it seemed the only way he could protect her. "Then I'll go with you."

She put her hands on her hips. "I can't arrive with a man. The whole point of doing this at all—"

"I'll meet you there," he said sternly. "No argument."

She opened her mouth to reply, then lifted her hands in a gesture of exasperation instead. "I swear by the Graces, you are *the* most stubborn, unbending, infuriating—"

"Yes, we have a great deal in common. But never mind the compliments. What time will you be there?"

She sighed, shook her head, then gave in, but she didn't look the least bit happy about it. "I'll be arriving with Lady Kimble and her friends at noon. You can't miss her carriage. It looks like something a Turkish sultan would ride in." She regarded him with a frown. "At least try to be discreet. If Montaigne sees you—"

"I'll be there." He leaned over and silenced her with a kiss. "You may not see me, but I'll be there every second."

Releasing her, he went to the counter and picked up the length of silk he had just purchased, folding it to hide the stained end. "Is silk very hard to clean?" he asked, sliding her a wicked glance.

Elizabeth looked away, her cheeks a fiery red, and spoke to him in a formal tone. "I suggest you take your purchase and leave with all haste, sir, before Georgiana gets here or Nell starts to wonder why we've been so quiet."

When her gaze finally flicked back to his, she looked at him from beneath her lashes, adding softly, "I'll never be able to look at that counter again without blushing."

"Good." He stole one last kiss before heading for the door. "Don't go out anywhere until Wednesday," he said firmly.

She muttered something under her breath, but apparently didn't consider that point worth another argument. "Very well."

Satisfied, he tucked the silk under his arm, gave her one last, lingering gaze, and left.

Elizabeth watched him go, mulling over the convoluted maze that was the male mind. A secret, feminine part of her felt pleased by his adamant orders; somehow they were easier to take when she knew they came out of concern for her, not greed for Montaigne's gold. And she had to admit, at least to herself, that it *would* be a relief to have him there Wednesday to protect her.

Perhaps it was even possible, she thought with a smile, that Pierce was in love with her. If the words he had whispered in the throes of passion held any truth at all, it was true.

With a hopeful little sigh, she turned to go find Nell, thinking that perhaps, just perhaps, all would turn out well after all.

Chapter 22

This wasn't going to turn out well at all. Pierce realized that before he had walked halfway home. By the time he approached his town house, it had sunk in with appalling certainty. This party Wednesday had all the makings of a disaster.

How could he keep an eye on Elizabeth at all times, in a houseful of people, without getting so close that he drew Montaigne's notice? Even if he managed it, what if she made another assignation with Montaigne as she intended, for the day of the Fair? Pierce didn't see any way he could take the gold and protect her at the same time.

He might fumble the raid entirely, if he had to spend his time worrying about her. She shredded his concentration; she had done so since the moment he met her on Hounslow Heath. Damn the woman anyway. Why the devil did she have to insist on placing herself in danger with such disturbing regularity?

And damn yourself as well, Darkridge, for acting like some kind of moonstruck lad and giving in to her.

He was in a thoroughly sour mood by the time he walked up the steps to his town house. Quinn opened the door.

Pierce handed him his coat. "I'll be upstairs," he said tersely.

"Very good, sir," Quinn replied, not questioning either his master's ill humor or the odd fact that he was carrying a bolt of blue silk.

Pierce took the steps two at a time and went up to his garret. He had to think, to devise a way to salvage both

265

the gold and Elizabeth's safety. He dropped the length of fabric by the door, poured a brandy and prowled about the room. To his profound irritation, he found himself edgy and tense and distracted.

Elizabeth had expressed a great deal of trust in him earlier, but now that he had time to think about it, doubt assailed him, like a little demon stabbing at him with a pitchfork. When she said she didn't fear danger with him, was she merely speaking physically? Did she only mean that she trusted him not to get her with child? Or did she truly *trust* him?

And once they each had their half of the gold, did she still intend to walk out of his life? Would she actually do that now, after all they'd been through together?

Scowling, Pierce stalked to the window and threw open the curtains. The late afternoon sun only highlighted the emptiness of the room. His sanctuary appeared colorless, gray, as if everything in it were coated with a layer of dust.

For the first time he could remember, he found the place . . . lonely.

Annoyed by that unfamiliar feeling, he started pacing again, and found himself standing in front of his bookshelf. Elizabeth's words rang in his mind.

"It's all very convenient, isn't it? You write them down as you want them to be, not as they are. Then you put them on a shelf to gather dust. You only take them out when it suits you . . ."

Ludicrous, he thought. He reached up and selected one of his volumes of poetry. As if he would people his world with paper friends. He didn't have to. He lived quite happily without them. That had been his way for fifteen years.

He could change that fact any time, if he chose. All he had to do was call upon . . .

His brows drew together as he tried to name one person who would call him friend. Frowning, he placed his glass on the shelf and started flipping through the notebook in his hand. He had known each of these people at one time or another, but only briefly.

His frown deepening, he threw the book aside and picked out another, then another. The pages were filled with casual acquaintances, drinking companions, pub owners, passersby, shopkeepers, married women, single women, gambling opponents . . . but no friends.

He plucked more books from the shelves, riffling through each before he tossed them on the floor. Suddenly he came across a poem he had never finished, and his hand and his thoughts and his breathing all stilled at once.

The word *Father* was written neatly across the top of the page, then crossed out with a scrawl of ink. The page was blank but for a few partial sentences, started but never completed, all blacked out with angry strokes of his pen. What could he say about a man he had respected and honored above all others—and hated as he had never hated another human being?

And loved as he would never love again.

With a curse, Pierce snapped the notebook shut and flung it into the pile. He turned his back on the bookshelf. What did it matter? What did *any* of this matter? Not one of the people on those pages meant half a damn to him, and that had always suited him quite well.

He reached for his latest volume, which lay on the desk, open to the page he had been working on most recently. His eyes locked on the name at the top.

Elizabeth.

The sudden, numbing recognition of a pattern riveted his eyes to the page. He had methodically finished every poem he had ever started, except for the one about his father—and this one.

Questions tumbled through his head, followed hard and fast by answers. Why should these two people be so hard for him to write about?

Because they were too complex. Because his feelings for them were just as complex . . . Because both meant more to him than any other person ever had.

Stunned by the realization, he ran a finger over the half-finished sentences and inadequate images on the page. From the very beginning, his feelings for Elizabeth

had been too raw, too intense to be captured by a means
so mundane as paper and ink.

She was simply indescribable: honest to a fault, yet a
highwayman; naively innocent, yet deeply sensual; em-
bittered by her past, yet optimistic that she could change
the world; kind and stubborn and beautiful and exasper-
ating and brave and reckless . . .

She affected him in ways that went leagues beyond
flirtation or physical attraction or sex or any feeling he
had ever had for any woman. God help him, he couldn't
even find words for the color of her eyes.

Elizabeth had filled his head and heart—his life—until
everything else seemed bleak by comparison. As he
stared at the unfinished poem, the truth suddenly hit him
as hard as a physical blow.

I love her.

He had to lean on the desk to steady himself. Bloody
hellfire, it was as plain as the black marks on the white
page! He hadn't been able to finish this poem because
he didn't want to file Elizabeth away with the others. He
didn't want her to be just another meaningless page on a
shelf glutted with forgotten people.

I love her.

He stood there, blinking like an idiot, his breath coming hard and fast, as if he had just run an enormous
distance. He had been deluding himself, maybe from the
very start. Thinking he was chasing after her because of
his plans for Montaigne. Thinking that what he wanted
was control.

What he wanted was to have her in his life. She had
quietly woven a spell around him with her feminine
magic until it overpowered all the hate and hard cynicism
in his soul.

I love her.

He straightened, slowly, turning the words over and
over in his mind, and gradually the shock began to wear
off. Until this moment, he would have thought it impossible. But here it was. Love. So real it demanded he
strike his flag, lay down his arms, and give way without
denial or argument.

Hard on the heels of that reason-numbing admission came another feeling, equally strong and just as new. Fear.

Love wasn't enough. It wouldn't protect Elizabeth from danger, not if she insisted on flitting about London playing her Lady Barnes-Finchley charade. He might very well lose her—lose another person he loved because of Montaigne.

No, God damn it to hell and back! His gaze snapped up to the window. Night was already falling. Tomorrow was Tuesday. He had only one day.

He wasn't going to let it happen, not again. Gritting his teeth, he realized that time and her stubborn nature left him only one choice. He would take her to a safe place—forcibly if need be—and keep her there until the Fair was over. She was going to have to bid farewell to her masquerading days, once and for all. That was that. She would be furious, but it couldn't be helped. They would have time to work it all out later.

Three quick steps carried him to the door and he bellowed down the stairs. "Quinn!"

Quinn appeared moments later. Pierce had resumed his pacing. He stopped and gave his servant a probing look. "I have something to ask of you. I won't order you to do it because it's going to be dangerous—"

"Ask it, sir."

"You don't understand. It will involve breaking the law, maybe risking your life."

"Ask it, my lord. After all that you've done for me, I owe you a great deal."

"Not your life."

"Perhaps not." Quinn nodded gravely. "But I should like to think I at least owe you my loyalty. And my friendship."

Pierce felt a smile tug at one corner of his scowl. He remembered something else Elizabeth had said: *"You don't even feel friendship . . ."* She had been wrong about that.

Pierce walked over and reached out to shake Quinn's hand. "All right, then. We shall work as a team. Now let's get underway. We've much to accomplish before Wednesday.''

A light rain misted the Wednesday morning air as Lady Kimble's carriage rolled along the London streets, collecting a cargo of bewigged, bejeweled, beribboned women. Elizabeth squirmed on one padded velvet seat, squeezed between Lady Vicary, a thin woman wearing what must be her own weight in jewelry, and Lady Houblon, a matronly sort of at least fifty who insisted on dressing as if she were fifteen.

Elizabeth was trying to concentrate on the daunting meeting that lay ahead of her today, but her head was swimming with the clash of competing perfumes, her ears ringing with Lady Kimble's endless praise of her gaudy coach, which the woman insisted on repeating for the benefit of each new arrival.

''You'll notice it doesn't jostle one about half so much as an ordinary coach,'' Lady Kimble said. ''Springs! Isn't it ingenious? And the crest on the door isn't just paint like some people have. That's *real* silver and *real* gold. Just like the ones in Paris.''

''Oh, you'll be the envy of simply everyone!'' gushed Lady Vicary.

''Harcourt and Irving will be sorry they missed this,'' Lady Houblon said. ''But that's what they deserve for passing up Lady Beauclerk's assembly to go to a silly boxing match.''

''Oh, but I'd be happy to show it to your husbands when they join us for supper.'' Lady Kimble beamed. ''I wouldn't want them to feel deprived. I'm the first in London to have one, outside the royal family of course. I've not seen its like.''

''Nor I,'' Elizabeth said with feeling. She had never been inside a bawdy house, but this was what she would expect one to look like: all scarlet velvet and gold-tasseled trim, complete with red drapes to block out the prying eyes of the curious masses.

She was saved from having to listen to another round

of compliments when the coach rolled to a stop, outside the home of the next addition to their flock of partygoers.

"Lady Selwyn wanted us all to come in and see her new home," Lady Kimble said, peeking out the drapes. "But we're running a bit late and I'm sure she'll understand that this rain would simply ruin my—I mean *our* coiffures."

Elizabeth wedged herself out from between Lady Vicary and Lady Houblon, glad for a chance to escape for even a moment. "I would be happy to make our excuses," she said brightly.

"Oh, but your hair, my dear. We could send the footman."

"I don't mind," Elizabeth insisted.

Lady Kimble didn't protest further, having already refastened her attention on her two remaining victims. "Have I told you about the decorative carving on the wheels yet?"

Elizabeth gratefully accepted the footman's offered hand and stepped out into the light mist. He held a parasol over her head, and she took care to keep her skirt up from the puddles; even a speck of mud would show on the pale lemon silk. Despite her objections, Nell had fashioned this gown a bit more modestly than the red one, adding a white satin stomacher and a froth of lace at the neckline and elbows.

The town house was surprisingly humble, for a friend of Lady Kimble's. The footman rapped on the door, then announced her to the servant who opened it. "Lady Barnes-Finchley, with Lady Kimble's party," he said imperiously, before standing to one side to wait for her with the parasol.

The servant, little more than a boy, ushered her into the entry hall. The house was apparently undergoing a renovation, for there wasn't a stick of furniture to be seen, only scaffolds and dropcloths.

"Is Lady Selwyn ready?" Elizabeth asked, bewildered, almost sneezing on the smell of paint, so strong it made her eyes water.

"I'll fetch her, mum," the boy said before dashing

off to find his mistress. A moment later, Lady Selwyn appeared from the rear of the house. She was a striking woman, of about Elizabeth's own age, dressed in a simple gown. The amber color set off her auburn hair, which tumbled about her shoulders with a complete lack of artifice. She was carrying a bundle in her arms.

As she came closer, Elizabeth realized with a sharp pang of distress that it was a baby.

"Oh, I'm so sorry that I'm not ready yet," Lady Selwyn said, rushing across the hall with an embarrassed smile. "Are the others here as well?"

Her eyes on the baby, Elizabeth couldn't find her voice for a moment. "Th . . . they asked if they might see your new home at a . . . another time. We're running a bit late, and there's the . . . rain."

Lady Selwyn looked relieved. "Yes, oh, yes, certainly. Actually, that would be best. We're terribly behind schedule, as I'm sure you can see. All of our servants are still at our old home packing, and the furnishings were supposed to arrive yesterday and they haven't, and simply everything is in chaos." She looked around, then up the stairs. "And Samuel was supposed to come see me off, but I suppose he's still up exploring that drafty attic."

With a sigh of frustration, she turned to Elizabeth and held out the baby. "Will you take little Samantha for a minute? I hate to have her breathing in all the dust up there. I've just fed her, so she won't be any trouble. I'll go see if I can't locate my husband."

"N . . . no, really. I . . . I . . ." Elizabeth had an armful of baby before she could choke out the last word. ". . . can't."

Lady Selwyn was already hastening up the stairs. "I shan't be but a minute."

Her heart thudding in her chest, Elizabeth stared after the woman for a full minute, holding the child at arm's length. She stood rooted in place, darting desperate glances around her. There was no place to set the baby down, and she could hardly lay her on the cold marble floor. Nor could she hand her to the footman outside in the rain. And the boy was nowhere to be seen.

Samantha started to wiggle in protest at being held so woodenly. Elizabeth knew she should cuddle the baby against her own warmth, but she couldn't. She *couldn't*! Just having this little person in her hands was agony beyond bearing. Babies were so blessed helpless, so tiny, so . . . fragile.

Swallowing hard, she tried to force down the wave of emotions that suddenly swelled in her throat, choking her like thick black smoke. She locked her gaze on the wall, not even daring to look at the child. She tried to interest herself in Selwyns' choice of wallpaper. A spring-green damask. How interesting. The baby began to fuss, gurgling and kicking for attention.

Elizabeth's hands began to shake. *What* a nice counterpoint that green color made to the gold-painted trim. The workmen were certainly doing a fine job with this room. Samantha's small sounds turned into a hiccough and then a full-blown cry.

Where the devil was Lady Selwyn? Please come back. Please, please. Elizabeth could feel cold beads of perspiration dotting her forehead, her pulse beating fast and shallow. She tried desperately to keep her attention on the decor. This was obviously going to be a *most* elegant home when finished. The Selwyns had excellent taste. Samantha began to wail.

"L . . . lady Selwyn?" Elizabeth called up the stairs. How long could it take to find one missing husband? What kind of proper lord spent his time exploring an attic, anyway? And why the devil was Lady Selwyn going to a party in the first place if her life and house were in such total disorder? "Lady Selwyn?" she repeated more loudly. "Anyone?"

The baby's crying became so pitiful, so desperate, that Elizabeth was finally forced to give Samantha the attention she demanded. "Shhh," she whispered, awkwardly trying to bounce the baby in her outstretched arms. That only made the child cry louder.

She finally gave in and cradled Samantha to her bosom,

fighting back her own tears. "Shh, n . . . now, it's . . . it's all right."

Samantha quieted within seconds, snuggling instinctively into Elizabeth's warmth. Elizabeth closed her eyes, aching with the baby's every little movement. She felt a devastating sense of emptiness, broader and deeper than all the waters around England. The weight, the roundness, the chubby softness of a baby was like nothing else in the world. Samantha even smelled wonderful, that sweet infant scent of milk and innocence.

It had all been so familiar to her—so very, very briefly.

Then, slowly, instinct took over. As if it were as natural to her as breathing, Elizabeth began to rock the baby, humming a half-remembered tune that faltered now and again. She felt a tug on her wig. Opening her eyes, she saw Samantha catch one of the bouncing white ringlets with both chubby hands. The baby smiled.

Elizabeth felt her heart turn over. The little girl was so perfect, so beautiful. She was about six months old, with a thatch of red hair, ruddy cheeks and bright eyes that rivaled the chandelier above for brilliance.

"Aren't you a pretty little girl," Elizabeth whispered, unable to resist brushing her fingers through the baby's silky hair, tickling her fat little chin.

Suddenly Elizabeth's vision blurred with tears. An emotion worse than any physical pain wracked every ounce of her being: *longing*. She had never had the chance to cuddle her own son this way. In the long months since, she had almost forgotten how very sweet it felt simply to hold a baby. She had forced herself to forget, clouded her memories with grief and loss and the fear of going through it all again.

But could she really live her entire life never feeling this special softness in her arms again, never seeing her love reflected back in a toothless grin, never cuddling a precious little person who was all her own?

A new feeling rose from deep within her to mingle with the longing: a sense of peace. She had been fighting a painful war with her own deepest, most natural instincts; she hadn't realized until now, holding Samantha, that it was a war she would never win. Nor did she have to. The feelings of grief and loss over Edward would always be with her, but wanting another child didn't diminish her love for him.

"You *are* a pretty little girl," she whispered, bending her head to brush noses with Samantha. "Yes, you are."

"Thank you," Lady Selwyn's voice said. "You're so kind to watch her for me. I'm sorry I took so long."

Elizabeth looked up and hurriedly dabbed at her eyes and tried to regain her composure. Lord and Lady Selwyn were coming down the stairs.

"This is my husband, Samuel," Lady Selwyn said, speaking around a hairpin as she hurriedly twisted her hair into a chignon. "Samuel, this is Lady Barnes-Finchley, a friend of Lady Kimble's. I've heard she's quite the hit of the social season."

Elizabeth blushed, still holding Samantha. "So pleased to meet you, sir."

Lord Selwyn was tall and blond, handsome in an unassuming sort of way that suited his casual attire of buff breeches and waistcoat with a white shirt. His sleeves were even rolled up. "And I you, Lady Barnes-Finchley," he replied with a small bow and genuine warmth.

"We really don't go in for parties much," Lady Selwyn said as she finished pinning her hair. "But I haven't been out very often since the baby, and Samuel insisted I go. Though there is *so* much to do here—"

"I shall take care of it all," Lord Selwyn said, smiling at his wife. "Your orders for the day are to let me handle this chaos while you thoroughly enjoy yourself."

As Lady Selwyn returned her husband's smile, Elizabeth noticed she had taken time to dab a bit of rouge on her cheeks, then realized it was a natural blush, for it deepened as her husband's hand strayed to her waist. Her lips were also a bit swollen, and Elizabeth didn't know of any cosmetic that could fake that.

She couldn't help but smile as she realized why Lady Selwyn had taken so long in returning downstairs. She couldn't help the little tug of envy in her heart either.

Lady Kimble could keep her silly coach; *this* was what Elizabeth found worthy of envy, this happy couple and their beautiful baby. They were the most charming aristocrats she'd yet encountered in London. Elizabeth couldn't even imagine any other lady of her acquaintance pinning up her own hair.

"I do hope Samantha wasn't any trouble." Lady Selwyn reached out to take her daughter.

"No, not at all." Elizabeth found herself reluctant to let the baby go. When she did, her arms felt weak, trembly . . . empty. "No trouble at all," she repeated softly.

Lord Selwyn lifted the little bundle from his wife's arms and shooed the women toward the door. "The two of you had better be going before that Kimble woman comes in after you. I'd rather face a firing squad than have her blustering about my entry hall."

"Samuel, honestly!" Lady Selwyn gave Elizabeth another pained smile, then took her arm as they went out the door. "Men! We marry them thinking we can civilize them, but it's a lost cause, isn't it? Now you simply must tell me all the latest gossip. I've been out of circulation so long . . ."

Elizabeth managed to utter a few tidbits as they collected the footman and dashed through the rain to the carriage. Then they were surrounded by Lady Kimble's nattering friends and subjected to one more rendition of the coach's litany of attributes.

Before long they were speeding toward the Beauclerks' country estate. Elizabeth felt relieved that she wasn't needed in the conversation. She was trying desperately to unclutter her thoughts and focus on the party and Montaigne and what she had to do today.

Unfortunately, her mind was filled with images of the baby and the Selwyns and . . . Pierce. She knew she shouldn't be thinking of him now, but wishing him away didn't work.

She tried simply repeating a single word over and over in her head. *Revenge.* She was so close to finishing the whole accursed business. Soon her part of the plan would be done, and Pierce would have the information he needed to steal the gold, and they would split it and . . .

And then what? There was a great deal unsaid and unsettled between them about what would happen after the Fair. Months ago, when she had set herself on this course of vengeance, she hadn't let herself think about anything beyond the day of Montaigne's downfall. Now it seemed that was all she could think about: *What happens after?*

But none of her thoughts left her feeling at all happy or secure. Too much depended on Pierce. She didn't like thinking about *after* without him, but she still wasn't sure he was capable of sharing—either the gold or his life.

Elizabeth had been lost in her thoughts for some time when Lady Vicary suddenly drew her attention back to the conversation.

"Shush, everyone!" the thin woman said urgently, holding up her hand for silence. "Did anyone hear something odd?"

The gossiping in the carriage ceased and they could indeed hear a sound above the squeaking of the carriage springs and the rhythm of the horses' hoofbeats: men's voices, shouting and rapidly drawing closer. Lady Kimble pulled aside one of the window curtains, peeked out and let loose an ear-splitting screech.

"Highwaymen!"

Chapter 23

❧

T he word "highwaymen" struck panic into everyone
around Elizabeth. Her companions dissolved into
screaming, babbling bundles of terror. Lady Vicary
snatched off her ruby earrings and necklace and tried to
stuff them in between the seat cushions. Lady Selwyn
had gone completely pale, and Lady Houblon and Lady
Kimble were in tears.

Outside, one of the male voices shouted, "Stand and
deliver!"

The coach jerked to a stop, almost tossing the women
to the floor. They clung to their seats and each other with
shrill cries and sobs.

Elizabeth, trying to dislodge Lady Vicary's painful
hold on her arm, was more annoyed than frightened. She
had nothing of value worth stealing and knew she
wouldn't merit much attention. But of all the confounded
bad luck! How ironic to be waylaid by highwaymen, and
on this of all days.

Lady Kimble's coach was a ridiculously blatant lure,
of course, but these would have to be bold thieves indeed, to attack a coach in broad daylight just outside the
city.

A shot rang out, and they all fell silent, like partridges
frozen in terror upon encountering a hunter.

"Down ye go, mates," the male voice said, apparently issuing orders to the footmen. "Step aside there
and be quick about it. You! Open 'er up and let's 'ave a
look at what we got 'ere."

The women crushed into a wide-eyed, cowering hud-
dle against the far side of the coach, leaving Elizabeth

the closest to the door as it opened. She blinked in the bright light, the image of a black-garbed brigand on horseback dancing before her eyes.

" 'Ello, me ladies,'' he said, leaning over his horse's neck, brandishing a pistol at them.

Her eyes on the gun, Elizabeth felt a stab of shock, followed by a dizzying sense of unreality, as if this were a dream. That was *her* pistol, the silver-embossed one she used to carry as Blackerby Swift! Pierce had taken it when he captured her, and had never given it back. How could this thief—

Her gaze snapped from the pistol to the man holding it and her surprise dissolved in a storm of fury. Outrage made her momentarily forget her companions. "I don't believe this! What the devil do you think—''

"Lady Barnes-Finchley!'' Lady Selwyn gasped, trying to pull her back from the door. "Don't provoke him!''

Pierce's dark eyes, just visible between the edge of his black kerchief and the brim of his tricorne, settled on Elizabeth. "Good advice indeed, me lady.'' She could have sworn he was smiling beneath the mask. "Do as I say and ye'll come t' no 'arm.''

Elizabeth had to settle for glaring her reply. Now that she was paying attention, she recognized Pierce's voice— though what he was doing with that accent and her pistol, attacking her group so dangerously close to London, she couldn't fathom!

Pierce glanced up toward the front of the coach. "Are ye almost ready there, mate?''

Elizabeth craned her head out the door, over her companions' strident objections. She saw a second man, dressed just as Pierce was, taking up the position vacated by Lady Kimble's driver.

"Ready,'' he called.

Who the devil could that be? Elizabeth was feeling more confused by the second. What the deuce was Pierce up to? And where had he found a partner?

He moved his horse to one side. "Ye'll be gettin' out,

ladies. One at a time, if ye would be so kind.'' He pointed the pistol at Lady Vicary. ''You first.''

Lady Vicary darted a hopeful look at the seat where she had stuffed her jewels before joining the two footmen, who stood outside in a puddle with their hands in the air.

Elizabeth had to dig her nails into her palms to keep from giving Pierce the tongue-lashing he deserved. So that's what he was up to! He had never intended to let her go to the assembly today. Well, if he thought to leave her stranded here on this muddy road, he was badly mistaken. She would walk the rest of the way in the rain if need be!

How could he lie to her so easily and go to all this trouble just to ruin her part of their plan? What kind of heartless blackguard was he?

''Step lively, there.'' Pierce turned his gun on Lady Houblon.

The rotund woman, who had been blubbering pitifully up to this point, suddenly gasped, staring at the weapon, and placed a hand over her considerable bosom. ''I know who that is!'' She turned a wild-eyed look on Lady Kimble. ''You were the one who told me about him. The daring highwayman with the silver-chased pistol and the accent. It's Blackerby Swift!''

The two women promptly rent the air with fearful cries and threats to faint.

Elizabeth sat frozen in disbelief, her mind whirling. Stunned, she couldn't begin to puzzle out this hopelessly topsy-turvy situation. She could only stare at Pierce and bite her tongue to keep from protesting, *He's not Blackerby Swift, I am!*

''P . . . please don't shoot us!'' Lady Kimble babbled.

''And don't take this,'' Lady Selwyn pleaded, indicating her simple gold wedding band. ''Anything else but not this. Please, I beg of you.''

Pierce made an impatient gesture with the pistol. ''Keep it. Just get out. And 'elp that one along while yer at it.''

Lady Selwyn quickly obeyed, dragging the wailing Lady Houblon with her.

Lady Kimble clung, cowering, to her seat. "I know what you want! You mean to take my coach. I won't let you do it. You'll have to kill me first!"

"Lady Kimble, really," Elizabeth said in disgust.

"Come along, lads," Pierce called to the footmen. " 'elp yer mistress out before I lose me patience."

The two men came forward and managed to wrestle her to her feet. As they lifted her out, she grabbed the window curtains, screaming and kicking. They had to pry her fingers loose one by one.

As soon as they were clear of the door, Elizabeth started to follow.

"Not you." Pierce moved his horse forward to block her path, speaking in that low, compelling tone that danced along her nerves.

Elizabeth suddenly realized he had a much more nefarious scheme in mind than leaving her stranded in the rain.

"He's going to abduct her!" Lady Vicary cried.

"She'll be ravished!" Lady Houblon added.

"My coach," Lady Kimble moaned. "My coach!"

Elizabeth never even had a chance to voice one of the vivid epithets that leaped to mind. By the time she recovered her wits enough to object, it was too late. Pierce signaled to his partner and the coach moved forward with a jerk, tossing her back into the seat.

Her last glimpse outside, before Pierce kicked the door shut, was of Lady Selwyn's stricken face, and the other three women, their wigs wilting in the rain, eyes wide and mouths already flapping with this juicily scandalous piece of gossip.

Elizabeth sat up and yanked aside the red curtain, ready to give Pierce a blistering earful, only to find that he had disappeared from view. She heard the sound of boots on the roof and the next thing she knew, he was nimbly opening the door and swinging himself inside.

She was absolutely struck dumb as he calmly seated

himself across from her and tossed his tricorne down beside him, scattering raindrops across the red velvet.

It took a monumental struggle just to recover her power of speech. "What . . . why . . . what . . . I don't—"

"You're babbling, Elizabeth." Pierce removed his mask and started taking off his gloves. He was smiling, the broadest smile she had ever seen on his face.

That self-satisfied grin finally snapped Elizabeth out of her stupor. "Of all the devil's own blackhearted, unthinking, underhanded things you have done, this really scrapes the dregs of the barrel!"

"I thought it went rather well, myself." He raised an eyebrow as he looked about the interior of the coach. "What is this monstrosity, anyway, a bawdy house on wheels?"

"Would you mind very much," Elizabeth said tightly, her voice shaking, "telling me what the deuce you think you are doing?"

"Abducting you," he said, as if it should be obvious. His gaze lingered over her clinging yellow gown as he shrugged out of his wet greatcoat. "And I must admit, that suggestion about ravishing was rather appealing."

Elizabeth was too furious to pay attention to what he was saying. "We had a plan!"

"We've changed it."

"*You* changed it. The same way you change anything that doesn't please you. Whether it's what I want or not!"

"By next week, you'll understand," he said confidently. "I'm doing what's best for you."

His patronizing tone only infuriated her. "Don't you realize what you've done? Not only can I not attend Lady Beauclerk's assembly, I won't be able to go *anywhere* in society now. I'll be the chief subject of gossip for weeks!"

"Well into autumn, I would imagine," Pierce agreed, reclining more comfortably in his seat. "Your departure from society will be every bit as notable as your arrival."

Elizabeth stared at him incredulously. "It wasn't

enough to keep me from going to this one party? You had to utterly ruin my place in society as well—''

"Not yours. Only Lady Barnes-Finchley's."

Elizabeth's head was still reeling too much for her to catch his meaning. "Oh, my God, when I think of what the *newspapers* will do with this!''

"I'm sure it will eventually become known as The Last Ride of Blackerby Swift." Pierce's smile widened. "I thought it appropriate that Swift and Lady Barnes-Finchley should disappear together.''

His words finally registered on Elizabeth's mind. "The last . . ." She regarded him through narrowed eyes, feeling a sickening sensation in her stomach that had nothing to do with the rocking of the coach. "*Disappear.* That's what this is really about, isn't it? You've decided you don't want to share the gold after all, and you couldn't even wait until the Fair to double deal with me!''

Pierce's smile vanished. "Believe me, Elizabeth, you couldn't be further from the truth.''

"The truth!" It was all she could do not to slap him. "Don't you dare speak to me about the truth! The gold is all that's ever mattered to you." As the idea sunk in and took hold, Elizabeth felt dazed; the whole thing was so painfully like that night at the costume ball. "The kisses and the rest—they were just lures to keep me distracted. And I fell for it. Like a fool I believed in you. I should have known you're no better than a lying, deceiving—''

"Elizabeth," Pierce warned, straightening. "Don't say things you'll regret later—''

"You haven't changed at all." Hurt and betrayal brought tears to her eyes and she covered her face so he wouldn't see them. "You're trying to edge me out of Montaigne's gold, just as you have since the moment we met. You're going to drag me off somewhere and leave me—''

"That's enough." Pierce moved with such speed he was beside her in a second, grabbing her wrists and forcing her to look at him. "Listen to me, Elizabeth. I know this is difficult to believe, but you're going to have to trust me—''

"Trust you? *Trust!* I'm surprised that word doesn't burn your tongue!" Elizabeth struggled against his grip, unable to bear his touch, unable to bear the fact that she wanted so badly to believe him. She had to stop wishing for the moon and see Pierce Wolverton for what he really was: self-interested and obsessed with money and capable of doing anything to get what he wanted. "This has all just been one giant ploy, to get me out of the way so you can abscond with the gold!"

His fingers tightened and his eyes smoldered with dark emotions. "I am not going to *abscond,* God-damn it. I'm taking you someplace safe so you'll bloody well stay out of trouble until the Fair is over!"

"I'm not going to believe anything more you say—"

"I am going to get that blasted gold on Sunday," he continued as if she hadn't said a word, "and bring it back and split it with you exactly as we agreed."

Elizabeth shook her head, steeling herself against the impulse just to believe him and melt into his arms. "You won't be able to take the gold at all now. You've ruined that, too." She stared at him accusingly. "When I don't show up for my meeting with Montaigne today, he'll start getting suspicious. And once he hears that Blackerby Swift is back—thanks to you—he'll hire dozens more guards for that shipment."

A hint of Pierce's self-satisfied grin reappeared. "That's not a problem. I've already worked around it."

"How can you work around scores of armed men?"

"All you need know is that I've taken care of it. Other than that, I'm not telling you a single word about my intentions."

"That's because you intend to keep all the gold for yourself!" Elizabeth tried again to extricate herself from his touch, but he still wouldn't let her go—pulled her closer, in fact.

She struggled to keep the anguish out of her voice. "I'm not going to let you do it," she vowed. "I'm not going to let you waste all that money on your bricks and

mortar and blades of grass. I want that gold to help people, women and children who have nowhere to turn. And
I mean to have it!"

"Elizabeth," Pierce said, his voice sharp with anger
now. "You are going to have to trust—"

"Oh, damn you!" She pressed her fists against his
chest and closed her eyes to shut him out. "Every time
I trust you I wind up regretting it. God, how I hate you!"

"Don't say that." He grasped her chin, forcing her
head up, but she stubbornly kept her lashes lowered. His
other arm fastened around her back and he locked her
body against his. "You're angry, but you don't hate me.
You know you don't."

"Yes, I do," she insisted, though her voice sounded
weak even to her ears. "I do—"

"Look at me and tell me that."

Elizabeth opened her eyes, intending to lash out with
all the fury and hurt she felt at what he had done; instead
she could only gaze up at him, feeling weak and cowardly and a fool a hundred times over. Because she
couldn't say it. She couldn't say she hated him, not when
he was looking at her that way. His expression was so
soft, his hands so gentle as he reached up to cup her
face, that she couldn't even find the will to pull away.

Pierce looked down at her, feeling an ache that started
somewhere in the region of his heart and spread through
his whole body. God, this was agony. The tears shining
in her eyes made his throat feel tight. He hadn't expected
Elizabeth to understand why he was abducting her—but
he hadn't anticipated feeling hurt to the quick by her lack
of faith in him.

In that moment he wanted nothing so much as to win
a single smile from her, just a tiny grain of trust or affection. After all they had been through together, she was
still as elusive as she had been that first night on Hounslow Heath. He had been chasing her all this time and
still hadn't caught her.

Only now did he fully understand what he sought: that
look in her eyes, the one he had glimpsed ever so briefly
the last time they made love. He wanted to see that every

time their gazes met—not this, not the way she was staring at him, her eyes full of pain and disappointment. A
sudden, sharp fear assaulted him, that perhaps he had
just extinguished that fragile flame forever.

It disturbed him to discover just how much he needed
that look of love, how cold and alone he felt without it.
All he could think about was wiping away the accusation
in her eyes and rekindling the spark that had flared before. He wanted, *needed* to bind her to him, body and
soul, until she couldn't possibly deny what she felt.

Not even completing the thought, he lowered his head
to hers and kissed her, ravenously, ruthlessly, using every
bit of his experience to arouse her. His hand moved to
the laces on the back of her dress.

She tried to twist away. "I hate you!"

"Then show me, Elizabeth," he taunted softly, recap-
turing her chin and lifting her lips back to his. "Show
me!"

He took her mouth aggressively, pinning her against
the seat, using one hand to subdue her when she pounded
her fists against his chest. Her whole body stiffened. A
sharp sound of outrage rose in her throat. Pierce only
kissed her harder, demanding a response, his tongue
thrusting boldly past her lips.

He unfastened her hairpiece, tossed it aside, then lifted
her with one arm, crushing her body to his. Despite the
rocking and jostling of the speeding coach, he made short
work of her gown, the lemon-colored silk and lace and
underpinnings giving way beneath his expert fingers.

She writhed and fought him, but there was no room
for escape in the cramped quarters, and her strength was
no match for his. He was determined to win this war for
her heart, and used every ounce of masculine power at
his command.

The back of her dress gaped open. He trailed one finger down her bare skin, slowly, from the nape of her
neck to the sensitive tip of her tailbone. She tried to arch
away, then shivered instead.

He splayed his hand across her waist, caressing,
kneading. Already, the tide of battle was turning in his

favor, and he reveled in it. He knew in the end neither would be conqueror, neither vanquished. Victory on this field would be shared, and all the sweeter for the sharing.

His lips began to move more slowly over hers, coaxing now, persuasive, as he lowered her down upon the velvet seat. The swaying motion of the coach brought their bodies together, then apart, in a way that mirrored more intimate contact. She whimpered, but he could tell it was more from confusion than protest. He held her still and at last broke the kiss, raising himself above her on one arm.

He expected her to launch a searing verbal attack as soon as he lifted his head. She only licked her bruised lips and gazed up at him through half-lowered lashes, her expression one of almost painful uncertainty.

Pierce forced himself not to smile; she was so busy trying to puzzle him out, she had forgotten all about fighting him. He gently slid the yellow dress from her shoulders and planted a lingering kiss on the soft skin just above her breast.

"Go ahead." He urged quietly. "Tell me how much you hate me."

She turned her head away. "Damn you," she whispered, but there was little strength and less ire left in her curse.

Now that she wasn't looking, he indulged in a grin of pure male satisfaction. One tug and her silken bodice slid to her waist.

He spoke in his deepest, huskiest tone, his words barely audible above the pounding of the horses' hooves. "Can't you remember?" He teased gently, kissing one of the gentle mounds that beckoned his lips, relishing the small gasp she wasn't able to restrain. "You loathe me." His tongue flicked out to graze her. "Despise me." He took the peak between his teeth and nipped her carefully. "And detest me."

She managed to wrest one hand free and buried her fingers in his hair. She clearly intended to make him stop, but she only held him, her hand trembling.

"I'm a blackhearted lout," he reminded her softly,

nuzzling her, taking her completely into his mouth, tormenting her with lips and tongue and teeth until she cried out. "And utterly selfish."

Her entire body was quivering beneath him now. Not giving her time to recover, he sat up and with a single movement of his arm, whisked her dress and stomacher and petticoats down past her legs. The yellow silk joined her wig on the floor, leaving her naked but for her stockings and garters.

Pierce was already so aroused he thought he would burst his breeches, but his desire reached new and almost agonizing heights as he gazed down at her. She returned his look, clenching her fists against the seat in mute protest, her body rigidly braced against the movement of the coach and the feelings that so clearly warred within her. Despite her outward show of hostility, he could see the resistance fading from her eyes, along with any pretense of animosity toward him.

She was the most intoxicating thing he had ever seen, all soft and pale and vulnerable against the crushed red velvet. The look of her spread through him like warm, heady wine. He felt again that fierce, urgent need to make her his—not just for this moment, not just physically, but wholly and completely and forever.

Surrender was near, for them both.

He ran his hands along her slim legs, her hips, her waist, hungry to learn the smooth perfection of each curve and hollow.

"There's one character trait I forgot," he whispered. "Wicked." Lowering himself over her, he traced a trail of kisses from her breasts to her belly, then lower. "Let's not forget wicked."

He grasped her thighs but she almost bolted right off the seat as she realized his intent.

"Pierce!" she cried, writhing in his arms. "No. Oh, God . . ."

He held her still and kissed her intimately, his tongue flicking over the sensitive bud of her desire.

"No." She struggled against him. "N . . . n . . . ohhh."

She tried to twist away, resisted until he made resistance impossible, then finally yielded and went limp, letting him pleasure her as never before. His hands slid from her legs to her hips, lifting her fully against his mouth. She shuddered and arched off the seat, sighing the wordless plea he had been waiting for.

He moved atop her quickly, unfastening his breeches as he gathered her to him. Their lips and tongues met and shared the muskiness of her arousal. Elizabeth moaned, deep and long.

"That," he murmured against her mouth, "didn't sound very hateful at all."

In answer, she tangled her fingers in his hair and expressed herself with kisses. He kicked free of his breeches, shaking with the desire to bury himself in her enveloping warmth, his need now so strong he feared he might hurt her.

"Hold on to me," he whispered in her ear. "My sweet, sweet Elizabeth. Hold on."

She wrapped her arms about his shoulders. He shifted so that he was poised at the opening of her feminine channel. Her lips parted and something changed in her eyes; the last mist of uncertainty cleared and he saw what he sought, sparkling as intensely as rare jewels against pure gold.

Love.

He drank it in like a parched wanderer granted his first draught of water. It sent him soaring higher than any physical pleasure he had ever known. With a groan of deep, pure joy, he thrust into her.

Elizabeth matched his cry, feeling his blunt hardness parting her, penetrating her. The indescribably sweet fullness sent her heart racing and her blood pulsing against her veins. Time faded, the rain and the coach and their surroundings and every angry word they had ever said to one another faded, and there was only this moment, this melding of body and soul.

There was only his voice, dark and rich as he called out her name, and his kisses, infinitely erotic as his tongue mirrored the motions below.

Even the scents of perfumes that lingered in the carriage gave way to the spicy tang of their mingled desire. He surged into her, his rhythm gathering force, and swept her to a place of bliss she had never imagined. The tingling fire she had felt with him before swirled and blazed through her limbs, through her heart, to the very center of her being.

She met his thrusts with mindless abandon, wanting to take him deeper, wanting the full length of him to be part of her. Every powerful movement of his hard-muscled body sent her breathlessly spiraling upward, ever upward.

Like moon and sun, shadow and light, earth and sea, they met, blended, changed until they were no longer separate and different, but one and the same.

She clung to him as though her heart would stop if she let go. His warm kisses turned hot, and hot turned sizzling. He moved faster within her, driving her wild with each ungentle stroke. Every fiber of her being felt taut, shivering, straining for release. The racing coach suddenly seemed much too small to hold her; the entire world wasn't large enough to contain the feelings she felt. She bit her lip, thinking she couldn't possibly withstand it, fearing she would tear apart, knowing she must die of this, and welcoming it all the same.

Pierce groaned, a sound somewhere between ecstasy and agony, and started to withdraw. Reason and fear slipped away and instinct and passion and love and longing took over, and Elizabeth raised her hips, wrapping her legs around his, holding him inside.

"Elizabeth!"

Pierce only had time to grate out that one harsh warning before she felt him exploding within her.

Then the tension at the center of her body snapped and her own thoughts scattered as a wave of release shimmered deliciously through her. In half a heartbeat, they were soaring together, sighing with one voice as they spun out beyond time, beyond reality, beyond any dream of rapture.

Floating downward like a feather on a warm breeze,

Elizabeth was still weak and trembling with little spasms of ecstasy when Pierce moved out of her and gathered her in his arms, crushing her to his chest.

"Damn," he said between ragged breaths. "Elizabeth—"

"I'm not sorry," she insisted against his throat. "I'm not, I'm not."

And then she couldn't say any more, because she was crying, sobbing inconsolably.

"I'm sorry, my sweet Elizabeth." He took her face between his hands, carefully, as if she would break. "I didn't mean for it to end that way."

"It's not that," she said, feeling even more miserable because of his gentle apology. "It's this. It's *after*."

"What's after?"

"It always happens this way." She struggled to put her sense of desolation into words. "When you . . . when we make love, it's like . . ." She looked up at him. "Like heaven. Like magic. And I start believing it will go on forever."

He brushed his thumbs over her cheeks. "It can."

His assurance only made her feel worse. A sense of sadness settled over her heart like a crushing weight. "But it never does. We always end up fighting again. We only have a little bit of wonderful before things turn awful."

"Only because of the gold."

"It's not the gold. It's us. You almost make me forget everything, but I can't." She started crying harder and had to make an effort to breathe before she could speak again. "I want to, but I *can't*."

"Stop trying to be practical." He admonished softly. "It doesn't suit you."

"I don't want to be practical. I just don't want to hurt like this anymore."

His fingers caressed her jaw. "Elizabeth," he said, that note of confidence still strong in his voice, "I know you don't understand why I've kidnapped you. You don't believe that I'm doing this to protect you, but you will."

"Don't you see?" she whispered. "It doesn't matter

whether I believe you or not. The problem is that you could do this at all."

She pulled away from him and wiped tiredly at her eyes, then picked up her gown and held it to her like a small child with a blanket. "Nothing has changed from the moment we met. Every time we make an agreement, one of us ends up breaking it. Every time we try to have a civil conversation, it doesn't last more than five minutes without turning into an argument—"

"That will all change, once this business with Montaigne is over."

She shook her head, feeling helpless and worn out, as if she had been trying to climb a huge, straight wall and had just slid to the bottom for the last time. "I kept hoping that it would be different, after the Fair. But *I* won't be different. *You* won't be different."

Her pain increased tenfold as she saw it mirrored in his features.

The hurt in his eyes disappeared quickly, buried under affront and accusation. "You mean that even after what just happened between us, you still want us to go our separate ways?" He looked at her in disbelief.

Elizabeth could barely choke out the words past a hot rush of new tears. "There's no other way we *can* go."

His expression hardened. "You love me."

It wasn't a question but a demand. Elizabeth hung her head, feeling the words strike to her very marrow. How could she deny them?

Oh God, it was true. She loved him, wanted him, needed him and more. The once-dreaded Lord Darkridge had stolen every bit of anger and fear and resentment from her, as easily as he had stolen her silver-plated pistol.

But how could she bear loving him and never having him? Pierce wouldn't change; he would always put his needs first, his goals ahead of hers. He would only listen when he chose to listen, believing that all he had to do was make love to her instead. He would do what he thought best, regardless of her feelings. And she would end up fighting him every time. How could they bring each other anything but unhappiness?

She looked up at him, and felt as though her heart were being torn in two. She couldn't bring herself to say she loved him, couldn't deny it, couldn't even nod or shake her head. Anything she said or did would only hurt him.

Feeling weak and exhausted, she could only clutch the pale lemon gown to her body and lift her shoulders in a slight shrug.

A host of emotions crossed Pierce's face, ending with hard-edged anger. "That's not an answer."

"You didn't ask a question," she accused quietly.

They stared at one another as silence stretched between them, silence filled with the mundane sounds of carriage wheels, jingling harness, and horses' hooves—and the tense rasp of two people struggling to breathe evenly.

When Pierce finally spoke, he sounded unflinching, commanding, and distant. "Obviously, I won't be able to convince you I'm telling the truth until I return. You'll just have to believe what you want for now."

He grabbed his breeches from where they lay in the corner and dressed without looking at her.

"Why can't you just let me go?" she said wearily.

"No, Elizabeth," he said with soft, sharp resolve. "For once, you're going to do what I tell you, and I'm telling you to stay put and stay away from Montaigne and the Fair."

Elizabeth didn't say a word. Another argument would be futile, and she found she had used up her will to fight. All she felt was numb—and more remote from Pierce than in the entire time she'd known him. Why couldn't he understand how important this was to her? She had to put her own demons to rest or they would torment her forever.

She did her best to don her garments in the cramped space without touching him. He didn't offer assistance. She didn't ask. When she was done, she slid to the seat across from him, since he had made no effort to move away from her.

Elizabeth lost track of time as she sat there, chewing the inside of her cheek, staring at the floor of the coach. After a while she became aware of a prickling sensation beneath her. She shifted away from it, then remembered. *Lady Vicary's jewels.*

Not moving, she glanced at Pierce. He had pulled back the window curtain and was glaring outside. There was no telling where he was taking her, but the gems might prove useful wherever she was going. Being careful not to draw his attention, she pulled the necklace and earrings from between the cushions and slipped them into the pockets in her skirt.

She almost jumped out of her skin when Pierce spoke.

"We're here," he said tersely, not looking at her.

It was only then Elizabeth noticed the carriage had slowed down. She looked out the window on her side to see where "here" was. The rain had stopped. By the sunlight, she guessed that it was midafternoon, though it was hard to tell, for they were surrounded by forest.

The coach lumbered along a path that obviously wasn't intended for such a large vehicle, slowed by mud that almost reached the wheel hubs.

They pulled up to a small cottage in a clearing and came to a stop. A moment later the door on her side opened. Elizabeth couldn't suppress a cry of surprise at seeing Pierce's accomplice without his mask.

"Quinn!"

"Madam," he said with a bow, reaching up to help her out.

Her surprise quickly gave way to a profuse blush. She knew he couldn't help but notice her badly mussed appearance, and felt grateful when he didn't even lift an eyebrow.

Pierce jumped down beside her and handed Quinn a ring with a few keys on it. "I'll dump this monstrosity of a coach in a field somewhere on my way back to the city."

"The lady will be completely safe here, sir." Quinn

assured his employer. He went to the door of the cottage and unlocked it, then stepped inside.

As soon as they were alone again, Pierce's gaze settled on Elizabeth. "Quinn will guard you until I return."

Elizabeth, who had already gathered that, only responded with a frustrated glare.

"And you needn't worry about the Viscountess Alden and Mrs. Osgood. I'll let them know you're safe. I'm certain they'll agree that this is best for you."

"I'm certain," Elizabeth echoed, feeling all the more irritated because she knew he was right. Everyone would be in complete agreement—except her. It only increased her determination to prove once and for all that she could take care of herself.

"Even if you somehow managed to get away—which you won't," Pierce added, as if reading her thoughts, "you can't go anywhere as Lady Barnes-Finchley or Blackerby Swift. You'll get too much attention."

She looked down at her muddy shoes. "You've seen to everything, haven't you?"

"Yes," he said cooly. "I have."

Her gaze flicked toward the cottage. "It's a prison. It may have furniture and carpets, but it's still a prison."

"I'm not your jailor, Elizabeth. And I'm not your enemy. If you haven't figured that out by now, we've nothing more to discuss."

With that he turned and slammed the coach door shut, then vaulted easily into the driver's seat.

He didn't say goodbye, didn't even try to kiss her or touch her. For some ridiculous reason, that hurt Elizabeth more than anything.

"You won't come back," she choked out. "Once you have the gold in your hands, you won't be able to resist keeping it all for yourself—if you can even get it. It'll be more dangerous than ever now. You might get . . ."

He turned and looked at her over his shoulder, but suddenly tears blurred her vision and she couldn't finish her sentence, couldn't bear to think about any harm coming to him. "E . . . either way, I'll never see you again."

He didn't reply. When she managed to see clearly

again, he was staring down at her from atop the stolen coach, his angular features a mask of rigid self-control. The only emotion she could detect was disappointment; it shone in his eyes, and struck her like a stinging slap.

Then even that disappeared.

"You're wrong," he said. Turning his back, he lifted the reins.

With a snap, he set the horses off as fast as they could go. Lady Kimble's prized carriage pitched and lurched down the muddy path into the forest, until it and Pierce were swallowed up by the trees.

He was gone.

Elizabeth couldn't stand the way that thought ravaged her heart. She started to sway on her feet, and suddenly was aware of Quinn at her side, gently taking her elbow to help her into the cottage.

She couldn't let it end this way. Pierce had always chastised her for being reckless, and here he was charging off, alone, into a ridiculously dangerous situation. Out of the torrent of emotions that raged within her rose a stubborn determination. She wasn't going to let him kill himself.

Somehow Blackerby Swift would ride again, one last time.

Chapter 24

On Thursday morning, Pierce paid a visit to a gunsmith. He chose the most expensive establishment he could find, one that would be used to dealing with eccentric clientele, and catering to unusual requests.

He dressed like a fashionable gallant, complete with brocade coat and breeches, a powdered wig and a silk patch on his cheek. Thoughts of the future and his feelings for Elizabeth hovered only at the edge of his mind; fortunately, since leaving her in Quinn's care yesterday, he found himself able to really concentrate for the first time in weeks. The next three days would see the end of fifteen years of planning and working for revenge—and he would need every ounce of skill and cunning he possessed to pull it off.

The hackney coach he had hired came to a stop on the Strand, in front of the renowned firm of Fulbright & Weeks, Gunsmiths. Pierce stepped out and handed the driver a generous tip. He had never been in the military, but imagined this must be what a soldier felt like on the eve of a decisive campaign: focused, taut, ready. Questions of right or wrong, courage or cowardice, life or death had been subdued by a fierce drive to get the job done. He could physically feel it, like a ball of fire in his gut, propelling him forward, step by resolute step.

The scent of gunpowder stung his eyes as he stepped inside the shop. He no sooner closed the door behind him than he was greeted by one of the shopkeepers.

"Good day, your lordship," the man said, dipping into a quick bow. "I'm Mr. Weeks. How may I be of service today?"

Pierce didn't waste more than a few seconds pretending interest in the various displays that filled the polished glass cases and velvet-lined leather boxes. He wasn't interested in flintlocks, carbines, dueling pistols, fancy powder horns or high-priced cleaning oils.

"I should like to purchase some lead shot," he said finally. "The sort suitable for a blunderbuss."

"Certainly, sir." The man was clearly disappointed in such a simple request from such a richly-dressed customer. "If you would follow me."

He went to the rear of the store, where casks and crates of all sizes were open to display a variety of ammunition.

"We've this, which is the more common sort." He held up a handful of tiny lead balls before turning to another barrel. "Or this larger type, which is more expensive but much more effective."

"The first will do," Pierce said.

"Excellent. And how much would you like today, sir?"

"I think about five barrels should do."

Weeks almost fell into his carefully-arranged display. "Excuse me, sir?"

From the man's astounded look, he seemed to believe his customer meant to start a private war.

Not start one, Pierce thought, *end one*. "I'll pay whatever you think fair. Cash. In advance. But I might need more than five. Will that be a problem?"

"Uh, no. No, sir. Not at all." The shopkeeper recovered quickly, his face brightening. "I could have them for you tomorrow. Would that be soon enough?"

"I would prefer to have them on Saturday. And I should like them delivered." Pierce indulged in a slow smile. "Along with one other item from your fine establishment."

It rained all day Friday, a driving downpour that beat on the roof of the cottage until Elizabeth thought it might wash the little structure away.

Wishful thinking, she told herself sullenly, staring out the front window as the last rays of cloud-choked sunlight melted into the trees. The dreary weather only worsened her mood, which had grown steadily more restless since Pierce had deposited her here two days ago.

It wasn't a horrible place, she had to admit, even though she felt horrible being here. At any other time, she might have called it charming. Most of the cottage was taken up by a keeping-room, with an oak settle, a cozy fireplace and hand made rugs. A kitchen and small bedroom made up the rest.

Pierce had thought to provide dresses so she would have a change of clothes, all the food she could eat, even a few books to keep her occupied. Quinn had turned out to be an excellent cook, and every so often would try to start a conversation or suggest a game of cards.

Elizabeth was not in the mood. A cage was a cage, gilded or not.

"Would you like supper soon, madam?" Quinn asked from where he sat by the hearth, reading.

"What time is it?" Elizabeth asked dully.

He checked his pocket watch. "Seven."

She sighed in frustration. It was almost nightfall. Before she knew it, the Fair would be here and gone, and she would still be stuck in the middle of these accursed woods.

Elizabeth turned and gave him a wan smile. "Yes, that would be fine. I'm sorry, Quinn, I know it makes no sense to keep taking out my ill humor on you."

Quinn looked up with a sympathetic expression. "Quite all right, madam."

"I suppose it isn't your fault that your employer is the most unyielding, infuriating man in all England." Elizabeth regarded Quinn with a furrowed brow. "Tell me, how *did* a kindly soul such as yourself ever come to work for the Earl of Confounded Darkridge?"

He chuckled at her description. "If I tell you, madam, I don't believe you'll call him that anymore."

Now Elizabeth's curiosity was truly piqued. "Really?" she said skeptically. "It would have to be quite a tale."

Quinn set his book aside, and his smile faded a bit, but he apparently decided to give it a try. "If it weren't for Lord Darkridge, madam, I'm quite certain I wouldn't be alive today. Before I worked for him, I was an apothecary. It was my profession. I had trained for it since I was a boy. But I got a bit overconfident, started experimenting, trying to improve existing formulas. I wanted to make a name for myself."

He looked up at Elizabeth, but she didn't interrupt; she could tell this was not a tale he had often spoken aloud.

"I thought I was being cautious," he continued, "in that I always tested the elixirs on myself first. I never expected to become . . . dependent on them. They started to affect my judgment. One day I tried one of my own formulas on a patient and I very nearly killed him."

He shook his head sadly. "I walked away from it that day, swore I would never go back. But I didn't leave the drugs behind. And when they weren't enough to help me forget, I tried to lose myself at the bottom of a claret bottle as well. I went to the London Register Office every day and tried to find work as a servant, but no one would hire me. I was almost ready to . . . give up. And then Lord Darkridge took me on."

"He was willing to take a chance on you?" Elizabeth asked softly, though she couldn't help the surprise in her voice.

"I'm sure if you asked him why he did it, he would have some perfectly practical explanation." Quinn gave her a meaningful look. "But I don't think Lord Darkridge always *has* logical reasons for his actions. He would never admit it, but once in a great while, he just does what his heart tells him is the right thing to do."

Elizabeth turned away, not responding to that. She thought of the way Pierce had chided her for trying to help London's downtrodden—and here he had done the same thing himself, at least once. Helping Quinn was not something a man who was completely cynical and self-interested would do. She didn't say anything for a moment. "Have you never wanted to go back to it, Quinn? Being an apothecary, I mean."

"No," he said firmly. "I am quite content as valet, footman, butler, and cook. I don't want to have anyone's life in my hands."

Elizabeth nodded. "I understand."

Quinn rose from his seat beside the hearth and cleared his throat. "Now, then," he said cheerfully, dispelling the somber mood. "I believe I was trying to persuade you to eat something."

Elizabeth smiled. "I suppose I could allow myself to be persuaded, if you could make one of your delicious mutton pies. And perhaps some more of that wonderful roasted rye bread with butter. What was it you called it?"

" 'Toast,' madam. It's the latest thing to take with tea." Quinn returned her smile warmly and went into the kitchen.

Elizabeth wandered to the other front widow and looked out, sighing, as reality intruded on her once again.

This was how she had spent most of the last two days: feeling useless. She wasn't allowed near the door. Nor could she escape out one of the windows—she had tried within minutes of her arrival, only to find that Pierce had bolted them all from the outside.

Indeed, he had thought of everything. She wasn't even allowed to have a candle in her room at night. Quinn explained that Pierce had forbidden it. Something about her trying to escape by starting a fire.

Pierce had forbidden it. The thought made her burn with helpless ire. How could he do this to her? Did he think this abduction showed he cared for her?

Even if he was only following his heart—as Quinn seemed to be trying to tell her—love was not a license to do whatever he wanted, under the guise of looking out for her best interests.

She leaned her forehead against the windowpane, watching the raindrops spatter and drizzle down the glass, listening to the clatter of copper utensils as Quinn went to work.

A momentous event was about to change her life, and she was forced to sit by, miles away, helpless as a china doll on a shelf, while it went on without her. Each minute dragged past, bringing nagging fears with it.

Perhaps Pierce did have good motives. Perhaps her accusations in the coach had been all wrong. But what if they never had a chance to work it all out between them? There was an all-too-real possibility that Pierce might never make it back.

Even if the lure of the gold didn't prove too much for him, Montaigne's guards very well might.

She closed her eyes, unable to stand a second more of this torturous waiting and wondering. Enough was enough. She would go mad if she had to stay here a day longer.

She raised her head and looked toward her bedroom. Her only hope was the jewelry she had buried in the stuffing of her mattress. If she could get to a village, or even a nearby farm, she could trade the earrings and necklace for a pistol and a fast horse and be back in London in time for the Fair.

All she had to do was think of some way to get around Quinn.

But *how*?

By Friday night, Pierce was feeling inordinately pleased with himself. Exactly as he had hoped, the gossip had raced across London faster than skaters across the Thames in January: Blackerby Swift was back. The bounder had staged his most daring raid ever, kidnapping the beautiful favorite of the social season, one Lady Elizabeth Barnes-Finchley, less than a mile outside the city in broad daylight.

The poor woman hadn't been seen since, and it was said she had been thoroughly ravished and either shot, garroted or stabbed—depending on from whom one heard the tale.

God-fearing Londoners demanded that the brigand be brought to justice. Magistrates vowed he would receive the most severe penalty under the law. Newspapers throughout the city printed scathing denouncements of the state of modern morals, accompanied, of course, by lurid descriptions of the rape and murder, some complete with artists' wildly imagined renderings, which sold a mountain of newspapers.

Reading the reports at home Friday night, Pierce shook his head at how easily gossip was accepted as fact. The truth was that he had left Elizabeth in fine and furious good health. The only fact in the stories, he thought with a fiendish shot of male pride, was the "thoroughly ravished" part. His grin faded when that thought was replaced by the memory of how they had parted.

Gossip aside, Pierce knew that by far the most satisfying part of the whole charade was taking place in a town house in Cavendish Square. It was too late now for Charles Montaigne to cancel his plans for the Fair; gin vendors from all over England were already on their way to London, ready to cash in on Montaigne's promise of payment in gold for a year's supply of their best wares.

Montaigne had sent word throughout the city that he would pay triple the usual amount to any man willing to serve as a guard for his coach for just one day: Sunday.

But as gossip spread of Blackerby Swift's murderous deed, along with freshly embellished tales of his previous exploits, few seemed eager to take up the challenge. One couldn't spend triple pay or *any* pay if one were dead. Only a handful of desperate types applied.

And so it was that when Pierce presented himself on Saturday afternoon—disguised in wig and cosmetics, a trick he had borrowed from Elizabeth—the steward hired him on the spot.

Everything was going precisely as planned.

The rain had lessened only slightly by Saturday evening. Elizabeth sat on the edge of her bed in the darkness, listening to the rivulets of water pattering against her window. She had hardly eaten all day, and spent most of the time in her room, thinking. As evening fell, sleep was the furthest thing from her mind.

The window was the best way out. She had decided

that with a certainty that made her pulse quicken. If she broke the glass, though, Quinn would come running in a second. And she couldn't think of how to get past the outside lock without breaking the glass.

Only after wracking her brain all day and into the night did she come up with an answer. She was sitting on it!

Diamonds.

She had heard or read once, she couldn't remember which, that diamonds could cut glass. Leaping to her feet with excitement, she retrieved the necklace and earrings from where she had stuffed them in the mattress. Praying that Lady Vicary wouldn't stoop to wearing anything but real gems, she carried them to the window.

She squinted in the meager light. It was deucedly difficult to work, with no candlelight and the moon obscured by clouds, but she managed to make a shallow cut in the glass.

Elated, she set herself to the task. After a few tries with the necklace, she stuffed it in her pocket, deciding that the earrings were easier to work with.

It seemed to take forever, for the windowpane was thick and she was afraid of making even the slightest noise. She hoped the steady splash of rainfall was enough to cover the tiny squeaking sound the diamonds made. She kept darting looks over her shoulder; Quinn slept just outside her door.

Her fingers were cramped when she finally finished, but her reward was a rough circle of glass that plopped into her hand. Setting it aside, she reached through the hole and unfastened the lock, then pushed the window open.

The fresh scent of rain and freedom was tantalizing, but she didn't take more than a second to enjoy it. She wished she had a cloak of some sort—but of course, Pierce hadn't provided that, since she wasn't supposed to go outside.

She had to make do with a blanket from the bed. Wrapping it around her and pocketing the earrings, she slipped out over the sill, landing softly in the mud on the other side. Quinn wouldn't come in looking for her until breakfast.

By then, she thought with a surge of anticipation, she could be halfway to London.

Pierce had been at Montaigne's town house for hours, but had yet to encounter Montaigne. He knew he should look on that fact as fortunate, but instead it irked him. He wanted to watch the bastard worrying about Blackerby Swift, sweating over his gold, never realizing the real threat was only a few feet away.

However, it seemed Montaigne was either so confident he didn't deem it necessary to rally his troops, or so overcome with nerves that he couldn't get out of bed. Pierce guessed it was the latter.

The yard behind the town house was a morass of mud by Saturday night. Pierce did his best to blend in with the other servants and guards who dashed about, seeing to last minute preparations.

He made himself useful by cleaning guns and helping saw planks to reinforce the floor of the carriage that would carry the gold. All the while he watched as the coin was carried into the town house through the servants' entrance. It had been arriving steadily from Montaigne's various banks, in trunks of every description, cleverly disguised as deliveries from various shops. He counted ten, exactly as Elizabeth had said.

When the trunks had all arrived, the coach was brought in, the planks laid in place, and the gold loaded. Pierce suffered a moment of uneasiness when three servants were posted on guard. When he casually asked, one explained that the men would take turns guarding the coach until morning.

Damnation, he hadn't thought the bugger would find it necessary to post not one, not two, but three guards in his own yard. Pierce went back to his tasks with a sinking feeling, but the foul weather played into his hand and solved what could have been a sticky setback. At eleven, he volunteered to take a turn at the watch, and one of the rain-soaked young footmen on duty was only too glad to go inside.

His confidence in his plan was fully restored at midnight, when the Fulbright & Weeks wagon arrived, exactly on schedule.

"What's this, then?" one of the two men on guard with him asked. "Another bloody delivery?"

The driver jumped to the ground. "From Fulbright an' Weeks. Mr. Montaigne specially asked that it be brought 'round at midnight t'night."

They untied the tarpaulin covering the bed of the wagon and lifted it, sluicing rain over the sides. Beneath it, Pierce could see ten sturdy-looking trunks of various descriptions, each padlocked, exactly as he had requested.

He met the driver's gaze and nodded imperceptibly in approval.

From beneath her borrowed tricorne, Nell acknowledged him with a flicker of a smile. She wore a greatcoat up close about her face, keeping herself both dry and concealed at the same time. When Pierce had asked that the lead shot be delivered to his home in trunks, the discreet Mr. Weeks hadn't blinked—nor had he so much as raised an eyebrow at renting the sturdy wagon for a few hours.

"Ten more of 'em," the servant said with a groan. "Me arms are already achin'."

"These must be the decoys," Pierce said confidently. "We can put them right in the coach. No need to carry them inside."

"Decoys?" the second guard looked at him in puzzlement.

"The ones Mr. Montaigne will carry to the Fair tomorrow."

"You mean these aren't more . . ." The first man stopped himself suddenly, looking warily at the driver.

Pierce turned to Nell. "Pardon me, friend, but might my mates and I have a bit of privacy for a moment?"

"Long as yer quick about it," she grumbled in a deep voice. "I'm goin' t' catch me death in this 'ere rain."

Shoulders hunched, she walked away a few yards and kept her back to them.

The first guard turned to Pierce with a look of surprise. "You mean these aren't more gold?" he hissed.

Pierce looked at him as if he thought him addlepated. "Do you actually think Mr. Montaigne is stupid enough to carry the gold in that coach tomorrow, with that highwayman fellow about—what's his name?"

"Blackerby Swift," the second man supplied, crossing himself.

"Right. Swift. Well to fool him, Mr. Montaigne's loading that coach"—he pointed to the one they'd been guarding—"with decoys."

The second man was catching on. "So even if Swift does rob it tomorrow, 'e won't get anything but these 'ere."

"Exactly."

The first man wasn't so easily convinced. "Then why the devil did we 'ave to load it up and guard the bloody thing all night?"

"What's the point of having a decoy if you don't make it look like the real thing?" Pierce pointed out. "Not everyone knows about this. I was supposed to take care of it personally, and I'll probably catch hell for telling you about it, but you look like trustworthy fellows."

The skeptical one called the driver back over. When Nell had rejoined them, he regarded her through narrowed eyes. "You sure you ain't from one o' them banks? And these trunks ain't full of . . . the same stuff as the rest of them deliveries what came today?"

"I don't know about any banks." She replied grumpily, an effective note of fatigue in her voice. "I told you, I'm from Fulbright an' Weeks." She slapped the side of the wagon, where the name was emblazoned in colorful lettering. "I'm bloody cold an' soaked through, an' these 'ere trunks are full o' lead shot."

The guard still wore an expression of disbelief.

Pierce addressed Nell. "Open one up and show him, would you?"

"Look, mates," she said, reaching into her pocket

and handing Pierce the key. "All I know is I'm supposed t' deliver these 'ere at midnight and pick up some others and take 'em with me. Can ye get 'em unloaded?"

Pierce leaned into the wagon and opened the closest trunk, revealing that it was indeed full of lead shot.

The skeptical guard still wasn't convinced. He frowned at the driver. "What are ye supposed to pick up?"

His friend nudged him in the ribs. "Don't ye get it, 'arry? Cor, yer slow. The real stuff must be going to the fairgrounds tonight."

Pierce nodded in response to the guard's look of surprise.

"I don't know," Harry said, shaking his head vigorously, dousing them all with a spray of rain. "I think we maybe better ask Mr. Montaigne about this."

"Fine," Pierce agreed, already turning toward the town house. "I'll go get him out of bed and tell him one of his servants thinks his plan is stupid. I'm sure he won't mind if you question him about it. Your name's Harry, right?"

"No, wait," the man called after him. Looking uncertain, he rounded on the driver. "Is that what yer supposed t' do? Take the real stuff to the fairgrounds?"

"Look, mate." Nell yawned. "When me boss tells me t' deliver somethin' an' says 'e'll pay me extra for comin' at this time o' night, I don't ask questions. I do what 'e tells me. And what 'e told me was, deliver these at midnight, pick up whatever they give me, and deliver that wherever they told me t' take it."

"Well . . ." Harry grumbled, "a'right then." He turned and tapped Pierce on the shoulder, none too gently. "But you better be right about all this, mate. Because as soon as Mr. Montaigne gets up in the mornin', I'm going to go see 'im. And if 'e wants t' know who said this was a'right, I'm going t' send 'im lookin' for *you*."

Pierce managed to quell an urge to knock the man to the ground. It wouldn't do to create a violent and potentially noisy scene, not this close to the house and the rest of Montaigne's guards. He realized, however, that he couldn't take the chance that these two might talk to *any-one* in the morning.

He responded to the threat with a smile and a slight shrug. "Do that. I'll go see him with you."

His confident attitude seemed to placate Harry, who finally gave in and backed down. "A'right, Richard, give me a 'and 'ere," he muttered.

The three of them started lifting the trunks out and depositing them in the yard. In a matter of minutes, they transferred the gold from Montaigne's coach to the Ful-bright & Weeks wagon, and put the lead shot in the coach. Pierce tossed the key in after it.

When they were done, Pierce handed Nell a slip of paper. "Do you read, friend?"

"I might not be no Oxford don, but me mum taught me me letters."

"Excellent." Pierce spoke loudly enough for his fel-lows to hear over the rain. "Here are the directions to the fairgrounds. Do this well and there will be a gener-ous sum sent to you and your boss, from Mr. Montaigne himself."

He couldn't help but smile at that last part, because it was true, in a way.

Nell bent her head to study the paper and muttered under her breath. " 'Long as Bess is safe and she gets 'er 'alf, guv. That's all I care 'bout." She lowered her voice even further. "I 'ave t' get this wagon back quick. Georgi's got the poor driver sippin' tea in yer parlor."

Pierce handed over a generous tip. "There you go, my good man," he said loudly, then slapped her on the back and added in a quick whisper. "Pull around the corner and wait a bit. I've two more packages for you to de-liver."

Nodding as if she understood the delivery directions, Nell pocketed the paper and the tip. She grumbled a few loud comments about finding an easier way to make a living and bid a terse goodnight to the guards before lifting herself back into her seat. Snapping the reins, she clucked to the team. The wagon pulled away, disappear-ing into the alley.

Pierce felt a surge of anticipation as he watched it go. The difficult part was over. Tomorrow, all he had to do was savor his vengeance.

He turned toward his companions with a smile. There was rope in the wagon. Pieces of the tarpaulin would do for blindfolds. He knew of a discreet little establishment down by the Thames where he could store a pair of inconvenient guards for a day or so with no questions asked. In a few days, he could send instructions to have them returned to Montaigne's doorstep.

They would be a bit worse for wear but much wiser about trusting their fellow man.

He stepped between them and clapped each on the back. "Say, fellows, when our turn at guard is over," he said affably, "what say we three go warm up with a bottle of rum?"

Chapter 25

⁓◦◦◦◦⁓

After so many dismal days of rain, the morning of St. Bartholomew's Fair dawned clear and unseasonably cool. In the hours before dawn, the town house in Cavendish Square was a mad rush of activity.

Montaigne, who had yet to put in an appearance, had ordered all his men, footmen and guards alike, to dress in his servants' livery, so that anyone daring to attack his coach wouldn't be able to tell from what quarter danger might come. Wearing the burgundy and gray coat and breeches fit nicely into Pierce's plan, for it helped him avoid attracting attention.

He was also grateful for the flurry of activity, because no one had time to worry about the fact that Harry and Richard were missing. One or two servants wondered aloud why the two were shirking their duties. Pierce mentioned they had gone off to warm up with a bottle of rum after guard duty last night. They were likely sleeping it off somewhere, and would no doubt turn up later. The explanation seemed to mollify the few who asked.

Pierce felt confident that nothing would mar this day. Fifteen years of bitter memories had sharpened his appetite for vengeance, and today he would be sated. An almost eerie calm had descended on him. The gold was safely stored at his town house, but not for a second had he considered slipping quietly away with the trunks last night. This was the moment he had waited for, worked for, hungered for, and he meant to savor every blessed minute.

All that was left to do now was wait and enjoy. The highlight of the show would be Montaigne's face as the trunks were opened in front of the gin vendors, revealing that his entire fortune in gold had been magically transformed into lead.

Only one thing disturbed Pierce's *sangfroid:* the sudden appearance of Monsieur Rochambeau. Pierce felt a bolt of shock as the Frenchman strode up to the carriage just as the horses were being harnessed. He had suspected the man to be a thief-taker, but hadn't realized he worked for Montaigne.

Thank God, he thought with a profound sense of relief, that Elizabeth was safe at the cottage. Both Montaigne and his thief-taker would both go empty-handed this day.

The idea filled him with satisfaction. Still, he felt a distinct uneasiness as he watched Rochambeau checking over the carriage, the horses, the harness, the wheels. Obviously, there was concern that the coach would be waylaid by sabotage. Without regard for his expensive coat, the Frenchman even got down on his back to examine the brakes and axles.

When he opened the door to look inside, Pierce tensed in alarm.

Rochambeau only gave the trunks and the interior a cursory glance before turning away from the carriage, apparently satisfied that the vehicle was sound.

Pierce relaxed slowly. The Frenchman never thought to inspect the gold itself.

Before returning to the town house, Rochambeau asked that a mount be saddled so he could accompany them on the road. Pierce made a mental note to keep his distance; he trusted his disguise, but didn't want to answer any awkward questions. Now was no time to take chances.

It was seven before Montaigne himself came out. The men were saddling their mounts when Pierce caught his first glimpse of his nemesis. He had expected to feel malice, animosity, perhaps triumph; he wasn't prepared for the rush of burning hatred that seized him.

As he stared at the pale, nervous, old man, he didn't feel pity or mercy. He felt murderous. His hand drifted to the pistol on his horse's saddle—his father's pistol. The grip was cold and solid and his fingers closed around it.

Suddenly he was fifteen again, sobbing over Thomas Wolverton's crumpled body . . . listening to his mother's heart-ravaging tears as they stumbled down the steps of Wolverton Manor for the last time. *No.* For her, for both of them, he had to win back all that had been stolen. He couldn't just kill Montaigne outright; it would be too easy, too quick.

Three score of rapid heartbeats went by before he could force himself to let the pistol go. A moment later, he was back in control, the impulse gone.

He watched his enemy's every move. Montaigne's face was pinched with worry as he snapped orders at his servants and pulled his driver aside to discuss their route in hushed tones. The impeccably pressed clothes and skillfully applied powder and rouge couldn't hide the strain he was under. The past few days had obviously taken a toll on him. Good.

Before the day was out, the past week would seem as carefree as a card party. Charles Montaigne would wish he had never heard of St. Bartholomew's Fair or gin or gold. He would get his first taste of the ruin and suffering he had meted out to the Wolverton family and so many others, his first taste of the horror and pain he had inflicted on Elizabeth.

More than a taste, Pierce thought with pleasure. A mouthful. A bellyful. *Choke on it, you son of a bitch.*

Someone handed him a blunderbuss, and Pierce mounted his horse. Four men, bristling with weapons, climbed into the coach. They maneuvered into the alley and then the street beyond. The servants and guards arranged themselves three deep on all sides. Montaigne, riding a fine bay, rode out ahead of the carriage while Rochambeau brought up the rear.

A coach was at its most vulnerable when it was moving slowly, so they set off at a gallop and sped straight through the London streets, avoiding the more roundabout routes that would have required going over bridges or twisting stretches of road.

Pierce could feel the tension all around him. It showed in the men's faces, their eyes, their white-knuckled hands clutching their weapons. The thunder of hoofbeats drowned out all sound.

He mimicked their alertness, but his was fed by eagerness rather than fear. To them, this ride meant danger and money; to him, it meant the beginning of the end for Charles Montaigne. The air rushing past tasted sweet, the pumping of the blood through his veins felt exhilarating.

At the pace Montaigne set, they reached the fairgrounds in little more than half an hour. The clear weather had drawn even more Londoners than usual out of their homes to enjoy the festivities.

St. Bartholomew's always attracted people from all classes, from common folk to gentry, sightseers to entertainers and mountebanks. Today it seemed anyone who had something to buy or sell had packed into the open fields just outside the west wall of the city. It was early yet; later the crowds would swell even more.

The carriage slowed only slightly as it moved through the press of people. Its speed and the cadre of armed men cleared a wide path. They passed lines of booths exhibiting lace, gold and silver ware, toys, walking sticks, shoes and secondhand clothes. The noise was incredible: shrill fiddling, accompanied by drums and bagpipes; the booming voices of actors in a costume drama; vendors fighting over a prime spot.

Loudest of all were the hawkers shouting the prices and merits of their strange and curious exhibits: threepence to see a pig which could do arithmetic, two for a puppet show, six to have one's fortune told, a full shilling for a peek at a man purported to be only two feet tall.

Smells of every kind of food spiced the air, from roast mutton and chicken pies to sugared wine and gingerbread. Pierce took it all in, wanting to memorize every second of this day so he could relive it all later.

Montaigne's guards, however, didn't pause even to glance at any of the enticements. None relaxed so much as a muscle until they reached the area where the gin distillers had their booths.

Even then, as the coach pulled to a stop, they kept glancing around, as if they expected Blackerby Swift to leap out from thin air. The vendors pressed forward, all eager to get their hands on the gold they had been promised.

Montaigne, looking relieved and infinitely pleased with himself, dismounted from his horse and stepped forward to open the door of his coach personally. Two of his footmen lifted one of the trunks out and set it on the ground.

The guards went into a paroxysm of cheers and victory yells, clapping one another on the back, shooting their pistols in the air. One would think they were a conquering army just returned home, grateful to have snatched life from the very jaws of death.

Pierce joined in the celebration, shouting right along with the rest, though for a completely different reason. None of them would ever know they had never been in danger for a moment.

Blackerby Swift was miles away, sitting on her shapely little backside and twiddling her thumbs. And probably cursing vividly at this very moment.

"Hellfire and damnation," Elizabeth muttered under her breath, panting as she pulled her horse to a stop just beyond the gin booths.

She took in the scene with a glance: Montaigne's jubilant guards, the crowd gathered around, and the coffer of gold that had just been taken from the coach.

She was too late! Pierce had obviously failed, since Montaigne was still in possession of the gold. Her heart sank. The men's clothes she was wearing, the mask in her hand, the pistol in her belt were all useless. Confound it, if only she had been able to escape during the day, it would have been different! In the darkness, it had taken her hours to stumble her way to a nearby farm. The occupants were eager to trade for the jewels, giving her clothes and food and a decent pistol—but the horse they gave her wouldn't have won a race even in its younger days. And the roads to London were in a disastrous state after so much rain.

She had missed her chance. She had ridden straight to the fairgrounds, hoping to help Pierce catch the coach as it slowed to enter the crowds, but her efforts were all for naught.

The transaction was about to take place, and Montaigne would be more successful than ever. He would poison more people with his gin—and send more to prison when they couldn't pay for it.

Defeat was like a bitter drug on her tongue. She watched the scene unfold before her as if through a haze. The men were unloading the rest of the trunks now . . . eight, nine, *ten*. They were all there. Montaigne had enough gold to buy a year's supply of gin and more.

The vendors started a chorus of "Open them! Open them!"

Elizabeth turned her horse, unable to watch any more. Her shoulders slumped and she let the animal walk where it would. She had failed. Women and children would suffer because she had failed. She swallowed hard, fighting tears. God, if only Pierce hadn't insisted on taking the coach alone . . .

Her head came up suddenly and her heart skipped a beat. Where the devil *was* he? An image flashed into her mind of Pierce lying dead by the road, killed by a bullet from one of Montaigne's fancily-dressed hirelings.

The idea sent ice through her veins. She nudged her mount forward, trying to push her way through the milling fairgoers. Her mind was so obsessed, she didn't notice a man beside her until he grabbed her horse's reins.

Elizabeth whirled in the saddle, trying to wrest free, an oath on her lips. The word died on her tongue as she recognized him.

It was horrifyingly clear that he recognized her as well, for his lips curved in a victorious grin. "*Bonjour,* madame, Or should I say, *bonjour,* Monsieur Swift?" His hand shifted from the reins to her wrist. "No matter, *non*? For you are under arrest."

* * *

The gin vendors turned ugly very quickly.

As soon as the first trunk was opened, the noisy crowd fell silent, then began whispering among themselves.

Pierce, standing at the front of the crowd so he would have a perfect view, thought this better than any of the other entertainments offered at the Fair.

They ought to charge admission.

Montaigne's opening line alone would be worth the price.

"What?" Montaigne choked out, staring at the black contents of the box. "What is this?" He turned toward the man who had opened the lid. "What in the name of all that's holy *is this*?"

The poor servant blinked at his master and answered honestly. "It looks like lead shot, sir."

"I know what the blasted hell it is! What is it doing in my coach?"

"There must have been some kind of mistake," one of his other footmen said, pointing to another trunk. "Open that one."

A second trunk was opened, then a third and a fourth.

As each lid fell back to reveal lead shot in place of shiny gold, Montaigne's eye's grew wider, his face redder and his voice higher.

Finally the tenth one was unlocked, and Pierce truly wondered whether Montaigne's head might not explode right off his shoulders. His screech was music to Pierce's ears.

"Where . . . is . . . my . . . *gold*?"

The gin vendors, who had been silent up to now, started grumbling among themselves.

"You mean *our* gold, don't you?" one of them called out.

Montaigne turned toward them, the brilliant color slowly draining from his face. The magnitude of his predicament was just now dawning. "There's been a mistake."

"Certainly looks that way," one vendor said tightly.

"What were you planning?" One in the back of the

crowd accused. "For us to get all the way home before we found out we'd been duped?"

"I've always been an honest business man," Montaigne shouted indignantly.

"Until now!"

"I made extra, just like you said," the first vendor growled. "I hauled it all the way down from Lincolnshire, just like you said. I want my money."

Now Montaigne really looked nervous. "I'll give you all notes. My personal guarantee—"

"You promised cash," another accused. "I'm not handing it over for anything but cash!"

"The gin won't spoil," Montaigne insisted, removing his hat to wipe the sheen of sweat from his forehead. "We'll postpone our business—"

The rest of his proposal was drowned out by groans and angry shouts.

"We sank all our money into making this gin for you and getting it here! Now you're telling us to haul it back?"

Montaigne looked from the lead-filled boxes to the angry circle of men, as if he just couldn't believe this was happening. "I . . . I have other assets," he said quickly. "Land, houses—"

"My wife and children can't eat your land!" one vendor shouted.

"Or your promises," another chimed in.

"All I'm asking is patience. Just give me two weeks. What difference could that possibly make to you? Two weeks—"

"We've got businesses to run," one of the men shouted.

"I say we go to the magistrate and let him fix it," another suggested.

Now Montaigne started to panic. "You can't be serious! I'm Charles Montaigne!"

One of the vendors shook his fist. "There's plenty of rich bastards like you what get in over their heads and try to cheat their way out. Maybe we best make an example of one."

This was met with shouts of "Hear, hear!" The crowd of men started to close in. Montaigne's well-armed servants and guards, who had been watching the exchange up to now, surged forward to protect their master. A couple of the gin sellers drew weapons of their own.

This was about to turn into a riot. Pierce snatched his gun from its holster and fired it into the air.

The report brought the two sides to a halt.

"Listen, mates!" he addressed the guards and servants. "Think a bit before you get yourselves killed saving him." He jerked his head in Montaigne's direction. "Where's the triple pay *we* were promised?"

The financial truth dawned on each man's face and they stood there, dumbfounded. More than one lowered his weapon. Montaigne went into a frenzy.

"No!" he cried. "No! Help me! I'll pay you all. You have my word—"

"Let me help you, sir," Pierce said, relishing every second. He walked over to stand in front of Montaigne, then offered his empty pistol. "It's more than fifteen years old, but maybe you could find some way to make it pay. I know I have."

Montaigne looked from the pistol to Pierce's face with an expression of absolute confusion. Then Pierce slowly ran a thumb over the scar that marred his left cheek.

Montaigne's jaw dropped. *"You,"* he gasped.

"I really would like to help you," Pierce said silkily. "But I don't believe I have much cash." Reaching into his pocket, he withdrew a handful of coins. "Let's see. One, two, three, four, five, six, seven. Seven shillings."

He counted them out, one by one, and contemptuously let them fall in the dirt at Montaigne's feet.

"All debts are paid now," Pierce said in a low, tight voice. He stepped away, his gaze still locked with Montaigne's.

The bastard looked ready to faint, but he never got the chance, for the distillers swarmed over him and grabbed him by the arms.

"Fleet's the place for people what can't pay their debts, rich or poor!" one of them said above the noise.

"No!" Montaigne shrieked as they started to carry him away. "Not the Fleet! They'll tear me to pieces!"

It was the last thing Pierce heard from him before the crowd hustled him off to the magistrate. The servants and guards milled around, obviously uncertain what to do. One kicked at a nearby trunk, swearing.

Pierce turned and walked away. He tossed his hat in the mud as he elbowed his way through the crowd that had gathered. He cast off the burgundy coat and gray waistcoat as well.

He took a deep breath, feeling as if iron bands had just been unfastened from his chest. Montaigne's business was in ruins. His life wouldn't be worth a fake shilling in prison. Before long, his lands and assets would be put up for sale—among them, the Wolverton estates. Pierce would be sure to be there, the highest bidder, using Montaigne's own gold.

A slow smile curved his mouth as he walked. The sun felt good on his shoulders. He started to laugh, a deep, hearty laugh unlike any he had enjoyed in a long time . . . since he had been with Elizabeth.

Ah, Elizabeth. That was going to be the absolutely best part of all this. He would go home and collect the gold this afternoon, then ride back to the cottage posthaste. He imagined the look on her face when he dropped the gold at her feet. Sacks and sacks of it.

She would probably greet him with a scowl, look down at the money with blank disbelief, then, slowly, she would start to raise her head.

Her lashes would lift, her full lips would part slightly, then she would smile. Her eyes would shine with forgiveness, with love. She would melt into his embrace and say she had been wrong about him all along. He would kiss her . . .

A flash of light at the corner of his eye drew Pierce out of his daydream. A jeweler's booth sported an array of bright gems, some hanging from its awning so that they spun and glittered in the sunlight. Pierce walked over and surveyed the man's wares.

"Best quality at the Fair," the merchant boomed.

"You'll not find better, sir." Taking in Pierce's lack of clothes with a shrewd eye, he added, "Or more reasonably priced."

A grin quirked at the corner of Pierce's mouth. He looked over the collection of inexpensive pins, bracelets, necklaces and other baubles, not really seriously interested—until one piece caught his eye.

It was a slim gold band, decorated with exquisitely engraved scrollwork. It was strong and simple, yet delicate, complex, uniquely beautiful, just like . . .

Pierce's heart was suddenly pounding against his ribs, and in that moment he revised his daydream. He wouldn't shower her with sacks of gold at all. He would simply offer her this one circle of burnished beauty.

It was a symbol, he realized that. A ring like this meant promises and trust and sharing, not just for a few nights or weeks but forever. He imagined her accepting it, accepting him. The image dazzled him.

"How much?" he asked hoarsely, picking it up.

"You've fine taste, sir. That's one of my best." The jeweler scratched his fat, gray-stubbled chin and pursed his lips. "Four pounds."

Pierce didn't haggle. It was too much, but he paid it.

Feeling ridiculously pleased with himself, he thanked the man and pocketed the ring, then moved along the row of booths. Perhaps he would pick up a few other trinkets for Elizabeth. Gifts always were helpful in soothing a woman's temper, and he knew she was going to be in rare temper by the time he finally got back to the cottage.

He was listening to a perfumer extoll the virtues of imported lavender water when he noticed the crowd behind him seemed to be growing louder. Turning, he saw they were all moving in the same direction. More than that, many were running. Some were shouting. What the devil? Was there a fire?

He moved into the flow of people and stopped a boy who was darting through the throng.

"What is it lad? Where's everybody going?"

" 'Aven't ye 'eard, mister?" he asked breathlessly, his

face aglow with excitement. "They've captured Black-erby Swift, they 'ave. 'An it's a *woman*!"

The boy ran off but Pierce remained rooted where he was.

Heart, breath, feeling, thought stopped.

The mob of people parted around him and moved past.

Then suddenly he was running with them as fast as he could.

Chapter 26

Newgate.

The name alone was enough to strike dread into even the most fearless criminals. They called it "a tomb for the living," this dark, hulking fortress that had been Elizabeth's home since yesterday. In the August heat, the stench of the place was so bad that neighboring shops had been forced to close.

The magistrate had ordered her placed in the most secure cell deep within the prison. Elizabeth had fought the turnkeys, but one struck her with a blow that left her half-dazed. They fastened metal cuffs about her ankles and chained her to an iron ring in the middle of the floor, as an added precaution against escape or rescue. Elizabeth spent that first night huddled in the corner, crying in the darkness until she had no more tears.

She willed herself not to give in to the horror she felt, but it was almost too much to bear. All her work and risk had gone for naught: Montaigne was still happily counting his riches, she was back in the gaol, and Pierce. . . . The worst, most heartrending thought was that she didn't know what had become of Pierce. The image of him lying wounded or dead left her desolate.

She had no doubt as to her own fate. No proclamation from the king would open the prison doors this time. Nothing would save her from hanging for her crimes. She was trapped, and there were no kind cellmates, no Georgiana and Nell, to help her through it.

No Pierce to comfort her in the darkness.

She was utterly alone.

In the afternoon, they opened her cell and let a stream

of curious Londoners have a look at the lady highway-man, for threepence a head. An artist came in and sat beside her to sketch an ink portrait, cheerfully informing her that he would make hundreds of pounds selling broadsheets at her execution.

Hour after numbing hour passed until the only sensation Elizabeth was aware of was the dull thud of her heart in her chest. The last visitors departed. Sleep didn't come, nor hunger nor even weariness. She wasn't sure whether it was day or night, until she heard the sound of the gaoler opening her door.

"Good morn to ye, me *lady*," he taunted.

Elizabeth squinted in the painfully sudden brightness as he stepped inside, carrying a lantern and a rickety wooden bench. He placed both across from her and went out. A second later, the magistrate came in, and the door swung shut behind him. Elizabeth didn't try to get up. She wasn't sure her legs would support her.

"I am here to take the required deposition," the magistrate informed her, sitting on the bench. He set an inkwell beside him and took out a plume and a long roll of parchment from his coat. He unrolled the paper and dipped the pen.

"Name?" he said sharply.

Elizabeth looked at him silently, taking shallow gulps of the fetid air. She wasn't going to make this easy for them. The might have her in a corner, but she wouldn't surrender life so long as there was breath in her body. If she had any hope at all, it lay in dragging out the legal proceedings as long as possible.

"Listen to me, missy." The magistrate leaned over, shaking the feathered end of his pen at her. "You don't want to make this difficult for yourself. You'll regret it. I'll see to it personally."

Elizabeth shivered but remained stubbornly silent.

The man's face puckered into a scowl. He tapped a finger on the parchment. "The indictment must list the name of the accused. If you refuse to answer my questions, I shall fetch the turnkeys and they'll take you for a visit to the press-yard. A bit of flogging and a few minutes under the weights should get it out of you quick enough.''

Elizabeth felt her back tingle at his threat. She looked down at the chains they had bound her with. Defeat and futility and fresh tears choked up in the back of her throat. It was over. Torture would make mincemeat of her defiance. How could she fight them? What was the point in resisting?

''Elizabeth,'' she said at last, still looking at the floor. ''Elizabeth Thornhill.''

''Miss or Mrs.?'' the magistrate demanded briskly, scribbling.

Elizabeth took a deep breath. ''I am a widow.''

''Mrs., then,'' he muttered to himself. ''Residence?''

Elizabeth felt a twinge of alarm. She prayed that Georgiana and Nell had moved to a place of safety. Since neither the turnkeys or the magistrate had mentioned them, she clung to the hope that they hadn't been brought in for questioning. In any case, she didn't want to supply evidence that might be used against her friends. They could very well be accused as accessories to her crimes—and face hanging with her.

If it was the last thing she did, she had to save them. ''Northampton,'' she said finally, her voice shaking a bit.

The man wrote it down, then set his pen aside and started reading the indictment in a formal tone.

''Mrs. Elizabeth Thornhill of Northampton, you are charged with crimes of the most heinous nature. It is alleged: that on numerous occasions you feloniously and unlawfully committed acts of highway robbery. That you most specifically attacked the coaches of one Charles Montaigne of Cavendish Square, stealing sums amounting to several hundred pounds. That you did place such funds in the London Bank under the assumed name of the London Women and Children's Trust, which funds have been seized by His Majesty—''

''No!'' Elizabeth cried, raising her head. ''They can't do that!''

The magistrate frowned at her. "They most certainly can, madam. Stolen goods are forfeit to the Crown."

Heartbroken, Elizabeth drew her legs up to her chest and pressed her forehead to her knees. It was all too much. There had only been a little over seventy pounds left in the account, but when that was translated into lives that might have been saved . . .

Not only had she failed to get the gold, now the Trust itself had been confiscated, and all she had accomplished had been torn away until she was left with nothing. She felt as though she were slowly being sucked down into a dark whirlpool.

"To continue," the magistrate said in irritation. ". . . That in carrying out such robberies, you did cause injury or death to be inflicted upon several of Mr. Montaigne's coachmen—"

"That's not true," Elizabeth said dully. "I never hurt anyone—"

"You are not to dispute the charges at the present, madam, you are to hear them." Clearing his throat, he found his place again. ". . . And on Sunday last, at St. Bartholomew's Fair, did steal from the aforementioned Charles Montaigne several thousand pounds in gold and cause it to be spirited away—"

"What did you say?" Elizabeth choked out, raising her head again. "I never—"

"Madam!" the magistrate snapped. "I will not be interrupted again. Now, then . . . St. Bartholomew's—no, I said that already. Ah, yes . . . and cause it to be spirited away and replaced with lead shot. The punishment for highway robbery is death. The punishment for causing serious bodily injury to another during commission of a crime is death. The punishment for murder is death. What say you?"

Elizabeth wasn't listening. She was staring at the man in open-mouthed wonder, stunned breathless at the news that Montaigne's gold had been stolen.

Pierce hadn't been wounded or killed! He had succeeded! He had gotten away with every last shilling! That was what he had meant about "working around" the guards; he had *exchanged* the gold somehow. A wave of elation swept through her—only to be cut short by the realization of what it meant for her.

Pierce had all the gold.

And she was being charged with the robbery.

The magistrate cleared his throat impatiently. "What say you, madam?"

"Wh . . . what do you mean?" Elizabeth asked unsteadily, still trying to sort it all out. She had certainly committed enough raids to hang several times over, but if she were found guilty of such a spectacular theft, she could kiss any hope of mercy farewell. The justices would be ruthless in their punishment, to discourage anyone else from even attempting an act so outrageous.

"You must enter a plea, Mrs. Thornhill. Guilty or not guilty?"

"I . . . I . . ." She couldn't think of what to say. A guilty plea would be a direct ticket to Tyburn. They were charging her with murder, and with a robbery that would surely be one of the crimes of the century.

The gallows loomed in her imagination.

Should she claim innocence? She would have to prove it, and how could she possibly do that? She swallowed hard, trying to stall so she could think. "I . . . I should like to know who brings these charges against me."

Looking aggravated, the magistrate glanced at the paper. "A Mr. Jean-Pascal Rochambeau, in the name of Mr. Montaigne."

"Why not Mr. Montaigne himself?"

"He is apparently involved in a dispute with some business associates, and is currently in Fleet Prison for debt."

That news brought Elizabeth a calming sense of balance and satisfaction. If nothing else, at least Pierce had gotten away and Montaigne was in misery. She might not find true justice, but Charles Montaigne had. She could cling to that. It also gave her hope.

Bringing a prosecution against someone could be a lengthy and expensive process; with Montaigne in the gaol, perhaps his thief-taker wouldn't be willing to go to the trouble.

She raised her chin. "What evidence does this Mr. Rochambeau claim against me?"

"Please, madam," the magistrate said with heavy sarcasm. "You were taken near the site of the St. Bartholomew's robbery, carrying a pistol and mask, and wearing these"—he looked her up and down with an expression of distaste—"these unseemly, masculine clothes. He also has witnesses to your criminal activities."

Elizabeth stared at him, aghast. "What witnesses?"

The magistrate was obviously at the end of his patience. "You are charged with a felony, Mrs. Thornhill. You are not allowed to see the evidence against you before trial. I have examined these witnesses myself, and they seem most credible." He snatched up his plume and stabbed it into the inkwell. "Now, what say you to the charges?"

Elizabeth chewed at the inside of her cheek, wondering what witnesses the Frenchman had found to use against her. If he could prove his case—and the magistrate seemed confident that he could—there would be only one sentence. Death.

She could see only one hope. Perhaps if the justices and jury knew the truth, knew *why* she had done what she had done, they might be merciful. Together with the fact that she was a woman, it might be enough to get her transported to the colonies or imprisoned rather than sent to the gallows.

In any event, the truth was all she had left.

"Sir, before I enter my plea, I should like the circumstances of my actions to be known. I do not wish to be sentenced on the basis of rumors and exaggerations."

"You are entitled to make a confession, if that is what you wish."

She wrapped her arms about her knees, hoping she was doing the right thing. "I should like it conveyed to the newspapers as well. Could you do that?"

"Certainly, madam," he replied.

Elizabeth hadn't expected any argument on that point; she knew the papers would pay handsomely for the gaol confession of a famous highwayman—especially when that highwayman was a woman. If she were to die, at least the truth would be recorded for all to know.

The magistrate looked at her expectantly, pen poised over a fresh sheet of parchment.

Elizabeth took a deep breath, and began her story. "I owed seven shillings to Charles Montaigne of Cavendish Square. I went to see him one afternoon last November . . ."

For an hour, she talked, and the magistrate wrote it all down: the death of her drunken husband in a gin shop, her debts, her cruel imprisonment by Montaigne, the loss of her baby, and finally the way she had turned to highway robbery, not only out of vengeance, but to benefit London's poor women and children.

She told it all simply, without embellishment, but left out all mention of Georgiana and Nell, and Pierce. She claimed to have acted entirely alone.

When she finally fell silent, the magistrate's expression had changed from animosity to vexation. He had to clear his throat, twice, before he could speak, and even then, his voice had taken on a much gentler tone.

"Madam, I still need your plea."

Elizabeth let out a slow, shaky sigh, feeling as if all the weight of Newgate were pressing down upon her. "I have told you, sir. I committed the robberies, I admit, but I never killed or hurt anyone. Nor do I know anything about the theft at the Fair."

He pursed his lips and studied the paper before him. "Shall I enter 'guilty' on the robberies, then, and 'not guilty' on the others?"

Elizabeth swallowed hard and nodded. "Yes. I suppose that will have to do."

The magistrate noted the various pleas with a sweep of his pen, then rose to leave. "I shall convey your story to the newspapers posthaste, I promise you." He paused at the door, tucking the plume and inkwell into his coat.

"I wish you luck, madam," he said quietly. "I fear you shall need a great deal of it."

He left, taking the lantern with him. As the door closed, Elizabeth listened to the heavy key being turned in the iron lock, felt the darkness close around her like a suffocating cloak, and prayed that the truth would be enough to save her.

She didn't have to wait weeks or months for trial like less famous felons. The indictment against her was drawn up quickly; the grand jury had apparently decided there was more than enough evidence to ensure a speedy verdict—which only added to her uneasiness.

She made a scratch on the wall each time her one meal of the day was delivered; she judged that only three days had gone by when the turnkeys came to deliver her to the Old Bailey, the famed criminal court next to Newgate.

They didn't allow her to clean up or even change clothes; she was forced to face the justices in the same shirt, coat and breeches she had worn to the fair. The bruise from the guard's blow was still painful on her left cheek, and she didn't want to imagine how bedraggled and dirty she must look. Pray God, she thought, it might inspire sympathy.

She knew it was far more likely that she had never looked more like a criminal.

They shackled her hand and foot and led her through the prison's cramped passageways. Outside, the walk to the sessions house was only a few short yards. The sun hurt her eyes, its brightness temporarily blinding her after so many days in the dark.

She heard noise all around; a mob of people had gathered, and only the strength of her guards held them back. Elizabeth recoiled, terrified, until she heard what they were shouting.

"Let 'er go, ye craven-hearted gullions!"

"Mercy fer the lady what 'elped 'elpless women an' children!"

"Yer one o' us, Bess!"

"She saved me and me little ones from the gaol, she did. Freedom fer Lady Bess!"

"Freedom fer Lady Bess!" The crowd took it up as a chant.

Elizabeth's eyes adjusted to the daylight and she could see that the people were reaching toward her, some waving newspapers. By the time she and the turnkeys made it to the sessions house, it was the turnkeys who were terrified.

As she was led into the Old Bailey, Elizabeth felt a renewed sense of strength, of hope. All her efforts hadn't been for naught. Those people outside, throngs of them, had been touched by what she had done. She *had* made a difference, at least for a short time.

Those simple Londoners believed in mercy; maybe the learned justices would feel the same.

Her guards roughly hauled her through the building and into the cavernous courtroom. The second they stepped inside, Elizabeth's brief hope flickered and went out.

The galleries on both sides of the chamber were overflowing with richly-dressed spectators, who gaped and pointed as she was dragged in. They were gathered around every thick marble pillar and seated in rows right up to the soaring ceiling. The size of the room and the richness of the people in it made her feel small and insignificant by comparison.

On the right, in the jury box, twelve white-wigged, dour-looking men stared at her with expressions that varied from disapproval to outright malice.

Across from them on the left side of the room sat Monsieur Rochambeau, looking triumphant, and a man she took to be the attorney who would present the evidence against her.

She wasn't allowed to have an attorney argue for her. The magistrate had explained that, since she was accused of a felony, she would have to speak on her own behalf.

The turnkeys handed her over to the bailiffs, who led her into the box where the accused must stand, a long, high counter cut off from the rest of the courtroom by a low wooden wall. Her chains clanked and rattled over the hum of conversation in the room.

On the opposite side of the court, across a distance so wide Elizabeth thought she would have to shout to be heard, the justices sat at their bench, six of them, so high above her she felt smaller still. They wore flowing scarlet robes lined in ermine, full-bottomed wigs in the old-fashioned style, and somber expressions that filled her with dread.

It wasn't the sympathetic people outside who would decide her fate, but these stone-faced aristocrats.

The chatter in the room lowered to gossipy whispers as she was left alone in the box, still wearing her shackles. The chief justice called for silence in a booming voice, then began a lengthy oration, advising all present of the virtues of authority and obedience, the fitness of the social order, and the goodness of King George.

As he began to expound on the charges against her, Elizabeth found herself searching the faces in the galleries, looking for even a hint of mercy, finding none. A few faces were turned her way, eyebrows lifted in curiosity, lips twisted with pity. Some even peered at her through opera glasses.

The rest of the powdered, rouged, and patched nobles were listening raptly to the justice, like a gathering of the faithful soaking up a speech on fire and brimstone.

Only when Elizabeth turned to the gallery on her left did she find a trace of anything other than reproach and condemnation, in just one person.

A man in the middle of the third row was staring at her, but it was an oddly gentle, concerned sort of staring. He was dressed as a fop, complete with outlandish cosmetics and a ridiculous hat and wig. He was—

Pierce.

Shock and relief and exultation and fear all tumbled through Elizabeth at once. She turned away the next second, afraid one of the bailiffs might notice her interest.

Oh, God, he was here. Even beneath the powder and rouge, there was no mistaking him. She would have known him if he were made up as the King himself.

What did he think he was doing? Didn't he realize how dangerous this was? Good Lord, he was only a few feet above Rochambeau; if the Frenchman chanced to turn around and take a good look at the spectators, he could set the bailiffs on him in a minute. Pierce had just stolen several thousand pounds in gold, for heaven's sake! He shouldn't be in London at all. He—

The *gold.*

That fact hit Elizabeth like a bolt from the sky, and suddenly she felt like laughing for pure joy and crying her heart out all at once. Pierce had the gold—*all* of it— yet he was here, with her.

She had expected him to be furious that she had disobeyed him. She half expected him to take the money and disappear and leave her to her fate. That was the sensible, logical, practical thing to do: slip out of the city and lie low until Montaigne's assets were auctioned off. He certainly shouldn't be anywhere near this sessions house.

Despite all of that, here he was. What could he be thinking of?

The justice was still droning on about her dreadful crimes. Careful to move only her eyes, Elizabeth glanced up at Pierce, and knew the answer.

She very nearly did cry then. Her knees started to shake. The truth broke through all her doubts and misconceptions, as clear and warming as the sun after a rainstorm.

Love had brought him here. Love kept him by her side, when he should be thinking of his own safety.

Elizabeth was so filled with regret and pain that she had to close her eyes. She had been such a fool. Her lack of faith must have hurt him terribly. She hadn't believed in him, and now it was too late. There would be no second chance, no opportunity to tell him how wrong she had been. He would never hear from her lips how much she loved him. It was so brutally unfair, and it was all her fault.

She raised her face toward him one last time, vowing that she didn't dare look his way again. She put every ounce of her heart into her expression, trying desperately to convey her thoughts.

I love you, Pierce, I love you, I love you. I'm so sorry for doubting you. But please, you must leave here. Save yourself. Take the gold and leave London. Please, please, whatever it is you're planning, don't do it.

He made no signal that he understood what she was trying to tell him, only gazed at her with a fierce, all-powerful confidence and determination. Elizabeth tore her gaze from his and stared straight ahead.

Confound him, he seemed intent on committing suicide! A tear rolled down her cheek and she reached up with her chained hands to awkwardly brush it away.

She could only be grateful that Georgiana and Nell and Quinn had stayed away; thank heavens they, at least, weren't in danger.

The justice was reading her confession now. Elizabeth was relieved to note that the magistrate had recorded it faithfully, word for word. She was also encouraged to see the very beginnings of sympathy and doubt in the eyes of the jurors.

Several women in the galleries looked at her with empathy and reached for their handkerchiefs upon hearing the part about little Edward.

When the justice had finished, however, Rochambeau's attorney rose to address the jury. He denounced her in scathing tones, holding up the mask and pistol found in her possession when she had been arrested. The jurors looked at one another, and at her, with furrowed brows and murmurs of uncertainty.

The chief justice called for the first witness.

Pierce clenched his fists in frustrated rage. God, Elizabeth looked so small and vulnerable down there alone, her clothes in disarray, her hair in tangles, a painful-looking bruise on her cheek. When he had seen that, and the shackles around her delicate wrists, a violent urge seized him: to personally tear every one of her turnkeys to pieces.

It was agony to watch this; he could see the optimism

in her eyes. Despite everything she had been through, despite uncountable lessons to the contrary, Elizabeth still possessed a deep, abiding belief that there was more good than evil in the world, that somehow things would turn out for the best.

Pierce had no such faith in his fellow man, and no doubt as to the final verdict.

Only with supreme effort did he manage to remain in his seat. He couldn't do anything, not yet. Reason told him it was lunacy to be here, since he couldn't help her, but he wasn't going to let her suffer this alone.

Through it all, she was magnificent, facing these pasty-pale codgers and self-righteous popinjays with a spirit that couldn't be doused by any amount of mistreatment.

A moment ago, when she had looked up at him, the love and faith in her eyes had knocked the breath from him. Even the vast distance between them couldn't dull the impact of the message she shared with him alone.

He didn't need to offer her gold or proof or promises, or even the ring he still carried in his pocket. She loved him, believed in him, without any of that.

She had raised her head, then her lashes, and he had felt every one of her emotions as strongly as if she were right beside him, whispering the words in his ear. He also sensed that she wanted him to save himself, leave her to whatever fate the court would mete out.

No, he vowed, not while his heart still beat and his hands had an ounce of strength. He wouldn't let these dawkins sacrifice her in the name of their so-called justice.

No matter what he had to do.

The first witness was one of Montaigne's coachmen. The attorney had him describe in vivid detail how Elizabeth had robbed his coach at gunpoint.

When it was her turn to question him, she could hardly think of what to say. She struggled to come up with any scrap of detail that might persuade the court to be lenient.

She tried to stand straight, with as much dignity as her

shackles would allow. "I robbed your carriage, sir, I admit. But did you ever see me cause harm or injury to any of your men?"

The coach driver thought for a minute, "No, mum. Not that I can recall."

She smiled tremulously. "Thank you."

Five other coachmen were brought forward, and she asked the same question of each of them. Not one could say she had ever wounded or killed any of their men.

Unfortunately, the last man was the one who had been driving on the night she was shot, the night Pierce had captured her. He didn't answer the question the way she had hoped.

"No, mum," he said. "You never shot anyone, but your partner did. He killed two o' my men."

The jury box and galleries broke out in a fresh wave of noisy speculation. The chief justice demanded order and sternly addressed Elizabeth.

"The witness raises an interesting point, Mrs. Thornhill," he said. "You were seen in the company of another highwayman on at least two occasions. One might assume that you were acting on his orders."

Elizabeth felt a frisson of panic shiver up her back. Only by sheer force of will did she keep herself from looking at Pierce for strength. "No, my lord. I acted alone."

"Come, come, madam. It is difficult to believe that a member of the gentler sex could carry out such crimes under her own volition. If you were corrupted by a man, the court might be persuaded to be more understanding." He spoke in an almost paternal tone. "More lenient."

Elizabeth almost sank to her knees in frustration. The very thing she had prayed for was being offered—but she wasn't about to pay the price. "I swear to you, my lord. I followed no one's orders but my own."

"Your answer may mean your life, madam. Consider carefully. All you need do is give us the man's name."

Elizabeth could almost feel the rope tightening about her neck. Her heart hammering, she lowered her head.

"Please believe me, my lord," she said doggedly. "I would save my life if I could, but I do not know who this other highwayman was. He was certainly not my partner."

The justice didn't reply for a moment. Charged silence held the chamber. "As you say, madam," he said at last, turning to the bailiff. "Call the next witness."

The next witness, bless her, was Lady Selwyn, followed by the Ladies Vicary and Houblon. Each had voluntarily come forward to vouch for Elizabeth's good character. She may have been driven to desperate acts, they said, but she was a fine person, and deserved good Christian charity from the court.

Elizabeth watched the jury listening to the women, and felt hope well anew within her. Perhaps, she prayed, she might yet escape with her life.

When Lady Kimble took the stand, however, Elizabeth's fragile optimism was ripped apart.

The woman wagged a finger in Elizabeth's direction. "I still don't see how she could *be* Blackerby Swift when she was abducted *by* Blackerby Swift! In *my* coach!"

The chief justice again glowered at Elizabeth. "The question is raised once more, Mrs. Thornhill. While it is not part of the charges here before us, it is said that Blackerby Swift kidnapped Lady Barnes-Finchley last Wednesday afternoon just outside the city. Since you have freely admitted to being both persons, perhaps you could explain how that was made possible?"

Elizabeth felt the last bit of color drain from her cheeks. "I . . . I cannot, my lord."

Rochambeau's attorney leaped in. "Unless it was her partner!"

"Yes!" Lady Kimble added shrilly. "They hatched some despicable plan between them to steal my coach!"

The attorney spun toward Elizabeth. "Perhaps that's the truth here," he shouted, his cheeks scarlet with excitement against the white of his wig. "The tart is trying to protect her lover!"

The galleries erupted in gasps and shouts. All the gossip about the abduction was exchanged anew in a flurry of conversation. The idea of a lady highwayman being kidnapped by her own lover was apparently just too titillating; the justice had to stand and pound on the bench before they fell silent.

When order was restored at last, he bestowed an impatient look on Elizabeth. "Mrs. Thornhill, I ask you for the last time. Name the man who directed your crimes!"

Losing any semblance of calm control, Elizabeth cried out, "I swear to you, my lord, that I acted alone."

This brought a wave of chatter from the spectators, who would not be quieted this time.

"My lord," Rochambeau's attorney called out over the noise. "I believe I can settle this question—and this case—if you would allow me to bring just one more witness."

"By all means, sir, do so!" the justice shouted back. "You are excused, Lady Kimble."

"But, my lord," she complained petulantly, "we've not yet discovered the whereabouts of my coach—"

"That is not the purpose of this session, madam. Now you will step down."

A bailiff had to take her from the box. The attorney was addressing the jury.

"This final witness, sirs, will leave no doubt that this woman is a vicious criminal who merits the gallows!"

He turned toward Elizabeth with a grin of hungry anticipation that made her feel ill. Her heart was in her throat. Who could possibly have such deadly evidence against her?

She didn't have to wait long for an answer. Surrounded by bailiffs, the witness was escorted in from the far side of the courtroom. She couldn't see him until he shuffled his way up into the box.

Even then, she couldn't place him. He started to fall and one of the bailiffs caught him, holding him up straight. Elizabeth frantically studied his profile, but she didn't think she had ever seen him before.

"Please identify yourself to the court," the attorney demanded.

The man faced Elizabeth, sneering, and recognition hit her with a jarring violence that almost made her faint. He was badly disfigured, but she knew his identity before he said his name.

"Gideon Lowe," he called out. "*Dandy* Gideon Lowe."

Chapter 27

Elizabeth's first fear was for Pierce. Moving only her eyes, she glanced toward his seat, panic-stricken when she saw that he was still there.

"Mr. Lowe," the attorney said. "Are you not the same Dandy Gideon Lowe who is infamous for acts that have terrorized the North of England, including highway robbery, burglary, murder and rape?"

Lowe was still leaning on the bailiffs, shaking now with the effort to remain standing. "The same," he said with apparent pride.

"Yet you have come here today voluntarily?"

"When I heard about her in the newspapers, I knew I had to do my duty as a citizen."

"But you realize, sir, that by coming to this court today, you risk the gallows yourself."

"I'm already dying," Lowe said bitterly. "The bitch did me in." He turned a hate-filled gaze on Elizabeth, wincing at the movement. "If I'm going to hell, I'm taking her with me!"

The galleries again burst into a flurry of discussion.

The attorney waited until the crowd had quieted. "And please tell us, sir," he said in dulcet tones, "precisely what you mean when you say, 'The bitch did me in.' "

"She was part of my knot," Lowe replied, slowly turning his scarred face toward the justices. "But she got greedy and turned on me."

"It's not true!" Elizabeth cried. No one paid her heed; they were engrossed in Lowe's lurid accusations.

"Can you recall for us, sir," the attorney asked, "the

340

specific occasion that brought you to this"—he gestured to the highwayman's face—"this state?"

Lowe was taken by a fit of coughing and couldn't speak for a moment. The bailiffs kept him on his feet. After a painful groan, he spat out his testimony: "She was with us when we raided a farmhouse, up north—"

"Near the accused's home town of Northampton, was it not?" the attorney prodded.

"Right, Northampton."

The attorney turned toward the jury and raised a meaningful eyebrow. "So she carried out her heinous criminal activities not only upon strangers in London, but upon people she knew, near her own home?"

"She was one of the best of 'em." Lowe nodded. "Until that night we took the Hibberts' house. Her share wasn't enough for her, and we argued. She shot me, right in the face." He raised a hand to his once-handsome features.

"And she wounded you in the side as well, did she not? Could you show us her handiwork?"

Lowe shook off the bailiff and dramatically opened his shirt to reveal a horribly infected wound. Cries of shock and revulsion echoed through the courtroom.

"So she left you for dead. And the wound is mortal, sir?"

Lowe's voice was heavy with bitter ire. "They can't exactly amputate, can they? The ride down to London near killed me, but I wanted that bitch to get what she deserves!" He lapsed into another fit of coughing.

The courtroom was abuzz with discussion again. The attorney picked up a sheaf of papers from his table and carried it to the jury. "If any doubt this man's word, you may examine his statement, sworn before the magistrate two days past, describing this woman right down to her violet eyes!"

"It's all lies," Elizabeth insisted helplessly. "I was never one of his gang!"

"She was," Lowe shot back. "Her and her partner both! A big, strapping bloke he was. Dark hair and eyes. I'd know him if I saw him again."

This brought a louder uproar from the spectators.

The justice silenced them only after a full minute of pounding on the bench. ''Mrs. Thornhill,'' he shouted. ''Do you still expect this court to believe, even after the testimony of this witness, that you acted alone?''

Elizabeth could only cling desperately to her story, watching her chance for mercy slip through her fingers. Anything else was unthinkable. ''Yes, my lord,'' she insisted.

The justice, frowning, turned to the attorney. ''I think we have all heard enough from this person, sir.''

The bailiffs half-carried Lowe from the witness box; as they took him out of the courtroom, he screamed, ''Hang the bitch!''

His demand struck Elizabeth's heart like a blade. Completely numb, she stood trembling as the chief justice summed up the case for the jury. The bailiffs didn't even go to the trouble to take her back to her cell while the jury deliberated. No one doubted they would reach their verdict quickly.

And they did, only a half hour later. On the charge of murder: not guilty.

Elizabeth's heart fluttered in her chest like a butterfly caught in a net. She held her breath as the rest of the verdict was read.

On the charges of highway robbery and attempted murder . . .

Guilty.

Elizabeth's vision went hazy and gray at the edges. She couldn't seem to breathe. An expectant hush fell over all present. And then the justice was passing sentence on her, in a tone that was no longer paternal, but filled with the passion and power of righteous vengeance.

''Mrs. Elizabeth Thornhill, your crimes have been so fully proved that no person here can have any doubt as to your guilt. You have been found guilty of taking up arms and committing highway robbery and attempted murder. The fact that you are a woman makes your crimes all the more unnatural and horrifying. If such behavior were to go lightly punished, it might encourage other women to acts of violence.''

He took a breath before continuing. "This court has made every effort to be lenient. We have given you every opportunity to cooperate, yet you have willfully thrown our mercy back in our faces. You obviously acted under the order of a man, yet you most unreasonably refuse to name him.''

He took another breath, and his whole body seemed to grow larger. The room dizzily expanded and overwhelmed her.

The sound of the justice's voice rose to a deafening thunder. ''It is therefore the decision of this court, that you be taken to Tyburn on Monday next, where you shall be hanged by the neck until you are dead.''

The word *dead* snapped the last fragile thread of hope in Elizabeth's heart. The finality of it rang in her ears, louder than the din from the galleries. The courtroom was spinning, her mind reeling with shock and denial.

It lasted only an instant before she fainted.

As Elizabeth fell, Pierce surged to his feet with the rest of the spectators, his heart lurching painfully in his chest. Her slender form crumpled like a marionette whose strings had been cut. A mad impulse to leap from the gallery and run to her side careened across his mind. Only the crowd of aristocrats prevented him.

He shoved through the crush of people to the railing, watching as the bailiffs lifted her limp body, passing her to the turnkeys with no more care than they would show a town drunk. They carried her out, and the nobles around him started moving toward the exits.

Their afternoon's entertainment was over, he thought with a sickened feeling in the pit of his stomach.

The crowd thinned, but Pierce remained at the railing. Directly below, Rochambeau and his attorney were shaking hands, smiling in exultation, preparing to leave. It was all Pierce could do not to throw himself over the edge. If the impact didn't do the job, he'd kill them with his bare hands.

His fingers gripped the smooth wood balustrade; he wanted to do it so badly, his mouth went dry. Finally he forced himself to let go. He pushed away from the sight, stalking to the nearest exit. Getting thrown in the gaol wouldn't do Elizabeth any good.

Outside, the spectators were making their way to their coaches, laughing and chattering, making plans to attend the evening's opera or a concert at New Spring Garden. He overheard a few wondering aloud about the price for seats at Elizabeth's execution.

He clenched his fists and kept walking. To think he had once cared what opinion these shallow coxcombs held of him. In that moment, he realized that admission to their exclusive circle was the last thing he wanted. He didn't know exactly when it had come about, but *their* acceptance didn't seem worth a false shilling anymore. Let the buggers believe what they wanted about Pierce Wolverton.

It wouldn't matter much longer. They would forget him and move on to juicier gossip, after he had been gone a while.

Quinn was waiting with the coach on a street two blocks away. Pierce swung up beside him on the driver's seat. The thought of riding inside like the rest of his noble peers suddenly revolted him.

He yanked the pearl stickpin from his cravat and tore the length of lace from around his throat. "Did you find a suitable bank?"

"Yes, sir." Quinn set the team off at a trot. "In Middlesex. They were more than happy to accept the gold, and your conditions."

"Good." Pierce felt only a little better knowing that was taken care of. The crown wouldn't be able to touch the money; he had deposited it in his own name, and while Pierce Wolverton might be considered a debauched blackguard, he was a peer of the realm. He had handed over every last coin of Montaigne's gold, with the full blessing of the Viscountess Alden and Mrs. Osgood.

The Anne Wolverton Trust for Women and Children would serve England's poor for decades.

His conditions had been that the bank oversee the charity, paying the debts of the needy, but they could keep a third of the interest on the account. He didn't have to do it. He knew that. He could have kept at least some of the gold for himself. But as soon as he had learned of Elizabeth's arrest—or perhaps even before, he didn't know anymore—he had lost the burning desire to reclaim his boyhood home.

His mother and father were gone; buying the house wouldn't bring them back. And without Elizabeth, Wolverton Manor would be no more than an empty shell, as barren and cold as his town house. It could never be home to him again.

Let the courts sell the estates to someone else, and let them live there with more happiness and peace than his family had known. He washed his hands of Montaigne, once and for all. Setting up a new trust was somehow a more satisfying end for the bastard's money anyway.

He also felt it was a more fitting tribute to his mother's memory. She would have been pleased.

While he sat brooding, Quinn asked hesitantly, "What of the lady, sir? Is there no hope for her?"

"None."

Quinn cleared his throat. "I can't tell you how sorry I am, sir—"

Pierce held up a hand to cut him off. "Don't apologize again, Quinn. It wasn't your fault. We couldn't have guessed she had some way of cutting through the bloody window."

Quinn didn't reply, just sat there looking miserable.

Pierce found himself in the unusual position of trying to cheer his servant. "What about the viscountess and Mrs. Osgood? Have you taken care of everything?"

"Yes, sir," Quinn replied, looking a bit happier. "We've finished closing down both the shop and their home. They're waiting for us at your town house."

"Good," Pierce said. "It was only a matter of time before they were brought up on charges themselves."

"They *were* a bit disgruntled, sir, that you wouldn't allow them to attend the trial." A hint of a smile tugged at his mouth. ''Mrs. Osgood was particularly vociferous about it.''

Pierce shook his head. ''Too dangerous. We couldn't risk having all three of us there. It would have meant three times the chance that one of us would be recognized. The viscountess is well known among the gentry, and Mrs. Osgood is one of their favorite shopkeepers.''

Quinn nodded in agreement. ''They are also greatly worried as to how you intend to rescue Mrs. Thornhill. They can't believe there's any way to get her out of Newgate.''

''There isn't, judging by the way they've got her shackled. She's probably in the most secure cell and heavily guarded. They might even have her chained to the floor.''

Quinn gave him a perplexed glance. ''Then what are we to do?''

''It's simple, actually,'' Pierce said slowly. ''Elizabeth Thornhill, Lady Barnes-Finchley, and Blackerby Swift are going to die.''

Chapter 28

*U*ntil you are dead . . . Until you are dead . . . The words floated through Elizabeth's thoughts in a hideous refrain until she nearly screamed to shut them out. Only the knowledge that her keepers would take pleasure in her suffering held her silent. She didn't remember being returned to her cell, didn't know when they had taken the shackles off her wrists and chained her to the floor once again.

The turnkeys were delighted with the outcome of the trial; they were making a fortune from Londoners eager for one last chance to see the condemned before her hanging. The price had gone up to fivepence a look.

A few kindhearted visitors tried to give her food, and one person tossed a bible into her cell; the turnkeys snatched it all away. No one, they snarled, was to give the prisoner anything. Too much chance of someone sneaking in a file or a weapon.

Two more artists were let in to sketch Elizabeth's portrait. Didn't they realize, she wondered bitterly, that competition would make for lower profits? She wondered dully where that stray bit of cynicism came from; it sounded like something Pierce would say.

No, she admonished herself. She wasn't going to think of him anymore. By now, she hoped, he had done the sensible thing and departed London with the gold. It was too painful to keep torturing herself with thoughts of their time together and outlandish hopes of rescue.

The way she had collapsed upon hearing her sentence only made it worse. That moment of weakness had robbed her of the chance to look at him one last time.

She would never see him again, never be able to say farewell.

But she was beyond regret now, beyond fear or sorrow. Resignation had settled over her. She blotted out everything around her, even the catcalls and jokes and prayers and words of sympathy from her visitors.

The stream of sightseers gradually thinned to a trickle. She guessed the hour to be late, for the turnkeys finally hustled away the last stragglers, gave her the daily meal of gruel and water, and shut her door. She didn't eat and only drank a little.

Grateful to be left alone, she huddled into a ball, trying to sleep. Unconsciousness would be a blessing now, the only means of escape she would find in Newgate. Even that was denied her; every time she closed her eyes, the justice's face loomed up, his mouth slowly and distinctly forming the words, ". . . until you are dead."

Eyes wide, she stared into the darkness and tried not to think or feel at all.

She had been alone only a short time when a light appeared outside her door. At first she ignored it, until she heard the gaoler turn the key in the lock. Blinking, she raised her head as he came in.

"Up ye go, me lady," he mocked. "We got another artist what wants t' draw ye. An' this one's payin' extra t' see ye t'night. Guess 'e don't want all the others t' beat 'im t' the print shops."

A cloaked figure stood behind him, carrying a sketch pad and easel.

The gaoler stepped aside and handed over the lantern. "Yer ten pounds buys ye 'alf an hour, mate. The magistrate'll 'ave me flogged proper if 'e finds out I'm lettin' folk in at night."

The stranger moved into the cell and the keeper closed and locked the door. Elizabeth had already turned her back, shutting her eyes, refusing to sit up so the artist could see her. It was humiliating enough being gawked at by curiosity seekers; being preyed upon by these vultures was too much. She had thought herself beyond tears, but felt them well again.

The man touched her shoulder.

She tensed. "I'm not going to pose, you greedy sot, so if you—"

"Elizabeth," a deep, familiar voice said. "It's me."

For a second, disbelief made movement impossible. In the next heartbeat, Elizabeth rolled over, blinking in the glow of the lantern, half afraid he was only an illusion conjured out of her most desperate wishes.

He didn't disappear. Kneeling beside her, he lowered the hood of his cloak.

"Oh, God," she choked out, not able to say any more past the lump in her throat. Suddenly the only thought in her head was a ridiculous wish that she could have bathed in the past week. He was so achingly handsome, and she must be a sight.

It didn't matter. He reached for her and crushed her into his embrace before she had a chance to ask a single question or think any more about how she looked. His arms around her felt so strong and solid, his embrace a warm haven against the whirlwind she was trapped in.

"Oh, Pierce," she whispered. He squeezed her tighter and she clung to him, feeling tears on her cheeks. She couldn't hold them back any longer, or the wracking sobs that rose up in her chest. She cried out all the pain and fear she had tried to bury, the sadness that she hadn't believed in him sooner, the longing for what might have been if not for her own foolishness.

"Shh, sweet," he soothed, cradling her head against his chest. "We don't want the gaoler coming back."

She buried her face in the clean-smelling linen of his shirt, muffling her sobs and trying to keep her voice low. "I love you, Pierce. I love you so much. I should have told you a long time ago. I don't know how you can forgive me after everything I've done—"

"My sweet Elizabeth," he murmured, his voice soft and intense. "There's nothing more for either of us to forgive. When I saw you in that courtroom . . ." He stopped suddenly and didn't finish the sentence. Then his fingers touched her chin and he tilted her head up. Their eyes met. "I love you."

His simple declaration lit her heart with joy. She laid her head on his shoulder and slid her arms about his back, her fingers gripping his cloak. They hung on to each other for a long time, not saying anything, just holding one another as they knelt on the floor of the cell.

Then they started whispering, repeating the words both had held back too long, a mingling of voices that felt as intimate as lovemaking, an intertwining of souls that made desperation and hopelessness seem very far away.

She ran her hands over his back, his shoulders, arms, chest, wanting to memorize the feel of him, savoring this moment as she had in her dreams a hundred times. His hands cupped her face and he kissed her, softly at first, then harder, making her his with possessive fire.

She could feel his heart pounding against hers before he finally set her away from him, his eyes and voice dark and serious. ''We haven't much time, Elizabeth, and I've a great deal to tell you—''

''Are Nell and Georgiana all right? No one came to question them—?''

''They're fine now. They're with Quinn at the moment.''

''And he's all right as well?'' She looked at him doubtfully. ''You didn't get angry at him for what I did?''

''No,'' he said, his expression by turns exasperated and oddly pleased at her familiar habit of interrupting. ''Now, stop worrying about everyone else. You're the one in danger here.''

''It doesn't matter now,'' she said, raising a hand to his face. ''There's nothing anyone can do. I'm only grateful we had this moment together. I couldn't go to my death without telling you I love you.''

''Elizabeth, I have no intention of letting you go to your death.''

''But what can you do?'' Fear gripped her heart. ''You don't mean to trade places with me! You can't. I won't let you—''

''Shh,'' he placed a finger on her lips. ''No, that's not what I'm going to do. I considered it, but unfortunately, you're far too small to walk out of here wearing my cloak.

Even in this dark hellhole, the gaoler would never believe it."

"Then what?" she asked forlornly. "You can't bribe them into letting me go. They're making too much from the visitors to risk death for money. Even if you offered them all of Montaigne's gold—"

"If I still had it." An uncharacteristic smile curved his lips.

She nodded sadly. "Were the estates auctioned so soon, then? You have your home back?"

"No, actually. It's all in the bank. I've set up a trust fund."

Elizabeth gaped at him. "What do you mean? What about Wolverton Manor?"

"It doesn't matter to me now," he said gruffly. "Not without you."

Elizabeth felt utterly confused. "But what's going to happen to the money?"

"Montaigne's gold will replace your charity. I've called it the Anne Wolverton Trust for Women and Children."

As the impact of what he had done sank in, Elizabeth thought she would burst with pride and love. The sacrifice he had made was enormous. He had given up any claim to lands that had been in his family for generations.

He had walked away from the money, and from his past.

She sat there beaming at him. "Oh, Pierce—"

"Elizabeth," he said sternly before she could utter a single compliment. "I don't have time to explain it all now. I have to tell you what we are going to do on Monday. You must listen to me, very carefully, and do exactly as I say." He grasped her chin, gently but meaningfully. "No arguments."

"I trust you," she whispered, meaning it with all her heart.

"Good." A flicker of a smile appeared before he turned deadly serious again. "Now, here is our plan . . ."

Chapter 29

Elizabeth was allowed to choose what clothes she would wear to her execution; it was one of the few rights the condemned had. She could have demanded to die in the same flamboyant style in which she had carried out her raids, wearing masculine garb. Instead, she requested more humble feminine attire.

She told the gaoler exactly which outfit she wanted: her black-and-white woolen sacque gown. The loose-fitting dress with its high starched collar would make her look as penitent as a Puritan. She also asked for her pannier, petticoats, corset, garters, plain cotton stockings, and the shoes with high, shaped heels, freshly shined.

For her last meal, she requested only one thing: a bottle of pale French claret from her own wine cellar. She gave the gaoler directions to the house where her "relatives" were staying, and he dispatched one of his men to fetch the requested items.

As she waited in her cell, sweat trickling down her back, she prayed that Nell and Quinn and Georgiana had had time to prepare everything, that the turnkey wouldn't lose any of it or decide to keep a souvenir or two for himself—and most of all, that she could remember every one of Pierce's instructions.

By the time the turnkey arrived back at Newgate, arms laden, the bells of St. Sepulchre's Church were chiming Elizabeth's death knell. The hollow, dolorous sound announced that the time of execution was at hand.

The gaoler searched the clothes thoroughly, going through the pockets and feeling the linings for a knife or other weapon, while the guards struck off the shackles about Elizabeth's ankles with a hammer and chisel.

"Ye 'ave t' 'ave yer feet free t' dance proper," one of the men laughed.

"Tyburn tree's the best dancin' master in all England," another added with a cruel smile.

She didn't respond to their taunts. The gaoler, satisfied with his search, shoved the clothes at her. "Be quick, now," he ordered as he handed over the bottle of wine and shut her door. "No laggin', hopin' fer a pardon. Yer public's waitin'."

As the men walked away, their parting laughter was lost beneath the sound of the bells, echoing through the clammy stone corridors, muted and otherworldly.

Elizabeth started to undress, her stomach churning. She tried to banish the worry from her heart. She just needed to do exactly as Pierce had said, act repentant, and give the crowds a show that would tug at their heartstrings. Pierce would take care of everything else.

Despite her resolve to remain calm, her fingers shook as she picked up her corset.

She barely had time to dress and whisper a brief prayer before the gaoler and his turnkeys came to collect her.

Elizabeth had sat in silence at the church service last night, listening to the prison chaplain's imperious commands to repent. Now, crouched in the darkness, she poured out her heart. She asked forgiveness for her sins, offered thanks for the joy she had known in her life, for Pierce's love, for Nell and Georgiana, and Quinn.

One of the guards picked up the wine. "Time to go."

Elizabeth remained kneeling, head bowed, eyes closed. She begged that, if something went wrong today, they all escape with their lives, even if she must lose hers.

She whispered "Amen," then rose to face her jailors.

The guards made crude jokes as they escorted her through the prison, but Elizabeth didn't spare them so much as a glance. They took her first to the small, high-walled courtyard known as the press yard, where prisoners were literally pressed for confessions with lead weights.

One of the turnkeys grabbed her wrists, jerking her arms forward with much more force than necessary. ''Ye won't be so high-and-mighty fer long, me *lady*,'' he said, binding her arms with a cord so tight it cut into her skin.

Next came the moment Elizabeth had dreaded. One of the other turnkeys went to fetch the noose. He looped it about her neck, leaving the rope to trail down her back. Sweat broke out on her forehead and her stomach turned as he tightened it to within a few inches of her throat; the final adjustment would be left to the hangman, who was thought to be expert in the correct tightness for a quick and painless death.

Elizabeth shivered, despite the August heat and her woolen gown and her determination to play this calm and cool. *It isn't real,* she told herself. *You're not going to die. Everything will go exactly as Pierce planned. Just don't panic.*

Her fingers were already going numb from her bindings. Real or not, this wasn't going to be pleasant.

The turnkeys shoved her ahead of them out of the press yard, through a short tunnel and into the main yard where the City Marshal of London and about fifty of his men awaited. In the center of the group sat the cart that would carry her to Tyburn Hill. The chaplain stood inside it. Elizabeth's gaze locked on the long wooden box beside him, and she couldn't suppress a shudder.

It was her coffin.

The marshal and his men mounted their horses. The three turnkeys pushed her up into the cart. They accepted blunderbusses and pistols from the marshalmen, then got in beside her. The cleric started to mutter a prayer.

Elizabeth sat on the pine box and reached toward the man who still held her wine. ''M . . . my claret,'' she said. ''I wish to drink a farewell toast to the people as we go.''

The man tossed it to her and she barely managed to catch it in her bound hands. Her heart hammered against her ribs. Uncorking the bottle with more than a little difficulty, she ignored the chaplain's disapproving glare and took a long swallow as the cart jerked forward.

As soon as the procession passed through the gates and into the street, a mob of shouting Londoners closed around them, some demanding that Elizabeth be pardoned, others screaming for blood. Boys darted through the crowd, waving sheaves of broadsheets for sale, each depicting an ink sketch of the lady highwayman.

The marshal and his men kept close to the cart, brandishing their weapons. Any attempt at escape or rescue would be pure suicide.

Elizabeth, doing her best to sit upright on the coffin as the cart jounced along the road, tried to keep a serene look on her face. Her heart beat a frantic accompaniment to the chaplain's monotone chanting. She raised her bottle time and again to people who shouted, "Be brave, Lady Bess!", "God be wit' ye!" or "Thank ye fer what ye done!"

She didn't see Nell or Georgiana or Quinn. She knew she wasn't supposed to until it was all over, but she felt an almost childlike urge for the comfort and reassurance of a familiar face. She had to console herself with the fact that Pierce would be waiting at Tyburn.

All along the route, more and more gawkers joined the procession, until the multitude was so vast, Elizabeth couldn't see anything but people all around. The turnkeys were growing nervous.

Elizabeth kept nodding to the crowd and kept drinking until she was so woozy she could barely lift the bottle. A mere sip was enough to make her dizzy, but she was grateful. The liquid spread through her, warm and reassuring. Her rapid pulse sent its effects racing into her every muscle, dulling her every nerve ending.

By the time they topped Tyburn Hill more than an hour after leaving Newgate, she felt drunk as a lord and then some. There were still more spectators waiting, in grandstands and at food and drink stalls. Those who could pay for a better view stood on ladders set up by the city lamplighters.

The people who had followed the cart flowed into the waiting crowd. The cheers and boos and shouts and whistles rose to an ear-numbing roar. Someone in the mob was still screaming, "Freedom fer Lady Bess!"

From another side she heard a man beg, "A pardon fer the good woman!"

From still another direction, a female voice demanded, " 'Ang 'er! 'Ang the bitch proper!"

The cart rolled inexorably toward the triangular gallows at the top of the hill and came to a halt underneath.

Elizabeth could no longer distinguish what anyone was saying; she could barely hear at all over the buzz in her head. The bottle of claret slipped from her numb fingers and she barely noticed.

She thought the gallows looked huge from below. It was hard to tell with only a glance, and she was finding it very hard to hold her head up after so much drink. The gaoler had cheerfully explained that the three-sided structure could accommodate twenty-four criminals at once—but today it would be hers alone.

She tried to look around. Where was Pierce? He was supposed to be here, right at the front. She didn't see him. Panic seized her. What if something had gone wrong?

A wave of stark terror swept through her, wiping away her courage and resolve. Elizabeth thought she would throw up. She bent over but the turnkeys grabbed her arms and dragged her to her feet, holding her at the very edge of the cart.

The hangman came out of the crowd and knelt on the ground before her. "Yer fergiveness, madam."

Elizabeth was still searching the scores of faces around the cart. Another man stepped forward—but it wasn't Pierce. It was the physician who would verify that she was dead.

Where was Pierce?

"Madam?" the hangman prompted.

Elizabeth looked down at him and tried to speak, but

her tongue didn't seem able to obey her bidding. She nodded her forgiveness, her head lolling to one side.

"She's drunk as a piper," one of the turnkeys growled. "Get on wit' it."

The executioner insisted on following tradition. "Has the condemned anything she wishes to say to the people?"

Elizabeth scrambled to collect her besotted thoughts. Wasn't she supposed to say something? She couldn't remember. She felt so very odd. Raising her head, she tried to speak but it only came out as wordless babble.

"She ain't goin' t' be makin' no speeches," one of the turnkeys said, looking nervously at the increasingly restless spectators. "Get on wit' it."

The hangman stepped up into the cart to adjust her noose, and the guards jumped to the ground.

"I'm sorry, Lady Bess," he whispered in her ear. "I'll make it painless as I can, I promise."

Elizabeth felt him fasten the rope so tight it choked her. Then she couldn't feel anything at all. Her whole body seemed to have gone numb.

No, her mind screamed. There was something else she was supposed to do! Pierce had explained it all. Where was he? *What was the last thing she was supposed to do?*

The buzz in her head swelled to a painful level. Earth and crowd and sky began to spin and she had to shut her eyes against a wave of vertigo. She felt a slight tug on her neck as the hangman threw the rope up and over the crossbar of the gallows. The cart jerked when he leaped to the ground. Opening her eyes, she saw him pick up the free end of the rope, wrapping it around and around his burly arm.

Someone handed him a whip. He lifted it until the tip hovered just above the cart horse's flank.

Elizabeth's tongue refused to utter the frantic denial in her head. *Where was Pierce?* The spectators were going mad, jumping and shaking their fists and opening their mouths wide with cries she could no longer hear.

She tried to step back from the edge of the cart; her leg struck the coffin. She didn't feel the impact.

The whip slashed downward.

And suddenly there was nothing but air beneath Elizabeth's feet.

Chapter 30

Georgiana couldn't stop screaming.

"Georgi," Nell admonished over the roar of the crowd, looking down to where Georgiana had fallen to her knees in the dirt. "That's good, but it isn't time yet."

"I am not playacting!" Looking up at the tall gallows, Georgiana saw that Elizabeth's body had finally been lowered to the ground. They had left her up the requisite fifteen minutes to ensure she had strangled to death. Georgiana could hardly speak past horrified tears. "She's dead, Nell! How could she not be after that? She's dead!"

Nell bent down and pulled Georgiana to her feet. "Not yet, but she will be, if we don't get t' 'er before they cart 'er off t' the cemetery. Now let's *go*."

She led the way through the jostling mob. When they pushed toward the front of the spectators, Georgiana saw the hangman bending over to cut the noose from Elizabeth's neck and the bindings from her wrists. The physician leaned over the still form. He held a mirror up to her mouth, then placed his ear to her chest.

After an agonizingly long moment, he stood and nodded to the City Marshal. "The prisoner is dead."

Georgiana had to cover her mouth to hold back another scream. The marshal addressed the gathered people. "Has the deceased any family present?"

Nell grabbed Georgiana's arm and yanked her forward. Both of them were in tears now. "We are her aunts, sir," Georgiana blubbered.

"And have you made suitable arrangements?" the marshal asked coldly. "Or shall the Crown be required to pay for the burial?"

''We 'ave an undertaker comin','' Nell replied tear-
fully.

''Excellent.'' The marshal gestured for his men to unload the pine coffin. Georgiana truly thought she would
faint as the turnkeys placed Elizabeth's body in the
wooden box. When they laid the lid on top and started
nailing it shut, only a pinch from Nell kept her from
swooning.

The onlookers had already started to disperse to the
food and drink stalls. The few who were left were watching the activity beneath the gallows. Georgiana hoped no
one would notice the tall, dark man slipping a fat purse
into the hangman's pocket.

Pierce had stood right beside the cart, just behind
Elizabeth, the entire time, with a pistol in his pocket
aimed at the executioner's heart. He had been ready to
shoot, grab Elizabeth and make a run for it if anything
went awry. Luckily, the hangman had decided to earn
his enormous bribe, rather than risk dying himself today.

The executioner had looked quite distraught up until
this moment; now he visibly relaxed as his benefactor
melted away into the crowd.

'' 'Ere comes our undertaker now,'' Nell said, pointing to a black-draped wagon pulled by a black horse that
was making slow progress up the hill, hampered by the
milling crowd.

''Clear a way, there,'' the marshal ordered. ''There's
nothing more to see. Move along.''

The driver, also all in black, came to a stop beside the
coffin and leaped to the ground. He and the marshalmen
loaded the box into the back of the wagon.

Georgiana and Nell scrambled up behind it, still sobbing, clutching one another's hands—not with fear, but
with hope. The driver leaped into his seat and lifted the
reins.

He glanced over his shoulder as they pulled away.
''Everything will be all right, ladies,'' he said tightly.

Georgiana didn't find Quinn's words or his concerned
expression the least bit reassuring.

Once they were out of the crowd, he lashed the horse

to get all the speed he possibly could, but a few morbid gawkers still rode after them for almost a mile before leaving them alone. When only one was left—a dark-cloaked rider the three of them knew—Quinn pulled off the road into a stand of trees and jerked the horse to a stop.

"Get her out of there!" Georgiana cried, tearing at the lid of the coffin with her bare fingers until Nell handed her a metal tool that had been hidden on the floor.

Pierce leaped from his saddle and vaulted into the wagon in one smooth movement, attacking the lid like a madman.

Nell started yanking out the nails on her side. " 'Ow can she breathe?"

"She doesn't need much air," Quinn said, working methodically. "Not in the state she's in now."

There were still a few nails to be removed when Pierce growled in frustration and tore the lid free by brute force.

"Oh, sweet Lord," Georgiana cried, stunned at the sight of Elizabeth's unearthly pale face and still form. "She's really dead!"

"No." Pierce lifted Elizabeth out and held her in his arms, shaking her. "Come out of it, Elizabeth." He cradled her against his chest, stroking her alabaster cheek. "Come back to me."

"It might be an hour or two yet, sir," Quinn said softly. "The drug affects everyone differently, and there's no telling how much she actually drank. She was supposed to finish the bottle."

Georgiana knelt beside Pierce and unbuttoned the back of Elizabeth's dress partway to loosen the tight corset underneath. Elizabeth had always hated wearing stays, but this time they had saved her life; Nell had sewn strong wires into the garment. All Elizabeth had to do was slip them free when she put it on, working them up into the back of her high collar. Then the hangman hooked them onto the noose while he was adjusting it, and cut them off when he removed it later.

Everything appeared to have worked perfectly, but Georgiana couldn't shake an ominously uneasy feeling.

"I . . . I thought she was supposed to give a farewell speech to the crowd and finish the claret while she spoke."

"She might have been overcome by the drug's affects too quickly," Quinn explained.

"*Might* 'a been?" Nell rounded on him. "Ye mean yer not sure? 'Ow do we know yer bloody drug 'asn't killed her?"

"I measured the dosage personally." Quinn looked deeply hurt. "And I would never have allowed it to be used on the lady if I hadn't experienced its effects myself. She's in a deep sleep, not unlike that of hibernation, but she is not dead."

Nell looked abashed but didn't apologize. Georgiana reached into her pocket for the smelling salts she had brought and waved them under Elizabeth's nose.

Elizabeth didn't make the slightest move or sound.

Placing a hand to her young friend's forehead, Georgiana was appalled to find her unnaturally cold. It looked for all the world as if life had left the slender, fragile form in Lord Darkridge's arms.

Trying her best not to cry, Georgiana looked helplessly at Pierce.

He wasn't paying her any attention. He stared down at Elizabeth, holding her tightly, as if his warmth and will alone could force her to awaken. The raw agony etched on his usually stoic features made Georgiana's heart ache.

"Sir, we could wait," Quinn suggested. "Another few hours—"

"We don't have time," Pierce said hoarsely, not taking his gaze from Elizabeth's face. "Get us out of here, Quinn."

"Yes, sir." Quinn moved back into the driver's seat.

Georgiana stood and nudged Nell, who looked up in irritation at first, then nodded in understanding, wiping tears from her own eyes. The two women left Elizabeth in Pierce's care and went to sit beside Quinn.

They were all silent as the wagon rattled toward the road. Georgiana only looked over her shoulder once. She saw Pierce kiss Elizabeth, so sweetly and tenderly that she felt terribly guilty for ever thinking ill of him.

But when he lifted his head, Elizabeth's eyelids didn't flutter open. She remained still—still as death.

She wasn't like the sleeping beauty of the fairy tale. A prince's kiss wasn't enough to awaken her.

The first sensation that Elizabeth became aware of was a rolling and pitching feeling in her stomach that she had never felt before.

She tried to focus on it, use it as a handhold to pull herself out of the pit of utter darkness that had nearly claimed her.

It took an enormously long time, but she gradually fought her way upward, becoming aware of other sensations: an almost painful tingling in her fingers and toes, a throbbing headache, and a heaviness in her chest. Then she noticed smells, a salty tang, like that of the sea, mingled with a musty, woody scent.

She wanted more, but couldn't seem to get enough air. Trying to breathe deeply, she only managed a weak gasp.

Suddenly a sharp, bitter odor assaulted her nose and she choked and tried to get away from it. The smell followed no matter which way she twisted her head. She felt a hand on her cheek, patting her none too gently.

"Elizabeth!" a familiar, deep voice commanded.

"Mmm?" she murmured sleepily, then grumbled when the hand left her cheek and started shaking her shoulder. "Stop that."

This was met with what sounded like the laughter of a small group of people.

"Only if you wake up," the voice ordered, softer now.

"I am awake," she insisted, and to prove her point, slowly opened her eyes.

It took a few blinks before she could focus on the faces looming above her. Pierce was closest, sitting beside her on what felt like a hard and uncomfortable bed. Behind him, she saw Georgiana and Nell and a very pale Quinn, standing along a wooden wall in what was obviously an unusually tiny room.

They were all smiling at her, even Pierce. Georgiana and Nell hugged one another, then Nell turned around and hugged Quinn, who didn't appear to mind at all.

"What happened?" Elizabeth asked, yawning.

Pierce felt her forehead. "How do you feel? Can you move?"

Elizabeth wiggled her fingers and toes experimentally. "I feel rather stiff, and my stomach is queasy, but I think I'm fine."

Pierce slid his arms around her, lifting her up off the bed and into a fierce embrace. "Thank God," he said raggedly, then turned his head. "And thank you, Quinn."

Elizabeth still felt drowsy and rather confused. "What happened?" she repeated, her mouth against Pierce's bare throat and her thoughts meandering.

"How much do you remember?" Pierce asked, holding her slightly away from him.

Elizabeth furrowed her brow and tried to sift through the snatches of memory that whirled in her head. "I was in the cart, and I was drinking from the bottle of claret, just as you told me, and then we came up over the hill and I saw the gallows." She shivered and Pierce rubbed her back soothingly. "I'm trying to remember what happened after that . . ." She closed her eyes, puzzled. "But I can't. It's all a blank."

"The drug perhaps blocked out her memory," Quinn said.

"Or the wine," Georgiana added. "Or the shock of it all."

"Whatever it was, it's a blessin'," Nell said firmly.

Pierce stroked Elizabeth's cheek. "I agree."

"All I know is that I'll never complain about wearing a corset again," Elizabeth said with a weak smile. Opening her eyes, she looked about the small room they were in. "Now would someone at least tell me where we are?"

"I shall do better than that," Pierce offered. "I'll show you."

He helped Elizabeth get out of bed, but when her legs proved too wobbly to hold her, he caught her in his arms and carried her. He ducked out of the room; their three friends stayed behind.

As he stepped into the corridor, Elizabeth realized they were on a ship. The hall was narrow and dark, but when Pierce climbed the stairway at the far end, she saw daylight above.

Then they were on deck, and she couldn't remember the sun ever feeling so good on her face, the air so pure and sweet. Pierce turned so that she could see all around—nothing but ocean on every side. They had obviously left England far behind. The sails snapped in the wind and the few sailors on deck only gave a polite greeting before going on about their duties.

Pierce carried her to the railing and cautiously lowered her to her feet, holding her close with one arm about her waist.

Elizabeth leaned back against him and watched the sun melt into the waves, the fireball softened and cooled by blue, the sea brightened and warmed by red. "You never told me we were leaving the country," she said in soft accusation.

"I did," he replied. "I said once we had whisked you away from Tyburn and revived you, we would all leave together."

"I thought you meant leave London."

"There's no safe place for you in all of England, Elizabeth. Your face is too well known."

She nodded, understanding. "If anyone were to discover that Elizabeth Thornhill is still alive, I'd have to spend the rest of my life like a hunted animal, running from thief-takers." She shivered.

Pierce rubbed her arms. "Nell and Georgiana weren't sure how you would feel about leaving. They thought it best to let you concentrate on what you had to do today."

Elizabeth looked out at the waves, the endless ebb and flow of the sea. Leave England forever? She thought of her family ties, of Northampton, of the beautiful countryside. Then she remembered the baby she had lost, the prisons, the wretched conditions in the city, the English "justice" system.

"It's best this way," she said at last, a bit sadly. "I won't have to keep running. I won't have to live in fear."

"Never again," Pierce said, brushing a kiss in her hair. "I promise you that."

He held her against him and they stood there in silence, watching the gulls swoop over the waves. After a moment, Elizabeth turned in his arms and looked up at him.

"But what about you?" she asked softly. "What about all the Wolverton estates, everything you wanted—"

He silenced her with a kiss, light and lingering and infinitely tender. "Everything I want," he assured her in a whisper, "is right here."

Elizabeth thought she would melt from the warmth of his gaze. She rested her cheek on his chest, listening to the steady beat of his heart, hope and love and yearning all twining inside her. "But I wonder whether I'll ever be truly safe, Pierce. Wherever I go, I still won't be able to use my real name—"

"Of course you will," he countered. "You'll be Elizabeth Wolverton."

Elizabeth tipped her head up, and the odd little grin on Pierce's face filled her with the most exquisite sort of joy she had ever felt.

He caressed her chin with the back of his knuckles. "In fact, most everyone will be calling you Lady Darkridge."

Elizabeth returned his smile, raised one eyebrow, and asked with mock formality, "Sir, is this a proposal?"

He swept her up into his arms again. "What say we go find the captain and see what he calls it?"

As he carried her across the deck, a sudden practical thought struck Elizabeth. "How *did* you manage to pay for all our passages?"

"Quinn got a good price for the town house," Pierce explained. "And I sold my books to a printer."

"Even your poetry?" she asked incredulously. He had always insisted his work was not for public viewing.

"It was time to let them go," he said simply. "And the man was more than fair about it. Gave me a goodly sum and said he'd print up a few and send me half the profits."

Elizabeth barely had time to be astonished at that when another thought occurred. "Do you realize, with everything that's happened, I've never even asked about our destination?"

Pierce's grin widened. "A place that is perfect for a pair of rogues like us."

Epilogue

Boston, Massachusetts, 1736

Autumn leaves drifted past the hall windows on the second floor of New Wolverton Manor.

Elizabeth paused just long enough to admire the view of the bright New England afternoon before she continued down the corridor on her quest. She found the men she sought—husband and son—sprawled on the floor of the master bedroom, surrounded by discarded pieces of paper.

Pierce lay on his back, gnawing at the end of the expensive new lacquer pen she had bought him. Their dark-haired baby slept snugly on his chest, tiny lashes lowered over his coffee-brown eyes.

Elizabeth stood in the doorway a moment, not making her presence known, simply soaking up the inexpressible joy of the little tableau. Pierce's strength and confidence had helped her tremendously during her pregnancy; he had patiently listened to her every niggling doubt, no matter how wildly emotional, and had refused to leave her side for a second during the long night when their son was born.

Now, four months later, she was finally learning not to worry every moment her son was away from her side. Everyone is New Wolverton Manor treasured him as much as she did. Pierce most of all.

Pierce's hand looked so large and powerful and gentle on little Thomas's back. Elizabeth loved seeing it there, or sweeping a pen across a page in a flurry of poetic

368

inspiration. It had been a long time since she had seen those fingers curled about the grip of a pistol. God willing, she would never see that again. Those days were behind them; Lord and Lady Darkridge were the most law-abiding of citizens, now and forevermore.

"I hate to interrupt the artistic process," she whispered, "but I believe you're getting more ink on Thomas than you are on the paper."

Careful not to disturb the baby, Pierce looked her way and took the pen out of his mouth. "It's never too early to begin the boy's education."

Elizabeth tiptoed across the thick Wilton carpet. "Trying to turn him into a writer already?"

"Actually, I've a feeling he'll be a seafaring man."

"Because we live in Boston?"

Pierce gave her a wicked grin. "Because he was conceived on board a ship."

Elizabeth felt a blush rise in her cheeks. "It's time for his nap."

"He's enjoying his nap quite well. So am I." Pierce reached out and caught the hem of her peacock-blue silk gown. "Why don't you come down here and we'll all enjoy it together?"

Elizabeth sat on the floor beside them, brushing a fingertip through her son's downy hair. "Actually, I've come with news. The post just arrived from England."

"Not another payment from Whitwell?"

"Yes, the largest one yet, in fact." Elizabeth let her pride show in her smile.

"We're going to have the devil of a time thinking of ourselves as rustic colonials if we're going to be rich."

"Mr. Whitwell also enclosed a note. *An Anonymous Poet in London* has just achieved the singular honor of becoming the most popular book in London since Swift's *Gulliver's Travels*."

Pierce's tone was gruff though his pleasure was obvious. "And I suppose he wants to know when *An Anonymous Poet in the American Colonies* will be finished?" He cast a frown at the papers scattered around him.

"Mmm-hmm." Elizabeth nodded. "I certainly think

you've more than enough poems finished. Although I still wish you would include my favorite.''

He reached up and stroked his fingers along her jawline. ''I've already explained, love, why I don't think it's a good idea to let them print the one about you. No one whose ever seen those eyes of yours could mistake whom I'm describing. 'Not amethysts, nor damsons rare, nor spring's first lilac days, could e'er match the love fire radiant in my lady's gaze.' ''

Elizabeth blushed and her lashes drifted downward. ''Not the one about me,'' she corrected gently. ''The one about your father.''

Pierce scowled and looked uncomfortable. ''That one isn't meant to be read by anyone outside the family.''

Elizabeth touched his mouth, trying to soothe the frown away. She liked that he used the word ''family'' so easily, that he had adjusted to the idea so quickly after all the years of self-imposed solitude. She also felt deeply pleased that he had finally gotten past the anger and resentment and grief he felt for his father, at least enough to write about his feelings. ''It's the most beautiful thing you've ever written, Pierce.''

''It was pure hell to write it,'' he said grimly.

''But you feel it was worth the effort.'' Elizabeth didn't phrase it as a question.

He sighed deeply, the baby rising and falling on his chest. Looking at his son, Pierce couldn't hold back a smile. ''Yes, it was. When I put my mind to it, I was able to remember him as he used to be, when I was young. Once I did that, I realized he never intended to desert my mother and me. He was just a desperate man in a desperate time, and who am I to set myself up as worthy to judge him?''

Elizabeth looked at her sleeping son, thinking of the fears and bitterness that used to haunt her; the feelings had faded with each passing day, until now they were only faint memories. ''Time heals all wounds.''

''No,'' Pierce said softly, reaching up to wrap his fingers in her long black hair. ''*You* heal all wounds.''

He was pulling her down for a kiss when Nell's voice

sounded in the hall. "Bess? Where 'ave ye got to? I've another idea fer ye."

Elizabeth sighed and sat up. "In here, Nell."

Nell peeked around the corner. "I should've known."

"And good day to you too, Nell," Pierce said sourly.

"What idea?" Elizabeth asked.

"Georgi thinks I'm ready fer the madhouse."

"I never said that," Georgiana said, coming up behind her friend in the corridor. "I said this idea of yours would land us all in whatever passes for a gaol in this uncivilized city."

The baby started to stir at all the noise. Pierce stood up and patted little Thomas's back to quiet him. "Don't just stand out there in the hall, ladies. *Do* come in."

Elizabeth rolled her eyes at her husband's none-too-subtle sarcasm. At least Pierce had lost a little of his bite, if not his bark. Maintaining a measure of tranquility between Nell and Georgiana had always been a chore, but adding Pierce to the mix made it a monumental task. No matter, she thought with a smile; too much tranquility made for a dull life. "What idea?" she repeated.

"I want t' sell patterns fer breeches in me shop," Nell said brightly, folding her arms over her chest. "Breeches fer women."

"Of all the addlepated—" Pierce managed to strangle the rest of his opinion. Crossing to the window, he opened it and stuck his head out. "Quinn! Would you come and collect your wife? She's regaling us with another of her ideas."

Nell looked miffed. "Theodosius thinks I'm barmy-brained too. That's why I'm askin' what Bess 'ere thinks."

Elizabeth winced for Quinn's sake. He and Nell had spent the entire first week of the voyage to the Colonies fighting like dog and cat. The second week, no one had seen much of them. By the third week, they had asked if the captain wouldn't mind performing another shipboard wedding.

Of course, Quinn had to use his first name when saying his vows, and Nell had insisted on using it ever since. She thought it adorable, much to her husband's chagrin.

Quinn, arriving from his and Nell's shop downstairs, stuck his head in the door. "And what are you concocting now, my good wife?"

Pierce waved him inside; Quinn came to stand behind Nell and slipped his hands about her waist. She sighed but kept her arms stubbornly folded. "I wanted to see what Bess thought of me idea. Everythin's new in New England. Why not new fashion?"

"Actually, Nell," Elizabeth had to admit. "I rather think the world's not ready for women in breeches just yet. Not even the New World."

Nell raised her chin mutinously. "I think they'd sell like cold ale on a 'ot day."

"Or land us all in trouble with the authorities," Pierce put in.

"I should think," Quinn said, giving his wife a squeeze, "that being one of the most popular drapers in the Massachusetts Colony would be enough for you, my dear."

"Me customers come t' Mrs. Quinn's wantin' new ideas," she insisted. "I 'ave t' give 'em what they want."

"She does have a point," Elizabeth said thoughtfully. "And breeches are rather comfortable."

Pierce looked down at his yawning son. "What *are* we going to do with this houseful of radical females?"

"My dear, what say we discuss your idea elsewhere?" Quinn suggested diplomatically, pointing Nell toward the door. "Say in our own apartments?"

Nell grumbled a bit at first, but Elizabeth heard an absolutely girlish giggle when the newlyweds were halfway down the hall.

Pierce watched the bedroom emptying with a look of relief. Thomas, despite all the activity around him, was falling asleep on his father's shoulder.

Georgiana looked at the child with an expression of pure love and tenderness. "Isn't it time for his nap?"

Pierce handed the boy to his godmother. "I believe his mother did say something about that, now that you mention it.'' He gave Elizabeth a conspiratorial glance. ''If you wouldn't mind, Georgiana?''

Fairly beaming, Georgiana lifted the small bundle and carried him out, cooing and tickling the baby's chin. Pierce followed her to the door, closed it behind her and walked back across the room, catching Elizabeth's hand as he went. He closed the window curtains and sat in one of the wing chairs before the hearth.

''Pierce,'' Elizabeth said, recognizing the look in his eye. ''It's the middle of the day.''

He only smiled and started unbuttoning his waistcoat.

Elizabeth blushed. ''I have a hundred things to do.''

He pulled her down onto his lap. ''This is first on the list.''

''But we have . . .'' She forgot what she was going to say for a moment as he nibbled the sensitive spot behind her ear. ''. . . A perfectly good bed right there.''

His voice was low and dark and filled with the promise of bliss beyond imagining. ''I've a yearning, Lady Darkridge, to relive the wild days of our youth.''

Elizabeth sighed and closed her eyes, giving in to the irresistible urgency in him, the passion, the love that was more enchanting than any dream of joy she'd ever known. His lips covered hers in a provocative kiss. She lay back over his arm as he slid her gown from her shoulders, and knew that the past would never, never compare to the wild, sweet days of their future.

Avon Romances—
the best in exceptional authors and unforgettable novels!

HIGHLAND MOON   Judith E. French
76104-1/$4.50 US/$5.50 Can

SCOUNDREL'S CAPTIVE   JoAnn DeLazzari
76420-2/$4.50 US/$5.50 Can

FIRE LILY   Deborah Camp
76394-X/$4.50 US/$5.50 Can

SURRENDER IN SCARLET   Patricia Camden
76262-5/$4.50 US/$5.50 Can

TIGER DANCE   Jillian Hunter
76095-9/$4.50 US/$5.50 Can

LOVE ME WITH FURY   Cara Miles
76450-4/$4.50 US/$5.50 Can

DIAMONDS AND DREAMS   Rebecca Paisley
76564-0/$4.50 US/$5.50 Can

WILD CARD BRIDE   Joy Tucker
76445-8/$4.50 US/$5.50 Can

ROGUE'S MISTRESS   Eugenia Riley
76474-1/$4.50 US/$5.50 Can

CONQUEROR'S KISS   Hannah Howell
76503-9/$4.50 US/$5.50 Can